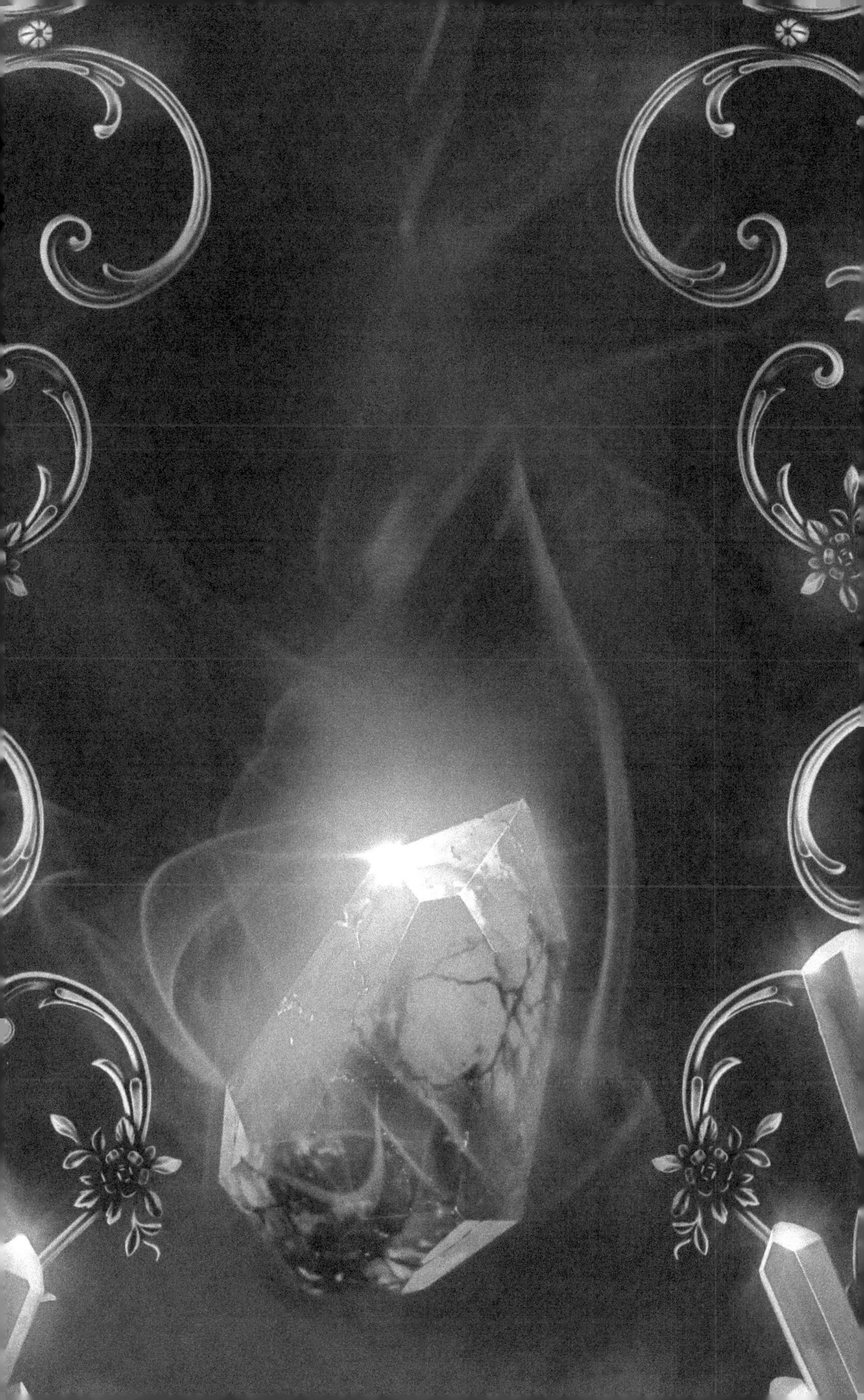

BLOOD AND CURSES
BOOK TWO

# AMY WOODRUFF

OF FATE AND FURY

Blood and Curses, Book 2



ISBN: 979-8-218-85820-9

Cover Design by MiblArt

*For Mom and Dad. Thank you for all you've poured into me and this series.*

SUZA
Bryxton
Olysa
VASSURYN
Lindor
Pontas
Terth
ELYRIA
Thassia
Astraeus
Cavamyne
The Elder Woods
Kyrun
Demra
Aphira
KASTRON
Halimore
Amhull
Kasus
ANDARRE
TAFARI

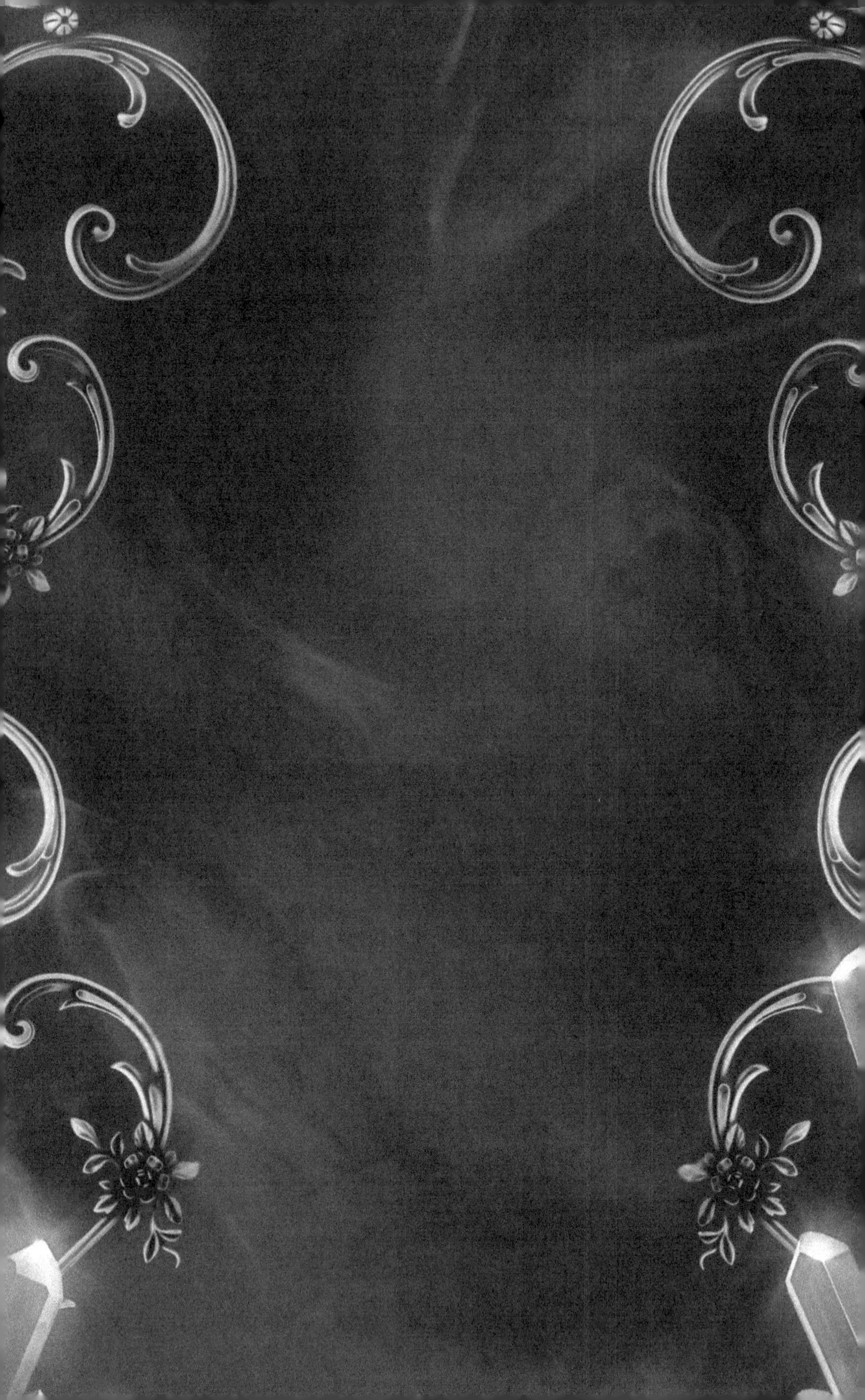

# CHAPTER ONE

## BRIDGET

A hard plastic chair dug into Bridget's spine as she sat, waiting for her name to be called. The buzz of hushed voices and unending activity grated against her skull, making her temples throb. Sterile white walls seemed to suck the air from her lungs, and the sharp sting of antiseptic did nothing to soothe her. Hospitals had always twisted her stomach into tight knots...especially when it was the *last* place she needed to be.

Bridget winced and pressed her fingers to the wound beneath her shirt. The same damn scar. Again. Droplets of blood trickled out and stained her maroon shirt. Heat radiated across her side, almost making her sweat despite the unescapable frigid Boston air. Sometime during her workout, she'd reopened the annoying thing. It was her own fault, of course. She'd never given it enough time to properly heal. Since September, the scar had split open and been stitched shut more times than she could count. Her bathroom cabinet looked more like a first-aid station than a place for toothpaste. But this time, an angry ring of red marred her skin, daring her to keep ignoring the ever present wound. An infection was the last thing she needed, especially when hospitals and doctors tended to ask too many questions.

Staring harder at her phone screen, Bridget tried to ignore the older woman sitting across from her. She was trying to catch her eye. Again. For the last thirty minutes, she'd watched the woman shift from person to person, asking questions that went on too long and digging just a little too deep. One by one, her victims had escaped, ushered behind double doors by a nurse. But now, with only a sleeping teenager in a surgical mask slumped against the far wall, Bridget had become the sole remaining target.

She sighed and slipped her phone into her purse. Avoiding eye contact clearly wasn't working. She didn't hate talking to people. In fact, during her time working at Hungry Pies, she'd mastered the art of small talk. A smile and some quick banter usually led to a better tip. But something about the woman's demeanor reminded her of Cora.

And that was someone she'd rather not think about during waking hours.

Maybe it was the unnervingly steady gaze, or the way she kept her hands folded perfectly still in her lap, Bridget wasn't sure. She just knew the woman's presence wasn't helping settle her nerves. With a to-do list a mile long, a pit stop at the hospital was throwing a wrench in her perfectly planned out day.

Apparently tired of being ignored, the woman waved her hand. "Have you been waiting long?"

"Just a little," Bridget replied. Seventy-nine minutes to be exact. Not that she was counting.

"I'm sure you'll get called back soon. They seem to be getting through the list rather quickly today. My throat is just a little sore, so I told them I don't mind waiting. I'm Maude." The woman's gaze darted to the scars on the back of Bridget's hands, then to the long thick one on her forearm from a Kastronian sword. "Did you serve?"

*Are you an officer?*

*Were you abused?*

*Did you hurt yourself?*

Bridget added the woman's question to the list of reasons people had tried to come up with for her skin's appearance. For some reason, people felt it was their right to know what had happened, even without knowing her name. Not that she ever explained. Some things were better left unsaid.

Actually, most of the things that had happened to her were better left unsaid.

*Do you work at Hot Topic?* was Bridget's favorite question when it came to her hair. After she'd passed through the gate, the bottom six inches of her hair had turned stark white. Magic taking a price, she assumed. She hadn't bothered to fix it yet.

Maude's stare continued to burn holes in her skin.

Bridget ground her teeth together. "No."

Her favorite one-word answer usually shut people down.

Maude didn't bat an eye.

"What happened?" she asked, scooting to the edge of her seat to get a better look.

Bridget put back on her leather jacket. She wished she hadn't forgotten her gloves on the kitchen island earlier. "A car accident."

She *had* been in a car accident... Once. Sticking to a somewhat truth was easier than always coming up with a lie. Bridget eyed the sliding glass doors that led to an escape. Maybe she was being paranoid and she wasn't seeing signs of an early infection. Maybe she didn't need medicine. Maybe...

"Mrs. Sanderson?"

*Saved by the nurse.* Bridget slumped back in her seat, her side twinging a bit. She tried to ignore the victory swirling in her gut at the sight of Maude's clear irritation to the interruption of her interrogation.

Bristling, the older woman stood up. "Yes, that's me."

"We're ready for you," the nurse said. Despite the dark bags hanging under his eyes, he wore a good-natured smile. Waving a hand, he directed Maude to a back left door, but not before his gaze trailed over Bridget. He suddenly stopped. "Wait... I know you."

Blinking, Bridget searched his face. Nothing about his features were familiar to her. *Andrew*, his name tag read. A common name, but surprisingly, she had never met one in her life. A hint of panic shivered up Bridget's spine. "I don't think so..."

"Yes, it was New London. I remember now," he said, planting himself in front of her.

Ice splintered through Bridget's veins. Memories of her brief time at the hospital in Connecticut flashed through her mind. Wires, pain, confusion. Too many questions about brain bleeds and contusions that she couldn't answer. Bridget's throat tightened. She'd already taken a risk checking into the emergency room with a fake name, but now someone *recognized* her. She needed to get out. *Now.* Too busy scanning the room for the best way to get around him and through the exit door, she almost missed his next statement.

"Yeah, I finished up my clinicals last semester at the hospital there. It's where I grew up. You're the ghost."

"The *what*?" Bridget sputtered.

Andrew reared back in surprise at her outburst. "I'm sorry, but it's what all the nursing students started to call you. You were in a coma for like a week. I think most of the doctors were surprised you even woke up... especially when the paramedics told them the man who found you in the woods had been doing CPR for over ten minutes by the time they got there. And then when you *did* wake up, you disappeared into thin air. Like a ghost."

Hearing her experience with the gate narrated to her so casually sent a tidal wave of dizziness over Bridget. He knew too much. And that was dangerous. Especially because of what she'd done right after she'd left that hospital, still far too weak from surgery. Hands shaking, Bridget hopped out of her seat. "That wasn't me."

"You had the craziest CT scan I've ever seen and that zodiac scar on your hand..." Andrew's voice trailed off, his dark eyes narrowing on the blood staining her shirt. "Isn't that where you were shot? Did something happen?"

"It's nothing. I'm fine."

Professionalism creeping back into his voice, he said, "It doesn't look like..."

Before he could finish his sentence, Bridget shoved past him and rushed toward the double doors that led to her freedom. If the bullet shaped scar on her side was indeed infected, she'd have to deal with it herself. Or with over-the-counter medication.

"Wait!"

Rush hour traffic drowned out Andrew's plea the moment cold winter air hit her face. Slipping just a bit, she sprinted down the icy block, not daring to look back. Not until the hospital was out of sight and all she could see was the familiar skyline of the Back Bay.

Finally stopping to catch her breath, Bridget bent over and braced herself on her knees. She groaned, realizing the right side of her shirt was now damp with something other than sweat. She'd have to stitch it up herself tonight if she was going to make it through her morning run. A habit she'd forced herself to develop, even when she'd barely been able to pick up a cup after leaving the hospital. It's what she knew Cade and Finn would do to keep up their endurance against the effects of magic.

As if her thoughts summoned him, a black Audi zoomed by on the street in front of her. Manhattan. Hungry Pies. Waiting on the curb for Cade to pull up in that exact same car. Unwanted images of her *old* life struck her core. Legs shaking, she almost fell to the ground. Within seconds, longing, despair, and anguish wrecked her mind. Not that it really ever left.

During the last four months, she'd said *I'm fine* to every doctor, shrink, and cop who questioned her. She repeated the two words to every person that asked about her scars or gave her a funny look when she flinched at the sight of diners. Even if her body had healed, for the most part, there was a truth she could barely admit to herself. She wasn't fine.

She wasn't fine at all.

# CHAPTER TWO

It took Bridget exactly three minutes and forty seconds to get to her feet and swallow back the tears stinging her eyes. And then seven minutes and two seconds to walk to the entrance of the Boston Public Library. She counted every breath and every step. As she waited at the crosswalk, she counted exactly how many times the person in front of her swiped right or left on his phone. It was a trick she had learned over the last few months. If she counted, she didn't have to think. About Elyria or Cade or what he happened to be doing at that very moment.

Five months. Five long months since she'd come back through the gate. Every day she woke up expecting to forget.

Every day her memories remained intact.

Bridget still hadn't figured out why she remembered. And perhaps she never would. When she couldn't sleep, which was most nights, she mulled over every possibility. On her worst nights, she tried to convince herself it didn't matter. She *remembered*. The *why* wasn't important. Even if her memories were both a blessing and a curse, she wasn't erased again. She found Nylah. She still remembered Cade's face. That was something she would never regret or take for granted again.

But memory came with a cost.

Remembering meant she knew what was coming for her.

It meant that every dark corner held a potential threat, or that every noise was the sound of a Fae or Witch running toward her, or that every knock on her apartment door was Finn, or Castor, or anyone that might be able to find her and let her know all was well in the land she hated that she missed.

Remembering meant that every day, she waited for the return of someone from Elyria.

Even if he couldn't come himself, Bridget *knew* that Cade would send someone. To check on her or to make sure that she was safe and had found Nylah. But she also knew that whoever Cade sent would be followed by someone working for his father. She knew it better than she did herself, at the moment.

It was only a matter of time.

It was one of the reasons the library had become one of her frequent haunts. The more she learned about artifacts, runes, and gates, the better chance she had of staying one step ahead. So far... she hadn't found much. But there was a promising book she'd finally tracked down that she was going to check out today. One about legends and stones in Ireland. No almost emotional breakdown on the sidewalk or mishap in an emergency room would deter her. Not when the spring solstice was only two months away.

A fact she *did* wish she could forget.

Bridget wiped the slush from her boots and stepped through the Boylston Street entrance of the Boston Public Library. The scent of paper and lemon-scented disinfectant hit her at once. She weaved around a dawdling family near the info desk and made her way to the glass elevator, jabbing the "Up" button with practiced ease. Then she froze.

Out of the corner of her eye, something flashed. Bright blonde hair caught the light. Hair that was all too familiar.

Bridget whipped her head to the right, but the corridor was empty. She pivoted without thinking, boots slipping slightly on the marble floor as she rushed back toward the entrance. Heart pounding, her eyes swept the room. Past the patrons, the guards, the tourists for the person she *knew* had just been behind her.

Before she could corner the only blonde in the vicinity, the girl turned her head. A glance at her side profile told Bridget all she needed to know.

She was imagining things.

First, a car set her off on an emotional spiral. Now hair. She needed to get a grip. Besides, out of all people, *Cassia* would be the last person to volunteer to come find her. Shaking off the tightness in her chest, Bridget headed back toward the elevator. She jabbed the button harder than necessary and pressed her lips together, swallowing the bile rising in her throat.

Once she reached the third floor, Bridget forced a smile at the librarian seated at the desk, tugging her jacket higher to hide the bloodstained shirt beneath. Heat radiated from the overhead vents, but the last thing she wanted was attention. Especially in a building with restricted archives.

The librarian returned her smile with practiced warmth. "Are you here for the Special Collections Open House?" she asked, gesturing to a nearby poster. A faded black crown hovered in the center of the image, surrounded by parchment and ghostly sketches. "We're featuring one of the library's favorite ghost stories today."

Trying not to grimace, Bridget shook her head. She'd had enough talk of ghosts and hauntings for one day. "I put a few books on hold... I actually think it was you who called me and said they were available."

"Anna Connors, right?" she asked, rolling her chair back a few feet. "I'll be right back."

A moment later, she returned with a small, dust-covered stack. The three leatherbound volumes looked like they hadn't seen daylight in decades. Bridget instantly recognized two of the titles from her request. The third, however, gave her pause.

"Druids?" Bridget asked skeptically. "What's this?"

Pink spread across the librarian's cheeks. "Based on what you've been asking for, I thought that might interest you too. I'm sorry if I over-stepped."

"I'll check it out," Bridget replied quickly. The word *druid* wasn't in her Elyrian vocabulary, but she didn't want to take any chances. When it came to her sister's safety, she couldn't afford to be ignorant about all things magical. It had already cost her too many times.

"Since these are shelved in our rare books section, they can't leave the library," the librarian added.

"I figured. I'll just be in here." Bridget adjusted the stack in her arms and made her way into one of the adjoining reading rooms.

Soft lamplight glowed beneath rows of green-shaded fixtures. The soundscape was familiar and oddly comforting. Whispers, the faint rustle of turning pages, the occasional scrape of a chair across hardwood. Bridget chose a table beneath a foggy window, dropped her purse quietly to the floor, and began to read.

She tried not to throw the book about druids to the floor when she opened it to find it written in another language. Why even suggest it to her at all? Sighing, she picked up one with a long title about ancient folktales and meticulously scanned each page for words or terms she recognized, like gate or Tuathan or rune. One passage mentioned a large cracked stone marked with ancient sigils, accompanied by a rough sketch. The villagers in the surrounding area had avoided it for centuries, claiming people vanished when they touched it during certain moon phases.

Bridget shifted in her seat. The throb in her side wasn't helping her con-centrate. She was halfway through a dull section on medicinal herbs when a shadow spilled across the pages. She looked up, hoping her heartbeat was only loud in her own ears. A man stood at the edge of her table, silhouette backlit by one of the overhead lamps. His straight blond hair poked out from under a Red Sox cap, and his icy blue eyes watched her.

"Do you mind?" he asked, nodding at the open seat at the end of her table.

Wordlessly, Bridget shook her head. In another life, she might've refused or argued. But the command to *lay low* kept her mouth shut. The man sat and pulled out a book that looked as old and worn as hers. He kept his head down and let the brim of his hat cast a shadow on his face.

Bridget tried to refocus on the herbs, but her attention kept slipping. Her fingers hovered over a paragraph without absorbing a single word. The feeling that she was being watched crawled up her spine. When she finally looked up, the man's eyes were already on her.

"Is it any good?" he asked, gaze moving to the discarded book to her left. When she didn't respond, he added, "I'm writing a paper for a folklore class. Figured I'd check it out if it's worth the trouble."

Bridget gave him a measured glance. Now that he'd lifted his chin, she could see him more clearly. His age matched his voice. He looked like he was in his early twenties, like her. Nothing about him screamed danger. Jeans, hoodie, Red Sox cap. Boston had a thousand students who looked just like him. Still, her heart hadn't stopped racing since he sat down. Swallowing hard, Bridget tried to relax her muscles. What had happened earlier in the day was making her paranoid. She was already seeing things in her dreams... she couldn't afford to let the delusions bleed over into real life too.

"Take it," Bridget said, sliding the book over to him. "I didn't expect it to be in another language."

She watched as he snatched the book off the table and began to flip through the pages. Slowly, color drained from his face.

"Do you know what language that is?" Bridget asked. He seemed to understand the book's contents. She hadn't even recognized —

His alarmed gaze snapped to hers. "What do you know about Druids?"

"Nothing," Bridget replied, eyes narrowing. Her fingers itched to grab the book back from him as her gut tightened. It was too much of a reaction from someone *normal*.

His mouth parted like he wanted to say more, but he stopped. His gaze dropped to the table between them as Bridget's phone vibrated violently against the wood. She snatched it up. A single word stared back at her on the screen:

*Again?*

Her stomach plummeted.

"*Shit.*"

Bridget bolted to her feet, the chair behind her screeching in protest as she nearly knocked it over. Without looking back, she sprinted out of the reading room and down the marble hallway, her boots echoing off the polished floors. She burst into the late afternoon air, breath frosting in the chill. Fumbling with her phone, she scanned the screen. Three missed calls and a calendar reminder glared up at her, all time stamped from over an hour ago. Had she really been so engrossed in reading she hadn't noticed her phone shaking with notifications? Bridget ground her teeth together and barely resisted the urge to smash her phone into the ground. She couldn't believe she'd missed an event. *Again.*

Bridget shoved her phone into her coat pocket and turned toward home. If she beat Nylah back, maybe she could come up with a good excuse why she wasn't at her choir concert. She was sick or detained at the doctor or *something* that made sense to a twelve-year-old who still miraculously believed her when she made promises.

When Bridget arrived at their rental house, one a little on the smaller side compared to the two-storied colonial pieces on the rest of the street, she spent at least five minutes undoing all the locks. The bottom three were her own addition, much to the suspicion of the neighbors. But she didn't care. The locks were the only reason she got more than an hour of sleep.

Inside, the hum of the dishwasher was the only sound that greeted her. The open kitchen and living room were still swathed in a kind of late-day gloom, the velvet furniture and rose-patterned wallpaper faded by winter light. It wasn't much. But beggars couldn't be choosers, and it had been a last minute find when she'd decided to bolt from the hospital in Connecticut.

Bridget dropped her purse onto the granite island with a thud. A lop-sided stack of worksheets sat beside it. Nylah's homework, probably. She ran a hand over her face. Behind her, a toilet flushed.

Bridget's stomach dropped. There would be no time for excuses. Moments later, Archer wandered out of the bathroom. He raised a brow at her haggard appearance.

"Ah, so you're not ghosting me. You know, a little emoji of acknowledgement every now and then would be helpful."

Bridget flinched. *Ghost*. The word of the day, it seemed. Even now, his presence was a reminder of the past.

Archer frowned. "Why the face? Did you run into one of those haunted tour groups that usually ruin your day with their slow walking?"

"Of my own life," Bridget muttered.

Silence stretched between them. The kind that used to be awkward, but now carried a quiet understanding. She knew it was Archer's way of giving her the chance to elaborate. With the amount of time they'd spent together over the last few months, she'd gotten to know him and his quirks very well.

Apparently sensing she wasn't quite ready, Archer slid a vial across the island to her. "If it's infected, this should help."

Bridget stared at it. The thick liquid inside was tinged green, flecked with crushed herbs. It looked just like the ones from his makeshift healing tent back in Elyria. Softening, she put the vial in her pocket. "How did you know?"

"Location," Archer replied, holding up his phone. "And correct me if I'm wrong, but I don't think that's grape juice on your shirt."

Bridget half-heartedly glared. "That's supposed to be for emergencies."

"It's fun watching your little bubble when I'm bored." He eyed her again, and then reached for a bottle of tequila hidden above the microwave. "I think you might need this too."

Without arguing, she poured herself a shot. Bridget hoped it would help erase the nurse's words about her time in the hospital and the image of Cade's car from her mind. Along with the notion that Cassia had been wandering around the Boston Public Library. Bridget downed the alcohol in one gulp. The burn helped steady her nerves. "I thought we agreed on no magic in the house."

"I thought we agreed to stop obsessing over what's happening in Elyria."

*Touché.* She guessed they both weren't keeping their promises, which wasn't much of a surprise, the more she thought about it. She *had* caught him using a spell to help Nylah with her homework last week. Bridget craned her neck to peek down the hall at Nylah's bedroom. The door was closed, and she couldn't hear anyone else in the house. A lick of panic shot up her spine. "Where is she?"

"She's out getting hot chocolate with a friend," Archer said, and then he held up his hands. "And before you jump down my throat, don't worry, I thoroughly vetted the mom."

After a moment, Bridget quietly asked, "How mad is she?"

"She's not mad." Archer sighed. "She's..."

If there was one thing she'd learned about Archer in the five months they'd shared a roof, it was that he loved to talk. Constantly. He filled every silence, even when she ignored him. He talked about music, about Elyria, about why toaster ovens were superior to regular ovens. Watching him struggle for words made Bridget's stomach twist. "She's what?"

"She misses you."

"I'm right here," Bridget said, backing away from him.

He'd said something similar a month before, and she'd shut him down then. She knew him and Nylah had bonded while she was in the hospital, it was one of the reasons she let Archer stay with them during their move to Boston. "Why didn't you say anything this morning? I could have used the reminder."

Bridget pinched the bridge of her nose and tried to swallow down the regret that wanted to drown her. She'd also missed the fall one, too busy obsessing and watching the gate to notice the time. How had she let it happen again?

"I did," Archer said, taking his own swig from the tequila bottle. "If I remember correctly, you said you were running a few errands and would be back in plenty of time. I don't remember you mentioning another visit to the library."

"I just want answers. You know that," Bridget said, the words flat from overuse.

For the past month, she'd suspected Archer no longer believed her—that he knew she wasn't just trying to understand why she still remembered. Especially not after they'd picked the question apart, again and again. Still, she clung to the lie. If he, or *Nylah*, knew half the things that plagued her subconscious, they would never look at her the same.

"You're not going to find them here."

Anger sparked in her chest. "You don't know that. There was a time when there were working gates all over. And today..."

Archer held up his hand. "It's just you and me here right now, Bridget. You don't have to hold back."

His words broke something inside her chest, already fragile by the day's events.

"You're right. I have been looking for... more." Bridget glanced at her closed bedroom door, where a stash of information and secrets were hidden under her bed. Part memories. Part truth. Part delusions she wrote down in the middle of the night. Throat constricting, she admitted, "I've been having these dreams..."

"I know," Archer said softly.

Bridget's gaze snapped to his, but he didn't flinch. Instead, he reached across the kitchen island and squeezed her hand.

"I can hear you," he added, voice low.

Heat traveled up Bridget's neck. Nylah was in the room next to her. If he could hear her, halfway across the house...

Her throat tightened. "They feel so real."

"I'm not surprised. Your brain has been messed with more than anyone I know."

Bridget shook her head. "It's not only dreams. I convinced myself I saw Cassia today. And there was this guy at the library... Something about him was so familiar."

Closing her eyes, Bridget chastised herself. She should've paid closer attention to him and asked more questions, especially when he had mentioned druids...

Something small pressed into her palm. She looked down.

"Take it and sleep," Archer said, closing her fingers around the object. "You haven't had more than a few hours since October."

Before she could protest, he added, "It's not magic. It's Ambien."

"Sleep isn't going to help me. I need *answers*," Bridget snapped. Dread filled her stomach just thinking about closing her eyes. It was the last thing she needed. "There has to be a reason why I feel like this... and an explanation for why I keep having these dreams and seeing things. Plus, last time I was in the way because I didn't know anything. I want to be able to help."

Archer stared at her incredulously. "*Last* time? The only time. You're not going back." He paused, then let out a hollow laugh. "Unless you think you are."

"I'm not going back," Bridget said, almost choking on the spark of longing she crushed down hard.

She wasn't. She *couldn't*. Nylah was here. And Cade... was going to be married soon. If he wasn't already. Bile rose up her throat.

"Who are you lying to?" Archer challenged. "Me or yourself?"

Bridget's hand shook as she grabbed the tequila bottle again, anything to steady her. He didn't get it. *He couldn't.* Even if she never set foot in Elyria again, someone from that realm *would* find her. She *knew* it. Felt it in her bones. Her connection to Elyria wasn't over. Not by a long shot.

"I'm not lying," Bridget croaked, chasing the words with another burning shot. "I just mean that I want to be ready when someone eventually finds us."

Archer's jaw clenched. "Bridget... it's been months." His voice was careful, like he was trying not to break something fragile. "No one is coming for us. No one is looking."

The words landed like a punch to the ribs. She staggered back a step, as if they'd knocked the wind out of her. For a heartbeat, the world tilted. It was a possibility she hadn't let herself to ponder. *Couldn't* let herself ponder. Because Archer was wrong. So wrong. She'd seen Cade fighting when she went through the gate. He wouldn't give up.

"You don't know that." She hated that her voice cracked. "Cade..."

"Let you go."

Bridget's heart stuttered. She could barely hear over the ringing in her ears. The kitchen blurred around the edges. Every atom in her body wanted to protest his statement, but she couldn't deny the growing doubt traveling up her spine. No matter how much she wanted to. It had already been slowly forming inside her months.

Bridget closed her eyes and willed his logic away. "You're wrong. You don't understand..."

Archer let out a hollow laugh. "I understand better than you think."

"I doubt that," Bridget snarled, despite immediately regretting the cruel words. There was an honesty in Archer's eyes she couldn't deny, but the truth he'd effectively seeped into *her* had left her reeling and spinning for a feeling other than misery.

"Did you know everyone in the Gemini coven has a twin?" Archer asked, effectively shutting her up and cooling the acid burning in her throat.

Bridget did know. From Cora. She closed her eyes, willing the Witch to disappear from behind her eyes.

"That's why I decided to work with her."

It took Bridget a moment to process his words, to get past the pounding of her heart. "Quinn?" she asked.

"A few years ago, my brother died of cancer. I was just a bartender living in Philadelphia when Quinn found me. I don't know why or how, but she told me what I was and said she wanted to work with me. Wanted to train me. She told me enough about Vassuryn and Elyria, that it was easy for me to cross back and forth, and officially become part of the Gemini coven."

Bridget's throat tightened as a prickle of guilt wormed its way into her heart. For months, he had helped her take care of Nylah. He'd even been the one to find her in New York for her. And not once had she ever asked him about his past, or why he worked with Quinn, or ask why he even bothered to stay with her at all.

"She promised things," he continued, eyes darkening. "Dangerous things. Things the Sanguis could do with the right runes... like bring him back."

Her breath caught. Bridget could almost feel the promise of that kind of power. Tangible, seductive, *cruel*.

"The more I worked with her, though," Archer continued, voice thickening, "the more I began to see the true cost of their magic. I watched her shrivel away to please someone whose name she wouldn't even dare utter. I watched countless people die just so she could get the Bloodstone. That's when I understood... some things aren't worth the cost. Some things are supposed to stay dead and buried."

Bridget flinched. "It's different," she whispered. She wasn't like him. Or Quinn. She wouldn't get so wrapped in blood magic, any magic, that she destroyed lives around her. She *knew* what it cost. Magic had already taken her memories, carved through her body, and torn Cade from her piece by piece. She wasn't chasing power. She was only trying to make sure it didn't take anything else.

"She started talking in her sleep too," Archer said. "And seeing things. It was like her personality would switch every other day. She'd be quiet one minute, and then vindictive the next, using spells I'd never even heard of... But she kept pushing. She couldn't let go."

A wave of nausea swelled in Bridget's stomach. Dreams. Visions. Voices. Was she unraveling the same way? Letting magic seep into the cracks until she didn't recognize herself anymore?

She took a few deep breaths before answering. "And you think Cade has... let go?"

"Bridget... You *died*. Your heart stopped. He must have sensed it. Why else has no one come through? Why hasn't he sent anyone?"

The truth turned her veins to ice. Did Cade really think she was dead? Ever since she'd been released from the hospital, she'd felt like a ghost. Like someone who didn't fit anywhere anymore. Instead of spending time with her sister, she'd hunted for information and waited for any sign from Elyria. She'd visited the gate to watch for someone coming through more times than she'd had dinner with Nylah.

All she had wanted in Elyria was to get back to her sister. Now that she had, she was doing everything *but* be with her. And she couldn't stomach thinking about Cade mourning her. *She was alive.* She wished she could shout it at him from across the void.

"He knows I'm alive. You're wrong," she argued, but her voice wobbled, like her conviction.

"Most of the time I am, and I would gladly let you spiral." Despite his words, he poured them both another shot and clinked her glass before he downed it. "I'm not saying this to you because I care. A little girl cares. And she wants you back."

Bridget's heart cracked in two. She closed her eyes to stop tears from falling. Nylah was here. Nylah needed her. She couldn't keep trying to live in both worlds.

"If I accept no one is coming..." Bridget croaked, stunned she was able to even get the words out. "If I... let him go. It's like everything meant nothing."

She couldn't accept that after everything they'd been through, this was it. They were never supposed to just... end.

"How can you say it meant nothing? Cade fought to make this happen, including making a deal with father. He wanted this for you. He wanted you to be reunited with Nylah. And now you are. That's not nothing. He didn't send you back to be a ghost. He wanted you to live. So *live*."

Bridget couldn't argue. This is exactly what she had wanted. The human realm. Nylah. No magic. No curses.

He'd given it to her. And the passports, IDs, and money that Archer had found stashed away in their old apartment... one last gift from him.

But every fiber of her being still yearned for him and screamed his name every waking moment. How was she supposed to let him go? The weight of missing him pulled at her every breath. At night, all she could see was him struggling against the binds from his father and trying to tell her one last thing.

"It's not going to happen overnight. Just... try," Archer said, giving her hand a quick squeeze. After a long moment, Bridget gazed up at him and wondered how they'd ended up like this. When the king had ordered him to take her through the gate, she never expected him to stick around or be her friend. Her closest one, at the moment. She had never expected he would willingly track down Nylah in Manhattan for her, or break into

Cade's old apartment to get the suitcase with their fake passports so they could start over. *Together.*

"Why did you do it?"

Archer didn't have to ask to know what she meant. He was the only reason she had survived. Without his CPR, she would have died in the Connecticut forest. He could have left her there and moved on in the human realm... without her trauma and insistence to stay near the Astraeus gate. No one in Elyria would have ever known.

Archer swallowed hard. "Quinn... she wasn't the one who deserved to win."

Bridget nodded, words of gratitude lodged painfully in her throat. Without a word, she turned and headed to the bathroom. The moment the door clicked shut behind her, she twisted the faucet on and braced her hands against the sink, knuckles white. Steam rose. Too hot. She cranked the cold. Her hot cheeks needed something to cool them down. For the first time in months, Bridget looked at herself in the mirror. *Really* looked.

The face staring back didn't belong to her.

Hollow eyes. Stiff shoulders built from relentless workouts. Hair that still flamed red at the roots, but from the shoulders down, it faded to lifeless white. Blinding white. Like life had been drained from the ends. Like magic had wanted one last price from her when she went through the gate.

In the hospital, Archer had said the moment they went through the gate, magic had exploded around them. That the second they landed in the human realm, a fissure formed in the stone and the ends of her hair slowly lost color. She looked down at her right hand. Even her ring hadn't escaped unscathed. A crack now tarnished the middle of the emerald.

Maybe it had been Cade's father destroying the gate after them. Maybe it had been another unexpected cost of crossing the gate with a human that had been gifted back her memories by the sacrifice of a Fae.

Maybe magic was really that unpredictable.

Bridget studied her reflection and made a decision. If she was going to let go—to move on, to smother the lingering grip Elyria still had on her and put her life with Nylah first—then every reminder of that night had to go.

And she knew exactly where to start.

Bridget reached down into her boot, and pulled out a pocketknife. Old habits did die hard. It glistened in the fluorescent lighting of the bathroom. Her mind traitorously presented an image of Cade and Elyria before she pushed it away. Before she tried to make sure she had every detail still memorized.

Gazing at the stranger in the mirror, Bridget lifted the knife to her shoulder blade. The ache in her throat swelled, hot and unmanageable, but she forced it down. Gripping the ends of her hair in one fist, she dragged the blade through and cut.

# CHAPTER THREE

The dreams always started the same.

Tonight was no different.

*Bridget walked around the palace in Cavamyne. Not the ruined husk she remembered, but something whole, untouched by time or war. Grand and resplendent, it gleamed like a memory too perfect to be real. Crystal chandeliers bathed the halls in golden light. The air shimmered with the scent of jasmine and rosewater. Gilded mirrors lined the corridors, and floor-to-ceiling windows revealed endless rolling hills bathed in sunlight, the sky impossibly blue, as if painted by magic.*

*There were two reasons she knew it was a dream. First, she had never actually seen or heard what the old Tuathan palace used to look like. Second, she was alone.*

*Most of the time.*

*Bridget always found the girl in the same place. The grand ballroom. It was the largest room in the palace, its golden marble floors stretching so far they seemed to vanish into haze. A crystal chandelier, larger than any Bridget had ever seen, refracted light into dancing rainbows across the vaulted ceiling.*

*Tonight, the girl stood in front of one of the arched windows. She turned as Bridget approached her. With black hair and blue eyes, and a pale purple dress that was large, lacey, and made of silk, the girl never spoke. Instead, she usually hummed a song under her breath or pointed at random things every time Bridget tried to talk to her. Eventually, she stopped trying and kept following the strange girl around the palace until the whole place caught on fire and she woke up.*

*A shiver went down Bridget's spine thinking of what was to come. When she made it to the girl's side, she gazed out the window. Her stomach twisted. The gate. She hadn't come across it in any of her dreams yet. It leered ominously. If she squinted, she would swear a blood stain dripped across it.*

*"Don't you hate this room? I know I do."*

*Bridget whipped her head around. "Excuse me?"*

*It was strange to hear the girl's voice after so many dreams. Bridget couldn't stop her mouth from falling open. She'd never spoken... and now her brain decided to have the girl talk to her about the ballroom?*

*The girl looked amused. "You're having trouble remembering."*

*"I remember perfectly fine," Bridget replied automatically. A lick of panic shot up her spine. She would wake up and remember her life. She always did.*

*"You're having trouble remembering the right words," the girl reiterated.*

*Bridget's anxiety quelled. The girl wasn't talking about memories or curses, but spells. Spells couldn't harm her in her dreams. But her obsession with finding any scrap of information about magic and Elyria was now fueling her subconscious. She sighed. "I've been told to let it go."*

*The girl frowned. "By who?"*

*Tilting her head, Bridget paused. This was her dream... didn't she already know who? "Archer," she said.*

*"Since when have you ever listened to a Warlock?" The girl laughed.*

*But Bridget didn't. The light outside had disappeared, darkening the ballroom a shade. Something wasn't right. Slamming her eyes shut, Bridget took a step back. She wanted to wake up.*

*"I'll help," the girl said.*

*Before Bridget could stop her, a spell fell from the girl's lips. The ancient language pierced her heart and conjured a swirling dread she couldn't fight. It poked at a memory in her mind she couldn't quite grasp. All she knew was that she needed to get away. To wake up.*

*Now.*

*Air billowed around her, threatening to thrust her into a growing whirlpool by her feet.*

*"Stop," Bridget ordered, almost falling into the swirling hole.*

*The girl ignored her. She repeated the phrase again. The wind grew harder and Bridget tried to scramble away.*

*"Stop!"*

Gasping, Bridget accidentally launched herself to the floor, still fleeing from the whirlpool. The hard, cold wood floor brought her back to her senses. She was awake. She was in her room. Safe. For the time being, at least. Bridget sat up and pulled out the notebook she hid under her bed. Despite the alarm that still rattled her bones, Bridget wrote down the spell that girl had repeated. And everything else from the dream. She always did. Just in case.

Once she was done, she flipped through the rest of the notebook. Her Elyrian notebook, she secretly called it. After she'd been released from the hospital, she started writing down everything. That way, if her memories were ever stolen again, she could have a reminder. At night, when she couldn't sleep, she wrote down every fact Cora had ever told her. During the day, she recorded every memory she could of the tournament. And then there were the Cade pages. His were the most detailed. She wouldn't let herself forget him. Not again.

When a noise from Nylah's room echoed through the dark house, Bridget stuffed the notebook back under the bed. She checked her phone. It was 6:00 a.m., which meant everyone would be up soon anyway. Bridget heaved herself off the floor and meandered into the kitchen. Coffee first. Then pancakes.

When Nylah finally tumbled into the kitchen, too full of energy appropriate for a Wednesday morning, in Bridget's opinion, smoke lingered in the air. She didn't know it was possible to burn pancakes, but somehow, she had. Luckily, her little sister didn't complain and doused a pound of syrup on each one.

As she ate, Bridget watched Nylah closely, trying to find any hint that she was angry or disappointed in her for missing the performance, even though she claimed not to be. But her sister seemed like her usual, bubbly self.

"You'll be there to pick me up today, right?" Nylah asked, zipping up her backup.

Bridget nodded and grabbed Nylah's puffy leopard print coat. "Of course. School is over at... 5:30?"

Nylah paused before giving her a droll look. "You're not funny."

There it was. The hesitation Bridget had been looking for. She had only picked up Nylah at school a few times, and each time, she *had* been late. But she was turning over a new leaf. No more obsessing about being ready for Shamans or Witches. She was going to give Nylah her full attention and be the stable, sane, loving older sister that she deserved. "I'll be there," Bridget promised.

"What are you doing today?" Nylah asked.

Bridget shrugged. "Just running some errands."

The second Nylah ran into the restroom to check her hair one last time, Archer sat up on the couch and narrowed his eyes at her. "Lie," he mouthed.

Bridget's cheeks heated. "Just one more time, I promise," she whispered. After cutting her hair, she had promised Archer she was done visiting the gate. But it was the closest she could get to Cade and she needed to say goodbye... at least for now. Her heart and head still couldn't process a definite ending.

Archer was about to say something else, but he stopped when Nylah walked back into the living room. "I like that you cut your hair. It suits you," she told Bridget. "The white was a little too tortured goth for me."

Bridget absentmindedly messed with the ends that barely reached her shoulder. She hadn't worn her hair so short since the fifth grade, but she was happy to be rid of the white. "I'm glad you think so, but seriously, if you don't leave now, you're going to be late."

Nylah jumped forward and wrapped her arms around her. "I love you."

"I love you, too," Bridget said, before something hard sent a pain through her hip. She pulled away from Nylah and reached into her sister's coat pocket. Her heart stopped when she pulled out the black rock she hadn't seen since the day Archer had taken her to Elyria. It still gleamed like a rainbow in the light, but in her hand, she could see the lines and crevices that told her it wasn't a real stone, but a crystal. Coldness radiated off every inch and stung her palms. Bridget swallowed hard. "You still have this thing?"

"Of course," Nylah said, demeanor serious as she carefully placed the stone back in her pocket. "I made a promise. I'll see you later."

Seconds later, she was gone. Bridget stared at the closed door, unable to move or breathe. It was a rune. It had to be. There was no other reason for Cade to have a random rock. She knew that now. But why give it to Nylah? Why have it all? She wanted to voice her suspicion to Archer, but she had just promised to try to move on. She would just have to keep an eye on it, and only mention it if something weird happened.

Bridget turned and found Archer watching her carefully. "I'm fine," she said through gritted teeth.

"The haircut says otherwise. Isn't a drastic change to your appearance supposed to be some sort of a call for help?"

"Lay off the self-help books. I barely cut off a few inches," Bridget replied, glaring at him.

Archer clicked his tongue. "And you're trying to take us down with you, judging by your attempt at breakfast."

Before she left, Bridget threw an extra burnt pancake at him.

The hour-long bus ride to the forest straddling the Massachusetts–New Hampshire border was one Bridget knew by heart. She made the trip several times a week. After her release from the hospital, she'd finally convinced Archer to show her the hidden gate back to Astraeus. Since then, she had made it a habit to visit and watch the gate weekly for any sign that someone was going in or out.

So far, the gate remained still and lifeless.

Each time she visited, she kept her distance. At first, she'd been afraid a Shaman would appear out of nowhere and shove her through, leaving Nylah alone again. If Finn, Delphine, or Castor ever showed themselves, *then* she would step out of hiding.

Now, though, she was afraid that touching it would confirm her worst suspicion.

Cade's father had destroyed the gate, and no one was ever coming through again.

Bridget moved to stand in front of the gate. It was different from the one in Cavamyne. Here, in the darkest part of the forest, five long, thin stones stood in a circle. Each stone was connected by lines of gray and white rocks, most of which were buried underneath soil. Shadows and sunlight warred for dominance over the circle.

Bridget took off her glove and grazed her right hand over one of the stones, almost hoping to feel a spark of magic, like Finn had in the ruins of the old palace wing in Astraeus. But nothing intensified under her finger-tips. She hated that hollowness seeped into her veins, slow and unwanted.

She wasn't sure whether one rock, all of them, or the center point of the circle took people back to Astraeus, so she picked the one illuminated by the most sunlight to approach. Up close, etches of symbols ingrained in the dark, faded stone appeared. Feeling a little silly, she struggled for a moment, unsure of what to do or say. Eventually, Bridget closed her eyes and wished for the impossible. She wished that somehow, Cade would hear her.

"I'm sorry," Bridget whispered, laying a hand on the stone. "I hope you know that."

Lately, guilt consumed her every waking moment. *She* was the reason he wasn't here. Because of *her*, they'd lost the Bloodstone. To save *her*, he'd been forced to make a deal with his father. She wanted to fix it. She wanted to fix it more than anything. But the belief that she would ever get the chance was slowly slipping out of her grasp. Some nights, the thought that Cade might hate her now kept her awake for hours.

"I never wanted any of this to happen... Archer told me you might think I'm dead. He thinks it's better that way but I'm not so sure. I don't want you to believe you failed. You didn't. Nylah and I are together. That was the plan, right?"

Bridget inhaled sharply. Longing flooded her until it almost splintered her from the inside. He should be here with them. Not alone in Elyria, maybe thinking she was dead. There was never any plan that was supposed to involve *goodbye*.

Some reckless part of her still refused to believe it. But if she stopped now, she was going to break completely.

"I hope you know that I love you," she continued, barely able to speak from the knot in her throat. "And..."

Behind her, a twig snapped. Bridget spun around, already reaching for the knife tucked into her boot. Her fingers wrapped around the handle before her mind caught up with what her eyes were seeing. A man stood at the edge of the clearing. He was tall, perhaps even more so than Cade, and didn't seem to be much older than her. A dark green uniform clung to his lean frame, and tousled blond hair poked out from beneath a brown ball cap. It wasn't until she spotted the familiar park service logo stitched to his chest that she let out a slow breath and eased the knife back into its sheath.

He held up his hands. "I'm one of the park rangers. I didn't mean to interrupt."

"But you did," Bridget snapped, turning her face from him so she could discreetly wipe away the wetness on her cheeks. She couldn't believe some guy had just listened to her crying to a rock.

"I'm just out on patrol."

Bridget narrowed her eyes. "I didn't know patrolling meant eavesdropping."

He moved closer to her, and for a split-second, déjà vu washed over her. The way his bright blue eyes flickered to the forest behind her, like he expected someone to be waiting there, tugged at a memory deep in her mind. Bridget searched his face, hoping something else in his features triggered how she knew him.

Her stare must have been too intense because he suddenly paused his forward movement. Clearing his throat, he replied, "I'm sorry, most people don't linger in this part of the woods. There are rumors it's cursed, but I know that's ridiculous. I just wanted to make sure everything was okay."

Bridget slowly moved her hand behind her back. Tucked between her jeans and belt, another knife lay hidden. If she was going to figure out how she knew him, she needed him to keep talking. Someone approaching her at the gate couldn't be a coincidence. Especially when they used the word *cursed*. "Are you new? I come here a few times a week and I've never seen any kind of... ranger."

"There was an incident in a state park in Connecticut a few months ago. A girl was shot."

Ice filled her veins as her stomach dropped to the ground. He was talking about her. But how? There had been no news stories or articles published about her. Archer had made sure of that. She'd withheld every piece of personal information she could from the doctors.

"Since then, areas like this have been on high alert," he continued. "We don't want any more accidents."

In the blink of an eye, his expression hardened. Bridget swallowed. No more pretending then. He circled her, trying to herd her away from the gate. The action made it clear he knew exactly what this place was. Muscles taunt, she gripped the dagger's handle, ready to throw it the second he came closer.

And then she *knew*.

She'd seen him the night she'd returned through the gate, standing behind Archer with a phone in his hand. And then again, through the windows of the ambulance after they'd restarted her heart a second time.

And yesterday in the library.

"You were there that night. You're the one who called 911," Bridget said. "I remember the phone in your hand. And in the library... you were interested in that book about druids. You're from Elyria, aren't you? How did you get here?"

The ranger froze. Bridget didn't miss the flash of surprise that lit up his eyes, like he hadn't expected her to remember quite that much. He let out a hollow laugh. "I think you're confused."

Bridget shook her head. She scanned his body, trying to find any sign of who or *what* he was, but his long sleeves and pants covered almost every inch of skin. "Who are you?"

"I told you, I'm a park..."

The second she heard the lie, Bridget flung her dagger at him, aiming for his leg. It wasn't meant to kill, just to buy her a second to run. But before it landed, the ranger lifted his hand. The blade shivered in midair with a metallic hum, as if it had struck an invisible wall. Then, yanked by an unseen thread, it snapped sideways and clattered against one of the standing stones.

Bridget launched herself at him. Her fingers caught the edge of his collar and tore the hat from his head before he sidestepped her with inhuman grace. Momentum sent her crashing to the ground. Pain bloomed across her knees and elbows as she rolled onto her back, gasping. Without his hat on, she could see arched ears peeking out of blond hair, along with a snaking, blue tattoo. Her stomach dropped.

"You're a Shaman," she breathed.

The man cringed. "I really hate that's what they call us now."

What the fuck? Bridget tried to reach for the other knife in her boot, but before her fingers grazed it, she was in the air. Her spine cracked as she hit one of the standing stones. "Who sent you?" Bridget growled, trying to move her arms and legs, but invisible ropes kept her in place.

"Stay away from the gate, Bridget," he warned, bending to retrieve his hat from the ground before placing it on his head.

She froze. He said her name like he *knew* her. Impossible. *Terrifying*. She shoved the thought down. She couldn't let herself feel the full weight of it.

"How do you know my name?" Bridget demanded.

He moved until he stood inches from her. Up close, she could see the power that glowed and swirled behind his pale eyes. The orbs were unreadable as they searched her face. Bridget couldn't bring herself to look away. Instead, she flinched against the rock, hoping to move *something*, but her entire body remained frozen. Her heart pounded as she waited for his next move.

After a long moment, he finally said, "We're out of time. For the good of all, never visit here again."

Before she could blink, he grabbed her arm. Bridget screamed as they both disappeared in a cloud of smoke.

It was like Elyria, but worse. She'd forgotten the sensation of traveling with Delphine, forgotten what it felt like to have every atom and cell torn apart and put back together. Bridget screamed, and when she thought her body would disintegrate entirely, she landed on her hands and knees on a gray sidewalk.

Bridget barely caught a glimpse of the man's dark green uniform walking away when hands started grabbing her. She tried to ignore the gasps and questions of the concerned crowd she'd fallen into in Boston. Jumping up, she ignored the blood pouring from her nose and tried to run after him, but he was nowhere to be found.

# CHAPTER FOUR

### CASSIA

"It's a little overcooked, don't you think?"

Cassia rolled her eyes. Every night, her father found something to complain about, whether it was the food, drink, or conversation. It had been that way as long as she could remember. Now, however, she was the sole person responsible for fixing those complaints since she was the only one who ever bothered to show up for dinner anymore. It wasn't a fun job, but she knew if *she* were to stop coming, her father would do more than just verbally berate her.

"It's always overcooked," Cassia muttered, barely resisting the urge to down her entire glass of wine. "Should I go say something to the chef?"

Her father continued to roughly cut his steak. "Don't bother. I don't have time to hire anyone else right now. Is your brother not joining us?"

Cassia scoffed. "The last time he had dinner with us, you forced a Shaman into his head. What makes you think he'll ever join us again?"

After throwing down his fork with a loud smack, he glared at her with steely, dark eyes. "He'll get over it eventually. At least he seems to finally be getting over that human girl. I heard he's throwing another party in Astraeus tonight."

Cassia bit her tongue. If only her father knew what her brother was *really* doing. She wasn't quite sure how Cade was fooling him, but she did know one thing: her brother was definitely not over Bridget. She was all he and his friends seemed to talk about. Well, *her* friends, too. Once upon a time. They avoided her most days.

But maybe there was something she could do to make her brother stop glaring at her every time she saw him. Casually, she suggested, "If you want Cade to come to dinner, maybe you should postpone tomorrow's banishment. You know he still wants more time to question the other one."

"Clever, but it's been postponed long enough," her father grunted. "The Andarrian girl has proved herself useless."

"But..."

"Enough," he hissed, "besides, any human that willingly chooses the gate instead of a release for information shouldn't be listened to. There's obviously something wrong with her."

Cassia fought the glower that threatened to form on her face. Well, she tried. "How are you even sending the Andarrian girl across the gate? Didn't you banish all the Shamans?"

Even Finn, one of the best trackers she knew, hadn't been able to find a single one.

"Do you really think I wouldn't ensure I could still summon them easily? They're bound to the throne, after all. They can't stay away for long."

*Just long enough for Cade to get married.* Her father looked way too proud of himself. Banishing the Shamans hadn't helped anyone. All it had done was ensure Cade couldn't use one to send one of his friends across the gate. Wanting to change the subject, Cassia said, "I received a letter from Elora. She wants to come home."

She and Elora had never been close, in fact, they usually despised being in the same vicinity as each other. But if her younger sister was home, maybe she wouldn't have to continue on with pointless dinners. A night without her father sounded like paradise.

For once, her father paused and considered her request. After a long moment, he said, "We'll see. I guess there's no reason to keep the deal with your brother. His little human is gone for good."

They sat in silence the rest of dinner.

Bottle of wine in hand, Cassia made her way to the south wing of the palace. Once she'd heard about Cade's party, she knew that's where he'd be instead. Inwardly scoffing, she took a long swig from her bottle. The red wine inside was tart on her tongue. She couldn't believe her father actually believed Cade would throw a party on the last night he had a chance to question the Andarrian girl about Cora and the Sanguis before she was erased forever. He'd spent months trying to get information out of her. Luckily for her, the runes embedded in her skin made her mind impenetrable. Cassia couldn't help but be a little jealous.

When she rounded a particularly moldy and vine-infested corner, Cassia spotted Delphine sitting outside the old dungeon door. Slumped over a book, her long, dark hair covered her face. As she walked, Cassia purposely dug her feet into the hallway's hard dirt. Delphine jumped and looked up when she finally heard the noisy footsteps.

"Again?" Cassia drawled, even though she knew exactly where she'd find her brother. If they wanted her to play the part of the uncaring twin sister, then she would. For good measure, she added, "And an effective guard shouldn't be reading a book. If I had been anyone else, it would have been too late to warn Cade."

Delphine's jaw clenched. "You know how he gets. He's not going to give up. And I'm really just here to make sure he leaves in time to make it to the party before Orion does."

Ah, so *that* was how he was fooling their father, by making an appearance at the party just in time for their father's little spy to see. Cassia couldn't believe it was that simple. Her father usually smelled her schemes from a mile away.

"Well, he'll have to give up by tomorrow afternoon," Cassia said. "I tried to convince my father to delay her banishment, but like always, he doesn't listen to me."

"Maybe she'll finally tell him what he wants to know tonight."

Cassia snorted. "I doubt that."

She'd observed the Andarrian girl enough times to recognize pure stubbornness. It did take one to know one. She wasn't going to tell Cade anything. Trying to put the cork back in the bottle of wine, Cassia looked down at Delphine just in time to see her stuff a letter into the pages of her book. The envelope was worn, like it had been opened, closed, and read many times. Delphine had been quick, but Cassia only needed a glance to recognize the handwriting. Once, she had known it better than her own. A tremble of something she didn't like went through Cassia's chest as she pondered whether *that* had been what Delphine had been focused on, not the book. She swallowed, and then got the nerve to ask, "Is that a letter from Castor?"

Delphine's cheeks reddened, and she didn't look Cassia in the eye as she said, "It is. He just arrived in Tafari and is boarding a ship here within the next week. He said he's just now responding because he's been in the human realm. The king still won't let him through the gate here in Astraeus. Not that there's any Shamans here to help with that. He said he has news for Cade about Bridget."

"If he doesn't say the news in the letter, that means it's not good," Cassia murmured. She'd gotten enough letters from him before to know he only sent niceties by mail. He believed bad news should only be told in person. Cassia curled her lips around her teeth. Him and his stupid honor.

"You don't know that," Delphine snapped.

Cassia resisted the urge to roll her eyes and secretly hoped Delphine hadn't shared the letter with Cade. It would only get his hopes up. And what she'd heard about that night gave her serious doubts about Bridget's survival. Especially when no one there had left unscathed. Speaking of... "Where's Finn?" Cassia asked.

Delphine paused. Her dark, slanted eyes were wary as she said, "Someone spotted something weird on the Kastronian border."

"That's not vague at all," Cassia muttered. When Delphine didn't reply, Cassia heaved the door to the dungeon open. Maybe she could finagle what happened at the border out of her brother. And get him to finally just let her do *something* to help.

Delphine jumped up. "What are you doing?"

"What does it look like I'm doing? I'm going down there."

"He won't like that."

Cassia ground her teeth together. Of course, he wouldn't, but she was tired of being told what to do. And she knew Cade better than anyone. There was no way he was calm when his last connection to information about Bridget was a day away from disappearing.

"Too bad," she called, already half-way down the curving staircase. The deeper she went, the colder and darker it got. Why the hell were they still allowed to keep people down here? She could feel her sinuses closing already.

When the stairs ended, the small expanse was lit by a row of torches. She could barely see Cade sitting in front of one of the cells. The one he always sat in front of. The one that held Alexia.

It was only after the incident in Cavamyne they'd discovered Alexia's Andarrian tattoos, the *runes* etched in the skin of her biceps, much like Bridget's necklace. And now here she sat. Cocky and safe. Mind impenetrable from Cade's assault, and on her way to the human realm by request. Their father had wanted to use her for information about Andarre, but she'd sat in the south wing for months without saying a word. He'd only accepted her request to go through the gate to spite Cade.

To Cassia's surprise, Alexia's eyes lit up when she entered the room.

Without turning around, Cade sighed. "What the hell are you doing here?"

"I was bored," Cassia quipped, knowing the response would annoy Cade the most. She wanted to gloat as she watched his shoulders stiffen. Finally, he wasn't ignoring her.

"And why is that my problem?"

"I thought maybe you would like some help with your interrogation."

Cade finally looked at her. She almost gasped. He looked worse than last week. Ghastly, purple bags hung under his eyes, and the stubble on his face was out of control. And his *hair*. There were many things about her brother she was jealous of, including his perfect, wavy locks, but now, each strand lay kinked and messy. It looked like he needed to shower and sleep for a week.

"I heard about your party from our father," Cassia said, hoping he would listen. He needed to get out of the dungeon and into the sun, around people, or *something*. "Maybe it's time you start heading there. She's a lost cause."

Fire brewed behind Cade's eyes, identical to her own, but before he could reply, Alexia's voice interrupted them.

"For that bottle of wine, I'll give you three questions."

Both of them whipped their heads to stare at her in shock. That one sentence was the most Cassia had ever heard her speak. Beside her, Cade venomously glared. A shiver went up Cassia's spine. At least she'd never been on the receiving end of one like *that*.

"I've sat down here for months, tried every spell possible to get past the rune on your skin, asked every question I could think of, and *now* you decide to—"

"That's a bottle from a winery in Vassuryn," Alexia said, reaching out her hand. "It's one of my favorites. After tomorrow, who knows the next time I'll be able to have some."

Cassia wasn't sure she believed her. Something dangerous glinted in the girl's eyes. Still stunned, she looked to Cade for guidance. For a long moment, he gazed at Alexia calculatingly.

"Do we have a deal?" Alexia asked.

Jaw clenched in determination, Cade swiped the bottle out of Cassia's hand and thrust it at Alexia. "Deal."

The air in the room changed.

The Andarrian took a long gulp of wine before she spoke. "What would you like to know? You've asked about Cora, Quinn, how we knew about the other gate and the Bloodstone... actually, you've asked so many things I've lost count."

Cade stayed silent. For once, Cassia wished he would enter her mind and tell her what he was thinking.

"Or maybe tonight you want to hear about Bridget. It really was a long seven months for her with Cora. I can tell you about the scars on her hands, or her back. Or that particularly nasty one on her calf from when Dante..."

Cassia jumped when the entire room began to vibrate. The bars of Alexia's cell rattled as a gust of a wind swirled around her. To Cassia's disgust, the human girl smirked. Beside her, Cade's eyes glowed as his entire body shook with rage. Without thinking, Cassia touched his arm. For a second, the power radiating off him burned her hand. When she recoiled, his eyes returned to normal. "Calm down," she whispered. "You only get three questions. Ask the right ones."

"I know that," Cade hissed, chest heaving. He turned to Alexia. "As for Dante, why do you think a pole went through the center of his chest the second I found your camp in Vassuryn? His face was one of the first things I saw in Bridget's mind after not being able to find her presence for seven months. Now that I know you're from Andarre, I'm guessing that was thanks to you."

"Is that your first question? Whether or not I gave Bridget the amethyst rune?"

Taking a step forward, Cade said, "Don't pretend to be clever. You know there wasn't a question in that statement. Why did Cora want Bridget? In Cavamyne, she said someone had been looking for her. That she was sent to get her."

Cassia closed her eyes. He was already starting off with a stupid question. But she should have guessed all his questions would revolve around Bridget. There were so many other things they needed to know, though, like why Cora seemed to know so much about the Sanguis. And there had to be a reason Alexia requested to go to the human realm. Why purposefully curse yourself?

"As you've already guessed, I'm from Andarre," Alexia murmured, motioning to her tattoos. "I met Cora there. She vouched for me when I was wrongly accused of a crime. If it wasn't for her, I would have been put to death. After that, I vowed to help her. Someone there found out she was a Witch and asked her to find Bridget."

"I think you should ask about the Sanguis," Cassia said, sensing Cade was impulsively about to ask about who sent Cora.

A muscle in Cade's jaw twitched. She could tell he knew she was right, but Alexia had piqued his interest. Finally, he spit out, "What do you know about Quinn and the Sanguis?"

"I don't know exactly how Quinn began her time with the Sanguis. After all, they are banished and stuck in Iegorus. Cora said they found a way to communicate with her from there. Something about finding a weak spot in the walls between realms. I only saw Quinn once, right after we found her with Bridget in Pontas with the Gemini coven. She used a blood spell and talked to them through a rune. She almost looked... possessed. It weakened her enough that we were able to take Bridget after she passed out."

Cade stilled.

"Ask her why she wants to go through the gate," Cassia whispered furiously, gripping the edge of Cade's sleeve.

Who in their right mind volunteered to erase themselves? There had to be a reason for that smug look. But as her brother stepped forward and gripped the bars of Alexia's cell, she knew he was no longer listening to her.

"So you intercepted Bridget in Pontas? There were scars on her stomach from blood magic. It happened there, right? There was blood everywhere when I found the Gemini coven hiding there with most of Bridget's things from New York. What else was Quinn looking for?"

"Cade..." Cassia sighed. That was question three. And a few extra. She didn't think he even realized it. It was the first time she'd seen his eyes show signs of life in months.

"We'd been informed to intercept Bridget there."

"How?" Cade pressed. "From who?"

"You've already asked three questions."

Cassia swore the bars of the cell bent from Cade's grip on them. After a long moment, he hissed, "What else do you want? Let's make another deal."

Cassia jumped in front of him. He was in no state of mind to be making deals. "You haven't made a deal with me. Why do you want to go through the gate?"

Alexia pressed the bottle of wine to her lips and chugged. She chugged until there was nothing left. She wiped her mouth with her forearm and then flung the bottle to the side. With a deafening crack, it shattered against the metal bars surrounding her.

Cassia received her message loud and clear. There would be no more deals

Cade snarled, and then stormed toward the stairs. Cassia ran after him. Barely able to keep up with pace, she panted, "Would you slow…"

Her brother didn't wait for her to finish. Instead, he shoved the top, wooden door open with a violent flick of his hand. Alarmed, Delphine hopped up and worriedly gazed between the twins.

"Of all the questions…" Cassia began.

Eyes stormy, Cade whirled on her. "Don't start. I knew exactly what I was asking. You weren't there that night in Cavamyne. Bridget might be back in the human realm, but things aren't over. There's still someone out there looking for her."

"But don't you think it's weird Alexia volunteered to go through the gate, especially knowing about the curse?"

"I don't give a fuck about why she wants to do anything!" Cade roared. "If she wants to forget everything about Elyria and leave, fine. Good for her. At least I got some answers from her."

And that's when she saw it. The gleam in his eyes she saw in the mirror every morning. The one he tried to hide when he noticed her gazing at him. He was… jealous. Whether over Alexia going to the human realm or forgetting, she wasn't sure.

Delphine stepped between them. "I think it's time to…"

"Right… I forgot about the damn party," Cade muttered. "Cass, whatever you do, don't let our father into your head again. You heard too much tonight. I don't want him knowing anything else about Bridget or who may be after her."

She wanted to scream at him that she never wanted him in her head in the first place, but instead, she pursed her lips and glared. Bridget wasn't the only one with a target on her back.

"What about who's after you? Quinn is still out there."

"Last time I saw her, she had one arm," Cade retorted. "I think I'm fine."

Before Cassia could argue, he grabbed Delphine's arm. And that's when she saw the hesitation on the other girl's face. Despite her claims to the contrary, Delphine was still struggling with traveling. Ever since Cavamyne, Cassia had noticed her reluctance. But who could blame her? The trip there with two other people had almost killed her. After a moment, Delphine closed her eyes, braced herself, and then disappeared with Cade with a loud pop.

By herself in the ruins of the south wing, silence pierced her ears. She should be used to the hollow noise by now. It was what she'd heard for months. Cassia's throat tightened. She hated it. She hated feeling useless. She hated wondering what everyone else was doing without her. And most of all, she hated wondering if her brother would ever forgive her.

# CHAPTER FIVE

The courtyard where the gate was located always gave Cassia chills. Once, when she was eleven, she'd accidentally run into the black spiked door. She'd been playing a game of tag with Cade and Finn and hadn't been paying attention to the path in front of her. If she lifted her chin, the tiny scar was still visible. For a few years, her pride prevented her from ever returning to the courtyard where she had lost the game. But now...

Cassia studied the garden's chalky, stone archways, the drooping flowers, and the thorny bushes. Everything looked so lifeless. And then there was the door. A noise radiated from it, almost like static. A static that seemed to drain and suck every ounce of magic that dared to get close to it. Absentmindedly, she wondered if that was the reason for the state of the plants. When Cassia heard footsteps to her left, she jumped behind a bush. She chastised herself for the ridiculous impulse, especially when she realized it was just Cade and Delphine walking toward the entrance to the gate. She blamed the courtyard. It always made her jumpy. Still, she remained behind the bush and strained her eyes to listen to their quiet voices. Eavesdropping had become her only source of information lately.

"I checked on Marin again this morning," Delphine said. "She still isn't awake. This isn't normal, especially for a Shaman…"

"What happened when Bridget and Archer went through the gate wasn't normal. She was the one closest to the blast…"

Cassia's interest piqued. Marin still hadn't woken up? When everyone had returned from Cavamyne, she remembered hearing about how the young Shaman had passed out after sending Bridget and the other Warlock through the gate, and that seconds later, a blast of magic knocked everyone to the ground. Cade had also returned unconscious, but he'd awoken after a day.

"Do you think that'll happen today?" Delphine asked.

Suddenly, Cade's voice entered Cassia's head.

*Stop spying.*

Cassia ground her teeth together and stepped toward them. *I wasn't. I was here first.*

*Your ridiculous attempt to hide behind that bush says otherwise. Are you here to watch?*

*Yes.*

Watching the Andarrian girl cross the gate hadn't been her original plan, but if Cade wasn't actively telling her to leave, then she would go. A shiver went down her spine as she remembered the last time she crossed over. The process hadn't been easy.

Cassia reached Cade and Delphine in time to hear her brother mutter, "I guess we'll see. They'll be sending Alexia through any minute."

"I'm glad you're here, Cass. I really didn't want to go down there. Let me know how it goes," Delphine shuddered. Cassia was glad she wasn't the only one affected by the courtyard's aura, but her spirits dampened when she caught Cade send Delphine a conspiratorial glance before she walked away.

Still sensing the tether to Cade's mind, Cassia added, *I'm surprised she's leaving. I actually thought you would have some stupid plan in place to get her through the gate with Alexia.*

*I considered it, but our father threatened to kill her parents if I tried.*

Cassia searched Cade's face. He avoided eye-contact with her, a blatant tell that he was *lying*. More than ever, she was determined to follow him down to the gate to figure out his plan.

But that was Cade. Always on edge. Always planning. Always keeping it secret. More than ever, she wished for the time before Riker's death when they'd been an actual family. One without the sense of impending doom riding on their shoulders.

"If Bridget was still alive…"

"She *is* alive," Cade snapped.

"Fine. If she *remembered*," Cassia corrected blithely, "do you really think this is what she'd want you doing? Not sleeping and obsessing over that Cora woman or the Sanguis? I talked to her enough to know—"

"You may have helped her a few times, for selfish reasons I might add, but you don't know her," Cade growled. "Whether she remembers me or not, I'm not going to let someone try to drag her here to Elyria again."

Cassia bit her tongue. Her brother really was stubborn. Maybe even more than her. If he didn't want Bridget involved with Elyria anymore, why send Castor to find and check on her? Why bother to hold on to someone he was never going to see again? She couldn't imagine feeling that way about anyone… or maybe she could.

But it was never going to happen again.

"At least fix… this," Cassia said, pinching the rough stubble on his face. "And the hair. You look like a caveman."

Cade recoiled and patted down his hair. "Whatever. It's not that bad."

Rolling her eyes, Cassia added, "Delphine mentioned something happened at the border."

"There was… an animal. That's the official story."

Cassia tipped her head. "And the unofficial one?"

She forced her tone to stay casual, even as her pulse kicked up. Cade was talking to her—*really* talking to her—and a small, reckless part of her wanted to believe it meant things might finally go back to normal. Before everything broke.

The world around Cassia disappeared as Cade placed images in her head. Images of a burning building. Screams. A shadow careening soldiers to the ground. Bodies with black markings that oozed blood.

Finally, Cade's voice pulled her out of the vision. *No animal did that.*

Cassia's heart pounded as she tried to refocus on the landscape around her. His assault has been so vivid, she'd nearly forgotten she was safe at home. *Please tell me that's not blood magic.*

She'd never seen it up close, only heard the stories. Magic always demanded a price, but blood magic destroyed. Cade met her gaze, the same grim understanding reflected back at her.

*Finn will let us know,* he answered.

"About what you said yesterday..." Cassia said, still shivering from the images, "I don't want to help our father. I want to help *you*. I didn't let him into my head on purpose that night. Believe me, I tried to fight him. I think... I think I know how to keep him at bay next time. I swear."

Cade's throat bobbed. His eyes moved to the ground. "I know."

"I know I'm not powerful." Cassia's voice cracked. The admission was one she actively avoided, even to herself. But she knew it was the one thing she could say to get Cade to actually listen to her. "And I know I can't do extraordinary things like Finn or Delphine, but I want to help..."

Suddenly, Cade whipped his head toward the black, spiked door in the center of the courtyard. "Did you hear that?"

"Hear what?" Cassia asked, hearing nothing but static coming from the entrance to the gate.

Face pale, Cade's eyes darted around the courtyard. "I swear I heard..."

Cassia grabbed his arm when he didn't finish his sentence. A trickle of anxiety went up her spine. She'd never seen her brother so rattled. "Are you okay?"

Cade squeezed his eyes shut and pinched the bridge of his nose. After a long moment, he grunted. "Let's just get down there."

Without a backwards glance, he strode forward and flung open the door. The torches lining the winding stairs flickered on and off as he passed each one. Cassia hurried after him, confused by his sudden change in demeanor. They had been the only two people in the courtyard. The deeper they went, the more goosebumps erupted on her arms.

In front of her, Cade sucked in a breath and fell against the stone. His knuckles turned white as he gripped the rough wall. "She's screaming!" he bellowed frantically. "You don't hear that?"

"No one is screaming," Cassia answered as he darted down the staircase, following something she couldn't hear. She took off after him, nearly sliding down the steps from her speed, but still never catching up. When Cassia reached the bottom step, she slammed into his back. She grabbed Cade's arm to keep from falling.

Only a Shaman, a guard, Alexia, and their father stood around the gate. The stone vibrated and glowed as the Shaman prepared it for Alexia's crossing. Out of breath, Cassia asked, "What the hell is going on?"

"I don't know," Cade mumbled. His entire body trembled as he stared at the gate.

"That was quite an entrance," their father said. He spared Cade a second glance. Cassia could have sworn there was a tiny hint of concern. Gripping his rune dagger, he continued, "I'm surprised to see you two together."

Cade kept staring at the gate, transfixed and frozen with something akin to... anticipation. Which frightened Cassia more than anything. Only one voice could pull that reaction from him. What exactly had he heard? And if Bridget was somehow on the other side of the gate...

She didn't have more time to ponder it, though, with their father now staring them down. Clearing her throat, she answered, "It wasn't planned. We ran into each other in the courtyard."

Their father shrugged, and then turned to whisper something into his guard's ear. Before Cassia could figure out what he was saying, Alexia caught her eye. The smirk on the other girl's face made her stomach curl. "Is there something you have to say?" Cassia snapped.

The Andarrian girl shrugged, a little too smugly for Cassia's taste. Especially since Cade's face was still pale.

Their father snapped his fingers. "We're ready. Let's get this over with," he grunted, motioning Alexia forward. Before the guard reached her, she turned to Cassia.

"Yesterday, you wanted to know I chose the gate."

"Does it matter?" Cassia whispered, avoiding their father's gaze. "In a few minutes, you won't even remember your own name."

She grabbed Cade's arm and tried to drag him out of his trance. Whatever secrets Alexia thought she could dangle in front of them, Cassia didn't care anymore. All she could hear was the shrill warning screaming through her bones that something was about to go very wrong.

Alexia smiled, slow and knowing. "Are you sure about that?"

Beside her, Cade stiffened and finally took his eyes off the gate. "What are you talking about?"

"I told you…" Cassia began, stopping when the guard stepped between her and Cade to grab Alexia and drag her forward.

Cade held the Andarrian girl back, despite the guard's protests. "Tell me what you know," he demanded.

Their father let out a growl that reverberated over the gate's drowning hum. "*Enough*. I've given you more than enough time to get what you want from her… and you still haven't shown any gratitude." To the Shaman, he ordered, "Hurry up and get on with it."

The Shaman nodded. Moments later, the gate began to vibrate more than ever before, and the echoing whirl almost brought Cassia to her knees. Over the noise, she barely heard Alexia's next words.

"Maybe I know something you don't. Maybe the rune on my skin protects humans from the curse. Either way, I have a feeling you'll find out soon enough." The guard pushed Alexia toward the gate. She stumbled, then dug her feet into the dirt before she careened into the stone head first. Sneaking a look at Cade over her shoulder, she asked, "Where do you think I should look for Bridget first?"

"You're bluffing," Cassia said, though the words tasted thin. Alexia wouldn't make it through the gate with her memories... it was impossible. And yet, the certainty in her eyes made Cassia's pulse spike.

The lanterns around the gate flickered. *Bridget is dead.* Cassia wanted to scream it, wanted to force Cade to hear it, to stop haunting himself with false hope that he would see her again. But the lie wouldn't help, not when Cade's fist was already raised, magic coiling tight around it, ready to snap Alexia's throat from across the room.

Cassia tried to push his arm down, but he wouldn't budge.

The corner of Alexia's lips lifted. "Am I?"

Cassia wasn't sure what sent Cade charging forward, the taunt or their father's laugh. Her father's guard jumped in his path.

"Don't you dare go near her," Cade snarled, knocking the King's guard into the wall with a flick of his wrist.

The Shaman's incessant, deafening chanting shook the stone, almost making it appear opaque. Alexia raised her hand.

"Stop!" Cade ordered.

Before Cassia could blink, Alexia had disappeared. A shudder ripped through the gate and sent a wave of power throughout the small expanse. Cassia fell to the ground, while Cade and her father merely stumbled backward. As she got to her knees, a crack split her eardrum. She looked up at the vibrating gate, expecting another wave of magic, but Delphine rushed past her.

What the hell?

Only then did Cassia realize what the crack had been... Delphine, appearing behind her.

Of course. Why had she let herself believe, even for a second, that they didn't have some sort of idiotic plan?

The second their father pulled his glowing dagger from its sheath, Cade raised his fist and knocked it to the ground. With his other hand, he froze the Shaman in place, preventing him from stopping the spell that kept the gate open.

Snarling, her father sent a pulse of magic toward Cade. It boomed when it collided with Cade's in the air, preventing either of them moving an inch. Cassia spotted a trickle of blood escaping from Cade's ear as he used all his strength to keep their father and the Shaman from the gate. Delphine was going to cross to find Bridget. That much was obvious. But Cassia doubted Cade getting distracted by Alexia had been a part of the plan, though. The timing was off. Cade and their father were fighting too close to the gate. Delphine only had a small pathway to get to the stone. And the guard...

"Delphine, look out!" Cassia shouted.

Delphine looked up in time to dodge the guard's sword that had been aiming for her back. The movement sent her stumbling to the ground beside her. Before the guard swung again, Cassia launched herself to her feet. Using all her strength, she pushed the guard into the cave's stone wall. Momentarily dazed, he grabbed his head before charging back toward her.

Her push had been impulsive. Now she had no idea what to do. Backing away, Cassia ran into Cade. Whipping around, she stared at her twin, whose gaze frantically darted between her, the guard, their father, Delphine, and the Shaman. He only had seconds to make a choice.

Cade could stop the guard whose sword was aiming for the two of them, only a few feet away, or hold the Shaman long enough for Delphine to get back up and get through the gate.

Blood poured from ears as he strained to keep his father and the Shaman subdued. Resigned, Cassia closed her eyes, the ache settling deep in her chest. She knew what he would choose.

But then Cade let out a resigned, angry roar. He flicked his wrist. A heartbeat later the Shaman flew into the wall. An earsplitting crunch echoed against stone before he dropped lifeless to the ground. The gate stilled. Breathing heavily, Cade lifted his hand to stop the guard. Before he could, though, the guard suddenly froze. Inches from them, blood spurted out his mouth. The guard twisted to the ground, their father's favorite weapon speared in his back.

Cassia's jaw dropped as she watched their father remove his dagger from the man.

"Now look what you made me do," their father said calmly, casually wiping the blood off his dagger on his forearm.

# CHAPTER SIX

## BRIDGET

"It's been almost two weeks since the *incident* in the woods. I doubt he's going to stroll up to you in the Boston Common for a nice chat," Archer said, passing her the last plate from their dishwasher to put in the cabinet. Early morning light reflected off the glass.

*The incident.* Archer's new nickname for her encounter with the Shaman by the gate rattled Bridget's nerves. She understood his reluctance to let Nylah find out what happened, but his skeptical tone every time he uttered the word, like he didn't quite believe her, made her want to throttle him. Despite his warning, she continued to hide a variety of knives on her person.

"You never know. Besides, I swear I felt someone watching me yesterday," Bridget whispered, glaring at him. If he talked any louder, he was going to wake Nylah. She wanted to get to the gate and back before her sister even noticed she was gone. On Saturdays, she tended to sleep like a log until it was time for their weekly movie marathon.

Archer shook his head. "Ever since the gate disappeared, you've been taking everything as some sort of sign."

Bridget tried to ignore her twisting insides, a warning that maybe she *was* too eager for a message from Elyria. After she'd come home with blood dripping from her nose and ears, ranting about the Shaman's warning, Archer had gone back with her to the gate. Except it wasn't there. For hours, they'd circled the forest and retraced the path they knew led there. They'd found nothing but trees. Bridget knew the Shaman had something to do with it, knew he put some spell or curse on the woods so it hid the gate entirely. Whatever he'd done, Archer hadn't been able to break it.

"I don't care about the gate," Bridget lied. Its sudden disappearance bothered her more than she wanted it to. Putting on her gloves, she added, "I just want to know who sent him. And why."

Ignoring Archer's gaze, she continued to gather up her purse and scarf. Moments later, he scoffed, "That's what you're doing today, isn't it? Going back out here to look for it? Have you ever considered that he gave you that warning for a reason? That maybe you should listen?"

She had. She *did*. But after months of radio silence from anyone in Elyria, the incident had sparked an ember in her heart that was steadily growing into a full blaze. Of what, she didn't know. Or couldn't admit.

"I'm just going to the library," Bridget said.

Before she could head to the door, though, a voice froze her in place.

"The Shaman is clearly avoiding you, so I doubt he'll show up again there, too," Nylah said. "And you should learn to hide things better."

Slowly, Bridget turned to face her sister. She thought she'd been asleep, but there she stood, holding Bridget's notebook of all things Elyria. Maps to the gates, research about the Shaman, lists of things about people and magic she'd written during the nights the fear of not remembering took over her soul. Dread twisting her stomach, Bridget searched Nylah's accusatory face, trying to find any hint about how much she'd read.

"Why do both of you act like I have no idea about magic and Elyria?" Nylah asked. "This house is small. I can hear you, even when you whisper."

Archer's gaze darted between the two sisters. Clearing his throat, he muttered, "I'm craving a coffee..."

Bridget stared daggers at his back as he left. This was the one time he could read the room? Since she'd returned, there was only one subject she'd gone out of her way to avoid with Nylah: Elyria. She was terrified that if her sister saw just how deeply it had changed her, it would change *them*. Every time she'd asked about it, Bridget had been able to change the subject. Until now. She couldn't deny the pleading currently plastered on Nylah's face.

"If you're going to look for the gate, I want to go with you," Nylah said, reaching for her boots.

Bridget swiped them before she could. "Absolutely not."

The words came out harsh, but she wouldn't apologize. She didn't want Nylah anywhere near magic... near the thing that had already carved itself into Bridget's bones and refused to let go. One sister ruined by it was more than enough.

"Why do you act like I'm not a part of this?" Nylah argued. "Like what happened didn't affect me, too?"

*Because you still sleep through the night.*

*Because you still believe that magic can be something good and true and real... without demanding something awful in return.*

So many reasons lingered on Bridget's tongue.

"You shouldn't be a part of it," Bridget said instead. "Cade should have never told you. You don't deserve to..."

"To what? To know? I'm glad he told me. Knowing was better than sitting around wondering why you disappeared. Cade promised me you would come back, and even though it was really hard to believe him some days, you did come back. I know bad things happened to you there. I hear you have nightmares every night. I see your hands, even when you try to hide them from me. Just talk to me and stop acting like I'm your stupid kid sister who doesn't understand."

The tears spilling from Nylah's eyes splintered Bridget's heart. She'd never wanted to be the source of his sister's pain. How could she think she'd be able to avoid the topic of Elyria with her forever? Nylah had always been able to see right through her, and had always trusted Bridget to be honest. It was their pact. The night before Bridget had aged out of the system, she'd promised Nylah she'd always be there, always be truthful. And now here she was, breaking that promise.

"I don't think that about you. You're one of the smartest people I know," Bridget croaked. "I just want to protect you."

"Well, I want you to *trust* me, and tell me the truth... You want to go back, don't you? That's why you won't talk about it with me."

Bridget held back a flinch and shook her head. "No, I don't."

"Yes, you do. It's why you have this." Nylah sniffled, holding up the binder.

"I want to be with *you*," Bridget corrected, grabbing her sister by the arms. "Listen to me. The second I remembered in Elyria, there wasn't a moment that went by I didn't want to come back to you."

It was the one truth that had never changed.

"I was always going to come back," Bridget said, needing Nylah to believe as much as she did.

Nylah jumped forward and wrapped her arms tightly around Bridget's waist. After a long moment, she whispered, "What about Cade? I miss him, too."

Even though the words were muffled, the sound of Cade's name thoroughly cracked Bridget's chest wide open. Would she ever be able to hear his name again without falling apart? "Cade has to stay there," she choked, barely able to get the words out. It was all her fault. "And his world is... dangerous. Especially for humans. Neither one of us wants you to go there."

Nylah pulled back and wiped off her tear-streaked face with the sleeve of her jacket. "Like this world isn't? That convenience store down the street was robbed last week."

Bridget almost wanted to laugh. Her sister never missed a thing. "You're too smart for your own good," she said, ruffling the top of Nylah's springy, curly hair.

"Seriously, though, let me help," Nylah pleaded. "Maybe I'll be able to find something you can't."

Bridget couldn't resist her sister's request now, not when every part of her body felt like an exposed nerve. "Fine. Let's go find Archer first, though. Something tells me he'll be peeved and make us watch *Selling Sunset* for the next week if we leave without him."

Nylah gagged and then quickly put on her boots. As she watched her, Bridget's stomach sank. She really hoped she wouldn't regret letting Nylah come, or help. But maybe she was right. Maybe an extra set of eyes would be beneficial. She wasn't sure Archer was putting much effort into finding the gate again, anyway...

Behind Nylah, the girl from Bridget's dream suddenly materialized. Rearing back into the refrigerator, a magnet fell on her head as she slammed her eyes and took a deep breath. She was seeing things. She had to be.

"Are you okay?" Nylah asked.

Bridget opened her eyes. The girl was still there, observing her sister with a puzzled frown. When the girl caught Bridget watching, her face changed. With a playful smirk, she reached toward Nylah and...

"Get over here," Bridget ordered, yanking Nylah behind her when she didn't move fast enough.

"Um, ouch. Are you on some kind of Witchy drugs from Archer?"

Bridget glared at her. When she turned back around, the girl had disappeared. The kitchen was silent and untouched. Like nothing had happened at all. "You didn't see that?"

Frowning, Nylah waved her hand through the air. "I saw you being weird."

Relief and dread tangling in Bridget's chest. If Nylah hadn't seen it, then maybe it was just her. Maybe this was what came after magic—flashbacks, fractures, her mind finally snapping under the weight of everything she'd survived.

She shoved the fear down hard, the way she'd learned to do with pain, with longing, with anything that threatened to break her. There wasn't room for this... not now. Not with Nylah watching her so closely.

"Right..." Bridget said, pasting on a half-smile. "Let's go find Archer before I completely lose my mind."

Outside, the streets of the South End were filled with early morning traffic. Around them, people hurried past them to get to work or school. Bridget grabbed Nylah's hand and led her to Archer's favorite coffee shop down the street. As the crowd started to thin, she felt it again. Eyes. Just like she had yesterday. Bridget's spine stiffened. She slowed down her pace and studied the street around her. She was about to pull Nylah through the park when she heard the last voice she ever expected.

"Hello, Bridget."

Ice spiraling through her veins, Bridget whipped around and came face to face with Alexia. She blinked, and then again, to make sure she wasn't hallucinating. Reflexively, her gaze darted to the sidewalk behind, half-expecting to see Cora there. Bridget slammed her eyes shut and tried to calm her racing heart. Cora was dead. She'd seen her die. Swallowing hard, she returned her focus to the smirking girl in front of her.

"How are you here right now?" Bridget gasped.

A flicker of surprise went through Alexia's eyes as she gazed at Nylah. "Who's this?"

Bridget pushed Nylah behind her. Still stunned to see Alexia very much alive *and* aware, she blurted, "You remember? How?"

"Did you ever have to wear an ugly cape like that?" Nylah whispered to Bridget.

Alexia took a step toward them. "Of course, I do."

"Don't come any closer," Bridget hissed.

"Or what?" Alexia chided. "I'm here to finish what Cora started. I'm here to bring you back."

In Vassuryn, Alexia had beaten her in most fights. Bridget knew it was why she confidently kept getting closer to her and Nylah and laughed off her threat. Since then, though, she'd trained with Cassia, and taken every self-defense and boxing class she could since they'd moved to Boston.

Jaw clenched, Bridget stepped forward and punched Alexia square on the chin.

When she collapsed to the ground with a loud smack, Nylah gasped. Her sister shuffled over to poke at Alexia's unmoving body. "Can you teach me how to do that?" she asked.

Bridget glared at her. After making sure no one was watching, she dragged Alexia off the sidewalk. She sat her up and made it look like she was sleeping against the alley's brick wall.

"Call Archer," she told Nylah, "we're going to need help getting her back to the house."

# CHAPTER SEVEN

Archer patted the side of Alexia's swollen face, but she didn't stir. "Exactly how much have you been lifting at the gym?"

It'd been an hour since they'd gotten Alexia back to their house and tied her up to one of the kitchen chairs. Bridget shrugged. There had been a year's worth of pent-up rage in her punch. She wasn't going to apologize. In the living room, Nylah pretended to pick up and throw a person to the ground. She growled and kicked the air. Archer stared at her incredulously.

"What is she doing? I swear I only let her watch wrestling once. Maybe twice."

Bridget narrowed her eyes. "You let her *what*?"

Archer ignored her question. To tighten the ropes around Alexia's wrists, he pulled up the sleeves of her dark green robe. He froze. "She's from Andarre. Did you know that?"

Eyes wide, Bridget leaned down and inspected the now visible tattoos. Each one shimmered purple against Alexia's skin in the fluorescent lighting. In all her time with her in Vassuryn, she'd never seen the markings. "How is that possible?"

"If you weren't so busy trying to escape every day in Vassuryn, you might have noticed," Alexia mumbled, finally lifting her head. She studied the tiny apartment before she fidgeted in the chair. "Why am I tied up?"

Archer let out a laugh. "I would think that's pretty obvious."

"Why are you here?" Bridget asked through gritted teeth. Alexia had only been around an hour and her attitude was already grating her nerves. Did she really think she would greet her with open arms? Or trust?

"I'm not answering any of your questions until you untie me," Alexia said. When they continued to stare at her, she relaxed and added, "I've spent the last few months in a dirty, damp cell in Astraeus. Not once did I spill any secrets to the king or tell anyone about Andarre or Cora until I made a deal with your boyfriend. Why don't you ask him how patient I can be? Oh wait, you can't. If you want to know how he's doing, I suggest you free me. I can tell what he yelled as I went through the gate."

Bridget stilled. Rage exploded through her veins as the world narrowed to a single, blinding point of heat behind her ribs. Alexia was offering Cade like bait, counting on her to bite.

Grabbing her arm, Archer said, "Bridget, I know she just mentioned your trigger word but..."

Recoiling away from him, she swallowed back the bile in her throat. She knew not to fall for Alexia's tricks and could see now how many times the other girl had manipulated her in Vassuryn. She wouldn't give her the satisfaction of reacting, even when she dangled information about Cade in front of her.

Too focused on calming the fire in her veins, Bridget didn't notice Nylah grab a knife from the kitchen drawer. Before she could stop her, Nylah cut Alexia's binds.

"We want answers," her sister said, pointing the knife at Alexia's face. "Now talk."

Archer threw his hands up in the air and muttered, "You've created a monster."

Bridget wasn't sure whether to be angry or impressed. Either way, she grabbed Nylah by the shoulder and pulled her backward.

"At least there's someone here with some sense," Alexia said, rubbing her wrist, and then her jaw. Her heated stare met Bridget's. For a long moment, tense silence filled the room.

"You heard her," Bridget chided. "Tell us what you're doing here and how you found us."

"That coven mark on your hand is more than it appears. With the right spell, it can be used to find you. Luckily, I was able to find some Witches in Salem to help me. That little town was Cora's backup plan if she ever had to track you down in the human realm."

"That was you following me yesterday... I should've known, but I still don't understand. You shouldn't remember or know who I am."

Alexia paused. "The curse is broken."

Every ounce of air whooshed out of Bridget's lungs. It wasn't possible. She looked at Archer, expecting him to say a contradictory remark. After all, he'd been the one to explain curses to her. But he stared at Alexia, mute, pale, and shaken.

"That's not possible," Bridget whispered.

It had been *Cade*, not her, Quinn had tried to kill. It was Cade's blood, royal blood, needed to break the curse on Sanguis. Or at least that's what her and Archer had surmised after months of speculation.

"It is. You owe Cora for giving you back the final piece," Alexia said, nodding at the ring on Bridget's finger.

"But I'm not..."

How many times had she read that the curse could only be broken by the blood of the girl Vega had killed? How many times had Cade told her the same thing? She glanced down at her cracked ring and remembered the fuzzy vision of a crevice in the stone before the ambulance doors closed... Bridget's stomach swirled.

"No, you're not," Alexia agreed. "But you must be related to her, like your prince to the person originally used for the curse for the Sanguis. A direct descendant. I'm certain."

"You can't be certain. It's a centuries old curse," Archer said, "and Bridget isn't from that world. I don't see how..."

"Except she is... She's from Andarre," Alexia stated, turning her fiery gaze back to Bridget. "Like I said, I'm here to take you back."

Feeling all eyes on her, Bridget laughed. It exploded in an uncomfortable rhythm from her chest. Alexia was wrong. *So* wrong. There was no possible way she was from Andarre. She remembered her childhood, remembered bouncing between multiple foster homes in elementary school and her first night in a group home in second grade. And she remembered her mother dying. The ring on her finger was proof of that. It was *hers*. Not some centuries old anchor to a curse.

"You're out of your mind," Bridget sneered. "I didn't break the curse. The reason I remember is because Cade already paid the price for me. The rune in your skin must have protected you somehow."

Alexia shook her head. "Cora and I were sent by your father to retrieve you."

"I don't have a father," Bridget snapped.

"You do."

"No. This ring was my mother's." Bridget fumed, holding up her hand. "I remember her dying. I remember taking it before the doctors took her away."

"Bridget, maybe let her explain," Archer said softly, stopping her from her unconscious assault forward.

Bridget whipped her gaze to him. With an accusatory glare, she asked, "Did you know?"

Immediately, she bit her tongue. *Did you know.* Why did she ask the question like she believed Alexia? She *didn't*. Desperately, she tried to think of any memory she had before the age of seven. After several moments of trying, nothing popped in her head. Panicking, she closed her eyes. The room spun. Everything spun. She didn't know what to think. At that moment, she desperately wished for Cade. He'd be able to search her head for memories. He'd be able to reasonably explain Alexia's lies. Or truths. She wasn't sure what her shaking body believed anymore. Nylah must have sensed her distress, because she felt her sister gently grab her hand. Her heart rate calmed.

"He didn't, but I'm guessing he overheard something," Alexia said. "I met Cora in an Andarrian jail. She traveled there to ask for help for the covens. The king had just stopped all trade with Vassuryn. She didn't have a warm welcome. Let's just say magic is not a popular subject in our homeland."

Hearing *our homeland* made Bridget sick to her stomach. She wanted no connection to the girl in front of her. "And why were you in jail?" she asked blithely.

"I'd been falsely accused of murdering a girl from school. We shared a cell and grew close. One day, Cora was plucked from the masses to chat with someone. Someone important. Someone with power. Days later, so was I. I learned Cora had been asked to go to Pontas to retrieve you and that she bartered for my release, as well. As a Witch, she'd be able to travel through Elyria and Vassuryn undetected."

"Pontas?" Bridget echoed, the word settling like a weight in her chest. Dread crept up her spine. Of all the towns in Vassuryn, Pontas was the one Cora had avoided at any cost. The Gemini coven had been attacked there... by *Cade*.

Because of her.

She'd been there. The scars along her stomach twitched beneath her clothes, an involuntary reminder. Whatever she couldn't remember, her body did. The sheer physicality of it still seemed imprinted on her.

"It's where we found you unconscious at an abandoned farm with the Gemini coven, along with Quinn and Archer."

Once again, Bridget glared at Archer. How much had he not told her?

He held up his hands and pleaded, "Bridget, I swear, I didn't know about any of this. When we came across them in Pontas, they said they'd been looking for a way to the human realm and were told Quinn might know about a gate. Quinn believed them, but I was skeptical. It seemed like too much of a coincidence. That's why I told them who you were."

Believing him, she turned her hateful stare back to Alexia. "How could you possibly have known I'd be there?"

A shadow passed over Alexia's face. "Andarre has been under attack for the last year. Creatures from the sea rise up from the waters and attack the coastal towns every few months. According to Cora, the royal family enlisted a Shaman to help. They said to find you. The Shaman told your father when and where you'd be."

"I don't believe you," Bridget said, trying to keep her voice even. A Shaman sent them to her? What would she do? Throw knives at sea creatures?

"Yes, you do. It's why you're so angry. You hate that it explains what Cora did to you. I admit, she took it too far sometimes. It was revenge, I think, for what she'd gone through in that jail, and for them not helping the covens."

Bridget was going to kill her if she didn't shut up. Alexia needed to leave. She needed to leave right now. Before she did more than punch her. "Whatever mission you think you're on, you've failed. I'm not going anywhere with you."

"It's not only Andarre that's in danger. It's Elyria. It's Vassuyn," Alexia snarled. "It's your duty—"

Bridget let out a sharp laugh. Her duty? What duty did she have to people she'd never met? "No. I'm never going back to that world again. You may believe some curse has been broken, but I won't risk my sister. I won't put her in danger."

Unreadable, Alexia took a step forward. "I had a feeling you'd say that."

Before Bridget could blink, Alexia grabbed Nylah and plunged a syringe into her neck. Panic exploded through her chest. She lunged forward and caught her sister before she hit the ground. Nylah coughed and rubbed at her neck. Bridget's stomach lurched as every horrifying possibility played out her in mind.

Pulling her sister closer, Bridget demanded, "What did you do?"

"It's a simple poison. I found the ingredients by the gate. The herbs by themselves are harmless, but together..." Alexia said, making Bridget's heart fall to the ground. "It was supposed to be for you, but I think this plan works better. Don't worry, she'll be fine. For now. It's slow-spreading. Luckily, the antidote is in Andarre."

Archer ripped the vial out of her hand and immediately started analyzing it. "Give me that. I'll come up with something," he told Bridget. "You know I will."

Grasping Nylah tightly, Bridget sent Alexia the most venomous glare she could muster. "I'm going to kill you."

"What she needs isn't grown here. There's nothing you can do," Alexia explained, unbothered. "Also, I forgot to mention that your father has my family. He's not going to release them until I come back with you. So... when do we leave?"

# CHAPTER EIGHT

### CASSIA

Cassia frowned as she walked the streets of Astraeus. Light mist filled the air and covered every surface, including her skin. The tops of the skyscrapers around her were split in half by a thick cloud. Even when it rained, the city always buzzed with life. But not today. The crowded stores and restaurants she usually frequented were lifeless and barely held a few patrons. When she'd woken to thunder, she'd immediately made plans to visit the city. Rainy days in Astraeus were an adventure for her. Those were the days she was just another face in a crowd at a packed bar full of people avoiding the weather.

She guessed too many people had been watching the news. Cassia even had to admit it was hard to tear her eyes away from the constant recycled footage from the Kastronian border. Even though it was always the same video, the beast in it sent shivers up her spine every time she saw it. It was identical to the one Cade had shown her. Almost human-like, but small and wraith like, with rows and rows of teeth. Instead of bright red eyes, the beast in the video had none. Its hollow eye sockets oozed a thick, black liquid she would guess was the same texture of blood.

Today, though, she'd wanted to drink and get lost in strangers and forget about how everyone in her life had shut her out. That plan had failed. As she walked back home, Cassia glared up at the building where she knew the news anchors were probably getting ready for their next broadcast and cursed them for ruining her perfectly good day. She'd almost made it to the front entrance of the palace when someone called out her name. She didn't have to turn around to identify the owner of the voice. He was the only person that insisted on always calling her Cassia, not Cass. The only person whose voice could make her heart rate spike with only one word. The only person she wanted to avoid when she looked like a drowned rat in the rain.

Maybe she should have just stayed and had a drink somewhere.

Slowly, Cassia turned around and spotted Castor jogging toward her. Chest tightening, she clenched her fists so her fingers wouldn't tremble. How did he always manage to look so unbearably handsome? Even with raindrops stuck to his black hair, he looked the perfect picture of a prince. On the path behind him, she spotted every woman turned to stare at his retreating form. Cassia couldn't blame them. It was hard not to.

"You're back," she said. She hated that the words sounded cold, but it was taking every ounce of her self-control not to reach out and touch him. Or smile. She'd lost the privilege to do that long ago, but it'd been so *long*. And the last time she'd seen him, he'd fought with her father to cross the gate. He'd only let him go because of Delphine's sudden appearance. Without the interference, she wasn't sure what would have happened.

"I just arrived a few minutes ago," Castor panted. When he approached her, he smiled, but it didn't reach his eyes. "I'm glad I caught you out here. I needed to see you before... everything."

"What for?"

"How's Cade? I wanted to get your opinion on his state of mind before I go see him. He knows I'm here. I feel him trying to get in my head, but I've been able to block him... so far."

The growing flush on her body suddenly stopped. Of course, it had nothing to do with *her*. It was about Cade. Like always. The distress barely hidden in Castor's dark eyes, though, made her pause long enough to stop from snapping at him. In her head, she silently screamed at Delphine that *she* had been right. He didn't have good news.

"How do you think he is? He's obsessive. Stubborn…" Cassia sighed. She thought about how her brother had been holed up in his room and the library the past two weeks, trying to find any information he could about Andarre and the Sanguis, no longer pretending to be in good spirits for their father. Swallowing hard, she added, "He misses her. He doesn't want to be here."

"We've known that for a long time," Castor replied softly.

"It's different now," Cassia whispered. Cade wasn't just stuck in Elyria, he was trapped. And it was slowly turning him into a ghost. At least when Bridget had been here, he'd been close to his old self again. Clearing her throat, she straightened her spine before she did something stupid, like cry. Motioning for Castor to follow her through the palace gate, she said, "This is all just a guess. He's barely spoken to me since his plan to get Delphine through the gate failed."

"His *what*?"

"See what happens when you go away for too long?"

Cassia's heart quickened when she felt Castor's hand brush her lower back, whether unconsciously or to comfort her, she wasn't sure. The moment he pulled back, her body screamed in protest.

"It's harder to travel back and forth without access to the Astraeus gate," he replied. "And my family's company is going through a bit of a crisis. I was here too long during the tournament. I missed some important meetings… Plus, Elyria isn't the only place being bombarded by random creatures."

"Is everything alright?"

"It'll be fine," Castor said, waving his hand. "My parents and older brothers don't need my help, like always. You know that."

Cassia resisted glowering at him. Even though she wanted him to share what was going on, it was typical Castor to keep everything to himself. He was always composed. Always calm. Never needed any help. She both admired and hated it about him.

Glancing back at the skyline, Castor murmured, "The city is quiet today. Before I left Tafari, I saw the video of what happened in Kastron."

"That hasn't been the only incident. My father sent Finn to check out another one. He still isn't back."

"Is that why you bought those herbs?"

Cassia locked eyes with Castor. The dark orbs knew too much. Breathless, she fingered the small paper bag in her coat pocket. How had he known what was in there? The purchase had been an impulse, a quiet yearning to be useful if one of those creatures did appear in Astraeus or someone needed her help.

"If you're trying to learn again, I can help," he said. "I know that last time..."

Cassia quickly shook her head. "I don't need any help. That's not why I bought them," she lied. She reddened, remembering the last time she tried to perform a spell in front of him. Castor was the last person she wanted to know how weak she really was.

Brows furrowed, he opened his mouth to argue, but his curious gaze moved to the two figures waiting for them by the white stone wall of the northern courtyard.

"What are you going to say to him?" Cassia asked quietly, eyeing where her brother stood in anticipation, Delphine beside him.

Castor sighed. "The truth."

As she followed him, Cassia wanted to scream at his back to lie to Cade, to spare him whatever bad news she knew that he brought. Especially when her brother looked more alive than she'd seen him in months. The excitement in his eyes made her stomach twist.

Her stomach twisted even more when she watched Delphine smile brightly and give Castor a hug. One that lasted a little too long.

When in the hell had *that* happened?

"Did you get trapped in a board meeting?" Cade grinned, grabbing Castor by the shoulder.

"Actually, a few. You wouldn't recognize the New York office right now," Castor replied. Cassia wondered if she was the only one who noticed the hesitation in his voice. He continued, "There was one week I had to fly back and forth from there and London three times. I think it's mostly taken care of now."

When Castor went silent, her brother stared at him expectantly. "And?"

Castor squared his shoulders. "I'm sorry, I couldn't find her."

Cade stilled. Cassia's heart dropped as she watched him pale... watched every inch of his face harden. Voice dangerously low, he asked, "What do you mean?"

"I searched everywhere. I spent as much time as I could combing through the internet and any source of information I could think of once I found out what happened..." Castor replied quietly. "But I think I was too late. I didn't get any of your letters until I was already back in Tafari, and there's too much going on there right now for me to go back to London, despite what my family believes. There's no record of any Bridget Adams in a hospital, shelter... or cemetery."

The second the word cemetery was out of Castor's mouth, Cade flinched. Delphine squeezed his forearm. Swallowing hard, Cassia gazed at Castor. The muscles in his jaw were clenched. Not only did see Cade as a brother, he hated to fail.

"What about Nylah?" Cade asked hoarsely. "Did you see her? She must be—"

Castor reached into his pocket and pulled out a folded sheet of paper. "She's missing too. I was able to find this."

Cade ripped the paper from his hand and unfolded it. Peering over Castor's shoulder, she peeked at the paper. At the top, *Missing Child* was written in giant red letters above a grainy black and white photo of Nylah. Because of Cade's trembling hand, she couldn't read the rest of the words.

"There should have been something," Delphine argued. "News articles, hospital records... *something*. Unless he just..."

Unless that Warlock had just left her to die wherever the gate had taken them. Cassia didn't need Cade's powers to know what words Delphine didn't want to utter.

Castor reluctantly continued, "I called your landlord about your apartment. Someone had broken in. He emailed me the footage... He was alone. It looked like he grabbed a bag..."

And then Cassia was sucked into whatever memory Castor was showing Cade. She wondered if her brother even realized he was losing control and pulling all their minds together. The palace garden around her disappeared and all of a sudden, she was standing in Cade's old apartment, watching a grainy image of Archer pick the lock on the door and grab a large suitcase. Seconds later, he was gone.

Even though the memory had stopped, Cassia couldn't break free from her connection with Cade's mind. For a moment, she was hearing *his* mind. She could hear him planning, calculating, reviewing every scenario that could have happened with Bridget and Nylah. His thoughts weren't the only thing he was projecting, though. Cassia braced herself against the stone wall she could no longer see. Rage, desperation, and longing choked her. Pain, so acute, made her want to fall to her knees. Each new feeling ripped through her soul. She was *drowning* in them. She couldn't...

"Cade, stop," Delphine gasped.

The world abruptly went back to normal. Eyes blurry, Cassia tried to catch her breath. When her vision stopped spinning, she spotted Cade's retreating figure. "Come back," she called, but he was already out of sight. To her left, Delphine grabbed Castor's arm. Cassia couldn't stop the white-hot rage that suddenly flowed through her veins.

Without thinking, she shoved Castor in the chest. "Why did you tell him the truth?"

"Are you serious?" Castor replied, staring at her in shock.

"You should have lied and said she was fine. Now who knows what he's going to do."

Castor took a step forward. His dark eyes bore into hers and she was suddenly afraid he knew that all of her anger wasn't because of what he'd told Cade... but because of something she had no right to anymore. Chest tightening, she raised her chin and refused to break their stare. Mere inches from her, he stopped. She felt his breath on her face.

"He deserved to know," he stated, voice almost at a whisper.

Throat tight, Cassia hissed, "If he does something stupid trying to figure out what happened, it's on you."

And then she ran. Too afraid to know if he watched her. Too afraid to find out if he didn't.

# CHAPTER NINE

Cassia leaned against the wall outside the throne room. Pressing against the hard stone helped quell her urge to pace. Inside, Finn was debriefing her father. She'd been kicked out. Of course, she'd been kicked out. Her father believed her knowledge of Elyria began and ended with the city's nightlife. She couldn't blame him, though. Once... maybe it had.

Not only was she curious about what Finn had seen at the border, Cade needed him. Now more than ever. She hadn't seen him since Castor arrived, which told her he was planning something. When he accidentally had pulled her into his head, she'd briefly seen the formations of it. Heard the whisper of Alexia's voice telling him about Quinn using the gate to communicate with the Sanguis. A bubble of anxiety sprung in her gut. Her brother was too relentless and reckless for his own good. He wouldn't listen to her, that much she knew for sure. But maybe Finn would be able to reason with him before the plan came to fruition.

When the heavy, wooden door of the throne room popped up, Cassia sprung forward. Grabbing Finn by the arm, she said, "I'm so glad you're back."

Finn blinked, and then pinched his leg. "Am I dreaming? Because that was the last thing I ever expected to hear you say to me."

Too concerned to roll her eyes, Cassia replied, "I don't know if you've heard, but Castor finally came back a few days ago. He couldn't find Bridget. Obviously, Cade didn't take it well."

She shivered, remembering the intensity of what he'd let slip through to her.

"Don't worry, I'll go find him now," Finn said. "It's not like Deckard was the first person I wanted to talk to today. Orion cornered me and basically dragged me to him the second I arrived."

"Don't say this to him, but I'm worried he's planning something."

Finn frowned. "Like what?"

"I don't know," she said, not wanting to say her thoughts aloud. What if she was wrong about what she heard? She didn't want to accidentally give her brother the idea. "It's just a feeling I have, and I know he won't listen to me if I try to talk to him."

"Alright, I'll see what I can do. I know I gave that Warlock a hard time, but I don't think he would have left Bridget somewhere without taking her to the hospital. He did help us, at the end." Finn sighed. "It should have been me to go. This wouldn't have happened. At least I have something that will distract him."

"What is it?"

Finn checked the corridor before he answered, "I saw Quinn, or at least I think I did."

Cassia narrowed her eyes. Pulling him further into the corner, she asked, "Are you kidding? Where?"

"It was in Kyryn, near the Kastronian border. One of the creatures attacked us in the night. We had to use fire to kill it. Nothing else seems to work. Through the haze, I swear I saw her face in the trees."

"You think she's the one creating the creatures," Cassia stated, reading his drawn, tight face. "She has to be using the Bloodstone."

"If she is, I don't know how it hasn't killed her yet."

Grinding her teeth together, Cassia said, "Burning every piece of information about the Sanguis was the most idiotic thing my ancestors ever did."

"The Shamans might know something," Finn suggested. "I can think of one that's old enough to have been around during that time."

"Echnav was the only trustworthy one. Too bad he's gone. I liked that he wasn't up my father's ass constantly," Cassia replied scathingly.

"That's one way to put it," Finn snorted. "What about Marin?"

"She's still getting her beauty sleep, apparently."

Finn sent her a droll look before he turned his attention to something behind her. Cassia turned around. Underneath a moss covered, stone alcove, just past the entrance of the throne room's large, marble corridor, stood Castor and Delphine. Their conversation seemed innocent, but when red-faced Delphine suddenly smiled, Cassia's own face heated. Breathing deeply through her nose, she tried to numb the onslaught of prickly emotions stabbing her chest. Cassia wanted to smack herself for feeling so possessive. After all, *she* had been the one to end things with him. And he'd accepted it... without a fight. The threat of reliving the memory hardened her heart. She'd made a promise to herself to never think of it again. When Cassia felt Finn's eyes on her, she straightened and smoothed out her thick, silver jacket.

"You should just talk to him," Finn said.

"About what? The weather?" Cassia drawled, hoping her face remained blank. "Besides, he looks fairly busy at the moment."

Finn's lips twitched. He leaned in and whispered, "You're not fooling anyone."

Cassia recoiled away from him. Glaring, she hissed, "Don't try to read me right now."

His ability to sense emotions had been a pain in her ass almost her entire life. It had taken her years to get over feeling like a walking open book whenever she was around him and Cade. Plus, it had made every game she'd played with them impossible to win.

Out of the corner of her eye, she spotted Castor and Delphine moving toward them. Reflexively, she took a step back. She hated that Castor zeroed in on the movement. His narrowed eyes locked on her retreating form.

To Finn, Cassia added, "Just find Cade and knock some sense into him."

And then she fled into the throne room, hoping the panic she denied didn't make her look too rushed.

Taking a deep breath, Cassia crushed more of the lovage she'd bought from a shop in Astraeus. The words in the old spell book she'd found in the library were barely visible in the candlelight of her room. Squinting, she muttered one of the Latin phrases aloud and then blew the tiny particles of the lovage into the candle closest to her. For a split-second, the flame roared brighter before returning to its flickering state. Cassia closed her eyes and mentally searched every part of her body for a sign that her magic had worked. Air had always been the easiest element for her to draw upon, and it was a simple strengthening spell. Peaking an eye open, she looked down at her hands. Did they feel firmer? Or was her mind playing tricks on her?

The light from the hallway suddenly illuminated her flexing fingers. Heart stuttering, she whirled around. It calmed, but only slightly, when she discovered Castor in her doorway. Grinding her teeth together, she muttered, "You can't come in here without knocking anymore."

His dark eyes, full of bewilderment, gazed around at the numerous candles littered across every surface in her dim room. "What are you doing?"

"What does it look like?" she snapped, pointing at the spell book on her bed. Cassia crossed her arms and hoped she wasn't as red as she felt at being caught doing the one thing she'd told him she wouldn't. Castor raised a brow and moved to stand beside her bed. Silently, he thumbed through the stiff, dusty pages of the grimoire.

Cassia swallowed hard as she watched him. Gold reflected off his dark skin in the candlelight and seeing him so close to her bed reminded her of the last time he'd been on it. When he'd slowly undone the straps of her thin, blue ballgown and moved his mouth all the way down her body until...

Clearing her throat, she backed into the corner by the closet. The heat rushing to her core was about to make her do something very stupid. The more space between them, the better. "I'm sorry I shoved you the other day," she said, hoping the mention of one of her transgressions would make him keep his distance, as well.

Instead, Castor tilted his head and studied her. She trembled when he took a step toward her. "Is that why you avoided me outside the throne room yesterday?"

Cassia breathed a sigh of relief when he stopped in front of her sapphire metal table to inspect the herbs she'd placed there. He picked up a few petals of echinacea and rolled them between his fingers.

"Are you going to let me help you?" he asked, keeping his gaze on the herbs.

She wanted to say no. Wanted to remind him about the last time he'd tried to teach her. She'd failed so spectacularly, she'd almost burned off all his hair. And then their sessions had turned into a different sort of teaching entirely. She'd learned all about beds, dark corners, and which clothes she didn't mind being ripped.

But when Castor locked eyes with her, she knew this time would be different. Cassia couldn't ignore the urgency in his eyes. Last time, there'd been no revival of blood magic or mysterious creatures threatening Elyria.

Last time, she'd had *two* brothers, and a sister not yet corrupted by her father. Everything was different now. She could no longer hide away in her room and hope life would work itself out. Time had already proven that lie to be false.

"What if I never get any better?" Cassia croaked, heart pounding as she admitted her greatest fear. "What if I'm always the dud Witch that can't defend anyone, let alone herself?"

Her confession softened his eyes. Inches from her now, Castor searched her face. His gaze brought a flush to her skin she'd forgotten could be so intoxicating. With his breath on her face, she could see the scar above his full lips from when he'd defended Cade in a bar fight on his seventeenth birthday, and count every thick, dark eyelash that breathtakingly lined the penetrating orbs she dreamed about at night. Cassia dug her fingers into the seams of her pants to keep herself from touching him.

"You will get better," he promised, "I've thought about this a lot, actually."

When he placed his hands on her biceps, she shivered. She wished she hadn't left her jacket on. It'd been so long since she'd felt his skin. The heat building in Castor's eyes made her wonder if he was thinking the same. She hoped she wasn't imagining it.

"As a Warlock, there's magic in my blood, but I still need to use elements to enhance my abilities and sustain it for larger spells," he murmured. "A Fae's power is in their blood, too. They draw inward. It's why magic physically weakens them faster than the other species. Even if your magic manifested as a Witch, you're still part Fae. I think that might make you different. I think that maybe... you haven't been pulling from the right thing."

Cassia briefly registered his words. His logic made sense. In a way. She wasn't as knowledgeable about magic as he was. But all she could think about was the way his hands moved to her hips and brushed across her lower back. Electricity rushed through her body. Instead of fighting it, she pressed herself against him. She knew she would regret letting the fire between them consume her tomorrow, but now, all she wanted was him beneath her on the bed. Cassia grabbed the lapels of his coat and gazed up at him. She whispered, "Teach me then."

Castor's fingers dug harder into her hips. Breath left her lungs as he pressed her against the wall and opened her legs with his thigh. Cassia pressed against him and moaned. She'd hoped for this exact reaction from him. It wasn't the first time she'd asked him to teach her. She'd said it to him before, with much less clothes, in the very same room. Replaying the memory in her head made her hips buck forward. Castor inhaled sharply and began to unzip her jacket. His mouth moved to her throat.

Chest heaving, he said, "Tell me to stop."

Cassia shook her head. She couldn't. Not when every inch of her was ready for him, like three years hadn't passed since the last time she'd kissed him. Not when she was already reviewing in her head all the ways she knew how to make him moan. Unlike...

Ice suddenly filled Cassia's veins. She froze, but kept her grip on his halfway open shirt. Hadn't she just seen Delphine blushing and flirting with him yesterday? She was just about to ask him if something was going on between them when a knock at her door pulled Castor's lips away from her collarbone.

Seconds later, the knock sounded again.

"That sounds important," Castor sighed, pulling away from her. Even though her legs shook, Cassia managed to zip up her jacket and stumble to the doorway. She flung open the door, ready to snarl at whoever wouldn't stop their incessant knocking.

"Have you seen..."

Delphine's mouth dropped slightly when she took in Cassia's twisted jacket, and then the figure standing behind her. Cassia hadn't realized Castor had followed her to the door. Her throat tightened when she felt Castor stiffen.

Face red, Delphine lowered her eyes and said, "Castor, I need your help. Cade thinks he's found some way to communicate through the gate. He's on his way there now. I couldn't stop him…"

Cassia's stomach dropped. She'd been right. She should've just gone to Cade herself and forced him to listen to her. Instead, she'd let herself be distracted and overwhelmed by the man she'd convinced herself to let go of. Now, who knew what consequences were in store for her brother if no one stopped him. Face paling, Cassia grabbed Castor and pulled him out to the hallway. Delphine nodded, and sped up her steps as they rushed toward the southern courtyard.

"Do you know what she's talking about?" Castor asked.

"I saw the idea in his head the other day," Cassia said. "That Andarrian girl, Alexia, she mentioned how Quinn used some sort of blood spell on the gate to communicate with the Sanguis."

The color drained from Castor's face. "If he uses blood magic, there will be serious consequences. More than his ability to cross the gate."

Delphine whipped her head around to glare at her. "Why didn't you say anything? Or try to stop him?"

"I said something to Finn. Besides, my brother doesn't care what I have to say. Or trust me."

"We all know that's a lie." Delphine scoffed. "You're the first person he went to for help when Bridget took that potion… And he saved you at the gate instead of sending me through to find her. He may be angry with you, but you're still his sister."

Cassia's eyes widened as she stared at the back of Delphine's head. First, she'd never seen Delphine raise her voice at anyone, let alone her. And not once had she thought about Cade's actions the night Bridget almost died. The first time. Or maybe the second. She'd lost track how many times that girl had been close to death. Had he really trusted her to help him? Or had she just been the closest?

"Can he even use blood magic?" Delphine asked Castor. "He's not a Warlock."

"If he's using his own blood, he doesn't have to be," Castor muttered darkly. "And there's so much we don't know about that type of magic. Most information about the Sanguis was destroyed years ago."

When they entered the courtyard, the buzz coming from the black spiked door almost brought Cassia to her knees. Whatever blood spell Cade was planning to try, he'd already started. She paused in front of the door, afraid she might pass out if she got any closer. Plus, it wouldn't be long before her father sensed the onslaught of magic radiating from the courtyard. Castor pushed on her lower back, though, and moved her forward. Her hands shook all the way down the winding stairs.

Castor grabbed the back of her jacket when they made it to the bottom floor. She gasped at the sight of Cade on his knees in front of the gate. Blazing candles surrounded him. A knife and a thick, brown leather-bound book were splayed out in front of him. To his right, Finn paced. Delphine tried to step forward, but an invisible barrier knocked her backward.

"Where did you get that grimoire?" Castor asked, eyes glued to the old book in front of Cade. "I've never seen one that old."

Cade flicked it open and didn't turn around as he said, "I broke into Echnav's old apartment last night and found it hidden in the floorboard."

Cassia tried to move toward him, but just like Delphine, a gust of wind pushed her back. She begged, "Cade, you can't do this. This is blood magic. What if it kills you?"

"I don't care," he growled, hurriedly flipping the grimoire. "I have to try something."

Castor knelt down and ran a finger through the dirt by the candles. Cassia wondered if he was trying to figure out some way through. Eventually, he wiped his dirty hand on his pants and said, "I can go back and search some more. Maybe I was too distracted by the company and there was something I missed. I'll find her."

"There's no more time for that. In another few months, I'll be married," Cade spat, finally turning to gaze at them. "How can I go through with that without knowing she's okay? How can I..."

A knot formed in Cassia's throat as she studied the panic rising in her brother's eyes. Even behind the blazing rage, it was visible. The spring solstice was less than two months away. It was one of her father's favorite topics at dinner.

After a moment, Cassia voiced the one thing she knew no one else would. "What if she really is just—"

"She's not dead!" Cade roared. Another gust of wind almost brought them all to the ground. Cassia braced herself on Castor's shoulder. Snarling, Cade continued, "Archer must have done something. What if he brought them back to Elyria, to *Quinn*? And I've just been..."

"You would know," Delphine said softly. "She doesn't have the rune anymore. You would feel Bridget or Nylah if they were here."

Cade ignored her and returned his focus to the grimoire.

Castor pulled some herbs out of his pocket and began to sprinkle them on the ground behind Cade. He said, "If you do this, there will be major consequences. Ones I might not be able to find a loophole around for you."

Cassia turned to glare at Finn, who stood stoically in the corner. "I asked you to stop him."

"Believe me, I tried," Finn replied lowly.

"It sure doesn't seem like it."

"Nothing was going to stop him. I decided to help so that at least I could be here to save him if something goes wrong."

"Then you didn't try hard enough," Cassia hissed, flinging herself toward the gate. She didn't care if she set the room on fire by knocking over the candles or had to strangle Cade to get him to stop, but there was no way she was going to watch him suffer the consequences of a blood spell. The second she hit the barrier around Cade, a force threatened to fling her backward. Cassia dug her feet into the dirt, though, and remained standing. Lifting her hand, she tried to reach past the candles. When her fingers crossed, her entire hand burned. Instead of pulling away, Cassia pressed harder. She screamed as invisible fire licked its way up her arm. Just as she was sure she was either close to breaking the barrier or collapsing, arms wrapped around her and pulled her backward.

"Let go of me," Cassia growled, struggling to get out of Castor's grip. Even though her arm pulsed in relief, she'd been *close*. She'd felt Cade relenting.

Castor whispered in her ear, "I'll pull him out if anything goes wrong. Once he's focused on the spell, the barrier should break. I promise."

But what consequences would he face before that happened? Cassia pushed against Castor again, but his grip tightened. Her vision blurred. So much so, she barely saw Cade grab the knife. Barely heard him mutter the spell under his breath from the ringing in her ears that warned her something bad was about to happen. She felt in the air. A shift. Something, or *someone*, besides the human realm was hovering on the other side of the gate.

"Please stop," Cassia bellowed in one last desperate attempt to stop him. "If she's alive, Bridget won't be able to survive a spell like this. You're risking her life."

"Then it's a good thing it's not her mind I'm looking for," Cade said, before he lifted the knife to the palm of his hand and sliced.

# CHAPTER TEN

### Bridget

The standstill traffic on I95 through Providence was doing nothing to help Bridget's migraine. Since Alexia had arrived in Salem, the incessant sharp pain radiating from her temple was beginning to feel like a permanent fixture. It pulsed and squeezed every time she mentioned Andarre or Cora or the curse. Which happened to be every five minutes. The only things Alexia wanted to talk about were the very things Bridget wanted to avoid. Groaning, Bridget pulled her white fluffy beanie further down her forehead and hoped once they got out of Rhode Island, there would be no more obstacles preventing them from reaching the Cavamynian gate by nightfall.

Beside her in the driver's seat, Archer fidgeted and impatiently tapped his fingers on the steering wheel. Every few minutes, he would hum a song under his breath. Even though the noise did nothing to help her head, Bridget was too tired to tell him to stop. When Nylah coughed from the backseat, he stiffened. After peeking at the young girl through the rearview mirror, Archer turned to Bridget and asked, "Are you sure this is a good idea?"

"What other choice do we have?" Bridget muttered. "We need him to cross the gate."

Her plan was a long shot, but it was the only one they had. Even though Alexia had poisoned Nylah with the notion of forcing them to go to Andarre, she had no real way to get back or cross the gate. Bridget nearly killed her a second time when she broke the news. They needed a Shaman. And there was only one Bridget knew. Or knew of. There was no guarantee he would show up back at the Cavamynian gate. After all, the last time she'd seen him, he'd been at the Astraeus one. But he was a Shaman. He'd been there when she'd come through before... And if he was so determined to keep her from crossing, then surely he would show up to stop her again.

The Shaman would be there. He had to be.

From the backseat, Alexia poked her head over the center console. "There are still a few options. He's seen Quinn perform the spell," she said, nodding her head at Archer. "He can—"

"We're not killing anyone," Bridget snapped, cutting her off. A shiver went down her spine as she remembered the first time she'd traveled through the gate. She still saw Quinn holding up a bloody knife in her dreams. With a snide smile directed at Alexia, Bridget added, "Unless you're volunteering."

Rolling her eyes, Alexia huffed and settled back in her seat beside Nylah.

"What if he's not there?" Archer asked quietly. "What if we can't find him?"

Bridget's throat tightened. Craning her neck, she snuck a look at her sister. Swollen, dark eyes glued to Archer's phone, Nylah coughed again. Her cheeks were flushed and there was a little bit of snot hanging from her nose. Wordlessly, Bridget handed her a tissue. Alexia had said the poison spread slowly, but every morning, Nylah's condition worsened. Forcing her gaze away, Bridget whispered, "We will."

She wouldn't fail her sister. Even if she had to parade around the gate for days and somehow lure the Shaman out with some spells by Archer, Bridget would find him.

There were a few blessed seconds of silence before the sound of Zac Efron's voice blasted through the car. Archer immediately perked up and started singing along. Bridget rubbed her temples. She recognized the song from a musical that her and Archer sometimes watched on nights when they had too much tequila.

"This is entertainment?" Alexia asked scathingly.

"To some people," Bridget sighed, giving Archer a sideways glance.

Alexia pushed another button and turned up the song louder. Over the noise, she yelled, "This little box says it's in your top ten most watched. What does that mean?"

Bridget whirled around and swiped her phone out of Alexia's hand. "Give me that."

After exiting the app, she stuffed the device between her legs. She'd hoped giving Alexia her phone would distract her enough to stop talking, like Nylah. Whatever show her sister was watching had kept her silent most of the ride to Connecticut.

After a moment, Alexia said, "You haven't asked me anything about Andarre."

"And that surprises you? You poisoned my sister and are withholding the cure until we go there. Only you would think blackmail makes a person talkative."

"Bitch move," Nylah mumbled, not bothering to look up from the phone.

"Nylah," Bridget scolded.

Archer shrugged. "She's not wrong."

"It's your home," Alexia argued, "only *you* would be stubborn enough not to ask any questions."

Bridget pressed her lips into a determined line and stared out the window. Supermarkets and gas stations blurred past, none of them holding her focus for more than a second. All her effort went into keeping her expression blank. She wouldn't give Alexia the satisfaction of knowing how much a single word had affected her.

Home.

Contrary to Alexia's unfounded belief, it was not the otherworldly place she'd once pretended to be from for the tournament. It never would be. *Home* had evolved in her head over the years. From a foreign concept, to locations and people. It never stayed the same, until one constant came along. Nylah. And then Bridget was sure she knew what the word meant. Even when they no longer lived under the same roof, Bridget had held on to *that* version of home like a lifeline... had fought like hell to make sure it would return to her. Until golden brown eyes and a snarky smile changed everything. In the blink of an eye, home transformed to include not just one person, but *two*. And it became full of color and life and a joy she hadn't thought possible.

But then it was erased... and replaced with a land full of magic and darkness. A darkness that would always linger on her soul. Still, even there, the word rebuilt and transformed in her mind. Just as she had begun to grasp the new version, it was ripped from her. Again.

Now, home was smaller, quieter. It consisted of a tiny house in a new city and bright smiles from her sister. Sometimes Archer's singing and bad jokes. But only half of her heart. *Real*, but only slightly.

One day, the word would have true meaning again.

One day, she would figure out exactly where she belonged.

One day, she wouldn't wake up and think that maybe her memories weren't the only thing she'd been cursed to lose.

Alexia's taunting voice cracked through her suffocating reverie.

"Why are you so angry that I'm making you cross the gate? Don't you want to see your prince again?"

Bridget turned around to glare at her, only to realize Alexia's eyes were glued to the phone on her lap. Throat tight, Bridget looked down to realize she'd unconsciously tapped on her device's little screen to look at the background picture. The one she'd spent days scrolling through a club's social media to find. Even though he hardly looked like himself in the Bob Ross costume, Cade's wide grin never failed to make her stomach flutter. She hated that it felt like the only thing she had left of him.

"We're going to Andarre, not Elyria. That is the end goal of your not so thought out master plan, right?" Bridget said, stuffing her phone in her purse so she wouldn't be tempted to look at it again. Of course, she wanted to see Cade. Bridget didn't think that would come as a surprise to anyone in the car. But if they were stuck in Andarre past the spring solstice... then she was never setting foot in Elyria again.

After a brief pause, Alexia said, "Since you won't ask, Andarre is beautiful."

"For fuck's sake..." Archer groaned, knocking his forehead into the steering wheel. "Learn to read the room."

Nylah snorted. "More like the car."

"It's an island surrounded by the bluest ocean," Alexia continued. "Every city is built with white brick and light blue roofs. Every beach is full of the softest, palest sand. It's always the perfect temperature, even in winter. And the food... better than anything a Fae can cook up."

Bridget rolled her eyes and tried not to be appealed by the description. "Sounds magical."

"So does Jamaica. At least I wouldn't get executed on the spot there," Archer let slip under his breath.

"There's nothing magical about it." Alexia sneered. "Magic is forbidden there."

"Except for the use of protective runes. And Shamans, when whoever's in charge needs help with the future," Bridget chided. "Seems hypocritical."

Alexia raised a brow. "You can take that up with the King when we get there."

"Yeah, I'm sure I will," Bridget replied blithely, returning her gaze to the window. The conspiratorial, taunting gleam brewing in Alexia's eyes rattled her. When they got there, there would be no time to complain to kings. Once Nylah was healed, they would get the hell out of there.

The expanse of forest outside New London gave Bridget the chills. She barely remembered being in the shrouded, dark state park where the gate to Cavamyne was located, but the hairs on her arm stood straight up, like her body subconsciously relived the memory with every step she took. Bridget squeezed Nylah's hand tighter and followed Archer down a narrow path. Since they'd parked the car, he'd been unusually quiet. Every few seconds, he nervously glanced at the shadows around them.

"Didn't you drive us right up to the gate last time?" Bridget asked.

"Last time, there wasn't four inches of snow on the ground. Do you really think that rental car could make it up this hill?"

Seconds later, Nylah slipped and pulled Bridget down with her. Falling on her knees, Bridget quickly lifted her arm to make sure her sister didn't fall on her face. He did have a point. The steep incline into the trees *was* icy. A few feet behind them, Alexia grasped a tree and tried to stay upright. Bridget hoped she would fall on her ass and break her tailbone.

Once they finally reached a plateau, Archer led them to a break in the forest. Past the mossy tree line, noise ceased. All Bridget could hear was her own breathing and the crunchy sound of snow beneath her feet. She gazed up at the sky, but it had disappeared. Only the dark, looming tops of trees shone down on her. In a way, it reminded her of the Elder Woods. At least there, she hadn't felt alone. No matter how much she trusted Archer, she couldn't get rid of the shiver that seemed lodged in her spine.

When the gate came into sight, Bridget's heart almost stopped. It looked unassuming. Any other hiker would probably pass it by without a second glance. But she knew better. Slowly, she approached the large, standing stone. It was taller than she remembered. And just like Archer had described, a jagged crack now went right down the middle. Even though it wasn't buzzing, she braced herself like it suddenly would start. Maybe it would. Bridget gazed around them for a sign of the Shaman, but the woods were empty. When Nylah tried to move closer to the stone, Bridget pushed her backward.

Out of breath, Alexia leaned against another tree. "What now? We've been circling the woods for hours. The Shaman's obviously not here."

"Give me a minute," Bridget snapped. Give *him* a minute, really. She twitched her gloved fingers. Maybe she needed to yell or shout to get his attention. Last time, she'd talked to the stone to make him appear. Bridget studied her present company. That was something she didn't want to do in front of them. Instead, she moved to stand a few feet from the stone. With her foot, Bridget kicked a layer of snow and leaves away. The hard dirt beneath was bare and lifeless.

Archer appeared beside her. "What exactly are you looking for?"

"I'm not sure," Bridget muttered, feeling sheepish. She'd been hoping, or dreading, to find some kind of sign she'd been there. Proof of the last time she'd come through the gate. Whatever blood or grime she'd left behind had already been cleaned or washed away with the seasons.

Bridget stared at the stone. And then at the space behind it. "I know you're watching," she whispered. The static in the air told her as much. It'd been a while since she'd felt the swirling tension of magic in the air. Turning to Archer, Bridget said, "Try a spell. Maybe that will get his attention."

"Like what? I'm better with potions."

"I don't know. A summoning spell."

"For what? A cute little forest creature? I think most are hibernating."

"I don't care if you summon a leaf," Bridget growled through gritted teeth. "Just try *something*."

Archer rolled his shoulders and then flicked his wrists in the air. Eyes closed, he muttered a spell under his breath. After a gust of wind almost blew Bridget's beanie off, a mud-covered leaf slapped her hard in the forehead. Beside her, Nylah laughed. Glaring, Bridget flicked it off and threw it at her sister.

Gazing around the still empty, Archer shrugged. "I don't think it's me that is going to get his attention. Try touching the gate. That's what you were doing last time."

But she'd also been crying and trying to talk to Cade. Neither of which she wanted to do in front of Alexia. Despite her misgivings, Bridget took a step toward the gate. Then another. Her chest twisted when she stood inches from the carved stone. She wished she knew what the symbols meant. Behind her, Nylah coughed. It sounded rough and full of phlegm.

"You hear that? We haven't got all day," Alexia berated. "This trip was a waste of time. Just get the Warlock to perform the blood spell so we can finally cross. I'm sure there's someone nearby in the woods we can find."

"You catch more bees with honey than vinegar, you know," Archer clucked, crossing his arms.

Not looking back at either of them, Bridget clenched her jaw and slammed her hand against the stone, directly over the crack. Nothing happened. No buzz or vibration or explosion of magic burst from the rock. Suddenly, out of the corner of her eye, a movement caught Bridget's attention. She swirled her head to the right, gaze darting erratically until it finally settled on a figure standing between two bare, dead trees.

Bridget's entire body went numb.

The girl was back. And no one else seemed to notice the other person clearly watching them. If she were real, they would. Her long, medieval looking pale pink dress looked out of place in the forest, and her striking features and black hair would make anyone stare.

The longer Bridget looked at her, the more the girl's smirk widened.

Without thinking, Bridget pulled a dagger from her boot and threw as hard as she could. The second it was out of her hand, the girl laughed and disappeared. Bridget's stomach dropped as she watched the weapon slice through thin air before it lodged itself in a tree trunk.

Beside her, Archer ducked and exclaimed, "What the hell? I thought we wanted to talk to the Shaman, not stab him."

Bridget shook her head and ran over to grab her dagger. "I didn't see the Shaman. Someone else is here," she said, frantically waving her hand between the two dead trees. Nothing but air sliced between her fingertips.

Nylah grabbed her flailing hand. Gently squeezing her fingers, her sister worriedly stared up at her. "Are you okay? There's no one there. It's just us."

Unable to stand the concern in Nylah's eyes, Bridget stepped away from her. Hands shaking, she took a deep breath. It had to be a trick of the Shaman. He had to be inside her head, making her see things. Into nothingness, she screamed, "I know you're here."

"Yelling is pointless," Alexia interjected. "Between your hallucinations and the Warlock's faulty potion, we'll never get back to Andarre. We should have gone back to the Salem coven for help."

"My potion was brewed to perfection, thank you very much."

"Have you forgotten I lived with a coven for over a year? I know what an effective potion looks like."

Just before Bridget strangled them both, Nylah fell to her knees and gasped for breath. Seconds later, hoarse coughs exploded from her tiny chest. Bridget dropped to the ground beside her and rubbed her back.

"Both of you, shut up," Bridget growled. Anxiety twisted her stomach. Once Nylah's breathing evened out, she glared venomously at Alexia. "You said whatever you gave her would affect her slowly. It's only been a few days."

For once, Alexia looked at a loss for words. Her dark eyes widened, and her mouth opened and closed as she stared at Nylah. "It shouldn't be making her this sick. I saw Cora use it on another human once. It was months before he noticed he was sick. I swear."

"Magic works differently here. Surely your precious Cora must have told you that," Bridget snarled. "You must have messed up whatever ingredients you found."

"I..."

"You didn't listen to my warning," a deep voice grumbled.

Bridget whirled around and pushed Nylah behind her. Still crouched on the ground, she registered torn jeans, a plaid covered chest, and then a gasp from Alexia. Swallowing hard, Bridget slowly gazed up to meet the bright blue eyes of the Shaman.

Below her arm, Nylah quietly exclaimed, "Woah. He just appeared out of nowhere."

Holding the Shaman's stare, Bridget raised her chin. He looked different than before. Without the fake park ranger uniform, he looked younger. His long blond hair was slicked back, and a silver earring hung from his left ear. After a long moment, Bridget dared to say, "Well, you didn't specifically mention *this* gate."

Face hardening, the Shaman turned to leave. Panic flooding her, Bridget rushed after him. "We need your help. My sister was poisoned. You have to send us through the gate so we can get the cure."

Before she could complete her sentence, the Shaman tossed a small vial at her. "It's not a cure, but it will keep her well. For now."

Bridget gaped at him, and then the vial in her hand. The swirling indigo liquid glistened and glowed with every movement. "Every potion I've had from a Fae has almost killed me. How do I know this won't do the same to her?"

The Shaman rolled his eyes. "Relax. I made it from ingredients I bought at the Walmart in New London. Like I said, it won't heal her, just contain her symptoms. For now, at least. Your Andarrian friend is right. The cure is only found on that tiny little island she calls home. Besides, I'm not Fae."

Bridget grasped the vial tighter in her hand, refusing to break eye contact with the Tuathan in front of her. Had he seen them coming? And why help them at all? She looked for any sign on his face for an ulterior motive, but his gaze was unreadable. Every Shaman she'd met or seen had seemed wild, cutthroat, and embedded with a resentment for humans. But the one in front of her reminded her of Cade, more than anything. She couldn't pinpoint whether it was his attitude or the shape of his face. Heart thundering in her chest, Bridget asked, "What's the price?"

His lips turned upward as he nodded at Nylah. "Just give it to her."

Wordlessly, Bridget uncorked the vial and handed it to her sister. Without hesitation, Nylah downed the potion in one gulp. Seconds later, color returned to her dark cheeks and her hazy eyes cleared. Bridget's entire body relaxed in relief. So much so, she involuntarily let out a small laugh. She turned back to the Shaman to thank him, only to find him walking away again. "Wait!" she called. When he didn't, she hopped up and ran after him. "Stop!"

"Bridget..." Archer warned.

But she was done waiting for answers. If he wouldn't stop, then she would make him. Bridget pulled another dagger out of her boot and threw it at him.

The Shaman whirled around and flicked it away before it hit him. "Would you stop doing that?"

"Not until you send us across the gate," she said. "I have to get the cure for Nylah. I won't depend on some concoction you made. Screw whatever vision tells you to keep me here."

The Shaman whirled around. "You wouldn't be saying that if you've seen the things I have. Besides, I made a promise to myself to not get involved anymore. Trust me, it's better that way."

"You've already made yourself involved. You were there the night we came through from Cavamyne. Don't deny it. And again, in Boston last month. You didn't have to talk to me at the library. Or at the gate. I was just trying to say goodbye."

She hated that her voice broke. Swallowing hard, Bridget straightened her spine. It would be easier to negotiate if he didn't know how desperate she was. Even if she had a feeling he already knew. "Plus, you had that vial ready for my sister," Bridget continued. "So just stop with the vague warnings and help us."

The Shaman stiffened. He stared at her, then Nylah. He even spared a glance at Archer and Alexia, who still waited by the gate. Only then did Bridget realize they were frozen in place behind her. That the air around her was thick and heavy with the presence of magic. That she was the only thing moving.

Frantically, she asked, "What did you do to them?"

"Nothing. We're inside your head," the Shaman said. "For all they know, you're still throwing the dagger at me."

Faintly, somewhere far away, Bridget felt wetness underneath pooling underneath her nose. "Why are you talking to me in here?"

"Because if you expect me to help, I need to know you trust them. What I know shouldn't fall on the wrong ears."

"Shouldn't you be able to see whether or not they'll be trustworthy?"

"I'm not omniscient. My visions are only bits and pieces of important events, and usually about people I'm already focused on watching."

Bridget tensed. "Then why see me?"

"Do you trust them?" he countered, each word said like its own sentence.

Bridget glanced back at the frozen Nylah, Archer, and Alexia. Only one of them made her hesitate. Would she ever trust Alexia with her life? No. But would she trust her to do whatever it takes to get back to Andarre? Absolutely. And that was all she needed to save her sister.

However, Bridget couldn't ignore the tiny seed of doubt, or hope, that Alexia was lying about everything… that the curse wasn't broken and that she wasn't from Andarre. That somehow, they could heal her sister here so that her heart wouldn't be fed the hope it was starving for… the hope to see Cade. Bridget pushed the thought away. He wasn't something she could afford to think about until Nylah was safe and healed.

When she turned back to the Shaman, she wondered if he could hear her thoughts, because a sad, stony expression had overtaken his face. Throat tightening, Bridget asked the one question she knew would reveal if Alexia was lying or not. "Am I from Andarre?"

"Yes."

Bridget closed her eyes and let the truth wash over her. Part of her wanted to sleep and not wake up for a very long time. The other part wanted to scream and thrash at everyone that had kept the truth from her. It was impossible, but at the same time, made complete sense in her head. Hadn't she always felt out of place? Hadn't she been secretly longing for the world she vowed to hate for the last few months?

When she was certain no tears would escape, Bridget opened her eyes. "Then I trust them," she said. "If I'm from Andarre, does that mean Alexia is right? That the curse—"

The Shaman held up a hand and cut her off. "Some things are better seen than heard. At least for you."

Bridget opened her mouth to argue, but a roaring whoosh slammed her to the ground. Noise and movement crashed into her senses. Bridget groaned and dug her fingers into the wet snow. The conversation in her head had cost her. Her temples throbbed and blood stained the white beneath her. A small hand grabbed her shoulder.

"Are you okay? Why are you bleeding?" Nylah asked.

"Magic, obviously," Alexia mumbled.

When Archer pulled her up, Bridget found the Shaman already glaring at Alexia. "That's enough. It's time we all had a little talk."

# CHAPTER ELEVEN

Bridget gripped Nylah's hand as she followed the Shaman, careful not to get too close. She kept her eyes glued to the back of his blond head and wished she could borrow Cade's powers for a few seconds to figure out his plan. What did he know about her past? And why help them at all? More than anything, Bridget wanted answers. She knew better than anyone, though, that Fae magic always came with a cost. Out of the corner of her eye, she checked Nylah's demeanor for any sign of negative effects from the Shaman's potion. In Elyria, magic had almost always had an immediate physical effect on her. When Bridget deemed her perusal of her sister was satisfactory, she straightened her spine. Even if he had helped Nylah, she wouldn't let the Shaman anywhere near her sister, or let him try to use her as a bargaining chip.

After a few minutes, the Shaman began to lead them down a trail that was all too familiar to Bridget. The root-filled, slippery path had taken them in circles for hours. Before she had a chance to protest their direction, Archer's loud groan echoed throughout the empty forest.

"We walked this trail about ten times," he called out. "The only things this way are dead trees and a porta-potty that should have been decommissioned about ten years ago. Ask the ray of sunshine behind me."

"I still can't believe you forced me to use that thing," Alexia growled.

The Shaman waved his hand. Seconds later, another path appeared to their left. This one was more shrouded and rockier than any others in the park. With a wry grin, he said, "Remember when you two couldn't find the gate back to Astraeus last month? I pulled the same little trick here. Camouflage is one of my specialties. Or curses. Depending on how you want to look at it. Many kings have taken advantage of it over the years."

"Along with prophecy," Bridget added. Like Marin. Like many of the other Shamans she'd come across in Elyria. Ominous warnings about the future seemed to flow from their mouths every second. Bridget couldn't stop herself from giving him a sideways glare. How much knowledge about her and her future was locked up inside his head?

"And this." With another flick of his wrist, the Shaman froze falling snowflakes midair. Seconds later, their assault continued. He continued, "Most Tuathans have some sort of gift of sight. Mine happens to be stronger than others... But like I said, I only see certain things. Important things. I can't control when or how they happen. And it's always..."

"Changing," Bridget finished for him. Isn't that what she'd always heard about the future? Isn't that why Cade constantly fought against his father?

He must have heard the optimism in her voice because he suddenly stilled. Blue eyes stormy, he warned, "Some things are too big to change. Some things are fate."

Bridget's throat tightened under the intensity of his gaze. Whatever desire she had about knowing her future disappeared from her body. His tone promised nothing but darkness.

"Why hide this trail?" Archer asked, breaking her out of her swirling thoughts. "This part of the park doesn't look like it gets many visitors."

"Maybe, but this path leads to my house. I didn't want any lost hikers coming across a cabin full of Elyrian relics."

"Relics? Like what?" Nylah asked.

"Most of it wouldn't be interesting to you, but I do happen to have a spoon that will change colors if it's dipped in poison."

Nylah grinned. "Cool."

"How long have you lived here?" Bridget asked.

The Shaman shrugged. "A few years."

A minute later, the tree line broke and a cabin appeared. Nestled in a meadow, its wooden structure radiated an otherworldly aura. *Magic.* Even as a human, Bridget could practically taste it in the air the closer they stepped. She snuck a glance at the Shaman. Theories of who he could be swirled in her head. Without using a key, he opened the painted front door of the cabin with a flick of his wrist.

Before she could follow him inside, a hand on Bridget's wrist froze her in place. The movement jostled Nylah's hand out of her grasp and brought her chest to chest with her least favorite person.

Alexia whispered, "This feels like a trap."

"Rude," Nylah muttered.

Rolling her eyes, Bridget said, "Don't pretend to be concerned about our wellbeing."

"That's the last thing on my mind," Alexia scoffed. "But if I'm going to save my family, I need you back in Andarre in one piece."

Archer grabbed Bridget's shoulders and pulled her away from Alexia's stiff demeanor. Clicking his tongue, he chastised, "Ladies, this is not the time for a cat fight."

Alexia blinked at him. "I don't have a cat."

Suppressing the urge to laugh, Bridget ripped her arm out of Alexia's bruising grasp. "He doesn't mean literally. Look, I'm not sure whether I trust him either, but he's the only one on this side of the gate that might be able to help us cross it and get us the answers we need."

Brows raised, Archer turned to her. "Answers?"

"Looks like someone is starting to believe my lies after all," Alexia said.

Bridget wanted to smack the smirk off her face. Instead, she took a deep breath and whispered to Archer, "Stay close to Nylah."

"I can take care of myself," her sister interjected.

"Humor me."

The interior of the Shaman's home was just like Bridget expected, full of random knick-knacks and mismatched items. However, she assumed each one wasn't really as *random* as it appeared. There were no pictures, or personal items. The only indication that someone actively lived there was the steaming pot of water on the stove.

In the kitchen, the Shaman wordlessly poured five glasses of tea. Sticking close to the door, Bridget scanned the walls and corners for any sign of a trap. Unless she counted the very large spider nestled near the ceiling, she found none.

"No television?" Nylah asked, flopping down on the couch.

"It gives me a headache."

So this guy was *old*. When the Shaman handed Bridget a small teacup, she was pleasantly surprised to find it already full of cream and sugar. Still, she refused to drink it and placed it on the fireplace mantle. Archer gulped his down and ran a finger over a row of books on the Shaman's shelf.

That's when she noticed it. An Elyrian history book on the shelf next to his wandering hand. One she'd seen only months ago.

"You're Echnav, aren't you?" Bridget guessed.

The Shaman's shoulder stiffened. "How did you guess?"

"Cade told me about you," she said, picking up the book. "He said you were his tutor. I saw a book just like this in his room. Plus, you're the only missing Shaman I know."

"Echnav... That's the name I started going by about a century ago when I briefly left Astraeus to live in Tafari. Once Marin was born, though, I came back to help raise her. My real name is Stellan. It's the name I prefer."

Archer snorted into his tea.

Bridget's jaw dropped. "You're Marin's father?"

He was so... young. And with the earring, did *not* look like anyone's father.

"Not exactly. Her father was one of my best friends. He died a few days after she was born."

"How? Aren't Shamans basically immortal?" Archer asked.

"Some would like to think so, but we do have our weaknesses. I couldn't stop you from cutting off my head or stabbing me in the heart. A certain iron also poisons us," Stellan said. "People like to think we're invincible because only a few things cause us to age at the same speed as humans."

"But you're not?" Nylah asked.

Stellan's lips twisted. "Definitely not."

"What makes you age?"

"Nylah," Bridget warned.

Nonplussed, Stellan continued, "If I were to bind my life to a human's, I would age with them. Die with them, even."

Bridget remembered Cade talking about Tuathans mating with humans a long time ago, but nothing about being *bound*. "Is that common?" she asked. "My experience with Shamans has been the opposite of... friendly. And none of them were old. Including yourself."

"Tuathans and humans used to be very *friendly* with each other. Why do you think there's so many Fae running around?" Stella said, almost cracking a smile. "Before the whole mess with the Sanguis, humans ruled Elyria... right next door to the Tuathans in Cavamyne. Even though the two populations had some issues every now and then, *intermingling* wasn't treated like it is now. But to be bound... it takes a price. No Tuathan would attempt it lightly. So to answer your question... No. It's not common."

"Marin did tell me she was only half-Tuathan. I just didn't realize what that meant," Bridget said. "How does it work?"

"This isn't the time for a history lesson," Alexia hissed in her ear.

Bridget ignored her. She didn't know why she was so curious, only that information pulled at something deep in her gut. Like she'd heard it before... possibly in a dream.

"When you bind yourself to a human, your life is tied to theirs... for better or worse. When Marin's mother died giving birth to her, Ambrose only managed to last a few hours. He was one of the few Tuathans, or Shamans... whatever name you want to call us, left that understood our purpose in Astraeus.... remembered the reason for the vow we took to protect the royal family. Now all that's left are ones that blindly serve him for their own gain. It's part of the reason why I left."

Stellan's quiet voice sobered the entire room. Even Nylah put down her tea and folded her hands together somberly.

Archer cleared his throat. "If being bound weakens your kind, why do it at all?"

"Love."

The word was out of Bridget's mouth before her brain had processed the response. Like it was a question she'd answered many times before.

Arms crossed, she studied Stellan with both suspicion and curiosity. "How old are you?"

"A little over 600."

To her left, Archer ran his finger across a dusty old clock. Bridget slapped his hand down. "Stop touching things."

Alexia groaned. "We get it. You're super old. I think we've learned enough of your backstory for one day. Can you send us across the gate or not? If I don't deliver Bridget back to Andarre, my family will suffer."

"More than just a few people are going to suffer if she goes back to Elyria," Stellan replied, so nonchalant Bridget wasn't sure if she'd heard him right.

"I don't want to go back to Elyria," Bridget said, hoping the half-truth wasn't too obvious on her face. She tried to push Cade from her mind. "We'll go to Andarre and then come right back."

"There's no future where I see that happening. The moment you cross the gate again, there's no coming back."

Bridget's heart stopped at the finality in his voice. All eyes turned to her, their stares begging her for different things. For a moment, she floundered as she wrestled with the truth inside her. "I think you already saw why I don't want to go back to Elyria." Earlier, she'd seen Stellan visibly react when she'd thought about Cade's marriage deal with his father. "It will be too late. Especially when we have to go to Andarre first. I am *not* going to go to Elyria."

A frustrated glint marred Stellan's expression. "It doesn't matter what you want. There are too many forces at play right now… too much at stake besides your sister. The second you step back in that realm—"

"Because of who she is?" Archer asked. "Some relative to someone who died for a curse a few centuries ago? Why does that matter?"

"What do you know about who she is?" Stellan retorted angrily.

"You're not answering the question. The curse is broken, isn't it?" Archer argued. "So why does it matter if she goes back or stays here? It shouldn't. It's done."

"I *knew* it," Alexia said, "she's related to the—"

"Everyone *stop*." Bridget's command silenced the room. She locked eyes with Stellan. "Answer Archer's question."

Stellan hesitated. "Listen…"

"In the woods, you said some things are better seen not heard. Well, it's time to explain. You *know* me." Bridget glanced at her teacup. "You knew—"

"How you take your tea? Maybe it was a lucky guess."

Bridget shook her head. "It's more than that. At the Astraeus gate, you knew my name. Knew—"

"I could've entered your mind without you knowing."

"I've had enough Fae in my mind to know it doesn't work like that." Bridget straightened her spine. "Show me."

"I've already been inside your head today. I think you might need a few more hours to…"

"Show. Me."

The world around her disappeared.

*A slice of pain splintered her skull. When she fell to her knees, grass broke her fall instead of dusty hardwood. Bridget dug her fingers into the wet, soft earth to steady herself. Breathing hard, she forced herself to look up. A long slab of a stone and two thrones appeared before her. Cavamyne. For a split second, panic rushed through her veins. Pain and loss and regret overwhelmed her senses. This was not a night she wanted to see again. Not a night she wanted to relive. Only when her vision focused did she notice the large group of people surrounding the gate. Notice that the stones weren't old and cracked. That the palace behind her stood looming and dark… and intact. Perfect. Exactly like her reoccurring dream. It couldn't be that night. Shakily, Bridget pushed herself to her feet.*

*From where she stood, she couldn't tell if the onlookers were Fae, Witches, or Nymphs. Their backs were turned as they all focused on two figures standing on the gate. A woman, with long dark hair, a blood-red mask, and silver metal claws adorning her fingers held a prisoner by her throat.*

*Bridget's heart stopped.*

*It was* her.

*She was the prisoner.*

*Not a relative. Not a great-great-great grandmother.* Her. *There was no denying it. No second guessing. Even if the prisoner's hair was longer and the skin on the back of her hands was smooth. Bridget knew herself.*

*Stumbling backward, Bridget ran into a hard chest. She whipped around and found herself face-to-face with Stellan. Or a different version of him. One that belonged in a medieval television show or renaissance faire. With a hood covering most of his face, he somberly watched the scene unfolding yards away.*

*"What is this?" Bridget asked.*

*When Stellan didn't answer, she reached for the edge of his hood to get his attention. Her hand slipped through his head, like he was a projection. That's when she realized he couldn't see or hear her at all.*

*This was his memory.*

*Bridget turned back to the gate. The masked woman chanted, barely loud enough to hear. Others around her, all in similar masks, did the same. The torches around the gate blazed and sparked the longer they went on.*

*Raising her metal claws in the air, the center woman silenced them. "Bring it forward."*

*Two soldiers, with black ooze dripping from the mouth and eyes, laid a box at the woman's feet. Bridget jumped when her old self turned her head in her direction. She followed her eye-line, expecting to find Stellan, but instead...*

*Cade.*

*Heart thundering, Bridget ran over to him. Her arms itched to throw themselves around him, but she knew they would just go right through him. Instead, she settled on just looking at him. It'd been so long...*

*But he wasn't her Cade, though. He was older, battle worn, and had scars on his cheek and forehead... and arched ears. Bridget peeked at his neck. Snaking, blue Tuathan tattoos disappeared under his shirt. His family's royal crest was embedded on the upper clasp of his jacket.*

*Bridget took a frenzied step back, her body already processing what her mind struggled to comprehend. He was... They were...*

*Composure breaking, Cade took a frantic lunge forward. Stellan caught him before he made it far.*

*"You can't," he whispered, barely holding back Cade who twisted and turned in his arms.*

*She'd been so distracted by Cade, she'd forgotten what was going on behind her. Bridget whirled around and found the other Bridget on her knees. The masked woman held a dagger in the air. Hands trembling, she realized exactly what memory Stellan was giving her.*

*The creation of the curse on the humans.*

*It'd been her all along. Her blood, her ring, at Cavamyne.*

*It's why her memories remained intact after she'd returned. Why Alexia's did, too. Why Marin had been so insistent about the timing when she'd sent her through the gate with Archer.*

*Her death had broken the curse.*

*An accident, she realized. Quinn's goal hadn't been about her curse.*

*Which meant...*

*The moment the knife went through the other Bridget's chest, Cade fell to his knees. Bridget followed him. Gasping for breath, he stared up at Stellan. "Do it."*

*Stellan's eyes remained on the other Bridget's now lifeless body. His grip on Cade had completely disappeared.*

*Struggling to breathe, Cade hurriedly grabbed Stellan's cloak and pulled him down to his level. "You said it has to be now. Do it!"*

*A scream echoed from the gate. In a ghastly, beastly voice, the masked woman howled, "WHERE IS IT?"*

*The explosion of activity surrounding the gate seemed to bring Stellan back to his senses. Shakily, he reached into his cloak and pulled out the Bloodstone. It glowed as Stellan closed his eyes and muttered something under his breath. Moments later, he unsheathed his dagger. On the ground beside Cade, Bridget couldn't take her eyes off him. He almost looked relieved and—*

*Stellan held the knife above Cade's chest. Bridget scrambled away. Unable to watch. Unable to—*

Screaming, Bridget launched herself off the couch. She didn't know how she'd gotten there, but Nylah's concerned face hovering over her told her she'd been unconscious for a long time. Blood poured from her nose as she tracked down Stellan standing in the corner. It was strange. Just moments before, she'd seen him upset over her death. Now, he looked at her like a stranger. There was no compassion in his eyes, only steely determination.

"You killed him," she snarled, wiping the blood from her face with the sleeve of her coat.

"Excuse me… What?" Archer exclaimed. "Who?"

"Cade."

"Not the Cade you know," Stellan corrected loudly over Archer and Nylah's sudden onslaught of questions. Clenching his jaw, he pointed at her. "That's not what happened. Think about what you saw."

Struggling to breathe, Bridget closed her eyes. For once, she wanted to forget. She wanted to go back to living in blissful ignorance of what was coming for her. What she *knew* she could not stop, no matter what Stellan or anyone did. But no matter how hard she tried, the images she'd seen wouldn't leave her retinas.

Cade wasn't just a prince. He was *the* prince. The Tuathan prince from the painting and every story she'd ever heard about the Cavamynian War. And she…

How was it even possible?

Archer laid a hand on her shoulder. It helped lessen her trembling. Only a little. "What did you see?" he asked softly.

"It was the curse," Bridget croaked. Oh, God. What did it all *mean*? "I need…"

Help. An explanation. A way out of this. Hope.

*Cade.*

Her stomach flopped. Did he know? The idea that he might have known their entire relationship had her wishing the floor would just swallow her up forever.

Slowly, Stellan moved closer to her. With every step, he searched her face. For what, she wasn't sure. Her eyes watered until she guessed he found what he was looking for. "If you expect me to help you, you need to say it," he said.

Bridget paused. If she said it, everything would change.

She gazed at Nylah, who watched her with so much concern her heart broke, then took a deep breath. "We've met before."

Stellan nodded. "Back in Elyria."

"Over five hundred years ago."

Silence enveloped the room. Bridget didn't think anyone was even breathing.

After what felt like forever, Archer sat down. Then stood up. Then paced a circle around the couch. "I think for once in my life, I'm actually speechless."

"How can you be speechless if you're still talking?" Nylah countered. "And as long as Cade isn't *really* dead, I think I can handle you being older than dirt."

Bridget let out a choked laugh. She really loved her sister.

Clearly rattled, Alexia backed into Stellan's tiny kitchen table. "That's not possible."

"I haven't created a curse quite like it since..." Stellan said, running a hand through his blonde hair. Bridget could've sworn he looked lighter. Like a weight had suddenly been lifted from his shoulders. He opened a cabinet and pulled out a bottle of whiskey. "It put me to sleep for a very long time. It's a side effect Tuathans encounter if we use too much of our magic at one time... it took me years to recharge."

"The Bloodstone... it's your blood, isn't it?" Bridget asked.

*The blood of one of the most powerful Shamans lies inside*, Cade's voice echoed.

Castor paced in front of Archer's cell. *Curses need two things: an anchor and blood.*

Quinn's smirk taunted her. *You'll never guess who was used to bind it.*

Her and Cade stood in front of the painting that depicted the memory she'd just seen. It had given her chills. She'd barely been able to look at it. Even then, somewhere inside her had known there was more to the story.

"You created it for the curse that sent the Sanguis to Iegorus…" she ranted, "a regular rune wasn't strong enough. But why use Cade to bind it? And how is it even possible we were *them*?"

Stellan took a long swig of whiskey, straight from the bottle. Then opened his mouth. And closed it again.

"Why aren't you answering?" Bridget demanded.

Archer let out a hollow chuckle. "All magic has a cost."

Stellan glared at him.

"That's what the curse cost you?" Bridget asked. "The ability to answer questions?"

Stellan rubbed his eyes. "My *memories*."

"Of everything? Then how did you just show me that night?"

"No, not everything. Just the ones that would help explain what I did and why you were killed. Magic takes what you want the most," Stellan replied tiredly. "Look… I did not wake up prepared for this conversation today… Luckily, I've had a few decades to work out what happened. Mostly with Marin's help. She's the one who's been able to dig out certain things. And another Tuathan, Bronwyn, explained some things to me when I woke back up after casting the curse. I'll start with what I know… your execution was not a surprise. Vega had revealed her plan to you early on…"

Archer let out a choking noise. "*Execution*? Exactly who were you? Or *are* you?" He glanced sideways at Stellan. "What's the proper term in this situation, old man?"

Pinching the bridge of his nose, Stellan took another long drink of whiskey. Nylah goggled at her like she was an alien. Alexia paced in the corner.

"I would like to know that, as well." Bridget ripped the bottle from his hand, scattering droplets all over the floor, before she did the same. She'd hoped the burn of the liquid would calm her quaking nerves, but they still kept pulsing like little alarm bells under her skin.

Stellan glowered at her. "From what I was told, the entire thing was your idea. It was the only way to stop Vega. She was very close to getting her hands on something that would have won her the war. You stopped that before it happened."

"So that's why she killed me?"

Not that she'd fully believed it before, but part of Bridget was relieved that she hadn't been killed just because Cade had chosen her over Vega. It seemed too silly of a reason for the head of the Sanguis coven. A shiver went down her spine thinking of the woman with the metal claws. Then the scars on Bridget's stomach flared to life. A night sky. Chanting. *Searching*. Quinn had been searching for something inside her.

Stellan hesitated. "It's complicated."

"Well uncomplicate it," Bridget hissed through gritted teeth.

"Bronwyn said your execution was inevitable. That we needed more *time*. And that the only way to give that to you and Cade... was to kill you both."

"This is crazy..." Archer muttered. Bridget couldn't help but agree with him. "Why would they agree to that?"

"To bring you back one day so that we could end it, once and for all," Stellan said, keeping his focus on her. "A curse within a curse. We would banish the Sanguis, and guarantee you and Cade's survival in one fell swoop. It's why it had to be his life that bound it. His Tuathan blood, along with mine in the Bloodstone, were the only two powerful enough to make sure it would work."

"So is it time to end it then?" Nylah asked. When everyone's confused gaze cut to her, she shrugged. "Haven't you been listening? He said he would bring you back when it was time. So it must be... right?"

"Not me... the curse didn't work like that." Stellan tiredly rubbed his eyes. "Magic isn't something that can be fully controlled. Even by me. I had no idea when Bridget and Cade would come back, or even if it would be at the same time. That must have been a risk you both accepted, but it's why…"

"You and the Shamans stuck around," Bridget finished, sensing his trepidation. She'd always wondered why the most powerful of all the species did the royal family's bidding and almost acted indentured, whose only purpose was to guard a gate. "The vow you mentioned… how it'd gotten all twisted up. Ambrose, Marin's father, was the last one left that remembered all this, wasn't he?"

The corners of Stellan's lips lifted. "Very good… but like I said, the curse weakened me. By the time I awakened, the new king had already destroyed so many gates… changed so many things. Vega was supposed to have no idea about what we'd done. But…"

Bridget heard his unspoken words. Magic couldn't be controlled and always had a cost. And whatever magic the new king had messed with had revealed too much to Vega in Iegorus. Knowledge she must have passed down to the rest of the Sanguis.

"What does this have to do with her staying away from Elyria? Or Andarre?" Alexia fumed, knuckles white as she gripped the back of a chair.

Stellan blinked at her. "Everything."

"How? The curse broke. She lived. The Sanguis are still in Iegorus," Alexia hissed. "Shouldn't you want her back in Elyria… to *end* it? Wasn't that the entire purpose of this whole thing? There are people that need—"

"This is about the other curse, isn't it?" Bridget asked.

*Once you cross, there's no coming back.*

Stellan's words of warning were not for her, but for *Cade*. If she went back to Elyria… fate would take its course. Just like it had done with her.

"To break the curse on the Sanguis, Cade needs to die in Cavamyne." Archer held up his hands when Bridget glared at him. "We were all there the first time Quinn tried. Obviously, we don't want that to happen."

"Then all we have to do is keep him away from there," Alexia said.

Stellan slammed his fist against the cabin wall. Books from his shelf tumbled to the ground. "You don't understand. It's not that simple. All three curses are connected. When Cade and Bridget were born, the veil shielding Iegorus from everything else weakened, but just slightly. That's probably why Quinn could communicate with the Sanguis."

Narrowing her eyes, Alexia spat, "Or why creatures covered in black ooze with a thirst for blood suddenly arose from the sea?"

"Now that the curse on the humans is broken, it's probably much worse."

Stellan's dark statement silenced Alexia. The girl paled, then slowly sat down in the chair she'd been using like a lifeline.

"Yep. That's two out of three," Archer muttered under his breath. "I would say life in Elyria isn't a picnic right now."

"If Vega hasn't figured out she has a real foothold between worlds now, she will soon... not enough for her to come through completely, but probably strong enough for her to do some real damage," Stellan said.

"Vega is *alive*?" Bridget sputtered. Ice filled her veins. She rubbed her neck, unable to stop herself from imagining the sensation of bloody claws digging into her carotid.

*I don't want to be around for what she has planned.*

Quinn... the fear in her eyes. She hadn't learned from a random Sanguis Witch, but from Vega herself.

"Time in Iegorus doesn't work like it does here." Stellan crossed his arms, then almost to himself, mumbled, "We might already be too late. She won't stop until she gets what she wants."

"Which is what?" Bridget asked.

Taking a deep breath, Stellan locked eyes with her. The guilt swirling there brought her stomach to the floor. He didn't know.

"Please tell me you have *some* kind of idea," Bridget growled.

An ear-splitting scream pierced the air.

Heart stuttering, Bridget whirled around and ran to Archer. On the ground, he writhed on his back like electricity was burning every single part of his body. Blood poured from his nose and his ears. Beneath his closed eyelids, his eyes moved rapidly back and forth. "What is this?" he croaked.

"What happened?" Bridget demanded, trying to get him on his back. He screamed again, his arms contracting into his chest.

"You have to help him," Nylah begged.

Bridget followed her gaze. Above them, Stellan stared at Archer in absolute shock.

"Stop," Archer pleaded, his entire body shaking. Red liquid sputtered onto Bridget's jacket as he continued to speak. "Of course, she's fine. She's standing right in front of me."

All of a sudden, Archer stilled. Bridget flinched when his eyes popped open. Except they were no longer his eyes. The foreign orbs glowed a bluish hue she'd only seen once before... the night a possessed Shaman had stopped her from crossing the gate. She gasped.

"Cade?"

It was *him*. She knew it. In confirmation, Archer's hand floated upward. A half-sob escaped Bridget's chest. Seconds before his fingers reached her cheek, his arm fell to the ground as Stellan slammed his hand against Archer's chest. His eyes and tattoos radiated a bright blue as he confronted Cade in Archer's mind.

"What did you do?" Stellan demanded.

Tears blurred Bridget's vision as she wrapped her hand around Stellan's wrist, hoping it somehow would connect her with them. Moments later, a blast of fire zinged up her arm. For a second, she heard Cade's screams as Stellan tried to help him control the magic surrounding them both. The sound rattled her bones. She recoiled, flying back into Nylah with a smack. Her sister, eyes wide and horrified, tried to copy her movements. Bridget pushed her away and caught Alexia's gaze. "Take her."

For once, Alexia listened and pulled Nylah to the corner with her.

"Of all the stupid, idiotic things to try…" Stellan growled. He stiffened, then pressed harder on Archer's body. "Stop fighting it. You have to let go of the spell…"

Blood continued to escape Archer's nose. Panic shot up Bridget's spine. Any longer and he might not…

Stellan sucked in a breath. "Marin, no!"

A wave of magic exploded from Archer, knocking everyone down except Stellan. Chest heaving, the glow from his power slowly disappeared from skin. Arm still burning, Bridget crawled over to Archer. The sight of his chest still moving up and down had her slinking all the way to the floor.

"Looks like you might be getting your wish after all," Stellan growled at Alexia.

As Bridget hugged Nylah close, she was left with one question…

What the hell was going on in Elyria?

# CHAPTER TWELVE

## CASSIA

*She remembers.*

The moment Marin had broken Cade out of the blood spell, he'd repeated the phrase over and over until he'd lost consciousness. Cassia sucked in a breath, trying to quell the nausea rolling through her. She'd never seen her brother so lost in magic, so trapped that he couldn't pull himself out of the void he'd thrust himself into to find that annoying Warlock's mind. And there'd been blood. So much blood. Every time she closed her eyes, she still saw it dripping down Cade's arms, staining the ground and grimoire beneath him. Still heard his screams as he battled a force none of them could see.

Cassia had just begun to panic that he'd been lost forever when Marin appeared before them. *Awake.* And radiating a power Cassia had never seen her wield in person. All of them watched, stunned and open-mouthed, as she grabbed Cade's head and released him from the spell... the black mark on the back of his hand transferring to her own. A sign, a *consequence*, of blood magic.

*Don't worry*, she'd said. It needed to be her.

And then she explained. About curses, deals, past lives, and Tuathan blood.

Cassia's head spun as they rushed Cade to the infirmary. She'd always seen him as her other half. The one person familiar to her since birth. Her *twin*.

That didn't seem to be the case anymore.

Since then, not one of them had dared to speak. Cassia didn't even think any of them knew what to say. What could they? Cade was much more than just *theirs* now. Even now, as he lay passed out in the hospital bed, a dozen different potions forced down his throat, he seemed different.

Groaning, Finn shook his arms and rolled his shoulders. "Okay, I am going to need all of you to *relax*."

"That's a little hard to do right now," Delphine said, cracking a smile.

Cassia couldn't imagine the onslaught of emotions he was receiving. Just her own threatened to suffocate her. And even though Finn kept a straight-face, she spotted a bead of sweat roll down his cheek. Standing behind Delphine, Castor rubbed his chin, deep in thought. Cassia could practically see the wheels turning as he kept his dark eyes on Cade. So she asked the one question everyone was avoiding.

"What happens now?"

In a chair next to Cade's head, Marin folded her hands in her lap. "What do you mean?"

"What do you think I mean?" Cassia sneered, heat traveling up her neck. "You've known about everything for years, apparently, but you just now decided to share it. Why? What do you see? It has to be something important."

"I decided to tell you now because if Cade had stayed connected to the gate any longer, he would have opened it, signaling to Iegorus and Vega that his full Tuathan powers returned. Which they haven't," Marin said matter-of-factly. "As for what happens next... I haven't seen anything past

Bridget going through the gate and breaking the curse. It's blocked… like someone hasn't made a decision."

"Who?" Finn demanded.

"I wish I knew."

Marin's calm demeanor spiked Cassia's blood pressure. She gripped the edge of the empty chair behind her, ready to make Marin show any kind of notion that *peace* wasn't the only state of being she possessed. Especially when Cade still hadn't woken up.

"Cass…" Delphine warned.

But it was too late. Cassia threw the metal chair to the ground. It clanged harshly against the tile floor, leaving her ears ringing. "Do you even care what happens *at all?*"

"Of course she cares," Delphine admonished. "She just saved Cade's life."

Marin held up her hand. "It's alright. I expected this reaction from her."

After sending Cassia a weary, sideways glance, Castor picked up the chair she'd thrown. "So these powers… he'll get them back eventually?"

"I don't know."

Marin's short answer had Cassia clenching her fists again. Before she opened her mouth, Castor's hand brushed her back. *Stop*, it told her.

She hated that she listened. And that her heart rate increased for an entirely different reason.

"Splendid." Castor sighed, keeping his position beside her.

Glancing at everyone but Marin, Cassia asked, "What do we do?"

Delphine nodded at Cade. "We wait for him to wake up," she said, like it was the most obvious answer in the world. Then she paused. "Although it could be a while. He lost a lot of blood."

"I think it's pertinent we find Quinn…. sooner rather than later," Finn said. "It can't be a coincidence she showed herself just a few days ago."

"Do you have a plan?" Castor asked.

"I'll think of something." Finn glanced down at Cassia's hand. "You should get that checked out."

Her fingertips, red and swollen from when she'd tried to break through Cade's barrier, stung every time she moved. But she'd honestly forgotten about the charred appendages since Marin's revelation. The action had been so unlike her. She wasn't like them... willing to leap in danger at a moment's notice. "I'm fine."

"It almost worked," Delphine said.

The encouragement in her voice pierced through the ice in Cassia's chest. Which made her want to throttle the girl who used to be her best friend. She was just so *nice*, it was hard not to be warmed by her positivity.

As the others began to strategize, Cassia leaned her head closer to Castor. She whispered, "I need to talk to you."

Castor gazed down at her, surprise coloring his expression. Still, he nodded and indicated for her to follow him to the emptier part of the infirmary.

"I'll stay until he wakes up," Marin said. "He needs to hear it from me. I know the entire story. He'll..."

Once they were far enough away that Marin's voice was nothing but a whisper, Cassia stopped. For a moment, she struggled with what to say... her request to speak with him impulsive. Now that he stood in front of her, with beautiful, round chocolate eyes patiently zeroed on her, she lost all confidence. Hands trembling, she thought of Cade. This was for him. And the good of the realm. "I need your help. Now more than ever, I need to figure out how to use magic on my own." Her throat tightened. "Will you?"

"Of course."

Castor's answer was quick, and confident, and everything she'd expected and hoped for. Behind him, Delphine watched them out of the corner of her eye. Cassia could tell she was trying to be subtle, but it was hard to ignore the twisted, unsure posture of the other girl. And... Cassia couldn't believe what she was about to say.

"But what happened earlier..." Flashes of them together in her room, just a few hours earlier, left her body aflame. Until then, she hadn't realized how much she *missed* him. She swallowed back the ridiculous thought. "That can't happen again."

"I agree."

An invisible whip slashed down Cassia's spine. Why did acceptance hurt more than she thought it would? The only indication he'd been affected by her words at all was a brief tightening of his shoulders. For a second, she wondered if she imagined it. "Good."

Messing with a button on his wrist, Castor cleared his throat. "Good."

She was literally torturing herself standing in the infirmary any longer. Heat pooling in her cheeks, which she really hoped was mostly psychological and not at all obvious, Cassia stepped around him. "Find me tomorrow... and send someone to get me when Cade wakes up."

Well, no one had come to get her when Cade had regained consciousness. The only reason Cassia knew he was awake was a whispered conversation she'd overheard between two servant girls about how he'd finally shaved. She gagged. *Seriously?* That was their hot topic of gossip? Rolling her eyes, Cassia pounded on his bedroom door.

Silence greeted her.

She rapped her knuckles even harder. "Open up. I know you're in there."

It's not like he ever went anywhere anymore. When he still didn't answer the door, Cassia twisted the handle. To her chagrin, it popped open with no resistance. She peeked inside, making sure he wasn't indecent, before she slid inside completely.

"Cade?"

No one answered. The room was tidier than she expected it to be, especially since its occupant never seemed to leave. Only one fireplace crackled in the corner, the desk next to it stacked high with books and parchment. His paned windows were opaque with frost.

Where was he?

Cassia wandered over to the desk. She picked up Cade's sketchbook, completely empty of papers, then glanced at the scattered mess beneath it. Drawing after drawing of Bridget lay stacked and discarded on top of each other, a puzzled mosaic of Cade's mind. Some were torn, some scribbled over... each one slightly different. Like he tried over and over to get it right but couldn't. For the first time, a rush of gratitude filled her veins that Bridget *was* alive. Maybe now her brother wouldn't act like a ghost.

A crumpled-up parchment caught her eye. Cassia unfolded it. A room she'd never seen before was sketched in great detail. A ballroom, perhaps. Floor to ceiling windows surrounded a marble floor. A crystal chandelier, one grander than their own in Astraeus, centered the room. Was this something he'd seen in New York?

Stuffing it back underneath some papers, Cassia exited his bedroom, hoping to find him in the library. She'd made a floor down and just passed the servant's quarters when she heard laughter. Not just anyone's laughter, though... her *father's*. Stunned, Cassia opened the dining room doors.

Her father and Cade sat at the table. Both had full plates in front of them.

*What the hell?*

"It's lunch time," she stated. Never once had their family eaten lunch together.

Their laughter died as they acknowledged her presence.

"And your point is?" her father asked, stuffing a bite of steak into his mouth. When she didn't answer, he nodded to the empty seat across from Cade. "Are you going to join us?"

Cassia recoiled from the openness in his voice. It'd been years since she'd seen her father remotely... *happy*. His white hair, drained of color from magic use, was slicked back into a bun, like he used to wear it. She resisted pinching herself to make sure she wasn't dreaming or transported back to a time before Riker's death. That had been the last time her father hadn't scowled at her when she walked into a room. And then there was Cade. Not only was he shaved, but his hair was combed. Cassia couldn't help but stare at him. It had been months since he looked like himself.

"What are you doing here?" she asked, trying to catch his eye. *Why do you look so carefree? Didn't I just find depressive episode portraits of your girlfriend in your room?* Cassia tried to ask with her mind. But he wouldn't look at her or let the connection form.

Cade shrugged. "Eating."

"I can see that. I'm not blind," she snapped. Reluctantly, she took the seat across from him. The velvet dragged against her wool pants.

"It seems your brother has finally come to his senses," their father said wryly. "I thought I'd have to drag him down the aisle on the spring solstice next month."

Cassia poured herself a glass of wine from the dark bottle sitting in the center of the table. She hoped it would help calm her shaking hands. "Is that still not the plan?"

Not that dragging Cade would work, either. He'd probably be there over his dead...

"I've agreed to marry Marin."

Cassia choked on the liquid she'd been chugging. Red wine sputtered out of her nose and onto the white tablecloth in front of her. Coughing, she gasped for breath and tried to clear the burn suffocating her throat.

Her father clicked his tongue. "You'll never get your turn with manners like that."

She wanted to be offended by the snide comment, but it was the only thing that seemed *normal* about reality at the moment. "*What?*"

Cade chuckled and took a huge bite out of a roll. Finally, she felt him enter her subconscious. *If you want to help, stop pushing.*

*What are you doing? Is this about what Marin finally told you?*

Cassia dug her nails into her thighs when Cade severed their connection with a slicing pop.

"We all know Cass is never getting married," Cade said. Even though she knew he didn't *really* mean it, the comment stung. "No one could handle *that* for the rest of their life. There are plenty of blondes in Astraeus who are way more fun. I would know."

Cassia took another large sip of wine. Maybe she really did go back in time to three years ago.

"Back to better topics. Even if it is part of our deal, I still think the spring solstice is the best date for the wedding," Cade continued. "It's symbolic... and it will give me the next few weeks to join Finn at the Kastronian border to quell the attacks before the big day."

Oh, so *that* was her brother's plan... butter up their father so he stopped having Orion follow him everywhere. He wanted to leave the palace.

He wanted to find Quinn.

"I agree. The spring solstice would be the best day and give the staff plenty of time to prepare. But..." Too busy cutting off another piece of steak, he didn't notice Cade's fists clench. "Your presence is still required in the palace. I think we should finish the tournament."

Control, obviously. That much was obvious to Cassia. It had been *months* since their journey to Cavamyne and the last task. All the girls had gone home just a few weeks later with the excuse that it was too dangerous to proceed.

"The point is our people need a distraction right now. It's our duty to provide that for them and stick to our traditions. Present a united front in the face of the unknown. Even though we know Marin will win, the people don't. Let them have some excitement." Their father grinned, but it didn't reach his dark eyes. "Why the sour face? Is there something else you'd rather be doing? I know that you think the border needs you... but I think Finn can handle his regiment and the situation on his own."

Cassia held her breath as she waited to see Cade's reaction. Her brother's eyes darkened and for a split-second, his inward struggle allowed her to grasp on to a tether of their connection.

*He knows*, she told him

He kicked her out again.

"You're absolutely right," Cade said. He plastered a smirk on his face. "Invite the girls back. I know there's a few I'd like to reunite with."

With a wink, he popped a piece of fruit in his mouth.

The prince was back. Cassia just hoped he knew what he was doing.

# CHAPTER THIRTEEN

## BRIDGET

"What are you doing?"

Bridget followed Stellan's hurried movements as he grabbed a backpack and began stuffing random items, including a particularly dusty bottle of wine, inside. Every time she tried to jump in front of him, he dodged her. Until she read his movements and snatched up the book he was reaching for before he could grab it.

"What does it look like I'm doing?" Stellan growled, swiping it from her hand. "I'm going back to Elyria."

"You can't."

The words slipped out of Bridget's mouth before she understood what they meant. He couldn't go back. Not yet. Not until *she* had decided what to do. She wasn't ready to face it all. Not the curse. Not the past. Not Vega... any of it. If he left now...

Stellan abruptly stopped in front of her. His hand on her wrist sent shivers up her spine. "Come with me."

Bridget's throat tightened. *Could* she go back to Elyria? Hadn't he been warning her against it this entire time? Besides, for months, she'd been convincing herself that she *didn't* want to be in Elyria... that it was too dangerous, especially for Nylah. To go now felt like a betrayal of everything she'd been building for herself. But... She glanced at her sister, who watched them curiously from her stationed spot next to the unconscious Archer on the couch. Nylah *needed* to go.

Stellan dropped her arm. "Or stay and go back to Boston," he said, blue eyes hardening. "Figure out another way to cross the gate. I don't care. But I can't be responsible for your fate anymore. Marin needs me."

His words struck a chord in Bridget. It wasn't about *her* anymore or a centuries-old curse... but the people who needed them. *That* was worth any risk.

"What did you see?" Bridget asked, desperate to know what had rattled him enough to push him back to Elyria.

Ignoring her, Stellan zipped up his backpack and headed for the door. Seconds later, Nylah coughed, reminding her just what was at stake.

"Wait!" Bridget called, following him outside. "Just wait..." Stellan stopped in his tracks. He tightened his grip on his bag as she approached. "I have to go with you. Nylah needs the cure for that potion Alexia gave her."

"I don't have time to stop in Andarre first," Stellan said. "Do you understand what that means?"

It meant seeing Cade, possibly married. It meant having to confront their past together before she'd comprehended herself. It meant walking back into the magical world that had almost destroyed her.

"Yes," Bridget whispered. She really hoped going through the gate wasn't as painful as she remembered.

As if reading her thoughts, Stellan said, "I'll do my best to make the jump as easy as possible for Nylah... And I can keep her healthy until she makes it to Andarre."

Bridget noticed his choice of words. *Her.* Not us. Fae were very careful with their words, after all. At least his slip-up, purposeful or not, gave her some insight into his visions. "But..."

Throwing his backpack inside the bed of a beat-up truck, Stellan sighed. "I didn't have to read your mind to know that was coming."

"I can't leave without saying goodbye to Archer," Bridget said. He'd made it very clear he never wanted to step foot back in Elyria. Even though she rarely told him, he was her *friend.* Leaving him would slice her open. "He's still passed out. I can't just leave him here... not without telling him where we're going. And why."

Stellan crossed his arms and leaned against the truck. Bridget followed his eyeline to where Alexia spied on them through the kitchen window. "I'm guessing the stray won't let you out of her sight either."

Bridget rubbed her temple thinking of Alexia's reaction when they told her they *weren't* going to Andarre first. "Archer... when is he going to wake up?"

"A few hours. Maybe days. I'm not sure. He was hit with a lot of magic."

"Will you wait?"

Stellan sighed. "We leave the second he's awake."

*Bridget was back. Again. The sight of her imagined Cavamynian Palace twisted her stomach. Couldn't her brain give her something else to dream about? This time, she didn't have to go searching for the other girl. She was already in the ballroom with her. Outside, the dark sky cast shadows over every inch of the marble floor. If not for the dim light of the chandelier, Bridget wouldn't have been able to see at all.*

*Picking a speck of dust off the black velvet sleeve of her elaborate gown, the girl pouted. "Didn't you like the spell I gave you?"*

*"I never asked for one," Bridget replied. If she wasn't incessantly dreaming about Cavamyne, the night Quinn dragged her through the gate would probably be her subconscious's other favorite memory to relive. Bile crept up her throat. There had been so much blood.*

*"If you say so," the girl said, patting Bridget's hand.*

*Bridget recoiled, stunned by the gesture. And by what traveled up her arm. Never once had she touched anything in her dreamworld. What was the point? It wasn't real. As the other girl smiled, though, Bridget couldn't deny the sharp, icy throb her fingertips had left on her skin.*

*"You've had a big day. Bridget. No one would blame you for lying to yourself."*

*Backing away, Bridget searched for a way out of the ballroom. Reality broke through the cracks. Trepidation crept up her spine that perhaps the girl in front of her wasn't completely made up.*

*Foothold.*

*Where had she heard that word? It repeated in her head like a mantra, calling her to remember.*

*"Who are you?" Bridget demanded.*

*The further she backed away, the more the girl followed. She cocked her head. "I'm just like you."*

*The scene changed. They were no longer in the ballroom, but in front of the gate. Recognizing the scene, Bridget fell to her knees. Vega, in her blood red mask and dripping metal claws, held up a dagger. Magic buzzed in the air, suffocating all life in the surrounding area. Chanting drowned out the sound of Bridget's heartbeat.*

*When moonlight finally illuminated the face of Vega's victim, Bridget choked. It wasn't her at the end of the knife... but the other girl. No longer in an ornate dress, but rags. Her blue eyes, full of unshed tears, pleaded with Vega to stop.*

*Without hesitation, Vega plunged the dagger into her heart.*

Eyes popping up, Bridget swallowed a scream. It didn't take her long to come back to reality. The stiff, wooden armchair in the corner of Stellan's cabin bit into her back and the heat from the fireplace burned the bottom of her feet. Sneaking a glance of Nylah and Archer passed out on the couch together, Bridget wiped a drop of sweat from her neck, unable to remember when she'd fallen asleep. Sometime between Nylah trying to draw on Archer's face and...

Ice went up her spine. Turning around, she found Alexia staring at her from across the room. At the kitchen table, she rolled a water bottle between her hands.

"You're not sleeping?" Bridget asked, even though she already knew the answer. In Vassuryn, Alexia had taken every night watch and opportunity to creep in the dead of night for Cora. "It's like two a.m."

"Of course not." Alexia scoffed. "You shouldn't be so trusting."

Bridget read between the lines. *Didn't Cora teach you better?*

Unlike Alexia, she wanted to forget every single *lesson* from Cora. After stretching her neck, Bridget heaved herself out of the armchair and headed for the kitchen. Through the window, she spotted Stellan leaning against the rail of his tiny porch, cigarette in hand as he stared up at the sky. So Alexia wasn't the only one refusing to get any rest. The air of the refrigerator cooled Bridget's skin as she reached inside for a soda.

"You were talking in your sleep," Alexia stated.

Popping the can open, Bridget downed her source of caffeine before answering. "It was just a nightmare. I tend to have a lot of those about my time in Elyria. I'm surprised you don't either."

Alexia kept a straight face, but Bridget didn't miss the tightening of her shoulders. It was strange, being with her now in the one place she never expected. Knowing *exactly* what made her tick. Alexia had always been an endless puzzle. One she'd given up solving a long time ago. But... in her wildest dreams, Bridget had never imagined their motivations would stem from similar interests.

"Your family…"

"I don't need your judgment," Alexia snapped.

Bridget tightly rolled her lips together. Nothing was ever easy with her. "No… I was going to say that it's… admirable you dealt with Cora that long just to save them."

The words, almost painful to admit, hung in the air between them. Avoiding Alexia's gaze, Bridget downed the rest of the soda.

"She wasn't as bad to me as she was to you."

*Oh really?* Bridget doubted that. Thinking of Alexia's broken body in Cavamyne, she let out a humorless laugh. "At the end…"

"I volunteered. I knew she wouldn't kill me."

"Cora had her fingers deep inside your abdomen. Your blood was spilling everywhere because she couldn't figure out how to use the Blood-stone. She wasn't going to stop," Bridget replied heatedly. "Not until she opened the gate. The only reason you're still alive is because Quinn distracted her."

Alexia paled, and for a second, the reality of what really happened in Cavamyne seemed to hit her. Or at least, Bridget hoped so. For once, a nervous tremble sat on the other girl's lips. Stuffing her soda can in the trash, Bridget almost felt bad for being the one to force the reality of Cora on her. Almost.

When Alexia tightened her cloak around her shoulders, the one she'd refused to change out of no matter how many times she'd been asked, Bridget decided to change the subject, realizing now that the cloak might be from Andarre. She eyed the dark green stitching, and the thick wool that had hidden Alexia's amethyst tattoos for so long. Did she use to have something similar?

A wave of dizziness hit Bridget hard. Not only did she have one bizarre past life with Cade to comprehend, there was another one in Andarre she still knew nothing about.

"So my father is not a nice person," Bridget said. From Alexia's descriptions, that much was obvious. He'd been so cruel to Cora, the Witch had practically tortured her to get back at him.

"Well... he'd probably be nice to you."

The thought was nice, but it certainly wasn't true. A father who cared wouldn't have let her be shuffled from home to home in a new world with no knowledge of her *actual* home. "Who knows... He did send me away."

"Are you saying you would have been better off growing up in Andarre? Knowing exactly who you were and what fate awaited you with the prince across the sea?"

A spark of anger ignited inside Bridget. "Is that why he did it? My family *knew*?"

Alexia paused, then slowly said, "I can't be certain. I was never privy to the conversations between your father and Cora, and she certainly kept most of the details to herself. But looking back... I believe they did. Why else would he do it? Why else would he threaten innocent families just to ensure your return?"

"If my father wanted me back, why even send me to the human realm in the first place?" Bridget's voice cracked, despite her angered resolve. The question reminded her too much of her childhood, the one she did remember. The one where she'd obsessed over that question until she'd finally learned and accepted there would never be an answer.

"Unfortunately, the person who would know the answer to that question is dead. So you can take that up with him when we get to Andarre." Alexia's face darkened as she glared at Stellan through the window. "If we ever get there..."

Bridget glanced at Nylah's sleeping form. They *would* get there. She still had to be cured. Then, almost like she knew Bridget was watching her, Nylah sleepily rubbed her eyes before burrowing further into Archer's side on the couch. The heat that had been building inside Bridget's chest dissolved. If growing up in Andarre and knowing about her past meant giving up her sister, she wouldn't do it. Not for anything. Not even for one less scar on her body. Bridget traced the outline of the Virgo symbol on her hand. "How did it start?" she asked. "Cora and the blood magic?"

Alexia stilled. A heavy silence surrounded them as the other girl got lost in a memory. Just when Bridget thought Alexia wouldn't answer, she whispered, "It started small... A blood spell here or there to keep us hidden from the prince. But then... she started to talk to someone. Sometimes in a mirror... or a pond. Sometimes to midair. Like there was a ghost in the room only she could see. That's when it got worse. That's when it consumed her."

Bridget's throat tightened. Panic flared in her stomach. A ghost. *The girl*. Appearing to her like one. Like a vision from her nightmares, so real that she'd attacked it. "Was it Vega?"

Eyeing Bridget up and down, Alexia frowned. "She never said."

*It couldn't be Vega*. Vega wore a mask. And claws. And dripped blood. Bridget scrunched her eyes closed. It was the dreams. They'd become so realistic, it was getting to her. If someone from Iegorus was using magic to communicate with her, she'd *feel* it. Pay the price for it. Still, she didn't want to look in any dark corner in the room, afraid of what she would see. Grabbing her leather jacket, Bridget darted for the door. "I'm going to talk to Stellan."

"Whatever hallucination you're seeing..." Alexia said. The warning in her voice stopped Bridget dead in her tracks, the door handle like ice on her fingertips. "Don't listen to it. Hearing voices is never a good sign. In any realm."

Without looking back, Bridget thrust open the cabin door and slammed it shut. Thick blinds rattled behind her and she darted over to the porch ledge and leaned over the railing. The cool air stung her flushed cheeks as she took a deep breath. No one was using magic on her. No one was *using* her.

And she *wasn't* crazy.

"Having a nice chat?"

Bridget jumped. She'd almost forgotten Stellan's presence. Behind her, he propped himself against the cabin, one boot flat against the wood. A puff of smoke disintegrated around him, the red glow from the cigarette hanging from his mouth barely visible in the moonlight.

Shivering, Bridget crossed her arms. "I don't know if you could call it that."

Taking the shortened, white stem between his fingers, Stellan offered it to her. When she shook her head, he shrugged. Only in a dark blue flannel shirt and jeans, he seemed unbothered by the cold.

"A bad habit I picked up here." Moving next to her, he flicked the cigarette into the snow below them. "I guess I'll have to stop now."

Out of the corner of her eye, Bridget watched him take off his ball cap and shake out his blond hair, revealing the tips of arched ears. "And this," he said, holding up the hat. He ran his fingers through the straight locks until they finally held in place off his forehead. "I guess there's no use trying to hide once we're in Elyria."

How was he so old, but still so *young*? If she didn't know better, Bridget would have guessed they were the same age. There was barely a wrinkle around his blue eyes. Or an ounce of trepidation in their silence. Mirroring her stance, he stood next to her, completely comfortable in it.

They'd known each other. Once upon a time. How was she supposed to talk to him?

But how could she not?

There were so many things he *knew*. About her. About Cade. About Elyria's future. Though she doubted he would be too forthcoming with *that* information.

A million questions ran through Bridget's mind, but each one got stuck in her throat. Where to even start? She glanced at her broken emerald ring, and then at Stellan, only to find him already watching her, patient and expecting. Had he seen this moment? The pressure of asking the right questions mounted in her chest even further.

The beginning, that was the only place *to* start. And how she even survived and remembered at all. "How did the curse break?"

Stellan's eyebrows raised. So maybe he hadn't seen this conversation. "I thought you learned your curse lore in Elyria."

"I did, but..." Bridget glanced down at her ring again. A ring that had almost been lost so many times. And brought back to her in two very unexpected ways. Luck... or fate?

"It was yours," Stellan said, nodding at the ring on her finger. "In some weird, twisted way, Vega must have thought she was being funny, using it for the curse. Bronwyn said your family took it before you were buried. It looks like they kept it in the family. They should have thrown it in the ocean when they had the chance."

Part of Bridget wanted to bristle at his words, she wouldn't have her memories without the ring. But a broken curse meant a greater chance of Vega escaping Iegorus. From the shadows dancing behind his eyes, Bridget knew that was the last thing Stellan wanted. As she slowly processed his statement, another slip-up, or fact, sent her reeling.

"I'm *buried* somewhere?"

She wanted to vomit. And find the grave. Or completely forget the notion. Forever. The thought of *seeing* it was completely...

"Believe me, obsessing over the past will only make you go crazy," Stellan said. A ghost of a chuckle escaped his chest. "You won't find it. I promise. Besides, I was still asleep when it happened. I couldn't help you if I tried."

Bridget buried the urge to inspect the ring down to the last chisel to see if the past was somehow imprinted on the stone for her to read. Or hurl it toward the woods. She wasn't exactly sure which action she wanted to accomplish most. What she did know was how strange it was to be wearing something so old... something that was *hers* that had traveled through time to belong to her again. The ring had always been the nicest, most expensive thing she owned. Throughout the years, she'd fought off foster family after foster family to keep it. "Was it you?"

When Stellan tilted his head, she continued, "A Shaman is the one who told my father in Andarre to send Cora to bring me back… According to Alexia, anyway."

She couldn't believe the sentence coming out of her mouth. *Her father.* The idea that he was out there somewhere was mind boggling. Had it been that same Shaman's idea to also send her away?

It was a long time before Stellan answered. "I haven't been to Andarre in over a century."

Part of her was relieved it hadn't been him… She wasn't sure if she could look him in the eye or trust that he would protect Nylah if he had. Beside her, Stellan gripped the porch's wooden railing, his knuckles white. Bridget didn't have to look at his face to know he was struggling with not being able to say more. "Who was I?" she asked instead. "Or is that also something you don't remember?"

It was the question that scared her the most. Who had she been to have this ring? To catch a prince and incur Vega's wrath, in one fell swoop?

For a split second, Bridget thought she saw the girl from her dream on the porch behind Stellan, her dark hair covered in snow. But after a panicked blink, she was gone. After checking her nose for blood, Bridget dug her nails into her thigh. No blood. No magic. Alexia's words had made her paranoid.

With a faraway look in his blue eyes, Stellan didn't seem to notice. The corners of his mouth turned up, just slightly. "From what I do remember… you were an ordinary, human girl."

There was no loathing, or disdain, dripping from his voice like the other Shamans in Elyria had when they talked about humans. Instead, there was so much *appreciation,* Bridget wasn't sure what to say. Clearing her throat, she waved her hand dramatically in front of her face. "Am I the same?"

Shocking her, Stellan cracked a *smile.* "For the most part."

In that moment, it reminded her so much of Cade, it took her breath away. "Cade... in your memory, he was Tuathan. If I'm the same... shouldn't he be?"

"He still is... and he still is Tuathan. It's how I knew exactly who he was when he was born," Stellan said, lips twisting as he rubbed the top of his arched ears. "There was no other possible explanation. Deckard couldn't believe it. You should have seen his face, especially after the hours I spent trying to explain... He made me spell Cade to hide his Tuathan features. It should hold, as long as we're both alive."

"Deckard *knows*?" Bridget seethed. Just like her father. Like everyone else but *her*, it seemed. "No wonder he hates me."

"It might be hard to believe... but he loves his son. He thinks he's protecting him."

Bridget frowned. From *her*? Or from what he believed they would unleash if they were together? And if Cade was really Tuathan... "I saw enough in Elyria to know that Cade is powerful. But his powers, they're not like the rest of the Shamans. Magic still takes a toll on him."

Every ounce of good nature dropped from Stellan's face. A muscle in his jaw flexed as he struggled to answer.

Bridget sighed. "Okay, the answer to that question is obviously somewhere in your lost memories. The spell... curse, whatever you want to call it, must have somehow diminished them?"

Stellan remained silent.

"Can you fix it?" Bridget asked.

Stellan sighed. It was a long time before he answered. "That is a very good question..."

Bridget waited for him to elaborate, but he kept his gaze fixed on a particularly snowy tree. When impatience crept up her spine, Bridget grasped on to one of the other questions racking her brain. "You tutored Cade... wasn't that weird? He said he'd known Echnav almost his entire life. He brought you to Cavamyne that night... all those years ago." *The night she died.* She couldn't bring herself to say it. "It seemed like you were friends."

"Cade is my cousin," Stellan said.

Bridget's mouth fell open. No wonder there was something about his face that kept scratching at something in her brain. They had the same jawline. And smile.

"He was also my best friend," Stellan continued softly. "It's why I waited and stayed with the royal family in Elyria... for so long I began to think I created the curse wrong and that you two were never coming back."

A sudden, horrid thought overtook Bridget. One that brought a wave of fury rising from her gut, barely uncontrollable. "You were the one that sent him to the human realm," she hissed, hands shaking. "Did you orchestrate this whole thing between us? Were we..."

Part of your plan. *A* plan. One she didn't fully understand yet. One that involved them not even having a *choice.*

"You don't know how hard I tried *not* to send him," Stellan bit back, cheeks flushed. "He never... It was the strangest thing. I think he knew you were out there somewhere, deep down. Nothing in Elyria was ever enough for him. I could see it brewing beneath the surface every time he looked at that painting of the curse or heard the mention of humans... It was only a matter of time."

His confession startled her into silence. Especially when his voice broke.

"But then his brother died and he was so broken. And all I could see was..."

"Your best friend," Bridget finished hoarsely when he couldn't. Before she thought too much about it, she reached out her hand toward him. When her fingertips grazed his sleeve, he stilled, then crossed his arms, effectively putting himself out of reach.

Stellan cleared his throat. "The one I'd made a promise to so long ago. The one with the same look I'd seen before when he asked me to make sure you found each other. I knew you were in the human realm... I'd seen flashes of you there. So when he asked me to open the gate, I agreed. But I told myself, I would just send him. No information or hints... Just let fate take its course."

"And it did," Bridget whispered, squeezing her eyes shut so that the liquid building there wouldn't spill over. Every moment she'd ever had with Cade replayed in her head... his laugh in Hungry Pies. The quiet mornings in their apartment. The intensity in his gaze that set her on fire in Manhattan *and* Elyria. Every image was a knife in her already throbbing chest. But she couldn't regret it. Not *him*, not any of it. She didn't care if it had been fate or destiny behind their meeting in New York. She *loved* him. Even now, worlds apart, when her entire soul felt ripped in two.

"I'm scared to go back to Elyria because I hate that parts of me miss it... especially if everyone there has already moved on. Cade might already be married," Bridget finally admitted. It was only a month until the spring solstice. Would he have waited that long, if he truly believed she wasn't coming back?

Despite his earlier words about quitting, Stellan pulled out another cigarette from his front pocket and lit it. "He's not."

Bridget's gaze cut to his. "You've seen it? Is that why he possessed Archer? To let me know?"

Stellan's lips twisted. "I haven't seen anything. I just know him. And as for why he possessed Archer and risked the consequences of blood magic... Well, that's Cade. He wanted to know you were okay so he made it happen. But Marin intervened before I could. I need to get back to help her."

"Because you think Vega knows she has a foothold now?"

Saying her name aloud sent a shiver down Bridget's spine.

"If she has, Elyria's in more danger than we realize." Stellan blew a puff of smoke in her face. Bridget cringed, then grabbed the cigarette out of his mouth and threw it on the ground. The smell reminded her of a foster father she'd rather forget.

A little stunned, Stellan raised a brow. "Blood magic is dangerous, especially for someone with human blood like Marin. The consequences for her will be deadly. I need to be with her. Besides, the deal Cade made with his father doesn't matter. That's your wedding ring," he said, nodding at the emerald on her finger. "I think you should know by now that magic can't be fooled. The curse preserved your souls, as they were. Technically, he's already married. To you. The bargain is useless."

Bridget choked. *They. Were. Married*? And somehow, she'd missed it. Or forgotten. Or whatever was the *technical* term. The broken emerald glistened in the moonlight. Vega had thought it was *funny* to use her *wedding* ring to bind the curse. Bridget's head spun. What had she done to her? "If we were already married... Why did Vega offer to marry him to end the war? That's the story Cade told me."

"It seems history got the story wrong," Stellan said. "Or out of order."

"I wish I remembered," Bridget whispered. The admission scared her, more than she wanted to admit. It meant she accepted that she *had* been reborn, and lived a whole life she barely knew anything about. One Stellan was forced to stay secretive about, based on the tightness of his shoulders.

Stellan's eyes darkened. "No... you don't."

His words left no room for argument.

They spent the rest of the night in silence.

# CHAPTER FOURTEEN

The sun, lowering over the horizon, illuminated Archer's sprawled body on the couch. He'd been asleep for almost two days. Blanket twisted between his legs, a light snore escaped his nose as his shoulders twitched. Bridget hovered over him and hoped it was a sign he was waking up soon. Stellan, along with Alexia, paced the porch, eager to leave and change their lives forever. Well, Bridget suspected *she* might be the only one concerned with that second part. The weight of both her past and future twisted her stomach, barely allowing her to sit down. Or eat. Nylah, now awake and stuffing stale cereal down her throat, tapped on her watch.

"Didn't Yogi Bear's nemesis out there say he would be awake by now?" she asked between full bites.

Bridget tried to keep a straight face. "I dare you to call him that to his face."

Narrowing her eyes, Nylah hopped off the kitchen counter and pulled Bridget's phone out of her purse. "I'll even show him. Based on the lack of television or anything remotely entertaining in this cabin, I doubt he would even understand the reference."

"How do you even know who Ranger Smith is?" Bridget asked, then teasingly added, "Besides, aren't you even a little afraid he might retaliate with some crazy mind magic?"

"Brenda was obsessed with that movie." Nylah shuddered. "And if I understood all the mumbo jumbo you told me this morning correctly, he's not the first Tuathan I've dealt with."

When Nylah accidentally slammed the cabin door shut a little too hard, Archer jumped. Almost falling off the couch, he cursed and squeezed his forehead, squinting as he gathered his bearings and fought to keep his eyes open. *Finally.* The sheer amount of relief hammering through her body, though, almost brought her to knees. Rushing over to him, Bridget handed him a glass of water.

Archer downed it in one gulp. Wiping his mouth with his forearm, he said, "Your boyfriend is a dick."

"I know." Bridget sighed, not having the heart to tell him about the marriage that technically still existed. Especially when she was still trying to come to terms with it herself.

Pinching the bloody rag they had used to clean his face between his fingers, he grimaced. "I was hoping it was a bad dream, but this crick in my neck is definitely real."

Out of the corner of her eye, Bridget caught Stellan watching them from the window. "Look…"

Archer followed her gaze. "Please tell me you didn't make a deal. You're prone to those kinds of reckless decisions."

"No deals," Bridget replied, giving him a half-hearted glare. "According to Stellan, Cade used blood magic to get inside your head and Marin took the consequences. He says she needs him. Not only that, but I think there's other things going down in Elyria he's not being upfront about. Not yet, anyway. He's ready to head there right now."

"And you're going with him."

A statement, not a question. Bridget gripped his empty cup in her hands, her knuckles white against the glass. "Nylah still needs to be cured. He says he'll keep her healthy until we can get to Andarre. And I..."

Bridget's throat tightened. She couldn't explain the pull to return to Elyria, despite knowing the fight that awaited her there. Not to anyone. Not even to herself. Ever since she'd returned to the human realm, memories intact, it was almost like she'd been *waiting* for it to happen. Living a half-life until the day she could. Guilt shivered up her spine.

"I know you don't want to go back. You're from here and that world already took too much from you," she said. "I'm not going to ask you to come with us, even though Nylah would miss you."

*And me*, but the words got stuck in her throat. Bridget had a feeling he knew anyway.

"Stellan wanted to leave days ago, but I made him stay until you were awake. Just in case. If this is goodbye, though... I understand. We won't be mad at you. It's your choice."

Archer sat up and leaned his elbows against his knees as he silently processed her words. For a long moment, he hung his head and stared at the ground before he returned her anxious gaze with a resigned smirk. "I've spent my life running. It's time to stop. Besides, someone's going to need to babysit the little squirt when you reunite with lover boy."

Bridget punched him on the arm before she squeezed her arms around his neck. "Thank you," she whispered, nose stinging as she tried to hold back the liquid threatening to spill from her eyes.

"Ouch. There's no need for violence, I already agreed to go," Archer quipped. "Besides, your life would be boring without me."

Rolling her eyes, Bridget used his shoulders to heave herself off the couch. "That's not true," she said, throwing his jacket at him. After the last seventy-two hours, she wished that was the case.

"Don't lie to me, Bridget," Archer said. "You're terrible at it."

Bridget gave him the middle finger before dragging him outside. Cold air nipped her nose and the frozen porch threatened to trip her. Stellan, leaning against his truck, gave her an impatient stare as Nylah rambled about something on her phone beside him. When her sister noticed them coming toward her, she squealed and launched herself at Archer.

"I knew you would come with us," she said. "At least you get my jokes."

"Is that what those were?" Stellan muttered under his breath.

From the corner of the porch, Alexia glowered. "Great. Another body to slow us down on our journey."

Archer rubbed the top of Nylah's head before he turned to Alexia with a bright grin. "You know, it's a shame I don't have a potion to fix that stick up your ass."

"Enough," Bridget hissed, stepping between them before Alexia's tense form reached Archer. Glancing back at Stellan for some back up, she noticed the cloud of exhaust forming around him. "Why is the truck on?" she asked. "Isn't the gate close enough to walk?"

Stellan let out a sharp laugh. "The Cavamynian gate is not an option. I wouldn't be surprised if Vega, or even Deckard, have people watching it. It's too risky. It's a few hours away, but I know of another one that will lead us into Kastron. It's close enough to the border with Elyria it won't put us too much out of the way."

"Weren't all the gates destroyed?" Bridget asked. "That's like Elyrian History 101."

"You can't destroy that kind of magic. Not fully. I can make it work."

But what would be the cost? Based on the way he avoided her eyes, Bridget had a feeling it would be hefty. Before she could help Nylah into the old truck, Archer held them both back.

"If we're going with you, you need to tell us what we're getting into," he said, dark blue eyes fixed on Stellan. "The last time I agreed to go to Elyria with someone without asking basic questions, I got into such deep shit, I thought there would never be a way out. So tell us… what does Vega want? We all know she's a crazy Blood Witch, but why did she start this war?"

Stellan sighed, then opened the driver door of his truck. "We don't have time for this right now. Besides, I *can't*."

Bridget slammed the door shut again. "No, Archer's right. We can't just go marching into Elyria blind. I've been there and done that. I won't do it again. You said you've had time to figure out some of what you're missing. So *try*."

For a long moment, Stellan stared at her. There was a war in his eyes, she could tell. The depth of pain and history there almost left her breathless. Bridget couldn't imagine knowing so much, but only able to share so little. She almost said as much, but Stellan suddenly lowered his gaze.

"The four artifacts… I think that's what Vega is after. Marin helped me figure that out a few years ago," he said, voice gravelly. "They were created by the Tuathans thousands of years ago. An ultimate show of power. It was said that together, these artifacts could defeat any enemy."

"Are they real? Or just some urban legend?" Archer asked.

Stellan's demeanor darkened, telling Bridget they were very real. She asked, "What are they? And where are they now?"

"One is in Andarre, isn't it?" Alexia asked, finally speaking up. "Growing up, I heard rumors of a powerful weapon locked in the palace. When the attacks from the sea started, people began to question why we weren't using it."

"You're not wrong. The Tuathan sword is there. But the artifacts… their magic is specific. Once they choose a master, it can only be wielded by them," Stellan said. "Your people couldn't use it if they tried."

An image tore through Bridget's mind. The same one Cora had dragged to the surface when she'd gripped her thoughts. Cade, standing beneath a cloud of dark trees, a sword blazing with light in his hand. The vision still clung to her, stubborn and vivid, despite everything that had followed hours later. It had felt too real to dismiss.

Her pulse skidded. A memory? One that she hadn't even realized was *hers* at the time? She forced out a slow breath, grounding herself. Nylah's fingers tightened around hers, anchoring her.

"Is one of the artifacts a sword?" Bridget asked.

A little surprised, Stellan nodded.

Bridget straightened, spine locking into place. "It's Cade," she said, certainty cutting through the lingering panic. "That's why this whole plan to bring us back exists, isn't it? Because it has to be him. He's the master of the sword."

"It's been centuries and..." Frustration marred Stellan's brow as he paused. "Nothing is guaranteed."

Anticipation rushed through Bridget's veins. "Okay, so there's four artifacts... Vega wanted them all?" Bridget concluded. "For what? And why would she even want them if Cade controlled one of them?"

"Slow down," Archer whispered in her ear. "Give him a chance to breathe."

Bridget slammed her lips shut. He was right. Her onslaught of questions had cracked Stellan's composure. A trickle of blood escaped his nose as he clearly battled the curse holding his memories hostage.

"The crown is the other well-known artifact..."

His gravelly tone told her it wasn't a normal crown. Silence enveloped them. Bridget's own heartbeat echoed in her ears.

"What did that do?" Archer asked. "Or is that..."

"People believe it could raise the dead."

Ice filled Bridget's veins. A knot in her stomach screamed at her. Telling her of things she didn't quite understand. When she finally found her voice, she asked, "Why would she do that?"

"To raise a zombie army of Blood Witches," Archer muttered. "Obviously."

Nylah asked, "Do you know where the crown is now?"

"No one knows. It was last seen five hundred years ago."

Despite answering Nylah, Stellan kept his gaze locked on Bridget. There was a strange sort of desperation. A plea for understanding. A begging for her to read between the lines and discover what he didn't remember fully.

*She was very close to getting her hands on something that would have won her the war. You stopped that before it happened.* Stellan's explanation about why she was executed echoed in her head. She'd found the crown. And then hidden it from Vega.

Despite any more evidence from Stellan, she just *knew*.

Beside her, Archer let out a tired breath. "Let me guess... Whoever saw it last took the secret of where it was hidden to their grave."

Stellan nodded, but he kept his gaze on Bridget. The secrets and plans swirling left her breathless. Without having to ask, she knew the search for the crown's location inside her mind would happen again. The scars on her stomach burned. *That's* what Quinn had been looking for when she'd nearly spilled all her blood during her first few days in Elyria. *This* is why they were going back. Whatever magic or rune he needed to dig deep inside wasn't here.

"This will be fun..." Archer mumbled, rubbing his eyes.

"Now... if we could please..."

Before he could finish, Stellan froze abruptly. Bright eyes glazing over, he reached out a hand and steadied himself against the truck. Without warning, he grimaced and twitched. Muttering things in another language under his breath as he shook his head, over and over. Bridget watched in awe. She'd never seen a Shaman have a vision before, and it was nothing like she imagined. He seemed to feel everything.

Slowly, Bridget moved toward him. When Stellan twitched again, she raised her hand.

Alexia dug her nails into her arm, so hard Bridget's muscle throbbed underneath her leather coat. "Don't touch him."

Bridget recoiled out of her grip. "Something's wrong," she argued, turning her focus to Stellan once more. His blond hair, now damp with sweat, clung to his forehead. Wrong seemed to be an understatement. Whatever Stellan was seeing was *torturous*.

Shuffling closer, Nylah whispered, "Why is he in so much pain?"

Breathing hard, Stellan mumbled, "No, no, no." Then, with a gasp, he convulsed and collapsed against the rusty metal.

Reflexively, Bridget darted forward to catch him before he hit the ground. But she wasn't the only one.

"Nylah, don't!" she screamed.

The moment both of their hands touched Stellan, electricity whipped through Bridget's muscles. The world around her disappeared and transformed into a shadowy, spinning mess of distorted images. The wall surrounding Astraeus, blown to bits. A city on fire. A Wraith with hollow eyes digging their claws into Marin's back. Each vision was more terrible than the last. When Bridget was sure her head would explode from the sheer force of the changing realities, an invisible force pulled her backward.

With a pop, Bridget landed in snow. Cold air filled her lungs as she struggled to control her breathing and process the blue sky above her. Irony metal filled her mouth. Swallowing hard, she wiped her nose. Not metal. Blood.

Then she remembered what happened.

To her right, Nylah lay face down in the snow. Her body shook with every breath. Bridget rolled over and frantically crawled to her. "Are you okay?" Bridget demanded, turning her over. Blood poured from her sister's nose, as well. "What were you thinking?"

Nylah rubbed her eyes and wearily sat up. "That's what magic feels like?"

Before Bridget could admonish her more, her sister began to cough uncontrollably. Rubbing Nylah's back, Bridget held her steady and used the sleeve of her jacket to clean up the excess blood staining her face. After a moment, when she still didn't stop, Bridget's stomach twisted.

"She's already sick," Archer said, briefly glaring at Alexia. "Magic is going to affect her more."

Bridget reached for her backpack, but Stellan beat her to it. He dug inside, then pulled out an identical bottle of the homemade liquid he'd given Nylah when they'd first arrived. His hand trembled as he handed it over to her. Bags that hadn't been there before now hung under his eyes. Bridget had been in his head only seconds and she wanted to scrub the images from her brain. She couldn't imagine what else he'd seen... and would continue to see.

The moment the liquid hit Nylah's lips, her coughing subsided. Relief almost knocked Bridget to the ground again. She reached out to rub her sister's back, but she knocked her away with a weak push of her shoulder. "Stop hovering," Nylah grumbled, taking another sip of the liquid. "I'm *fine.*"

Above them, Alexia scoffed, "I told you not to touch him."

"Do you ever say anything helpful?" Archer asked.

Closing her eyes, Bridget replayed the shadowy visions. "Has that happened?" she asked Stellan, who leaned against his truck, arms folded. She hadn't been able to recognize the *when* of the images. Just that it was Astraeus being attacked and nearly burned to the ground.

A muscle in Stellan's jaw flexed. "It will. We've wasted too much time. We won't make it in time to help stop it."

"What do you mean? Is it happening right now?" Bridget demanded. Stellan didn't answer. She clenched her teeth together. "Then fuck it, let's just go through Cavamyne."

Archer helped Bridget to her feet. "What did you see?" he asked.

Stellan shook his head. "Like I already said, Vega—"

"Obviously you two were too focused on the gloom and doom to actually see anything useful," Nylah said, casually wiping excess snow and dirt off her pants. "Luckily... I did."

Bridget's mouth fell open as she watched her dig around for something in her jacket pocket.

"I was confused for a second, but then I realized I was in your head," Nylah continued, glancing up at Stellan. "So then I thought about what I wanted to see. Before I knew it, I saw a flicker of brightness. And then I almost... like reached out and grabbed it. If that makes sense."

"And what was that?" Stellan asked, blinking rapidly like he didn't quite know what to make of her. Bridget didn't either. Nylah had been around magic for *one* day and already seemed to navigate it better than she ever had.

"The best outcome." Nylah straightened, then pulled the black stone from her jacket. In her palm, it glittered and glowed. "And what I could do to help."

Color drained from Stellan's face. He bent closer and peered at the stone, but did not reach out to touch it. His throat bobbed as he asked, "Where did you get that?"

"Cade..." Nylah replied, eyebrows creasing at his obvious wariness.

Stellan looked to Bridget for confirmation. She nodded. "I didn't realize what it was until I came back. A rune, right?"

"Not exactly. Did he say why he had it?"

"Never," Bridget said. "But it must have come from the vault in Mount Lugh. There was something missing in the case where I found the Blood-stone."

Cursing under his breath, Stellan ran a hand through his damp hair. And then laughed. A sharp, humorless, shocked laugh. Like he wasn't quite sure if he was amused or completely flabbergasted.

Archer gazed at him sideways. "That's not just a rune, is it?"

"It's one of the Tuathan artifacts," Stellan said, then laughed again.

Bridget's mouth fell open. "How is that possible?"

Suddenly, Stellan grabbed Nylah and spun her around in the air. At first, Bridget was shocked by the gesture. But as Nylah squealed, she remembered he *did* help raise Marin. Her gaze softened as he gently put her back on the ground.

"You might be the most peculiar child I've ever met and what you did was extremely dangerous, but the whole city of Astraeus is about to owe you a very large thank you," Stellan said, causing Nylah to glow proudly. "That stone should create a gate for us. Right here. To anywhere we want."

Hope stirred in Bridget's chest. "And you can use it?"

"No..." Stellan said. "But I think she can."

Silence enveloped them all. After a minute, Nylah shuffled closer to Bridget. When she audibly swallowed, she stepped in front of her. "How?" Bridget asked. "She's a human." Which meant consequences. And payments. And *pain*. Something she wouldn't let her sister experience.

A hint of a smile on his face, Stellan held out a hand to Nylah. "Do you trust me?"

# CHAPTER FIFTEEN

## CASSIA

The palace always radiated a dreariness and reminded Cassia of a long, soulless tunnel. But on days the weather particularly nagged her, the suffocating emptiness of each room made her want to scratch her skin off. Leaning her head against the dusty window of her and Cade's old training room, Cassia studied the sky. It was sunny, and bits of snow melted into the ground from the unexpected warmth, but something just felt *off*. In the distance, where she knew miles away Kastron lay, dark clouds swirled above the horizon. They had for days. Each morning, she'd woken up and anticipated rain, but it hadn't come. The clouds hadn't moved an inch in their direction, despite the howling wind blowing their way.

Just as another gust of wind rattled the glass underneath her forehead, two figures strolled into her line of sight, invading the deteriorating garden below. One she recognized immediately. But the other... Hai? Or Ondine? She couldn't remember which Kastronian girl had died during the tournament, but the alive one was currently *trying* to flirt with her brother. Even three stories above them, the girl's loud, nervous giggle pierced the room through the window.

However, a girl trying to impress her brother wasn't what had Cassia swimming in confusion. Over the years, she'd seen many girls attempt to woo her brother. Each one more nauseating than the last. What confused her was Cade's receptive grin at whatever joke the girl spouted off. Still, it didn't reach his eyes.

Cassia tapped on the glass, knowing he probably already sensed her watching them, and waited for the tell-tale prick in her temple that he was connecting with her mind. Below, he determinately turned his back to her and brushed some lingering, melting snow off of his companion's shoulder. The Kastronian girl immediately turned red. Gritting her teeth, Cassia tapped again.

Finally, her brother's annoyed, laborious sigh echoed through her mind. *What do you want?*

*That was fast,* she said. *Didn't you just agree to restart the tournament yesterday?*

*Didn't you know? Father had all the girls and their families sequestered in Astraeus for months. Most of them returned to the palace this morning.*

Cassia snorted. Of course he had. Their father's plan had been to finish the tournament all along. He'd just been waiting for the right time. And he was the master of getting what he wanted. *You played into his expectations like a fiddle.*

*That's not what's happening.*

When Cade glanced up at her with a quick glare, Cassia fought the urge to roll her eyes. There was only one plan that seemed to be winning and in place right now. And it wasn't Cade's.

Moments later, Cade picked off one of the only blooming camellias from a shrub and handed it to Hai. *That* was the girl's name, if she remembered correctly. *What are you even doing? Didn't you basically already pledge yourself to Marin?*

Behind his back, Cade held up his middle finger. Hai was too busy stuffing the flower in her hair to notice.

*Really nice,* Cassia snapped.

*I never claimed to be.*

Cassia pulled on their connection, trying to find some way into Cade's mind to get a glimpse of what he was really thinking and planning. Because there was no way he was out for a stroll with Hai just for the hell of it. The harder she pulled and searched, though, the more distant his presence became. Cassia growled and sent him a wave of frustration. *Poor Bridget, all alone in the human realm while you let other girls try their best seduction skills on you.*

With a whipping tug, Cade severed their connection. Cassia flinched, just as the window between them cracked. Just a sliver. Just enough that satisfaction roared through her knowing that at least *that* had gotten a real reaction from him. When she looked back out the window, Cade was already leading Hai away with a new stiffness in his shoulders.

Maybe if her brother would just be honest with her, she wouldn't have to hit him upside the head with things he didn't want to hear. Roughly spinning on her heel, Cassia made up her mind to go find someone that *did* want her help. Because maybe—

She wasn't alone.

Cassia recoiled back into the window, thumping her head against the glass. Heart pounding, she stared into Castor's dark, penetrating eyes. Heat traveled up her neck when she spotted the amused twist of his lips.

"Hi."

She dug her nails into her thighs and hoped she didn't look too flustered. Even though it seemed to be her constant state around him.

Castor cocked his head. "Why do you look so surprised?"

"Why did you sneak up on me?" Cassia shot back. Now that he was moving closer, her hands trembled. She knew the only reason he was there was because she'd asked him to help her, but now that they were alone, she hated that she'd even suggested it at all. How could she have possibly thought she would be just fine with being *friends*?

Cassia took a deep breath and thought of Delphine. It didn't matter if she was fine with it or not. This was her reality now. She needed to get a grip.

Still, the resolve was hard to maintain when Castor continued to move closer to her. "Why were you so engrossed with the window that you didn't notice me calling your name?" he asked softly, now inches from her.

Cassia's breath hitched. Before she could answer, Castor's gaze moved to the outside garden behind her. Sighing, he crossed his arms. "You're spying on Cade."

"I was not *spying*," Cassia corrected, the heat returning to her neck. "I was here first. Besides, I wanted to know why he was in the garden with Hai."

"Her family owns most of the land in Kastron," Castor said. "I think he's trying to figure out how to use that to find Quinn."

Cassia had a feeling Castor didn't just think that, but *knew* that was Cade's intention. Whatever her brother's plans were, he was always one of the first to know. Mirroring his stance and crossing her own arms, she blithely replied, "Well I think he's playing with fire."

"He can handle himself," Castor said. For a long moment, he studied her. "Now you on the other hand…"

"Can't do shit."

Unfazed by her bluntness, Castor narrowed his eyes. "Need to focus on yourself. Did you not sleep?"

Too absorbed in her own thoughts about her brother's plans, Cassia didn't notice Castor raising his hand until he was already tracing the bags under her eyes. Briefly, she let herself enjoy the sensation of his touch before she stepped away. "It doesn't matter."

Because it *didn't*. She wasn't the one with a psycho Witch after them. Or the one with a curse dependent on their life. Or even the one with a secret Tuathan identity they knew nothing about. Wow, her brother had really been ringing up the surprises lately.

A muscle in Castor's jaw quivered, but he didn't push her. Fingering the crack on the window, he asked, "Do you know why Cade is asking me about an ancient artifact?"

"Like he tells me anything," Cassia replied automatically. When Castor shot her a weary look, she sighed. "Which one?"

"The Tuathan ones."

Cassia's gaze cut to his. It was the last thing she expected him to say.

"Those haven't been seen for centuries," she said. A spike of trepidation shot up her spine. Every story she'd ever heard or read involving the Tuathan artifacts ended badly. Why would Cade suddenly be interested in them?

"There's one in Tafari," Castor said, surprising her. "Or at least, that's the rumor. Obviously, no one has ever found it. But that's not the one he's interested in. He was asking about the crown."

Cassia's throat tightened. Of course he was interested in the most powerful, dangerous one. The one with the least amount of lore surrounding it. The one *actually* missing for centuries. "Why would I know about that one?"

"You read more than anyone I know."

Except there weren't any stories about the crown. And she hadn't picked up a book in a very long time. Not since...

Now was *not* the time to harp on family drama.

Cassia straightened her spine. "I used to."

"Cassia..."

Holding up her hand, she cut him off before she let him say something stupid like he *knew* her or something equally nostalgic. "Why don't you tell him he needs to stop whatever idiotic plan he has to fool our father instead of focusing on an ancient toy that probably doesn't exist anymore?"

"He's not trying to fool anyone. Believe me, your father is well aware of the fact that Cade's reasons for marrying Marin are ingenuine," Castor replied. "But he doesn't care. Not when he's getting what he wants. And

Cade… He's going to do whatever it takes to find Quinn, especially now that he knows she still poses a threat to Bridget. If your father gets in his way… *that's* when you should be worried."

"I'm already worried," Cassia admitted, bile rising in her throat. "He's not seeing the bigger picture. Do you really believe all these attacks on the border have been random? That it isn't Quinn trying to lure him back to Cavamyne?" She paused, making sure her voice wasn't croaky before she continued. "Quinn doesn't care about Bridget anymore, despite what Cade now thinks about their past and fate being tied together. She wants the curse on the Sanguis broken. Which means she wants him *dead*."

Castor shook his head. Grabbing her chin, he forced her to look at him. "Even though Quinn has the Bloodstone, she doesn't have the power to orchestrate the attacks I've seen. That amount of magic… It would have killed her by now."

"Then she's not working alone," Cassia croaked. When she realized just how close they were standing, that she'd practically wrapped her arms around him, she turned around. Wiping away the stray tear that had dared to escape her traitorous left eye, she asked, "What about your family? Is any of this happening in Tafari?"

Behind her, Castor cleared his throat. "Not like here… But my parents, they've felt a shift. They know it's not long before it reaches them. If things escalate, I'll need to go back."

*Sooner rather than later.* His unspoken words pierced her soul. Time was catching up with them. All of them. It wouldn't be long before everything changed. The future, just like the dark clouds that lingered on the horizon, hovered around them, ready to become real at any second.

"Then we better get to it," Cassia said, trying to plaster a smile on her face. "You said you've been thinking… what can't I have possibly tried before?"

Castor reached into his pocket and pulled out a small vial. "Take this witch hazel and try a summoning spell."

"A what now?" Cassia stared at the vial, not daring to take it. Witch hazel was an aid only used by covens who specialized in pulling from the earth. She could barely channel air. A fact Castor knew. Glaring, she said, "You know I can't."

"You and Cade are twins," Castor argued, prying open her fingers and forcing the vial into her palm.

After a moment of resisting his efforts, she reluctantly relented. "A fact I've known my entire life."

"You were created together…"

"I learned about the birds and the bees a long time ago."

This time, it was Castor's turn to glare. "Marin said he's Tuathan… that he's exactly the same as he was back in the day, give or take a few powers. He's an anomaly. His birth or reincarnation or whatever you want to call it happened because of a curse created hundreds of years ago… But it wasn't just him."

"It was me, too," Cassia finished, barely able to speak over the knot in her throat.

She was just as an anomaly.

Cassia read the anticipation swirling in Castor's eyes. Did he really think that whatever magic Cade possessed had transferred, even just a tiny bit, over to her?

"Maybe we've been going about your magic the wrong way the entire time," Castor said as he began to pace excitedly. "There used to be another race of magical creatures. Druids."

Cassia froze. "Their existence has always been a rumor."

"According to who?" Castor challenged. "Your family basically rewrote history five hundred years ago."

"Good point… Go on."

"Fae are essentially a mixture of humans and Tuathans. We all know that. The human blood in Fae is why magic comes at such high prices." Castor cracked his knuckles. "If I remember correctly, Druids are a mixture of Witches and Tuathans… Just think about it, Cassia. It could explain why you've had such trouble with magic. Witches and Tuathans pull from the inside… from their blood. The elements and runes are just tools for them to enchant their abilities and use as leverage when it comes to the cost of magic."

Castor started to pace.

"But Druids… there's a reason not many of them exist anymore. A reason why other species shudder when they're mentioned. I don't think Druids pull from their own abilities. I think they pull from… everything."

"Everything that is magical, you mean." Because she had tried to pull from elements before, like a proper Witch, with no luck. Which made sense, if his reasoning was correct. There was nothing magical about plucked herbs or tainted air. Not when they were already plucked or bottled. Druids needed something truly *alive*.

As if reading her thoughts, Castor continued, "I don't think there's anyone alive that truly understands magic. It comes and goes as it pleases. Blesses some lands, evades the others. Is natural only to a few. But there are some things that it seems to be a constant in. Land, rivers, runes…" His gaze cut to hers. "People."

Something about the way he was looking at her sent heat to her core. Swallowing hard, she asked, "How do you know all this?"

Castor's lips twisted. "Elyria might have thought it was safer to erase their history. But it doesn't mean Tafari did. While I didn't have a whole class about Druids growing, I still learned they existed."

"Suza," Cassia blurted. She'd seen the blotted-out space on the map. Been told to never ask or acknowledge the land to the west. She'd only heard the name once, from Echnav. "What happened to them?"

"That's a question for a Shaman." He stopped abruptly in front of her, then grabbed her hand. He gently tapped the center of his chest with her knuckle. Her stomach swooped to the floor. "Try. Pull from me."

"I can't," Cassia whispered, suddenly unsure if she was terrified he was wrong... or right.

Castor nodded. "Yes, you can. You're a Witch, but you share very old and powerful Tuathan blood with your brother." Keeping her hands intertwined with his, he spread her palm over his heartbeat. "What if you are a Druid? What if you haven't just been pulling the right places?"

Hearing the words, she swore she felt a tingle against her skin, like it was ready to fuel whatever spell she desired. Throat tightening, she argued, "There has to be a reason there are no more Druids. Maybe you're wrong and they never actually existed."

Castor tightened his grip. "Try."

*Try.*

She'd tried her entire life. And gotten nowhere. This time would be no different. No matter what Castor believed. No matter how long he stared at her with such sickening encouragement that it made her want to throw something at his head. She *couldn't.*

Reluctantly, Cassia closed her eyes. She focused on the sensation of his shirt against her hand... She tried to imagine her body soaring to life with a magic she wanted to borrow. *Come alive,* she urged. *Do something.* But no matter how much she concentrated or shouted commands in her head, nothing happened.

"You're not pulling from me."

Peeking one eye open, she asked, "How do you know?"

Castor's lips turned up at the corners, just slightly. "You can do this."

One small smile and her stomach fluttered, urging her to do whatever he said. She really was pathetic. Closing her eyes again, she heeded his advice. Instead of focusing on only her, she thought about his body. How his heartbeat pounded beneath her fingertips. The heat that radiated up her arm. Anything that remotely felt like magic or power or whatever Druids pulled —

And then she felt it.

A spark.

Cassia pulled on it. Heat exploded from her gut, licking up her spine until she felt it buzzing underneath her palm. Vibrations radiated from her skin, alive and alert. Her hands shook, unfamiliar with the weight and sensation pulsing through her appendages. She gasped, unable to believe what was happening. Unable to believe what she was feeling. *Magic*, like she never had before. And it was *hers*. She couldn't decide what she should do first.

The last two days played in her mind. There were so many things going on. So many things she needed. She needed—

With a crash, the door flew open. Cassia dropped her hands. The magic flowing through her veins disappeared. Castor dropped to the floor, gasping for breath. She dropped with him and grabbed his neck. Blood poured from his nose. Before she had time to process what was wrong or why the door had flown open, Castor pulled her up and jumped in front of her. Lifting his hand, he caught a flying black brick midair just inches away from her face. He turned to her, clearly stunned. Breathing labored, his lips began to move.

Heart pounding, Cassia couldn't hear what he was saying over the roar in her ears. It wasn't a brick. It was a book. And *she'd* brought it to them.

Castor's hand on her arm brought her back to reality.

"Do you know what this is?" he asked again.

Silently, Cassia took the book from him and flipped through the pages. She'd been thinking of artifacts and Quinn and—

"What the hell?" Finn mumbled, rubbing his bleeding temple as he entered the training room. "Why did I just get hit in the head by a flying book?"

Cassia moved her gaze from the trembling book to Castor, whose quiet elation made her even more queasy, then to Finn. And then back again. Unsure of how to explain or comprehend their current situation.

She had magic.

And it was *powerful*.

Castor squeezed her arm again. She didn't realize how much she'd been shaking until the gesture stilled her vision.

Frowning, Finn checked the hallway for any unwanted visitors before he asked, "Is everything okay?"

Cassia took a deep breath. She needed to calm down. She needed to get a grip. It was one time. No reason to get excited, or proud, until she could do it again. "We were practicing."

Finn's frown turned to mild disgust. "I've heard that one before."

Heat flooded Cassia's face. She'd forgotten that had been their excuse the last time Finn had caught them together in a dark room, three years ago. "We were."

"Cassia asked me to help her with some spells," Castor said mildly, rubbing the back of his neck. Discreetly, he wiped his nose. "I didn't mean the book to come crashing our way like that."

She silently thanked Castor with her eyes. There was no reason for the others to know it had been her. Not until they knew for sure what it meant. And if she could do it again.

But Finn was Finn. And based on his raised brow, she could tell he sensed they were hiding something. Damn emotion reader. Clearing her throat, Cassia asked, "What are you doing here?"

"I'm looking for Castor," Finn said. "The king wants to see him."

Castor let out a frustrated sigh. Waving a dismissive hand, he said, "Not now. We're not done here."

"As much as I like the idea of blowing him off... it's about Tafari. He received a letter from your parents."

# CHAPTER SIXTEEN

Cassia gave the bartender another mocking smile as he glared at her from across the room. She saluted him with what was leftover of her drink, then downed the potent liquid in one gulp. Fire exploded in her throat as she slammed the glass on the sticky table. Not long after Castor and Finn had disappeared due to her father's bidding, she'd headed straight for her favorite club in Astraeus. Unable to stop feeling like she wanted to crawl out of her skin. Unable to sleep. Unable to do anything but replay the memory of magic soaring through her bones.

"Another?" the older man asked tiredly, already heading for the near empty bottle.

Cassia ground her teeth together. For an establishment that advertised being open all night, he sure seemed inconvenienced by her presence. Granted, she was the only one left in the place, but it wasn't like she wanted to be there. She'd nearly smashed a window when she'd discovered her usual haunt boarded up. Permanently. Just like every other bar and restaurant she tried until she stumbled across the seedy one she was stuck in now.

She didn't pretend she didn't know why. Even though her father constantly told the city they were safe from what was happening at the border, the majority clearly didn't believe him.

"You know, if you showed a little enthusiasm instead of mumbling under your breath every time your only customer ordered, this place might not be so dead," Cassia snapped, slurring her words just a little too much for her taste. She stumbled to her feet and pulled out a handful of gold coins. "Forget it. I'm done."

"At only one in the morning? I'm shocked," the man deadpanned. "And we have plenty of customers. At reasonable hours."

Not bothering to walk the money over to him, Cassia left the coins sprawled on the table. "Then change your damn sign."

Wind almost knocked her over as she stormed into the night. It cut across her face, leaving her cheeks stinging as she tightened her long black coat around her shoulders. As she turned in the direction of the palace, Cassia paused to stare up at the dim buildings towering around her. Months ago, they'd lit up the night sky and captivated the attention of everyone on the street. Now, each one almost seemed lifeless. And she was alone on an abandoned avenue. A shiver ran down her spine.

To her left, a whistle sounded from the train station, alerting patrons in the station that it was leaving in five minutes. Cassia glanced over at the silver monstrosity. She'd never been on it, nor did she want to after her experience with machines in the human realm. If she ever needed to leave Astraeus, a horse would do just fine. Bristling at the thought, she was surprised to see it operating so late. Would anyone even be on it?

Cassia caught sight of a figure at the ticket counter. Well, apparently someone was a fan of riding late night death traps. When the figure kneeled to pull out a ticket from the dispenser, their hair fell away from their face. Cassia froze.

Delphine?

*What the hell.*

Feet already moving, Cassia watched as Delphine rushed inside the station. Before the other girl could get out of sight, she hopped up the steps and slid through the closing glass doors without bothering to stop at the counter for her own ticket. No matter what, she wouldn't get on. She just wanted to know what Delphine was up to.

Because there was only one reason she was sneaking on a train in the middle of the night.

Practically sprinting to keep up, Cassia managed to grab Delphine's shoulder seconds before she reached the train's nearest boarding door. Flinching at her touch, Delphine whipped around. Shock radiated from every inch of her skin. Catching her breath, Cassia leaned against her knees and silently thanked whoever was listening that Delphine had decided to walk instead of using her special ability. Not that she seemed to be using it much lately anyway.

"What are you doing here?" Delphine asked, dark eyes worriedly roaming the space behind them.

"What are *you* doing here?" Cassia countered. "It's the middle of the night."

Delphine inched toward the boarding door. Another whistle sounded, warning that the train would be departing soon. Gripping the machine's long silver handle like she could somehow stop the train from leaving if she had to, Delphine stuttered, "I couldn't sleep."

Cassia narrowed her eyes. "You couldn't sleep so you decided to take a trip to…" She ripped the poorly hidden ticket from Delphine's fist. Her heart dropped. Then twisted in her chest. It was just as she suspected. Throat tight, she finished, "Kastron."

A tense beat passed between them. She took Delphine's silence as a yes. Of course her brother had all their friends doing his dirty work while he… Cassia stopped. She processed the nervousness in Delphine's eyes and remembered the fact she wouldn't *need* to take a train. Not if she was going to Kastron alone. Not if she really wanted to.

"Where is he?" Cassia asked, even though she already knew the answer. Without waiting for a reply, she gripped the silver handle and tried to step on the train. Delphine shoved herself in front of her.

"If I let you on, you have to promise to help. We're probably only going to have one shot at this. A scout spotted one of those creatures close to the Elder Woods. Your father is planning to increase the protection spell around the city and basically lock everyone in. This might be the last train out for months."

*A shot at what?* Cassia wanted to ask, but nothing would come out of her mouth. Delphine's interference had let her body catch up with her brain. She stared at the long, shiny machine as fear poisoned her limbs. If she did manage to actually get on the thing, how much help would she be? She barely knew how to use her own magic now. Was she a *Druid*? And even if she did get on, there was a real possibility she would spend the entire ride fighting off a heart attack. Bridget had made sure she never wanted to be in a moving metal machine again.

And if her father *was* closing off the city, would they even be able to get back in?

Delphine hopped on the platform of the boarding door and held out her hand. "Are you coming or staying?"

The train whistled again, warning that it would be leaving within ten minutes. The high-pitched squeal snapped Cassia out of her spiral. Even though her hands were shaking, she gripped Delphine's outstretched palm and pulled herself onto the thing she swore she'd never ride.

But that had been before Castor figured out her magic. Or what she was.

And now, anything seemed possible.

Heart pounding, she tried to ignore Delphine's surprised stare as she followed her down the carpeted center aisle of the train. Every few seconds, she gripped the wall to stop herself from falling on her ass. Cassia took a deep breath. If she didn't find a seat soon, she was going to vomit.

They passed compartment after compartment. The further they went, the smaller and less spacious the rooms became. Finally, Delphine stopped in front of one with a chipping wooden door at the very back of the train.

"Seriously, he couldn't have sprung for anything nicer?" Cassia mumbled as Delphine slid open the door.

Eight eyes went from relieved to incredulous faster than Cassia thought possible when the others caught sight of her. She inventoried everyone present. On the left bench, Cade glowered at her. Next to him, Finn seemed to be holding back a laugh. Castor, on the other side of the tiny compartment... Cassia couldn't bring herself to meet his curious gaze. And then there was Marin, quiet in the corner as she leaned her head against the train's foggy window.

Everyone.

Even Marin.

But not her.

"Well... two princes, a Shaman, a guard, and a favored tournament contestant sneaking into first class in the middle of the night wouldn't be very subtle, would it?" Finn joked, breaking the tense silence.

Cassia ignored him and kept her gaze locked on Cade's fiery glare. Her throat tightened more and more the longer she tortured herself by not breaking away from the direct line of his clear, and growing, irritation.

"What the hell are you doing here, Cass?" he growled.

Delphine shushed him, then quickly slid the compartment door shut. "Despite the hour, we are not the only ones on this train. She spotted me going into the station and followed. You know I'm a terrible liar."

"That's why we all came separately," Cade replied through gritted teeth. "The plan was very precise. Any deviations..."

"How?" Castor asked, interrupting his oncoming rant. "The staff entrance isn't anywhere near the road... and weren't you supposed to just pop in, anyway?"

Silence enveloped them as he waited for an answer. Delphine twisted her hands. A hint of pink flooded her cheeks.

Finn laughed. "She stopped to buy a ticket," he said, patting Delphine's cheek. "Our little rule follower." After a quick glance around the crowded compartment, he shrugged and then nestled himself against the door on the floor. "Since this thing will get going any second, looks like I'm down here for the rest of the trip." With a wave of his hand, he directed Cassia to the sliver of open seat next to Delphine, who had squished herself beside Castor. "You're welcome."

Wordlessly, Cassia inched a corner of her bottom onto the ratty cloth bench, careful not to press against Delphine too much. The last thing she wanted to be responsible for was pushing her closer to Castor, despite the sore lower back the position would give her.

"My uncle works at the station. You don't know how many times I've heard him rant about people sneaking on the train without paying," Delphine said, still a little flushed. "It comes out of the attendants' pay."

Cassia tried not to feel sick when Castor squeezed the other girl's arm in support. His gaze cut to hers, telling her they both knew the reason for her mishap. She still was having trouble with magic. Forcing her gaze to the floor, Cassia channeled her attention to the betrayal swirling in her stomach. Anger was good. Anger would keep her traitorous thoughts at bay.

"You knew about this earlier," Cassia hissed, glaring sideways at Castor. "And you didn't say a word."

Between them, Delphine sat up straighter. The moment she noticed the frown forming on the other girl's face, Cassia added, "He was helping me with a spell."

Finn raised a brow. Once again, Cassia ignored him and hoped he sensed the wave of annoyance she tried to silently direct toward him.

"Why do you always assume the worst?" Castor retorted, shaking his head. "I didn't know anything until Finn summoned me. There was no letter. It was just a ploy to fill me in."

"Of course it was," Cassia seethed, even though his words somewhat calmed her racing heart. Castor wouldn't lie... no matter how many times she accused him of it. Or wanted to believe he would.

"We knew you would disapprove," Delphine said placatingly.

*That* was putting it lightly. Why go after Quinn when she clearly had the upper hand? The Witch had the Bloodstone *and* seemed to know what the Sanguis wanted.

Staring out the window, Marin finally spoke. "They didn't think you could keep the secret."

At least the others had the decency to look ashamed, but beside Marin, Cade cracked a humorless smile. "Well, she's not lying."

*Ouch.* The comment sent a stinging all the way down to Cassia's toes. Maybe she deserved that one. But she knew better now... even if there was no way to prove to them that she did.

"It's pretty obvious Quinn doesn't want to be found. A reckless mission to Kastron isn't going to change that," Cassia hissed. Marin rubbed her arm, then fiddled with the hem of her pants. The casualness of the gesture irked her. "Have you seen where she is? Or what's going to happen when we get there?"

"I told you... I haven't been able to see anything."

For once, Cassia heard a hint of frustration in the Tuathan's usual monotone voice.

Whatever consequence she'd taken for Cade was affecting her more than she wanted to let on.

"I saw her near the border," Finn said. "You know that."

Taking a deep breath, Cassia nodded. She did. And that was only a week ago. Logically, she knew Quinn was probably still in the area. Despite the growing darkness that seemed to linger around Astraeus, Elyria's border with Kastron was the area being haunted by unknown forces. *Monsters*, she'd heard whispered in the palace. And even in her own head by Cade when he'd shown her what Finn had seen.

"And you think it's okay to use him as bait? Because that's what is essentially happening," Cassia prodded. "Aren't fiancées supposed to be a little more protective?"

Cade banged his head against the seat.

"Lay off, Cass," Delphine whispered.

A sharp pain entered Cassia's temple. Cade's annoyed voice echoed through her head. *Finn says your emotions are suffocating him.*

She glanced at Finn on the floor. He rubbed his temples. Without thinking, she shot back, *Tell him to say it to my face.*

Cade raised a brow, acceptance of the dare clear on his face. When his gaze cut to Finn, she held up a hand. *Don't.* That was the last thing she needed said aloud. *Why are you even doing this? You've spent months holed up in your room and now you want to go after Quinn?*

*That was before... everything.*

Such a small word... but so weighted. An invisible hand clawed at Cassia's chest. In theory, her twin brother sat across from her. The same one she'd known since birth. The boy she'd seen save a bird with a broken wing at age seven. The person she'd always believed would know her better than anyone... But apparently, he was someone else entirely. A Tuathan, with latent powers and a past life. A prince with a fate tied to a curse. One with an enemy willing to do anything to break it.

The train lurched forward, nearly nudging Cassia from her chair. She took a deep breath. No matter what, Cade *was* her brother.

"Finally," Finn mumbled. Castor hummed in agreement.

*And what happens after you find Quinn?* Cassia shot back at Cade. *Do you kill her? Do you use her or the Bloodstone to bring Bridget back?*

Across from her, Cade tensed. *Bridget won't come back here.*

*How do you know? She remembers. After your little stunt, she could be trying to get here on her own. Didn't you say she was with Echnav?*

Cassia peeked at Marin, still leaning against the window, a little paler than usual. The annoying, secretive Shaman *still* didn't have an answer for that.

*I don't know what she was doing with him, but she won't risk her sister. If it was Riker... Would you?*

No way in hell. But she didn't need to answer Cade for him to know that. *If this isn't about seeing Bridget again, then why go after Quinn? The Bloodstone will kill her eventually.*

Cade's brows knitted in frustration. *But it hasn't. Which must mean she's found some kind of loophole... or is working with Vega, who is still alive in Iegorus and trying to get out. According to Marin. If that's the case, then I have to do what I can to protect Bridget from her.*

*But Vega doesn't need Bridget to break her curse... she needs* you.

Why couldn't her brother comprehend that he wasn't untouchable? Huffing, Cassia crossed her arms and fixed her gaze on the window so she wouldn't glare at him too hard. He was finally *talking* to her. No matter what she felt, she didn't want to mess that up. Outside, the darkest part of the night shrouded the outer wall of Astraeus which began to approach them at a slowly increasing speed. It wouldn't be long before they exited the city completely, or passed the fortified tomb-like structure where she knew the rune protecting the city was hidden. She imagined her father there tomorrow afternoon with one of his Shamans, effectively locking the city without them inside.

Cade snorted. *Tomorrow afternoon? He'll notice we're gone before breakfast and send a whole battalion after us.*

From the floor, Finn sighed loudly. "You know... your little secret conversations aren't so secret. We all know when you two do that twin—"

The world around them exploded.

Crunching, spinning, swirling metal mixed with a crisp night sky. Cassia was in the air, flying toward an unknown destination. Unable to scream by the sheer amount of confusion freezing her limbs. And then *heat*. Blistering and overwhelming. It pressed in from all directions, impossible to place, but close enough to sear her skin as she spiraled toward it.

Finally, the whirling stopped. The ground caught her at last. The impact jolted through her spine. Pain lanced up her arms as her palms scraped raw across pavement or stone. Sparks burst behind her eyes as she skidded through rubble. Her body only stopped moving when it slammed into something solid.

When she came to a stop, her entire body shivered with adrenaline. Gasping, she rolled to her back, her vision swimming. Smoke curled around her in dense, choking tendrils. What the hell had happened?

Sirens began to blast throughout the city. Wailing and more ominous than she ever imagined they would be. A warning to run. A warning to hide. Which is what she needed to be doing. But she still couldn't connect her brain to her muscles.

A shuffle reached her ears. Cassia flinched. She needed to get up. *Right now.*

She dug her bloody palms into the icy ground and tried to push herself up. Before she could, a blurry Castor crawled over her. She almost sobbed in relief. Half of his face was covered in dirt and blood dripped from the corner of his mouth, but he was *alive*. Wordless, he took her wrist gently and inspected the worst of the scrapes on her right hand, then shifted to steady her back as he helped her sit up.

"Are you okay?" he asked, voice barely audible over the sirens. Now that she was upright, the sight of the wreckage in front of her sent acid up Cassia's throat. Around them, the night bled with fire. Beside the broken and ripped train, a giant hole permeated the city wall, jagged and burned. Fire blazed from the opening to the small domed building containing one of the most powerful runes in her family's possession. Between the rubble and the smoke, she couldn't tell if the building had been breached. If—

Castor squeezed her arm and forced her to look at him. "Are you hurt?"

Cassia shook her head and slowly heaved herself to feet, hoping that would wipe the concern from his face when there were other things to worry about. Like where her brother and their friends were. "What happened? Have you seen anyone else?"

"Some sort of explosion. I landed beside Finn and Marin. She's trapped underneath part of the train so he went to find Cade. Whatever consequence she took for Cade has severely weakened her. She can't lift it herself. Him and Delphine couldn't have been thrown too far from us."

The sirens suddenly stopped. Then came a growl.

Low and guttural, it slithered out from the southern edge of the Elder Woods just beyond the city's perimeter. Trees groaned. Branches rattled against each other as the shadows between them shifted.

A second snarl echoed. The wet, gurgling sound turned Cassia's blood to ice as two creatures crawled into view. Both moved on all fours, limbs too long. Their eyes were hollow, empty voids, and thick strands of black ooze dripped from their matted fur, hissing as it hit the ground. Every inch of them looked like rot and death and nightmare.

And exactly like the one from Cade's stolen memory.

"The wall…" Castor said, voice dying as he reached the same conclusion as her. The train hadn't been the target of the explosion. It had just been in the wrong place at the wrong time as someone tried to breach the city by destroying the structure fueling its protection spell.

"This has to be Quinn," Cassia said, coughing through the thickening air. "How did she know where to target?"

Like the Witch could hear her, the fire lining the wall's hole and pathway to the rest of the city died in one fell swoop. The creatures' hackles raised in anticipation.

"That doesn't matter right now. We can't let those things in." Even though his gaze was steely, Castor's throat bobbed. "Whoever did this, destroyed the bridge too."

Whirling around, Cassia caught sight of the large smoke cloud in the distance. It was the middle of the night. The majority of the soldiers based in the city would be asleep in their barracks beneath Mount Lugh. On the other side of the river. "We're alone."

"For now," Castor promised.

Cassia wasn't sure she believed in his optimism. The creatures were already closing in on the hole in the wall. Without help, they wouldn't be able to hold them off for long.

Another snarl pierced her ears. The first creature dug its claws into the dirt, readying itself to launch. Beside her, Castor pulled a bag of herbs from his pocket. Under his breath, he muttered a spell. One Cassia didn't recognize. A piercing screech tore through the silence as the lead creature lunged.

Midair, the beast was thrown backward. With a bone-crunching crack, it smashed into a tree, snapping bark and branches on impact. The monster hit the ground with a shuddering growl and struggled to rise.

Cassia's head snapped toward the smoke. A knot in her chest loosened. "Cade!"

Out of the smoke, her brother appeared. He strode forward, golden eyes alight with power. The air seemed to bend around him, heavy with energy that made her bones vibrate.

"Get out of here, Cass," Cade growled, launching another piece of rubble at one of the creatures with a flick of his wrist. "Delphine is waiting for you behind the train."

"Impeccable timing," Castor said, halfway grinning. "If we have any chance of keeping them out of the city, we need to reactivate the spell."

Cade turned his head, as if searching for something. He flicked his wrist again. Seconds later, a twisted piece of wreckage lifted from the ruins. The piece, Cassia assumed, that Marin had been trapped under. With another pulse of power, it shot forward and struck the beast square in the chest. The monster staggered and growled. But no matter what Cade continued to throw at them, the creatures didn't seem to be deterred.

"Take Marin and go," Cade told Castor. "She's free now. She'll know how to get inside and fix the rune, but she'll need your help."

Determination etched on his features, Castor nodded. He squeezed Cassia's arm, then whispered in her ear, "Do what you can."

It wasn't hard to miss his hidden meaning. Her *powers*. She'd almost forgotten. Before she could argue with him or say she didn't know how to do it again without him, he'd disappeared in the rubble of the train.

Cassia turned to Cade, just in time to see another wave of magic surge through him. A section of the shattered wall cracked loose and shot toward the second creature, slamming it into the dirt. Dust clouded the air. Cade staggered slightly, and blood began to drip steadily from his ear.

"You need to run, Cass," he said through gritted teeth. His voice trembled with strain. "I've got this."

Cassia opened her mouth to argue, but a movement in the trees caught their attention. Especially since the creatures suddenly stilled. A man, at least, he might've been once, emerged from the dark. His body was skeletal, his skin stretched tight over bone, veins pulsing black beneath the surface like poisoned roots. His face was sunken and hollow-eyed. Black sludge clung to his jaw, sloughing from his fingertips in thick, oozing drops. Long black fingernails dripped blood as he raised his hands. The moment he did, the creatures growled in tandem and charged forward again.

Cade titled his head. "It's not Quinn controlling them."

The man, or Wraith, or whatever the hell he was, raised his hand again. Not to control the beasts, but to attack. A jagged shard of twisted metal hovered in the air and then launched straight at them.

Cassia reached for Cade. "Watch out," she gasped. Without thinking, she pulled. Unlike with Castor, it didn't take her long to find a spark of magic within him. The moment she touched his shoulder, something within him responded. Magic leapt from his skin and surged like lightning up her arm. It was *everywhere* inside him, thrumming just beneath the surface. Cassia seized and redirected it.

Seconds later, the shard veered off-course and slammed into a pile of debris beside them.

Cade's arms dropped to his sides in stunned silence. "How did you do that?"

Cassia snatched her hand away from him and cradled it against her chest. Her palm still tingled from the contact. She didn't answer. She couldn't. How could she explain something she barely understood herself?

Her brother, too busy staring and trying to breach her mind for an explanation, didn't notice the shadow uncoiling behind him. One of the beasts had scaled the wall, its blackened claws digging into stone. Its teeth glinted in the dim light as a snarl peeled from its throat.

Suddenly, silver flew through the air. The beast shrieked. It twisted violently and toppled from the wall with a sickening crunch. A dagger jutted from its shoulder, slick with black ooze. Whimpering, the creature dragged itself toward the waiting Wraith, its strength fading.

Swallowing hard, Cassia searched the trees behind the Wraith for the source of the dagger. For an explanation. For some kind of rogue soldier that had been hiding in the Elder Woods.

Then, out of the darkness, stepped Bridget.

# CHAPTER SEVENTEEN

### BRIDGET

B ridget's entire body froze at the sight before her.

Seconds ago, she'd been in the snowy woods of Connecticut. Now, a hellish landscape similar to the one she'd briefly seen in Stellan's vision pierced her eyes. Grey stains littered the city's stone wall, a once imposing sight of the brightest brick and metal. A giant hole gave her a clear view into the chaos happening inside Astraeus. Three creatures seemed to be in charge of the ruin.

Bridget's breath caught as her gaze locked on the two creatures prowling just inside the breach. Their appearance sent a wave of déjà vu down her spine, like she'd come across one before. Maybe in a dream. Or a past life.

Or maybe they were just the type of a creature everyone couldn't help but envision in a nightmare at some point.

They were... wrong. Built like wolves, but taller. Their fur, soaked and clotted with filth, hung from their frames like rotting moss. With every movement, their muscles rippled with unnatural speed. Black foam dripped from their fangs, and when they snarled, she caught a glimpse of too many teeth.

The other antagonist was more human-like. The skin that hung on its skeletal frame was a patchwork of scars and blisters. It wore no armor. Its head was bald, and what might've once been tan flesh now burned with open sores and oozing rot. Long black nails curled from its hands like talons.

Bridget pushed Nylah behind Stellan and turned to him for an explanation. Is *this* what they had seen in his vision before they'd left? Were they already too late, despite Nylah's use of the Tuathan artifact? Something she *still* needed an explanation for. But Stellan's answer was drowned out by her own heartbeat when she spotted the back of a head. One she'd know anywhere, even with blood and soot caking his temple. One that was too busy pounding loose rubble and saying something to his sister to notice a beast slowly creeping up the ruined stone wall behind him.

Without thinking, Bridget darted forward and pulled a dagger from her boot. Faintly, she heard Nylah gasp as she launched the blade in a single motion. The weapon struck true in between the monster's shoulder and neck. A hidden soft spot she'd luckily hit. The moment the weapon pierced the beast's skin, her knees buckled. Black goo spewed forth as the massive creature wailed and twisted. Behind it, the skyline of Astraeus wheezed with smoke.

Bridget slowly lowered her hand, her breath ragged in her chest. Her heart felt like it might punch through her ribcage as the shrieking creature twisted away and fled back to the side of the Wraith-like man. Stellan, now glowing with power, held up his hand and yelled something at her again, but all she could focus on was the head swiveling in her direction. His glowing irises, so saturated with power just moments ago, dimmed back to their familiar warmth in an instant. Recognition dawned on his face as his eyes locked with hers across an expanse of rubble and smoke.

Bridget stopped breathing completely.

In her loneliest nights, when the world was quiet and the only thing she could hear was her own heartbeat, she had often imagined this exact scenario. Even though she knew it was hopeless and wrong and the opposite of what she should be wishing for in the place he'd fought to return her to… Whenever it happened, she wasn't able to look at Nylah the next day. Still, she kept the imaginings close to her heart, deep inside where she could visit them every once and awhile.

But now it was a reality.

*Cade.*

In front of her.

His familiar wavy hair was wild and blood smudged his cheek as his stunned gaze bore into hers.

Despite the chaos around them, her entire body felt truly awake. *Alive.* Bridget sucked in a breath. Nothing compared to the feeling of his eyes on her or the way she knew the moment she moved toward him, he would meet her halfway.

Nothing would ever compare to him.

A sob escaped Bridget's chest. Vision quickly blurring, she reached him before she realized she *had* been moving. She barely registered Cade's own wrecked expression before his lips were on hers, blazing and fierce. When his hand dug into her lower back, she wanted to melt into the ground as the weight of their separation crashed into her. It'd been so long. Yet, as she kissed him back with just as much ferocity and longing, the innate sense of *him* embedded itself back into her soul, healing some of the broken pieces inside her she thought would be raw forever.

"You shouldn't be here," Cade mumbled against her lips, refusing to break the contact. He pulled her closer and ran his thumb over the skittering pulse in her neck. "You really shouldn't be here."

Despite his admonishing words, he didn't sound mad at all. A ghost of a laugh got trapped in her throat.

"It's a long story." Reluctantly, Bridget pulled away from him, the sound of distant crash bringing her back to her senses. They were not alone and she needed to get Nylah as far away from the destruction as possible.

Behind Cade, Finn charged toward one of the smaller beasts, blocking it from entering the city wall with a swipe of his sword, while Cassia ducked behind a fallen stone.

"What the hell did we just walk into?" Bridget asked, gripping the lapels of his sooty leather jacket.

Cade frowned, then wiped away the trickle of blood that had escaped her nose during her travel across the gate. "We?"

Tilting her head, Bridget led his gaze to the eclectic travel group. She wasn't sure who Cade seemed more stunned to see, Nylah or Stellan. *Echnav* to him. His golden-brown orbs flittered between the two, like he couldn't quite comprehend the sight before him. Guilt swirled in her stomach as she caught Nylah's gaze peeking at her from behind Stellan with fascination. Less than ten minutes in Elyria and she was already witnessing destruction. Behind them, Archer mouthed silently *what should I do*, while Alexia, thin lipped and pale, glared at her like this was *her* fault.

A wild hand waved between her and Cade.

"I don't know if you two realize this, but this is not the time for a loving little reunion," Cassia hissed. "Finn's barely holding them off. There's no point to Castor fixing the protection spell if whatever those things are get inside."

Right. First things first. Bridget searched the area around them for some sort of hiding place. "We need to get Nylah somewhere safe. Now."

Suddenly, Cade knocked her to the ground. She lost her breath as they landed with a hard thud. A jagged shard of glass sliced through the air overhead, crashing into a piece of metal with a shattering crack. It would've taken her head off.

Cade didn't waste a second. Still half-shielding her body, he flicked his wrist and sent a chunk of stone flying through the smoke. It collided with one of the beasts with a thunderous crunch. If the beasts were to the right, they now stood between her and her sister. Bridget rolled over, only to find the forest empty.

Before her heart completely left her body, a ripple of magic zinged through the smoke, reaching her ears with a pop. Stellan, Nylah, Archer, and Alexia appeared out of thin air, next to a heap of metal wreckage.

"Luckily you brought help," Cade said, helping her to her feet. "Delphine is behind the train. She can take you both away from the city."

"I'm staying."

Now that she'd seen him, the idea of letting him out of her sight made her stomach knot.

Cade's expression tightened. He opened his mouth to argue, but before he could speak, a blur of movement barreled into him. Nylah leapt into his chest and squeezed her arms around his neck. Cade stumbled back half a step, then caught her, wrapping his arms around her small frame. A knot tightened in Bridget's throat. Despite the chaos around them, she couldn't help the pure joy spreading through her limbs. *This* is what she'd been missing and wanting.

The sight of Stellan striding toward them, the epitome of seriousness and determination, stopped any more liquid from blurring her vision.

"You're welcome," he said. Tight-lipped, he turned to Cade. "Where's Marin?"

Cade put Nylah back on the ground, but still held onto her hand. "She's helping Castor reactivate the protection spell around the city."

"She's not strong enough for that right now." Stellan seethed.

"She can handle it," Cade argued over the deafening growl of one of the creatures. "Right now, we've got bigger issues. Getting the spell reactivated won't do us any good if these creatures are inside when it happens. Castor is helping her. Between the two of them, it will get done."

A blast of magic erupted from the Wraith's fingertips, slamming into them like a shockwave. The force hurled all four of them backward into Archer and Alexia. Bridget hit the ground hard. The breath knocked from her lungs. Instinctively, she curled her body around Nylah, gripping the girl's wrist and pulling her tight against her chest.

Stellan and Cade were already on their feet by the time she'd managed to sit up.

"Watch it," Alexia grumbled.

"Like I chose to fall on top of you," Bridget snapped, taking Cade's outstretched hand. In a flash, he pulled her and Nylah up.

"What exactly are these creatures?" he asked Stellan. "Nothing seems to be able to get them to back down."

"I'm not sure about the beasts, but the one controlling them is a Wraith."

"That doesn't sound ominous at all," Archer muttered.

Bridget couldn't help but agree with him.

With a flick of his wrist, Stellan summoned a dying ember from a smoldering patch of grass. It hovered, trembling in the air above his open palm. With a precise motion, he pinched it between two fingers and drew it upward. The spark stretched and bloomed. In a heartbeat, it exploded into a blazing fireball, casting sharp orange light across his face. The air crackled. Heat shimmered across Bridget's skin as he launched the fireball straight at the nearest beast.

"Fire will destroy the beasts," Stellan said, creating another ember. "But it's going to take more than that to hold off the Wraith. Let's hope that spell is reactivated sooner rather than later."

Another blast of magic slammed out of the Wraith. This time, Cade threw out his arm, magic pulsing from his core, before it reached them. Bridget and Nylah were lifted off their feet, weightless for half a second, before they landed safely behind him, cushioned by a burst of Cade's power. Alexia and Archer crashed to the ground again.

A sharp zing pierced Bridget's temple. She recognized Cade's presence immediately.

*Get her away.*

With another pinch, he was gone. In her peripheral vision, she spotted him yelling another warning at Finn as one of the creatures tried to jump through the hole in the wall again. Pulling Nylah toward the train, Bridget dug her hand into her sister's pocket.

"Hey!" Nylah protested, trying to wiggle out of her grip. "For someone who likes to pickpocket, I would think you would be a little less rough."

"Where's the stone? Those things might want it."

Which meant it absolutely could not be in her sister's possession when that happened. Bridget tried again. This time, the stone burned her skin. Muttering a curse, Bridget snatched her hand back.

"I swear I didn't do that," Nylah said, wide-eyed.

"I know you didn't," Bridget said. Magic had a mind of its own. The ancient rune clearly wanted to stay with Nylah. "Do not let anyone know you have this."

Still looking stunned, her sister nodded.

"Over here!"

Delphine careened out of the wreckage of a twisted metal tube, stumbling over debris as she sprinted toward them. Blood streaked from a gash along her temple, and black soot clung to the entire left side of her body. She'd been near the blast, close enough to burn. But she was alive. And the sight of her lit something in Bridget's chest.

Relief broke free in a sob as Bridget launched herself forward. "I can't believe it's really you."

Delphine caught her mid-lunge, arms wrapping around her in a crushing hug. "You have no idea how good it is to see you," she whispered back, voice thick with emotion.

Her glassy gaze shifted to the girl behind her. "And I know exactly who you are."

Nylah grinned. "It's good to know I have a reputation."

A thunderous crack split the air behind them. Bridget turned instinctively, just in time to glimpse Cade, Stellan, and Finn locked in battle through a thick curtain of smoke. Archer and Alexia lingered at her back, both tense and eyes darting.

"Please take her," Bridget said, pushing her sister forward. "She needs to get away from this."

Delphine's smile faltered. "I..."

"*Please*," Bridget said again, more desperate this time. "I know magic won't be easy on her, but it's the quickest way to get her somewhere safe. Where's the king's men? Is backup coming?"

Before Delphine could answer, Alexia stepped forward with a scoff. "What about *me*? This whole place is about to collapse—"

Bridget didn't even glance at her.

Delphine pointed over her shoulder, where a pillar of smoke spiraled above the treetops. "There was another explosion near the river. The guard unit is trapped on the other side of the bridge. I think they're close, but they'll need a few more minutes to reach the city."

At least some kind of help was on the way. Bridget nodded, already stepping back. "Then I'll stay here. With Cade and the others. Just get Nylah to the palace."

Delphine hesitated one last time. Then her jaw set, and she reached for Nylah's hand. "There's a back way through the city that I know. We'll take that. It should be safe."

Bridget pulled her into one more embrace. "Thank you," she whispered, filing away the need to figure out the source of Delphine's wariness for when they actually had *time*.

"I want to stay with you," Nylah said fiercely, her fingers clutching Bridget's sleeve. "We said we'd stick together."

The desperate plea in her dark eyes almost broke Bridget's resolve. "Not this time." Kissing the top of her head, she shoved Nylah into Delphine's arms.

Delphine gave her a last look, then pulled Nylah away. Her sister didn't take her eyes off Bridget, even as the smoke swallowed them whole.

"Like I'm sticking around for this," Alexia muttered, rushing after them.

A harsh reply was on the tip of Bridget's tongue, but Cassia dug her fingers into her arm. With so much chaos and smoke around them, she'd barely registered her presence still hovering around the wreckage.

"Now is not the time to let her get to you," Cassia said. "If you're finally done chatting, we could use the help."

Bridget glared at her. "And what exactly are you doing?"

Archer dropped a pile of sticks between them. "According to our very old friend, we need fire. It's the only thing that will stop them."

Before her and Cassia had a chance to respond, Archer dropped to his knees and started rubbing two sticks together. His brows pinched when he noticed their shocked faces. "I was a Boy Scout."

Cassia looked like she was tempted to knock his makeshift pile over. "That's an apartment complex," she said, pointing at a five-story brick building behind them. "There are probably people inside that need our help, not to mention who else could still be trapped from the train."

Bridget followed her gaze to the curling piece of metal that hung haphazardly over the two glass double doors that she guessed was the entrance. She could tell from the way it sagged inward that part of the roof had caved in. People were probably still trapped inside.

To her left, another fireball caught her eye. This time, it was Cade's. It wasn't as large or incandescent as Stellan's, but it hit the Wraith square in the chest, sending it reeling with a guttural hiss. Bridget's stomach flipped when she saw the blood running from Cade's nose, crimson streaks cutting through soot on his skin.

"You're right," she said quickly, snapping back to Cassia and Archer. "Besides, by the time you get that fire ready, Archer, it's going to be summer. Cade and Stellan know what they're doing." Bridget grabbed him under the arm and forced him to his feet, despite his protests. "You go with Cassia through the main entrance. Help her get that debris out of the way. I'll check and see if anyone is trying to get out through the back."

She didn't bother to check if they agreed before she took off running, boots pounding against cracked stone. The air thickened with smoke as she rounded the corner, but the heat faded slightly with each step she took away from the central fight. The screams and snarls of the creatures dulled to a distant echo in her ears, replaced by the thunder of her own pulse.

Bridget reached the far end of the building. It was long and shadowed, with no movement or sounds, just broken gutters and dark windows. The complex loomed above her, too still and too quiet. Had the power gone out? Or had the building already been evacuated?

Her steps slowed as she approached one of the windows. All the rooms behind the glass looked pitch black. There was no flicker of movement or signs of life. Standing on her tiptoes, Bridget knocked on a window and peeked inside. "Is anyone in there?"

"Why? Do you want to let me in?"

Bridget whipped around and found Quinn standing on the other side of the wall, barely visible through a jagged crack. The Bloodstone shimmered at her throat like a dying star, casting an eerie glow on the hollows of her face. The beauty Bridget had once admired was gone. In its place stood something gaunt and unnatural. Quinn's once-luminous eyes had turned black and veined, stretching into the skin around them. Her thick raven hair hung in limp, greasy strands across her cheekbones, framing the twisted grin curling her lips.

"Are your little minions not getting the job done?" Bridget jeered, reaching into her boot. Before the other girl could reply, Bridget flung her final dagger. It cut through the air with a sharp hiss and grazed Quinn's cheek, drawing a thin red line across her waxy skin.

Quinn didn't even flinch. She simply tilted her head, blood dripping lazily down her jaw, and smiled wider.

"Catch me if you can, Bee."

Bridget's stomach turned. Even though she hadn't seen Quinn in months, the words didn't sound like Quinn. The cadence was wrong. Too playful. Too sweet. And she'd never once called her *Bee*. In fact, the name brought a sharpness to her chest that she didn't like.

Keeping her gaze locked on Quinn's retreating form, Bridget jammed her foot in the crack and clawed her way to the top of the wall. Leaping off, she landed in the Elder Woods with a thud. Her teeth rattled from the long plunge. A laugh echoed through the trees. One that sounded familiar, but still not Quinn's. With a growl, Bridget sprinted after the sound and toward the direction she'd seen Quinn hop off in.

Moments later, the trees thinned abruptly, giving way to a moss-slick boulder perched at the lip of a ravine. Bridget skidded to a halt, chest heaving. Moonlight flooded the clearing, casting sharp silver edges across the gnarled roots twisting into the ground. The ravine beyond yawned wide and black, its depth impossible to gauge.

Quinn nonchalantly leaned against the boulder. With her one hand, she fiddled with the Bloodstone around her neck. Her thick black jacket hung in tatters, the sleeves frayed and streaked with blood and dirt. Her pants were torn at the knees, revealing skin marred by bruises and burn scars.

"You really shouldn't be out here alone," Quinn taunted.

Bridget kept her eyes on the ruby red crystal between the Witch's fin-gertips. The rune had been the source of so many of their problems. She'd almost died for it. It was most likely the thing that had brought the Wraith from Iegorus. It bound Cade to a future he might not survive. As long as Quinn had it, none of them were safe. Bridget wasn't leaving without it.

"You really shouldn't take things that don't belong to you," Bridget chided back, taking a cautious step toward her.

A sudden pulse of magic erupted from the Bloodstone, slamming into Bridget's chest. She flew backward. Her spine cracked against a tangle of roots as she landed on the ground. Before she could gasp for air, her body jerked, yanked forward by an invisible force. Stones and brambles tore at her jacket and bit into her back as she was dragged across the forest floor like a rag doll.

She skidded to stop in front of the boulder, next to Quinn's feet. Bridget coughed, blinking up through strands of hair as the Bloodstone loomed inches from her face, casting red shadows across Quinn's sickly features.

"You can't win, Bee."

That *name* again. It clawed at Bridget's ribs like something half-forgotten and wholly wrong. Above her, Quinn's grin stretched wide, deranged and missing more than a few teeth. The Witch leaned closer. Her breath was sour and uneven, but it wasn't the smell that made Bridget freeze. It was the glint of something familiar. A gold chain slipped free from beneath Quinn's ruined jacket. Nestled beside the pulsing Bloodstone was *her* amethyst necklace.

White-hot fury surged through Bridget's veins. With a snarl, she slammed her knee into her chest, coiled her body like a spring, and launched her boot straight into Quinn's face. Her heel connected with a brutal crack, right between the Witch's eyes. Quinn shrieked and reeled backward, slamming into the boulder behind her. The bloodstone's glow flickered. The magic holding Bridget's ankle dissolved instantly.

Rolling to the side, Bridget scrambled to her feet. Every muscle screamed, but adrenaline overruled pain. She took a deep breath, only to find Quinn watching her with wide eyes. *Clear* wide eyes. Quinn stared at her, dazed and blinking. The thick, pulsing veins that had clouded her skin just moments ago had thinned to faint lines.

Quinn rubbed the darkening red outline between her eyes and chastised, "You actually followed me? *Why*?"

The Witch tried to stand up on her own, but her knees trembled. She collapsed against the boulder again.

Bridget's heart thundered. "You basically lured me out here," she spat, chest heaving. "Unless I kicked the last working screw out of your head. Why did you call me Bee?"

Quinn's head snapped toward her, eyes wild. "I *didn't*," she hissed.

Bridget almost pinched herself. Had she fallen into some sort of alternate reality when she'd jumped into the Elder Woods to follow Quinn? Her brain couldn't bridge the gap between the snarling Blood Witch who'd taunted her through the wall and the trembling girl unable to stand up straight now.

Quinn choked, blood splattering from her lips as she dropped to her knees, clutching her ribs. Her breaths came in short, shallow gasps. For a heartbeat, she looked small. Almost like the girl Bridget had once known. Both stones, the pulsing Bloodstone and the familiar glint of her amethyst necklace, dangled in the open, exposed against Quinn's chest. Unprotected. Bridget didn't hesitate.

She lunged forward, eyes locked on the crimson rune. Her fingers closed around the Bloodstone. The moment her skin met the stone, a shock of energy pulsed up her arm.

Suddenly, Quinn's head snapped up and her eyes blackened in an instant.

The Witch's hand shot out, clamping around Bridget's throat. With terrifying ease, she hauled her to her feet. Bridget's grip on the Bloodstone slipped as Quinn's fingers tightened around her neck. Black dots bloomed across her vision. Her pulse screamed.

The veins spread again, spidering through Quinn's face. Just as darkness threatened to swallow Bridget, the Witch released her. She hit the ground hard, coughing and sucking in air.

"That's better," Quinn said with a satisfied sigh, rolling her neck

Still gasping for breath, Bridget grunted, "Are you out of your mind?"

A sharp pain pierced her temple.

*Where are you?*

A hint of panic was laced in Cade's thundering voice. She closed her eyes and pictured her path through the forest. Blood dripped down her nose. Seconds later, his presence disappeared.

Quinn let out a humorless laugh. "Let me guess, someone is missing you." She tilted her head. "That puckered confusion on your face isn't becoming. It's going to give you wrinkles."

Bridget wiped the blood from her lip and stood. Her voice was hoarse but steady. "Are you serious right now? I'm not the one changing personalities every few seconds."

Once her spine straightened, Bridget launched herself at Quinn, driving her back into the moss-covered boulder with a satisfying crack. Without hesitation, she twisted and swept her foot beneath the Witch's ankles, sending them both crashing to the ground. Bridget grunted as Quinn's elbow slammed into her ribs, knocking the wind from her lungs. Before she could recover, Quinn shoved her to her back and pinned her with a knee to the chest.

"No, you're just the one refusing to stay levelheaded long enough to ask the right questions," Quinn hissed.

Gritting her teeth, Bridget managed to lift Quinn's knee an inch off her, but another wave of magic from the Bloodstone rolled through her body, short-circuiting her strength. Her arms flailed uselessly to the sides.

"C'mon," Quinn purred, her weight pressing harder into Bridget's sternum. "I know you can think of something clever."

The words heated Bridget's blood. She was crazy. Absolutely crazy. But they *did* need answers. And the moment Cade finally arrived, he would probably kill her. She reached blindly to her side and found a broken tree branch. With a snarl, she swung it upward and cracked it against Quinn's neck. The Witch went flying.

Gasping, Bridget stumbled to her feet and pressed her hand to the boulder for support. Her ribs screamed in protest. "How did you bring those creatures here?" she demanded, her breath ragged. "The curse isn't broken. They shouldn't even exist outside Iegorus."

Quinn spat to the side, blood mixing with the dirt. "They're not from Iegorus," she said, voice rough and gravel-laced. "I created them. Tuathans can't resist the power blood magic gives them. Wraiths are what happens when there's nothing left to give."

The Wraith was *Tuathan*?

"How? There's hardly any left and they all live in the palace."

Instead of answering, Quinn just smirked. The Bloodstone began to glow. Again, an invisible hand pulled Bridget to the Witch. "I think it's time for us to go."

*Us?*

Panic sprung up Bridget's spine. This time, when she reached Quinn, Bridget had her fist ready. She knocked Quinn in the temple and pushed her toward the boulder. Whatever she'd done with her foot had changed Quinn. And it needed to be repeated. Grabbing the Witch by the collar, Bridget shoved her as hard as she could into the stone.

Quinn's skull cracked against the stone with a sharp sound that echoed through the clearing. Her body crumpled. Veins rippled on her face like black lightning. Eventually, Quinn stuttered, "Bridget."

Suddenly, the trees swayed as wind began to swirl around them. *Cade.* He was close.

"What happened to you?" Bridget asked. Because two minds seemed to be fighting for control. She couldn't help but feel an ache in her bones for someone so lost and controlled by magic. A place she never wanted to be again.

Still struggling, Quinn shakily bared her teeth. "You," she snarled. Wrapping her hand around the Bloodstone, Quinn muttered a spell under her breath. Darkness began to glow under her skin. A crack reverberated the air. She was *leaving*.

"No," Bridget breathed, reaching to stop her. They needed the Bloodstone. They needed more answers. But before Bridget could blink again, Quinn had disappeared.

A hazy cloud of magic lingered in the spot Quinn had been standing. Bridget let out a frustrated scream and tried to sweep her fingers through it. But strong, familiar arms wrapped around her waist and yanked her back.

"The spell is about to be reactivated," Cade said breathlessly. "If you're out here when that happens, you'll be trapped with the Wraith."

"No," Bridget repeated angrily. As Cade pulled her through the woods, she struggled in his tight grip. "We can't let her get away again."

"She's already gone."

The words sliced through Bridget's chest as she let him grab her hand and pull her faster through the trees. Bridget stumbled alongside him, her heart pounding and her mind racing. As they reached the clearing, the full horror came into view. Near the breach in the wall, two piles of ash smoldered. Bones and scraps of fur scattered in the dirt. The beasts were dead.

But the Wraith was not.

It snarled as Stellan encircled it with a barrier of fire, sweat gleaming on his brow. Its hollow gaze found them through the smoke and screamed without sound. And still, it pressed forward, relentless.

Cade shoved Bridget behind him and grabbed her wrist in a grip that nearly dislocated her shoulder. She barely had time to breathe before he yanked her back through the fractured remains of Astraeus's wall. They stumbled over debris, smoke curling around their legs like claws. The instant they cleared the boundary, Cade shouted, "Do it now!"

A light shot up from a building further away from them. A twisting column of purple smoke shot up from the far side of the city, unfurling like a storm. It coiled in the sky, then spread wide, rippling outward until it blanketed the heavens in swirling violet clouds. Bridget flinched as the magic collapsed downward in a great sweeping wave. It crashed over them, seeping into the air like thick mist and stretching outward until it sealed the broken wall in an invisible dome.

Bridget craned her neck. Just beyond the edge of the new magical barrier, the Wraith clawed at nothing, trapped in the Elder Woods. Its head snapped toward Stellan, then Cade, before its mouth split in a silent snarl. One final, guttural roar tore from its throat before it vanished into the trees.

Across the rubble, Stellan stood like a statue. His arms slowly lowered as sweat gleamed down his temples. Moments later, soldiers poured into the streets behind them. The echo of boots and shouts flooding Astraeus with life once more.

Cade's hand on her neck almost made her jump. Once she realized it was just him, she leaned into the touch and let him inspect the welts she already felt forming. "Are you alright?"

Bridget's body trembled from the adrenaline lingering in her veins. The sight of him before hit her again like a freight train. Patches of blood stained the skin under his nose and ears. His shirt was ripped down to his navel. But he was *alive*. He was *here*. And so was she. Bridget grabbed his ash covered lapels and kissed him. Shivers erupted down her spine at the heat and raw hunger that began to consume her as his lips moved against hers. Electricity filled her veins, but Cade suddenly pulled away from her and squeezed her shoulders.

His eyes blazed as he asked, "Are you out of your mind? What the hell were you thinking?"

It took Bridget a minute to get her brain working again. Quinn. The Bloodstone. Hundreds of soldiers were surrounding them. Out of the corner of her eye, she spotted Stellan piecing back together the wall with his magic. "She had the Bloodstone," Bridget said. "If she doesn't have that, she loses her reason to keep coming after you. She loses her *power*."

Even though anger marred his face, Cade's thumb brushed her neck again, tracing the outline of a bruise just beginning to form. "That doesn't mean you go after her on your own. She's already proved she doesn't need the Bloodstone to hurt you." His gaze flickered to her side, where her leather jacket and green sweater hid the scar that almost killed her. "How did she even manage to get you alone? Where's Nylah?"

Behind him, Cassia and Archer heatedly argued in hushed whispers as they walked toward them. Bridget didn't look away from Cade. She reached up and brushed a smear of dirt from his cheek, letting her fingers linger just a moment longer than necessary. She didn't want to stop touching him. "I sent her with Delphine and stayed back to help Cassia and Archer get people out of that apartment building. Quinn saw me from the forest. She called me Bee and then dared me to come after her."

Cade's brows furrowed. "She called you *Bee*? Has anyone ever called you that before?"

"No... And something about that name just got to me. I can't describe it."

*Bee* still echoed in her mind... like a truth that seemed to dangle just out of reach.

Archer came to a stop beside them, cracking his back with a wince before bending over his knees, winded. "Who are we talking about?"

"Quinn," Cade said flatly, shooting him a glare that could shatter glass.

"Well, she always was a fan of nicknames."

Cassia rolled her eyes. "Right. I almost forgot you were her little errand boy for a while."

Archer opened his mouth to respond, but Bridget shook her head, cutting through the tension. "It was more than that. The name felt too... personal." She sighed. Her gaze cut to Cade. "She also tried to take me with her."

The words hung heavy in the space between them.

*I'm sorry,* Bridget told him with her eyes. She'd almost been taken from Elyria just as quickly as she'd arrived. The slight downturn of his lips told her that he understood. A pinch stung her temple. A sign he'd also read her other silent plea. Once his presence filled her head, Bridget replayed her conversation with Quinn and how her behavior had kept erratically changing.

Cade narrowed his eyes. *Do you think someone was controlling her?*

Bridget raised her brows, *Don't you?*

*She was wearing your necklace. It shouldn't be possible.*

Blood drained from Bridget's cheeks. She hadn't even made the connection... and she'd seen the amethyst herself. Instead, she'd only focused on the explanation she *wanted* for the wild changes to Quinn's demeanor. She hadn't wanted to see what was happening to Quinn for what it really was: the consequences of magic. Suddenly, her head felt very light.

Was the same thing happening to her?

"Of course you ran straight off into danger. You were supposed to be *helping*," Cassia said.

Before blood could seep out of her nostril, Cade left her mind. He pulled her into her chest and pressed his lips to the top of her head. "You need to rest and we all should get back to the palace before our father finds out you're back. I just felt him a few blocks away."

Cassia grimaced. "At least a dozen soldiers have come to this area. He might already know."

Bridget eyed the quiet and still Elder Woods. Somewhere out there, the Wraith still lingered. She watched Stellan fix the last part of the wall. Loud enough for him to hear, she said, "That Wraith was a Tuathan."

Stellan rubbed the back of his neck and reluctantly joined them. "What makes you say that?"

"She had a heart to heart with Quinn in the Elder Woods," Cade answered.

Archer scoffed and reached to lift a section of Bridget's hair, revealing the bruise at her neck. "I still can't believe you let someone with one arm do that to you. So much for those self-defense classes."

Bridget elbowed him in the stomach. "Touch me again and I'll demonstrate the advanced course."

"Most Wraiths are Tuathan," Stellan cut in, his voice tight. "But now's not the time for a history lesson. Cade's right. We need to find Marin and get back to the palace before anyone realizes we're here yet."

Bridget noticed the way his eyes kept flickering to every open space, probably looking for Marin, but Quinn had looked so *smug* when she'd asked about the Wraiths. She couldn't let it go. "I just don't understand how that happened. Have some of the Shamans gone missing?"

Cassia eyed her curiously. "Our father banished them all once we got back from Cavamyne."

"He was afraid I would use one of them to send Finn or Delphine through the gate," Cade said. After a quick pause, he shrugged. "He wasn't wrong. But I don't think he left them unprotected. He brought one back to send Alexia through the gate."

"I didn't recognize the Wraith. It wasn't one of your *Shamans.*"

Stellan spit out the last word like it left a bad taste in his mouth.

"There are more Tuathans out there?" Archer asked.

Rolling his eyes, Stellan tried to shuffle. "Of course, there's more out there. Not everyone decided to stick around and protect the royal family."

"Where are they then?" Cade asked.

"I know you just found you're technically Tuathan, but we're not built with an internal radar for each other," Stellan replied through gritted teeth. "*I don't know.*"

Before the tension could splinter further, a voice cut through the ruins. "Found them."

Bridget breathed a sigh of relief when the sounds of Finn's voice broke the heated stare between Cade and Stellan. For someone who claimed Cade used to be his best friend, Stellan was acting extremely prickly with him. Through a maze of scattered debris, Finn led Castor and Marin over to them.

Stellan's eyes lit up. He ran over to Marin and wrapped her up in a giant hug. Until that moment, Bridget realized she'd never seen a real smile on

Marin's face. Despite the pallid color of her skin and frail countenance, she glowed. Finn's grin distracted her from the reunion. Bridget returned it and wrapped her arms around him.

"Aren't you a sight for sore eyes," he said.

Archer rapped a finger on his forearm. "No cast?"

Finn blinked at him. "I broke my arm almost six months ago."

Bridget couldn't believe it. Archer actually *blushed*. Clearing his throat, he turned to the sweating Warlock behind him. "Castor, handsome as ever. It's always a pleasure."

"I can't say the same about you."

Beside her, Cade burst out laughing. Bridget tried to keep a straight face. Until she noticed Cassia's disgusted stare.

"Seriously, what the hell happened to your hair?"

With a frown on his face, Cade's hand instinctively went to the white ends. Bridget raised a brow. "Did you not experience the same magical explosion we did right after we passed through the gate?"

"No, we did," Finn said. "It was not fun. It knocked out Marin for a solid five months. Cade for about a day. I'm guessing it was because they were closest to the blast."

"Something like that," Marin replied. She opened her mouth to say something, but her knees gave out. She fell into Stellan's chest. "Before anyone says anything, I'm fine. I can see it on your faces. I just need to rest."

Bridget crossed her arms and glared at Castor. "Do you ever check your email? Or answer your phone?"

"What are you talking about?" Castor frowned.

"I called practically every Bardot office I could find listed on the internet and tried to get in touch with you. I didn't think it was safe to use my real name, but—"

Castor's mouth fell open. "*You're* the stalker?"

Bridget punched Finn on the arm when he started laughing. Before she could explain further, Marin fell over again.

Jaw clenched, Stellan picked her up and cradled her to his chest. "We need to go. *Now.*"

Cade grabbed Bridget's hand. "Nylah and Delphine are probably wondering where we are," he said.

*And Alexia.* What in the world were they going to do with her? Cade didn't know about Nylah's *condition* yet. If that was even the right word for it. Alexia would be lucky to not end up in the dungeon again, especially when he found out they would need to leave for Andarre as soon as possible to cure her. Bridget's head spun. Wordlessly, she let Cade pull her in the right direction. There was time, she told herself. As long as they were together, things would be okay.

Before the trees disappeared out of sight, Bridget glanced one more time at the Elder Woods. She could have sworn she saw blue eyes and dark hair peeking at her through the trees.

# CHAPTER EIGHTEEN

Being back in Cade's room made Bridget's head spin. When she closed her eyes, it almost didn't feel like five months had gone by… that it was just yesterday she'd been sick in his bed or standing by the fireplace contemplating how to get back to the human realm. Back to the life she *had* wanted.

Now, she wasn't so sure what she wanted her future to be.

Nylah was safe and currently being tucked away in a secured room until morning. That was enough for now. In the morning, Stellan would have more answers for them… about Tuathan artifacts and those creatures. In the morning, it would be clearer what she was supposed to do.

When the heat radiating from the fireplace finally calmed her racing heart, she explored the tiny bits of newness scattered throughout Cade's room. New books were stacked on the table by his large bed. By the bathroom, a hole indented the dark blue wall, along with a cracked vase in the corner. Frowning, she wondered what had happened. Absentmindedly, she flipped through the loose papers on his desk. There was a map of the continent and a few sketches. Some even of her. In one of them, she was wearing an outfit she didn't recognize. A dark blue gown with a wide neckline and puffy sleeves.

The door squeaked open behind her. Bridget whirled around and stuffed the sketch underneath the others. Something about it raised goosebumps on her skin.

"Nylah is in the room across the hall with Delphine," Cade said, throwing his jacket on the edge of his bed. His white shirt underneath, covered in dirt and blood, was hanging on by a button. "She took the potion Echnav made for her, but not before she told me all about the carjacker you knocked to the ground in Boston. I definitely need to hear that story from your perspective, by the way." Cade slipped his shirt over his head. He used it to wipe some dirt off his face before he threw it to the corner of the room. "Since everyone is focused on what happened at the wall, no one saw us enter the palace. My father should be clueless until the morning."

"And Finn is with Alexia?" Bridget asked, trying not to stare too much at his exposed chest. Her fingers itched to touch him, especially when he came to stand less than an inch from her. Too close when the weight of five months still hung between them.

Cade nodded. "He'll stay outside her room until morning. I don't know why you don't want her back in the dungeon after what she did."

"She's trying to save her family… I guess I can relate."

Closing her eyes, Bridget leaned into Cade's touch when his thumb began to trace her cheekbone. The rest of his fingers tangled in her messy hair, loose from the tiny braid she'd tried to secure it in before crossing the gate. Heat traveled all the way to her toes, so simultaneously comforting and awakening that she almost swayed on her feet.

"What really happened out there in the woods?" Cade asked. "Why were you so affected by what Quinn said?"

Bridget searched his earnest gaze. Something inside her unlocked and the pressure to keep just how many dreams and visions she'd been having a secret deflated. "I've been hearing things," she admitted. "And seeing things."

"Like what?"

Despite the openness and belief in his voice, Bridget couldn't help but wryly crack, "Archer thinks it's magical induced trauma... That my brain has been permanently affected by too much magic and that it's causing me to imagine things."

*Like Quinn.*

She couldn't bring herself to say it.

Anger flickered over Cade's features. He gently grabbed her chin and forced her to look at him. "Archer has never lived through breaking a curse and been told he had a past life five hundred years ago."

Bridget let out a broken laugh. Leaning against his chest, she reveled in the safety of his arms. Just for a moment. Moving his right hand to her temple, Bridget said, "Try and look. That might be easier than explaining."

A quick pinch sliced across her forehead, then Cade was skipping through her memories. To make it easier, she tried to bring the dreams to the forefront of her mind. The ballroom. Vega stabbing her mysterious companion. The image of that same girl in the woods, taunting her by the gate. When a trickle of blood escaped Bridget's nose, Cade dropped his hand. The sudden departure of his presence left her head throbbing.

"And nothing ever changes?" Cade asked, grabbing her waist to keep her now trembling body steady. "It's the same room and girl, over and over?"

"Do you recognize her?"

"I don't... She said she was just like you. Maybe you knew her before..."

*Before*. In the life neither of them could remember. Unable to scrub the image of dripping metal claws from her mind, Bridget swallowed her fear. "You don't think it's *her*, do you?"

The idea that Vega had been messing with her mind from Iegorus had slowly been driving her crazy.

Cade was silent for a long moment. "I didn't feel anyone else," he said, brushing her hair out of her face. "But that doesn't mean she hasn't tried. If it happens again, I'll be here."

Unable to speak from the knot in her throat, Bridget nodded. She wanted to correct him. To say *when* it happened again. Because it would. The idea she would be back in the ballroom the moment she closed her eyes, even next to Cade, made her stomach twist.

Pushing it from her mind, Bridget picked up the backpack she'd brought with her and zipped it open. "I didn't take much with me when I left... Part of me wasn't sure we would even make it here. But this notebook goes into more detail. I wrote down every dream in it."

Bridget handed it to him and silently watched him thumb through a few of the pages. After a moment, he put it down on his desk.

"What did Echnav say?"

There was a strange tone in his voice, like the question was forced out of his mouth. Bridget titled her head. "I didn't tell him. I don't know why." Or maybe she did. The thought of having another person look at her like she was crazy, especially him, had kept her mouth shut. "His real name is Stellan, actually."

"Right. He did tell me that in a not so polite way in between fireball lessons at the wall."

Staring at the small grin blossoming on his face, the reality of where she was came crashing down on her. She was in Elyria. With *Cade*. Reaching up to trace the bags under his eyes, so similar to her own, emotion barreled up her spine. His hair was longer than she'd ever seen it and there was a new scar above his eyebrow. Dirt and smoke stained his face, evidence of what they'd just fought and lived through. Astraeus had been close to being overcome.

So why was there so much *joy* stirring in her gut?

"What's wrong?"

Bridget didn't realize she'd started crying until Cade's fingertips wiped away drops of hot liquid running down her cheeks. "I've spent months beating myself up for missing you and wanting to be here," she croaked. "And when I found out about everything… about you and us and why Cora came after me in the first place, I was so *relieved*. It suddenly made sense why I always felt so out of place and couldn't stop obsessing about what was going on here even after I was back with Nylah. But now that I'm here… did we do this?"

She gazed at the window. Though she couldn't see anything but a dark night sky, she knew chaos still plagued the city. That workers and soldiers were fortifying the wall and sorting through the debris.

"Are we the reason for those creatures? Did we bring an entire war to the future just so we could try to be together?"

"Bridget…"

He didn't have to finish his sentence for her to understand it was more than that. They'd needed more time to defeat Vega, according to Stellan. And resurrecting them in the future had ensured that. But she couldn't ignore a stirring in her gut that there was more to it. That even back then, she hadn't been able to let him go. Bridget let out a strangled laugh. "What does it say about me that I'm happy about it?"

Cade grabbed her chin and forced her to look at him. "Hey, I'm happy too. I've felt like a ghost these past few months. It was like my heart had completely stopped beating until I saw you come out of that forest."

Bridget's heart throbbed. "I know how you feel," she whispered. She'd barely felt alive since she'd woken up from her coma. But the knowledge about the past she'd learned from Stellan came crashing down on her. "What if me being here is wrong? Stellan tried to stop me from coming. He hid the gate from me. He only helped get us here because Nylah is sick and Marin needed help."

*He told me if I came back, people would suffer.*

The sentence wouldn't leave her throat. It *couldn't*. Not when the emotion swimming in Cade's eyes was tearing her to pieces.

"You being here could never be wrong," Cade argued. He grabbed her hand and placed it on the center of his chest. His heartbeat pounded under palm. "*This* isn't wrong. I love you. I've always loved you."

"I love you, too," Bridget choked. The room blurred as she placed a bruising kiss on his lips. She poured every ounce of longing she'd felt for him since she'd left and hoped it said everything she couldn't.

She wanted to scream in protest when he broke the kiss. Cade's labored breaths on her heated skin silenced her as he kept his lips a hairsbreadth away from her own. He looked almost as wrecked as she felt when he said, "I don't care if fate or a curse brought us together. I would still choose you. In every life. Every time. I don't need history to tell me that."

Bridget wasn't sure who moved first, but his kiss consumed her again. His tongue slid against hers, igniting a hunger that roared through her chest like wildfire. Every nerve lit up at once. Her hands roamed over the warm, solid lines of his back, nails scraping lightly along his skin. When his mouth found the hollow of her throat, a moan escaped her lips, unbidden and raw. His lips scorched a path from her jaw to her collarbone, each kiss like a brand against her skin.

Bridget tangled her hands in Cade's wild hair. Breathless, she shoved off her jacket, and he helped her tug free of the green sweater clinging to her damp skin. His hands slipped to her waist, trailing over bare skin. Possessive and reverent all at once.

Cade froze when his fingers brushed against the new scar stretching from the bottom of her rib cage to her breast. His fingers brushed against the jagged skin where a bullet had ripped her open.

Bridget stilled. Her heart climbed into her throat. For a beat, she thought about reaching for her shirt. About telling him not to look. But he was already lowering to his knees.

Softly, Cade pressed his lips to the edge of the scar. Then again. Slower. Firmer. His mouth trailed down the twisted seam. She watched him, body trembling, as his fingers skimmed over her ribs with aching tenderness. Heat surged to Bridget's core as she reached for him. Her fingers curled into the front of his torn shirt, tugging until he looked up at her again. The moment their eyes locked, electricity pulsed through her veins.

She didn't want gentleness right now. She wanted *him*. Like she always would. And not because they were finally safe, but because nothing about their world ever was.

When he started to rise, she met him halfway, capturing his mouth with hers in a kiss that was deeper. Fiercer. Her nails scraped across his shoulders, pulling him closer, until their bodies pressed flush together. Cade groaned low in his throat, hands gripping her waist like he might come undone if he let go.

Bridget spun them, backing him toward the bed until the backs of his legs hit the edge. He sat with a thud, but didn't stop touching her. His hands roamed her back and her hips. She climbed into his lap and kissed him again, teeth grazing his bottom lip before his hands slid into her hair and he deepened the kiss until the world tilted.

She wasn't sure when his shirt came off, only that her palms couldn't stop tracing the hard lines of his chest. His muscles flexed and twitched beneath her touch. Her breath caught when he shivered.

Cade's mouth brushed her shoulder, then lower. Bridget barely registered when he lifted her, gently laying her back against the cool sheets, his body hovering over hers. His fingers trembled slightly as they skimmed the edge of her ribs and the curve of her waist, like he was memorizing every piece of her.

The heat of his hands ignited something low in her belly. She arched into his touch, dizzy with the sensation of being completely unraveled. Cade kissed her again, this time slow and aching. And then, with one final breath, he entered her.

A rush of fire bloomed in her chest, stealing the air from her lungs. Flames licked through her veins, melting her into him until she wasn't sure where she ended and he began.

And then when all that remained was heat and breath, she let the fire consume her completely.

# Chapter Nineteen



Late morning was usually Cassia's favorite time to visit the library. The sun struck the stained-glass windows just right, scattering color across the tables. Today, though, if she found one more book cataloging the flowers of the Elder Woods, she was going to hurl it through the nearest window.

Not that shattering a centuries-old pane of stained glass would help. If anything, it would just invite the smoke and bruised clouds still clinging to the city inside, turning the library into another place she couldn't breathe... let alone read.

An ache traveled up her neck. She'd barely slept, unable to stop replaying the night in her head. Every time she closed her eyes, she felt the heat of the explosion. Saw Castor's bleeding face above her. Watched a monstrous beast climb the city wall. She knew she should be out helping with the clean-up... or maybe even checking in with her father, not that he would spare the time to assess the situation with her. Still, spending hours looking for the origins of a book shouldn't be high on her priority list.

Cassia glanced at the book again. The one she called for when she'd pulled on Castor's magic. It's dirty, burgundy cover had no title. The pages were filled with a language and sketches she didn't understand. But she couldn't help but obsess over it. Why *this* book?

And why did it almost spark underneath her fingertips every time she touched it?

Climbing up another ladder, she compared the spines of books on the extremely dusty top shelf to the one sitting on the table below. None of them matched. Growling, she grabbed a particularly heavy one and slammed it toward the ground. It hit the marble floor with an ear-splitting thud.

"I hope it's nothing I did."

Nearly falling off the ladder at the unexpected intrusion, Cassia swiveled her head to meet Castor's amused gaze a few feet below her. "You have to stop sneaking up on me."

"I promise I don't mean to," he said, holding out a hand to help her climb down. Cassia ignored it, too afraid that his touch might make her pull from him again. It had been different with him than with Cade. She'd brought Castor to his knees... she'd weakened him. That was the last thing she wanted to do. When she put a good distance between them, Castor frowned. "What are you doing?"

Cassia held up the mysterious book. She tried to ignore the buzzing that went up her arm. "I'm trying to figure out where this book came from. It's the one from the other day."

*That she used him to get.* She wondered if Castor's heard her unspoken words. When he took the book from her hands, it didn't seem to affect him like her. The longer he flipped through the pages, the more the crease between his eyes deepened. "What is this? Do you know which language this is?"

"I have no idea." Cassia sighed. "So you see my predicament. I figured it came from here. It can't be the only one like it, right? There's a I on the spine."

Wordlessly, he shut the book and traced the numeral with his finger. Cassia crossed her arms when the silence between became stifling. She wished he would say something or have some brilliant idea about what the book was about like he usually did. Instead, she had no idea what he was thinking. It bothered her more than it should.

Castor caught her watching him. His dark eyes roamed over her face. "Did you sleep?"

A traitorous heat filled her cheeks. Cassia resisted the urge to fluff her hair or pat away the purple under her eyes just so he would stop looking so closely.

He took a step toward her.

She took a step back.

"Cassia..." Castor sighed, a hint of frustration layered in his words.

"Maybe this book will be useful for something," Cassia blurted. Lack of sleep had the truth spilling from her lips. "I didn't do anything earlier. I just stood there... Like a coward."

She couldn't help but wince. It's what she'd been told she was her entire life. The tiny little word shouldn't make her want to crawl up in a hole and die.

"It's fine," Castor said. "And it's not like you did nothing. You helped those people trapped in their apartments, didn't you?"

Cassia let out a strangled laugh. "Barely. That idiotic Warlock did most of the work. I have these powers. Apparently. I could have used them."

She had — for a moment. Long enough to save Cade. But the shock on his face after had made her too scared to even try again. What if she'd accidentally drained him like she had Castor? Astraeus could have ended up in ashes.

"You don't know how. Which is why—"

Cutting off his excuses, she snapped, "That doesn't matter."

"Yes, it does."

Castor was in front of her now, too close, for comfort. She could almost feel his breath on her face. Why did he have to make her feel like the world was upside down every time he got near? Clearing her throat, she argued, "Bridget didn't have any trouble throwing herself into danger to save Cade."

"Bridget doesn't think before she acts," Castor replied tiredly. "It's gotten her in trouble many, many times."

"At least she knows what she wants," Cassia mumbled, mostly to herself. But *of course* Castor didn't miss it. He didn't seem to miss anything.

"And you don't?"

This time, she really did feel his breath on her cheek. For a second, she let herself imagine the brief hint of longing in his gaze was real. Shivers wracked through her body. Cassia couldn't keep her eyes from the curve of his lips. A tiny birthmark sat on the corner, only noticeable up close. It was one of her favorite things about it.

So maybe she *did* know what she wanted. What she lacked was the guts to act on it.

"I know what I want."

That damned Warlock's voice carried like a grating siren to their spot in the library corner. Suddenly feeling like she was suffocating, Cassia rushed backward. Only to hit a table. The hard wood smacked into the back of her thigh, sending a slice of pain down her leg. She gritted her teeth and pretended like it didn't happen.

"A different room. You would think a palace would have thicker walls," Archer said, appearing from around the corner with Finn.

"It was one night," Finn replied. "Try living with them for a few months."

"You're always welcome to go back to the dungeon," Cassia snapped, hoping she wasn't as red as she felt.

Archer raised a brow. "You know, your ray of sunshine brother was a lot scarier when he..."

With a light cough, Finn elbowed him. "I think we interrupted something."

Damn emotion reader.

"No," she and Castor said at the same time. Cassia hated that his quick answer made her stomach twist. And since when had those two become so chummy? "What are you two doing in here?"

Finn gave her a knowing look. "We're looking for—"

"Me."

Echnav, or Stellan, or whatever the hell he was going by now, emerged by a far shelf. Like an invisible veil had been cast off of him. Cassia tightly rolled her lips together, remembering the same camouflage trick from when he'd been one of her tutors. "What the hell," she hissed. "How long have you been there?"

Stellan's only answer was a slight upturn of his lips. Did every single one of her conversations with Castor have to be overheard or seen by someone in her vicinity?

Cassia glared at them all. "So what is this? Another secret meeting that I didn't get an invitation to?"

"I summoned them to the library because you were already in here," Stellan said. "The information we need to discuss is vital to you, too. It's clear Vega knows she has a foothold. The Wraith could have only been created with her help. We've already wasted too much time."

Well, Cassia couldn't really argue with that. And at least this time, she wasn't fighting to be included.

Archer sighed. "Yeah, can we stop with the head invasions? A note under the door would have sufficed."

"A foothold?" Castor asked.

Stellan pinched the bridge of his nose. "Where's Bridget and Cade?"

"I know... we're late."

Hand in hand, Cade and Bridget peeked around the far library shelf. After a quick glance over his shoulder, her brother gently nudged Bridget forward, never once letting go of her hand. For once, Bridget's hair wasn't pulled up and the sweater she wore, oversized and clearly from the human realm, was a faded navy with cracked white lettering that spelled out something Cassia couldn't quite make out. It clashed horribly with the elegance of the palace, but who was she to judge?

But her mouth almost fell open at the almost overnight transformation of her brother. He looked so damned *happy*. Part of her was a little jealous. She snuck a glance of Castor out of the corner of her eye. He was now a few feet from her. Which was good, she told herself. That was the way it was supposed to be.

"Most of the guards are back on the grounds. We had to take the long way," Cade muttered. "Could we have picked somewhere a little more inconspicuous?"

To Cassia's surprise, Stellan glowered at him. With a flick of his head, he directed them toward the back shelf where she knew Cade's favorite secret room was hidden. When the others followed him, she let herself fall to the end of line. That's probably where they wanted her anyway.

"Someone's looking perky this morning," Archer said to Bridget.

Even though she couldn't see it, Cassia knew Bridget rolled her eyes. "I actually slept without any dreams last night."

Archer snorted. "That's surprising. I didn't think you'd slept at all based on the noises I heard around breakfast time."

"We didn't need to know that," Finn muttered.

Cassia seconded his opinion.

With her free hand, Bridget shoved the blond Warlock. Laughing, Archer wrapped his arm around her shoulders and kissed the top of her head. Cassia watched him whisper something in her ear. Seconds later, Bridget elbowed him hard in the stomach.

Magic pinched her temple.

*You're unusually quiet.*

Cassia tried to shove away her brother's presence. He was the last person she wanted to know about her sudden, lonely spiraling thoughts. *Since when do you care?*

She barely registered Cade's surprise before he was gone.

"Where's Nylah?" Bridget asked, a hint of panic in her voice.

"She's with Delphine watching over our favorite person," Archer said. "Can you believe she asked to stay with her instead of me?"

"I can," Castor whispered to Cassia, holding open the loose shelf so she could climb through easily. She couldn't stop herself from releasing a giggle.

Cassia slipped into the study and claimed an empty seat by the window. Sunlight streamed through the glass, warming her back and casting lazy golden beams across the wooden floor. To her surprise, Castor came to stand beside her. Without a word, he leaned against the slanted roof, his shoulder brushing the stone wall. The sunlight slanted across his features, highlighting the angles of his face and casting his deep brown skin in a soft, golden glow.

Cassia balled her fists. She really needed to stop staring.

At the other end of the long wooden table, Cade was murmuring something to Bridget. Whatever he said, it made her laugh. Cade grinned back, a little crooked and helpless. Whatever secret passed between made both of their faces soften. She wasn't the only one who noticed.

Stellan strode over and slammed a thick pile of papers onto the table, scattering a few of them across the polished surface. Cassia tilted her head, taking in the sight of their old tutor — relative, apparently, next to Cade. Now that she was really looking, she couldn't believe she'd missed just how similar their jawlines were and how the slope of their noses matched like mirrored edges.

But for all their resemblance, their differences were louder. Cade, all shadows, with unruly dark hair and a storm behind his eyes. Stellan, composed and bright, his every move calculated and smooth as silk. One dark, one light. Two sides of a very complicated coin.

A muscle in Cade's jaw twitched. "How's Marin?"

Busy unwrapping a map, Stellan didn't look up. "Better. But I told her to stay away today. She needs more rest." Whatever he found on the map, he must have not liked, because he suddenly shoved it to the side. "We don't have much time. And there's only so much I know."

Finn raised a brow.

"The cost of the curse," Bridget said. "He's lost some vital memories. Mostly about Vega."

"Convenient," Castor muttered, messing with a loose string on his coat. "Why don't we start with how you appeared in the Elder Woods? There's no gate there."

Leaning over, Stellan drummed his fingers on the table. "Okay, the Tuathan artifacts I can do... For the most part. They're riddled throughout history enough that most of the legends surrounding them don't specifically apply to Vega or what happened at Cavamyne."

Castor pinched the bridge of his nose. "Aren't those a myth?"

Bridget shook her head. "Apparently they're very real... not that I know anything about them. Nylah had one." She glanced at Cade. "That you gave to her."

"The stone?" Cade frowned. When everyone waited for an answer, he lightly stuttered, "I swear I just thought it was a regular rune. Right after I'd made the decision to go to the human realm, I went to the vault. I wasn't sure how magic would work there... so I knew I would need more than just my pendant if someone ever came looking for me."

Finn barked a laugh. "And you just happened to choose the one rune in that entire mountain that is actually the stuff of legend? Only you, man."

Cassia tried not to glare at him. The reminder of her brother's actions almost four years ago and *why* it had happened left her chest stinging.

"There was something about it," Cade murmured, suddenly looking lost in a memory. "Something familiar. Like I'd seen it before. The moment I saw it, I knew it was the one I had to take… I tried to use it once. Right after the Shaman found us at the Halloween party. Nothing I tried worked." After a long pause, he cemented his gaze on Bridget. "I gave it to Nylah in case something happened to us. I knew if a Shaman or another Fae saw her with a rune, they would hesitate long enough for her to get away. I never expected…"

Head spinning, Cassia cut him off. "Okay, we get it. You didn't pay attention to anything in this library while we were growing up. If you had, you wouldn't have recklessly taken an unknown rune from the vault across the gate."

Cade glowered at her. "Like you ever—"

"Can we get back to the main reason we're all stuck in this stuffy excuse of a room?" Cassia snapped. "Every history book I've ever read theorizes that the Tuathan stone can open and create gates."

"And your father has been keeping it to himself all these years?" Castor asked speculatively. "Is that why Quinn tried to blast her way into Astraeus? Are there more here?"

Stellan shook his head. "Based on the timing of Quinn's attack, I assume her target was Cade. Without him, she can't bring back the Sanguis. The stone was the only artifact left in Astraeus. Deckard had no idea it was in the vault," he said. "Believe me, he would have already used it for his own advantages by now."

"Okay but no one else has brought up the biggest issue with all this," Bridget interjected. "It wasn't Stellan that brought us here. *Nylah* used it. She's human. Us and magic usually don't mix."

"The stone…" Stellan choked. Taking a deep breath through his nose, he clenched his fists. Hoarsely, he spit out, "Only someone with pure intentions can wield it, even if they're human. It's how it was designed. As long as it remains in her possession and her intentions stay the same, it will only obey her."

Alarm trickled down Cassia's spine. Blood dripped out of Stellan's nose, like the admission had cost him a great deal. There had to be more the curse was costing him than just his memories. Not only was magic taking a toll on a Tuathan rare, but he spoke of the artifacts like they were living, breathing entities.

Archer loudly snapped his fingers. Cassia jumped. She'd almost forgotten the exasperated Warlock in the corner. "We already went over most of this back in your Lincoln Log cabin. There are four. They all sound equally dangerous. We happen to have one of them. We still need to find the others. What else do we need to know?"

Cassia couldn't help but agree with him. Just a little. They already had one of them. It didn't matter what the others were or what they did. The sooner they could find them, the sooner Quinn's use of the Bloodstone and assault on Elyria would stop. It had to. Out of the corner of her eye, she watched dark clouds swirl in the sky. Even through the window, the air outside seemed heavy.

"The more we know about the artifacts, the easier they will be to find," Finn argued. "There's so much lore surrounding the artifacts, even I'm not sure what's true."

Cassia watched a bead of sweat form on Stellan's temple. If no one helped him explain anything soon, he was going to pass out. She cleared her throat. "It all starts with the lake, right?" Ignoring Cade's stunned stare, she quietly continued, "It's rumored Tuathans received their power from an enchanted lake. They proved themselves and the land rewarded them... at least, I think so."

Stellan ran a trembling hand through his hair, leaving the normally slicked back blonde strands slightly ruffled. He gave Cassia a quick, grateful half-smile. "Even I don't know exactly how the artifacts came to be. That happened long before our time. All I know is what we figured out while we tried to beat Vega to them."

Bridget and Cade froze. Cassia watched them share another meaningful look before they locked eyes with Stellan. Their unspoken conversation sent a wave of anxiety up Cassia's spine. The weight of their history stifled the air. Would she ever be able to wrap her head around the fact that her brother and Bridget had lived a whole life over five hundred years ago?

Beside her, Castor cursed under his breath, his frustration clearly visible. She wondered if the next question pressing her mind was the same as his.

Would any of them ever be able to find out the truth about it?

Bridget's throat bobbed. Her voice was raspy as she asked, "How much about that can you remember?"

"It started when…" Stellan flinched. Closing his eyes, he balled his fists. "Damn it. Okay… let me go a little forward. There's only so much Marin was able to break free and some of those memories still want to stay locked up. Eventually, Cade concluded that the first Tuathans decided the power the lake had given them wasn't enough. They channeled more magic from the lake into four artifacts… to be an endless source of power. For any creature. Even humans."

"But magic is unpredictable," Cade said, crossing his arms. "The artifacts took on a mind of their own, didn't they?"

Cassia took Stellan's silence as a yes. After a moment, he nodded. "If you want to channel their power… you have to pass their tests. A fact we didn't understand until it was too late."

"*Tests*?" Finn asked.

"Or price. Whatever you want to call it," Stellan replied stiffly. "If you haven't already figured it out, we didn't get much of a chance to test our theories."

"Which artifact did Vega want?" Castor asked. "Or was it all of them?"

Bridget's cat-like eyes cut to Stellan before she sat her hip on the edge of the table. "We think it's the crown. Stellan said it could raise the dead. Apparently, it went missing around the same time Cade and I died."

The last words fell out of Bridget's mouth in a quiet, slow cadence, like she still didn't quite believe them. A muscle in her brother's jaw twitched as he rubbed Bridget's lower back. Cassia couldn't stop the twinge of sympathy that sprung in her gut. Still, did they *ever* stop touching?

"And you think they had something to do with it?" Castor asked Stellan.

"I think *she* did."

Cassia scoffed. "Of course, she did. Leaving chaos in her wake is Bridget's specialty. What about the others? The sword hasn't been seen since around that time either."

"That one is in Andarre," Archer said. "The joy that is Alexia helped us figure that one out."

"It was taken by another Tuathan there for safekeeping. It's the first artifact we found and it…" Suddenly, Stellan bent over and coughed roughly. Bridget tried to reach out for him, but he waved her away. Droplets of blood were splattered across his hand. "*Don't*. I need to get out what I can. The sword…" Stellan struggled for a moment. "It's the first one we found. It's how we figured out that once someone passes an artifact's test, it only answers to them."

Cassia's stomach twisted.

"He'll be fine," Castor whispered in her ear, his hand on her lower back.

But Cassia's gaze was no longer on Stellan… it was on *Bridget*. She'd paled considerably. Once Cade gripped her hand, she seemed to find her voice. "It's Cade. That's why this whole plan to bring us back was created… Because it has to be him."

The slight glow radiating behind her brother's eyes told Cassia he was trying to search Bridget's head for answers. The crease between his brows deepened with concern. Without thinking, she pulled on the heat radiating from Castor's hand, her only thought the desire to find out exactly what Bridget knew. Before she could blink, an intoxicating spark of magic funneled through her veins. Cade's presence flooded her mind.

*What did she see?* Cassia demanded.

Before Cade could respond, she tugged on a memory that he was analyzing. Bridget's memory. It was dark, and hazy. More dreamlike than real. He was in a dark forest holding a sword that glowed. A beast almost identical to the one outside the wall charged at him.

With a gasping breath, Castor removed his hand. The image she'd been analyzing disappeared with a searing pop.

Cade's eyes narrowed at them both. Had he realized he hadn't invited her in?

"And the scroll?" Finn asked. "That one is even less documented than the crown."

Stellan rifled through the same papers, then roamed his eyes over a far bookshelf. "From what I recall, that one alluded us, as well. There might be something in a book that I remember, but—"

"This is just your theory, though, right?" Cade challenged, effectively stopping Stellan's perusal. "You don't actually remember what Vega was after. Why do you assume it's the artifacts? She was powerful enough to almost decimate the Tuathans. She completely destroyed Cavamyne. Why would she need them?"

"Because of who she is. It's why she's obsessed with blood magic," Stellan answered, his mouth falling into a hard line.

"A psychopath?" Archer chided.

Stellan's throat bobbed. Silence pierced Cassia's ears as she waited for him to answer. Finally, he said, "A Druid."

# CHAPTER TWENTY

"The book in Boston. It was about Druids. That's why you asked me why I had it," Bridget said, looking stunned.

But she wasn't the only one. The entire world seemed to tilt on its axis as Cassia processed his words. *A Druid*. Just like she was supposed to be. Apparently. If Castor was right. Blood drained from her face as she stared at her hands. Vega had committed so many atrocities... and now she was the same as her?

Finn's brows furrowed. "But the Sanguis are Blood *Witches*. That's a pretty big key word."

"And Druids don't exist anymore," Cade added.

Castor's stare burned a hole in the side of Cassia's face. She didn't dare look at him. Her lungs already felt like they were collapsing in her chest. If there was any sort of pity or *fear*, she would die.

Stellan's gaze flickered to hers.

*He knew.*

Cassia dug her nails into her sides and used all her strength to keep her face as neutral as possible.

"Why do you think that is?" Stellan asked Cade, finally taking his eyes off of her. "I was knocked out for over four decades after I cast that curse in Cavamyne. When I woke up, walls were already being built around every city. Humans were essentially exiled to Andarre. After that, it was years before people were able to travel freely between each region. The Regina Torneamentum started because they wanted a controlled way of allowing interaction."

"All of this division started because they wanted to keep Witches and Tuathans apart?" Castor asked. Cassia tried not to flinch at the sound of his voice. "That's essentially what a Druid is, correct? We didn't try to completely erase them from history in Tafari, but they weren't exactly a hot topic."

A frustrated hum emitted from Stellan's chest. "Believe me, if I had been awake, I wouldn't have let them decide to keep the next generations in the dark. Look, the Sanguis were given their name to set them apart from the Druids that didn't turn to blood magic for more power. Not all of them are evil... And the Sanguis aren't the sole proprietors of blood magic. It can be performed by any of the species, but it's extremely intoxicating and deadly to everyone but a Druid. Magic may be fickle, but it loves balance. For everything it gives..."

"It takes," Bridget finished. "Quinn said the Wraiths are what happens when there's nothing left to give."

Stellan nodded. "When you're no longer willing to pay the price, it will take your soul." The statement seemed to suck the air out of the room. He continued, "Druids are different, though. They're unique in the sense that they're a combination of *all* the species, even humans. Because of that, they don't have their own magic. That bit of human blood, mixed with everything else, somehow nulls their natural abilities and creates this perfect storm of hunger. If they want to wield magic, they have to take it."

Cassia couldn't breathe.

"From blood?" Cade asked.

"Not necessarily. Everything alive has a bit of magic in it. Before the Sanguis, Druids lived in balance with their land in Suza." Stellan pulled out a map from a pile on the table. He unrolled it and pointed to an unmarked land in the southwest corner of the continent. The one she'd been told her entire life was completely dead. "It was the perfect give and take... Until they wanted too much. That's when some started turning to blood magic. While it physically doesn't affect them like it does Tuathans or Witches, their price is that it destroys everything around them."

The patch of land screamed at her. Cassia wanted to melt into the floor and disappear from existence. She didn't want to be a Druid. She *couldn't*. It wasn't her fault that her twin happened to be full of Tuathan blood and that somewhere in time one of their ancestors decided to breed with a Nymph, completely screwing her over. Plus, her ancestors had basically separated all the species to guarantee she didn't exist. Yet, here she was. Screwing up things again even when she didn't try. Too lost in her spiraling thoughts, Cassia barely heard Stellan's next statement.

"Vega's quest for more power destroyed Suza. It destroyed Cavamyne. It only makes sense that she wanted an endless source."

Cade sighed in resignation. "The artifacts."

"The Wraiths want the endless source, too. They're addicted, but they probably think it will save them," Bridget said. "Is that what's happening to Marin? Is she turning into one?"

Stellan's entire countenance shifted. Simmering rage began to brew on his features. "It's different with Marin. She's half-human. The price is already greater for her. In fact, it will most likely kill her, but she took it to protect Cade." He glared at her brother. "You should have known better to mess with blood magic."

Color drained from Cade's face. "You're the one who had a whole journal of blood magic spells hidden under your bed," he growled. "If you had told me about *any* of this earlier, things would be different."

Bridget hopped off the table and tried to stand between them, but neither one batted an eye at her presence.

"I was entrusted with that book to—"

"Cass?"

Finn's gasping question silenced the room. Wincing, he rubbed his chest as he stared at her.

Cassia inhaled sharply. Her emotions were suffocating him. She'd been so lost in her thoughts, so preoccupied with her own shame spiral of what it meant to be a Druid, she hadn't realized anyone in the room might be paying attention to her. Even though Stellan had just told them not all Druids were evil, a bubble of fear rose in her stomach.

"It's nothing," she stammered. Her cheek muscles quivered as she tried to keep a straight face.

It didn't work. Before she could stop him, Cade's presence invaded her mind. He took no qualms in filtering through her thoughts to find what he was looking for, despite the mental hurdles she tried to throw at him. Just as needles began to prick her scalp, she felt his rush of surprise.

"You're a Druid."

To her, he said, *I guess that explains what happened at the wall. Which one of our ancestors do you think was a Nymph?*

Cassia curled her lips into a grimace. Everyone was now staring at her wide-eyed, except for Castor and Stellan. The two shared a look, one she wished she could interpret, but the rush of relief pounding through her veins was almost too strong to control. There wasn't any fear emanating from the echoes of Cade's mind. Only pure shock and curiosity.

"How is that possible?" Bridget asked.

Since they were still connected, Cassia became lumped into Cade's infiltration of the others. She watched him share the memory of what she'd done at the wall and how she had channeled him, along with the *private* conversation she'd had with Castor in the training room.

Without thinking, she pulled on his power and severed his connection with the others. *Would you stop?*

*It was the best way to explain.*

Cassia scowled at him. She doubted that. After a moment, the needles pressed harder into her skull. While she enjoyed her little talks with her brother, she sometimes hated it when he left their connection open for too long because eventually, his thoughts and feelings began to follow. Right now, the sheer amount of calculating and planning going on in the background of his mind was giving her a headache. And the underlying guilt of Marin's condition worsened it. Cassia could barely hear the others over it.

"Well, I'm for one glad we have someone like Vega on our side," Archer said. "Fight fire with fire, as they say."

Finn frowned. "They do?"

The words made Cassia flinch. Castor's hand grazed her lower back. If she was going to learn to control her supposed *hunger* for magic, he really needed to stop touching her. Something about his had been more intoxicating to her than when she'd taken Cade's. Sometimes, it felt like she was craving it.

Cade winced. Apparently, she wasn't the only one drowning in the other's problems. *It doesn't seem like you're handling this well.*

*Would you be if you were just told you were destined to destroy everything around you?*

*We won't let that happen.*

Finally, with a searing pop, Cade was gone. His optimism wasn't contagious. In fact, she wanted to throttle him over it. When had anything in their life gone her way?

Cassia jumped when Castor touched her again.

"Are you alright?" he whispered.

Wordlessly, she stepped away from him. After being in Cade's head, her blood was already roaring with the need to recharge.

Cade rolled out another map. "I think it's pretty obvious that we need to find those artifacts before Vega does. Bridget and I will go to Andarre. When we're there, we'll get the sword. Castor—"

"No one is going anywhere," Stellan declared, reigniting the tension in the small room. "Your father just shut down the port in Aphira. Even if there was a ship ready to go, it would take us days to get there. Marin is sick. Quinn is still out there. The best course of action is to stay in Astraeus until we can get the Bloodstone back from her. That guarantees—"

"Nylah has to go to Andarre. Whatever you brewed for her is just a band-aid. What if you forget to whip a batch one day?" Cade asked, his voice low and lethal. "And last time I checked, no one had put you in charge."

Bridget's shoulders tensed. "Cade..."

Stellan's jaw flexed. "I'm the oldest one here. I'm the only one with any real experience with Vega or the Sanguis in this room. I'm the one who's seen what the future holds if you leave Elyria right now." His gaze swept across the room, landing hard on Cade. "Trust me, it doesn't end well. Do you think just because you're the prince we should all listen to you? Guess what, you're not the only one of those in this room."

Castor raised his brows. "I trust Cade's judgement. Besides—"

"You left," Cade snapped. "You disappeared for three years without even bothering to tell us the truth about anything. You didn't even want to come back here. If it was up to you, we would still be in the dark right now. We're going to Andarre."

Cassia locked eyes with Bridget. There was a plea for help there, but words got lodged in her throat. Something ancient swirled in the air. There was too much history loaded in Stellan's statements. She couldn't help but think their confrontation was a long time coming.

"What do you expect to tell your father? If you leave, he'll know Bridget's here. He'll know about Nylah. I don't think he'll like the interruption to his wedding plans for you."

The books on the shelves around them trembled in place. Finn backed Archer closer to the door.

"It's time. I'm through playing his games."

"Is it?" Stellan asked, a ghost of a laugh on his face. "The second he knows, every responsibility you've avoided comes crashing down on you."

"I can handle it," Cade snarled.

"I know you can't. Your little stunt with the gate and blood magic proves that." Stellan looked Cade up and down. "You're not *him*. Not the Cade I knew. Right now, I'm not sure you ever will be."

Cade and Stellan stood chest to chest.

"Take me to my father," Cade said, his voice low and lethal.

Cassia's stomach swooped to the floor. Their father was unpredictable. Every time they truly fought, a major life change happened. She didn't think she could take another one.

Cade grabbed Stellan's arm. The Shaman laughed.

"Do you think because you've seen me do the spell a few times, you know how to? Your powers—"

A crack almost exploded Cassia's eardrum. She covered her face from the sheer force of magic that exploded throughout the room. After it passed, she looked up. Cade and Stellan were gone.

"Where did they go?" Bridget demanded from the floor. Finn and Archer helped her up.

Cassia couldn't take her eyes off the spot where they'd been standing. Cade was confronting their father. She couldn't shake the image of their fight four years ago from their mind. The next day, Cade had left. Her father had changed. Elora had changed. Everything—

"Where's your father right now?" Castor's hand on her arm brought her back to reality. The sound of her own heartbeat almost drowned out his voice.

Bridget's anxious face appeared in front of her. She hadn't even seen her move. "You have to have some idea."

It took a moment for Cassia to find her voice. "Probably his study. He always spends the afternoons there when he's stressed."

They were all out the door faster than Cassia could blink. Castor grabbed her hand and pulled her along behind him. She could barely keep up with his quick steps. Her mind wouldn't stop spinning. The others were arguing and shouting things at each other, but the voices sounded like gibberish.

A blur of rooms and hallways turned into her father's study. It was hidden behind a portrait of her great grandfather. His sly smile and twinkling eyes had always intrigued her. Now, as she looked up at it, he seemed to mock her with secrets. Shouting echoed from inside. Wordlessly, Cassia ran her finger down the painting's gold frame until she found a latch.

She was shoved through the tiny opening before the portrait had even opened an inch. Her father's study was darker than she expected. Usually, sunlight illuminated her father's study and the floor to ceiling windows and glass roof shimmered with the afternoon sun. But dark clouds swirled over the heads. For once, the lamps in the corner were on. They flickered every time her father spoke. His tan skin looked purple as he glared at Cade and Stellan. Cassia didn't think he could get any redder. Until his gaze zeroed in on Bridget, who had stumbled in behind her.

"You," he hissed, raising his hand.

Before any magic left his fingertips, his hand was slammed into his desk by a gusting wind.

"You're not touching her," Cade growled, his eyes ablaze with growing power. The morganite pendant under his shirt glowed a dark orange.

Their father shot out of his seat. "I am your *father* and I—"

With a flick of his wrist, Stellan had him wrapped in an invisible rope. Their father snarled and struggled against the binds. Stellan tightened them. "It's time, Deckard. I know you thought you could outsmart fate, but it's here. It's time to accept it. There's nothing more you can do."

"What's he talking about?" Bridget asked, trying to get closer. Finn pushed her behind him.

Cassia's throat was a hard knot. "I don't know."

"Cassia, maybe you should take a step back," Castor said, tugging on her arm. Since they'd arrived at the study, he hadn't strayed more than a few inches from her. "You don't have to be here."

"Yes... I do."

There was something in her father's eyes she'd never seen before. Something he was trying to hide, but failing.

Fear.

His throat bobbed as his gaze flickered between Stellan and Cade. Cassia wasn't sure which one was making him nervous. Still, he continued to thrash against the invisible binds. At his hip, his obsidian dagger practically vibrated from the power he was trying to channel.

"Elyria is on the brink of ruin," her father bellowed. "War is coming. It might already be here. I'm doing what I can to prevent it and make sure the continent stays as stable as possible." His fiery gaze cut to Cade. "And you think running off to Andarre with your girlfriend is the answer? Remember, we have a deal."

"Do we?" Cade narrowed his eyes, then cocked his head toward Stellan. "If he's to be believed, I'm technically already married. There is no deal."

Beside her, Cassia heard Bridget choke. Her father glowered.

Cade barked a humorless laugh. "Which you already know, apparently. I should have known. You already had Stellan camouflage me at birth to hide who I was. Have you ever told me the truth about anything?"

The slight break in his voice pierced a hole through Cassia's heart.

Her father let out a roar. The binds around his feet broke free. "I did all of that to protect you. I've shown you what she'll do."

A bead of sweat rolled down Stellan's temple as he tried to keep her father contained. Cade noticed and sent a wave of roaring wind at his father. He stumbled back a step. The whiskey glass and pens on his desk slammed to the ground.

"It's not going to happen," Cade hissed.

A drop of blood escaped Cade's nose. Cassia's stomach swooped to the floor. He was going to push himself too hard to prove a point.

"In every vision, it's never changed. Not once," their father hoarsely choked out.

Bridget broke free from Finn and darted toward Cade. Stellan raised a hand and blocked her from reaching him. She glared at him and pushed at the barrier, even as Archer and Finn tried to pull her back again. The wind around Stellan and Cade had picked up tremendously, swirling around them like a terrible storm. Cassia could almost taste the magic buzzing around them. The air was heavy with it. Her blood began to sing.

"What is it?" Bridget demanded, having to shout to be heard. "Cade, what will I do?"

Cassia saw her brother hesitate before a vision flooded her senses. She grabbed Bridget's hand, just in case, but she had a feeling Cade was unloading it on everyone. It felt too messy, too raw, like he was struggling to share it and maintain control.

*They were no longer in Astraeus, but Cavamyne. Cassia could tell by the runes in front of her. She'd seen them sketched in a book. Cade and Bridget stood in a low pit, between two stone thrones. They circled each other. The sword in Bridget's hand gleamed in the moonlight. All of a sudden, Cade stopped. The moment he did, Bridget thrust the sword through the center of his chest.*

Cassia struggled for air when it finally ended. Her fingers clawed at her chest. She'd felt the sword as if it'd struck her. That *couldn't* happen. Cade couldn't die. And Bridget would never—

"No," Bridget gasped.

Cassia had forgotten she'd taken her hand. It trembled in her grasp. She squeezed it tightly as she watched Bridget stare at Cade in horror. Her brother glanced over his shoulder at them. The wind lessened slightly as the power radiating in his eyes flickered.

"I would never..." Bridget rasped.

Cassia silently agreed. She'd seen what the two of them would do for each other. She couldn't fathom a world where the vision would ever come true.

"Enough," Stellan hissed. The blue tattoos snaking around his neck turned the brightest blue. "You're not in control of the future. How many times have I told you our visions aren't to be trusted?"

Cassia narrowed her eyes. But hadn't he been asking them to trust him based on his visions almost the entire time? What made *this* one so different?"

"She needs to go," her father hissed, breaking free his right hand. He raised his dagger.

Cade stepped forward, fire behind his eyes. He snarled, "It doesn't matter what time or place, I am her and she is mine. We will not be separated."

With a roar, the magic that had been building in his chest unfurled.

The barrier Stellan had cast between them shattered like glass. Their father flew backwards, slamming into the stone wall with a sickening thud. A second later, the glass ceiling above them fractured with a deafening crack. Cassia barely had time to react before shards of crystal began to rain from the sky. Cade collapsed to his knees, power still pulsing around him in unstable waves. Bridget dove toward him without hesitation, reaching for him.

Cassia felt Castor's hand on her head, attempting to push her down.

But instead of fighting the magic rushing toward her, like she usually did, she embraced it. Cassia let it fill her veins. When it reached her fingertips, she let out her own roar. The shards never touched the ground.

Instead, they disintegrated midair, turned to dust by the raw power pulsing from her outstretched hands. Sand whirled across the chamber like a miniature cyclone. Cassia lifted her face to meet her father's stare. Behind the fury and disgust in his eyes, she caught the flicker of pride he couldn't quite hide.

When the chaos quieted, everyone raised their heads tentatively. Her father struggled to get to his feet. Betrayal and rage were clear on his face.

"It looks like I'm the only one trying to save my son." For once, his full attention turned to her. "I tried to save you, too."

Cassia inhaled sharply when she finally realized what he meant. "You knew?"

Her whole childhood replayed in her head. The criticism. The training. The reluctance to let her have anything to do with magic.

He'd been trying to keep her Druid identity hidden, just like Cade's Tuathan one.

"Of course I did. I tried to stomp it out of you so you wouldn't become a monster."

*Monster.*

The word repeated in her head like a bad chant that she couldn't escape from. Her muscles quivered. Is that what she was doomed to be? Is that what everyone would eventually think of her?

"You must not know your daughter at all, then."

Castor's words did nothing but shatter her heart more. Cassia wasn't sure *she* even knew who she was anymore. Every day, everything she knew seemed to change.

Stellan raised his hand. Her father hit the ground hard. Once. Then twice. Until it became clear the fight had gone out of him. He didn't shout. Didn't threaten. He simply stayed there, shoulders slumped, head bowed low. Only then did Stellan release his invisible grip.

"The future is here. Accept it," Stellan said. "Or lose your children forever."

Cassia's gaze drifted to Cade. He stood with his arm firmly wrapped around Bridget, her head tucked beneath his chin. Over the top of her hair, Cade met Cassia's eyes. His mouth curled slightly. Not in triumph, but in bitter understanding. Cassia mirrored the look. Neither of them said what they were both thinking. But they both knew... he already had.

With a grumble, their father slapped sand from his sleeves and brushed off what remained on his shoulders. He rolled his neck with a sharp crack and leveled a scathing glare at Stellan. "Was it absolutely necessary to do this in front of the riffraff?"

Behind Cassia, Archer leaned toward Finn. "Are *we* the riffraff?"

Finn sighed.

Deckard stopped in front of Cade and Bridget. He stared at them for a long moment. "Leave for Andarre for all I care. Abandon Elyria when it needs you most. That's your choice." His voice lowered, thick with warning. "But whatever happens next is on you."

Sand spiraled around his boots as he turned and stalked from the room. "And someone clean this mess up," he snapped, just before the heavy doors slammed behind him.

Cade leaned in and whispered something to Bridget. Whatever it was made her nod before he guided her out after him. Cassia looked to Stellan. He hadn't moved. He stood in the middle of the wreckage, eyes turned toward the gaping hole in the roof, lost in a sky that didn't answer.

"After what happened in the library, you still took Cade's side?" Cassia asked.

The tension had been suffocating. He'd clearly been angry. She'd half-expected to find him agreeing with her father when they'd finally made it to the study.

Stellan didn't look at her right away. "No matter how angry I am," he said finally, "I always will." He exhaled, gaze distant. "And for a second, I thought I caught a glimpse of the old Cade. It's hard to let go of that kind of history."

Cassia glanced at Castor. *That*, she understood.

But when Castor came toward her, she stiffened. His earnest gaze punctured her sole. He wanted to help. She could practically hear the words in the air between them even though he hadn't spoken. But excess power still vibrated through her veins. And she suddenly wasn't sure if she'd taken it from the air or from him.

He'd *touched* her. Right before she'd exploded.

Rushing past him, Cassia croaked, "Stay away from me."

Before she became a monster and destroyed him completely.

# CHAPTER TWENTY-ONE

## Bridget

The dry fields outside of Olysa were bare and brown, just like Bridget remembered. She stood in front of a tent, the only source of shade for miles. Its dark purple, thick material clapped against the harsh wind. The crusty dirt beneath her feet billowed upward and clung to her every pore.

Bridget hated this place. Cora had kept them there for almost a month. She hadn't been allowed any relief from the sun until she'd finally hit a target with one of the dull daggers she'd been given. Behind the straw-filled round bag that she'd trained on, a looming mountain range sat covered by smog. Instead of white peaks, dark stone crumbled every so often. One of them even had a stream of bright red liquid spewing forth.

Suza, Bridget now realized. She'd been so close. When she'd asked Cora what lay beyond the mountains, she'd snapped at her and told her it was a place that no life could go if they wanted to keep living. A wasteland. Every night, Bridget had stared at the mountains, imagining that somehow the wasteland was an escape. Because anything would be better than the penetrating heat that burned her skin.

"This place is depressing."

*Of course, she was here. It had been foolish to think that just because she was dreaming of another place, that she wouldn't show up.*

*Bridget turned to face the girl. "Try being stuck here for a month."*

*Instead of her usual ball gown, the girl wore black riding pants. Her corset-like top was embroidered, with jeweled buttons and a high collar that almost reached the length of her entire neck. She closed one eye and pretended to throw something with exaggerated flair. "Is this where you learned your little knife tricks?"*

*Bridget's muscles tensed. This was her head. She should know. Unless the mirage in front of her really was someone. That notion struck her to her core. Because there was only one person who had that kind of power.*

*"Who are you?" Bridget asked.*

*Part of her hoped her brain would just tell her the answer. The other part of her just wanted a real name to say. She couldn't keep calling her the girl, not when she wasn't one. In fact, Bridget thought she might be a tiny bit older than her.*

*The girl cocked her head. "Like I said, I'm just like you."*

*"What does that mean?" Bridget demanded through gritted teeth. She pinched the side of her leg, hoping it would wake her up or make her scream so Cade would know she was dreaming. He couldn't be far...*

*"This would be no fun if I told you," the girl pouted, despite the conniving glint in her dark blue eyes.*

*A strange mix of rage and trepidation crept up Bridget's spine. She didn't want to be crazy. And there was only one way to find out. A knife lay covered in dust between them. Bridget lunged for it. Hot from the sun, the metal handle singed her palm.*

*The brunette narrowed her eyes. "Do you really think that is going to hurt me here?"*

*Bridget twisted the blade until it faced her own body.*

*"No, I don't."*

*Before the other girl could stop her, she plunged the knife into her stomach.*

With a searing gasp, Bridget clutched her stomach and lurched upright. The phantom sting of the blade radiated through her abdomen, heat burning from navel to spine. Her lungs spasmed as she gasped for air, hand flinging sideways in search of Cade. Only a cold, untouched pillow met her fingers.

Panic twisted in her chest. Bridget's pulse roared in her ears as she scanned the room. Empty. The fireplace was cold, the coals long dead. Pale light filtered through the cloudy window, revealing daytime. For a moment, she feared she was stuck in another dreamworld. Bridget screamed Cade's name, the sound low and guttural. If she'd been asleep, she'd wake to darkness. To fire. To *him*.

Seconds later, the bathroom door burst open. Cade rushed in, green shirt half-buttoned, damp hair dripping onto his forehead. The sharp scent of citrus and cedar clung to him as he dropped beside her and framed her face with both hands.

"Hey—hey. Look at me. What happened?" His voice was urgent but steady. "Are you hurt? What's wrong?"

Bridget leaned into his touch and closed her eyes. She *was* awake. They'd headed back to his room after they'd grabbed breakfast with Nylah so that he could shower. He'd only been gone a few minutes when she sat down on the bed with an old Elyrian history book.

"I fell asleep?"

Her words came out like a question. She hadn't been tired. In fact, she *never* napped. Usually, it was impossible for her to shut off her brain long enough to do so. For her to lean back and close her eyes without even remembering seemed like a wild notion.

The unease brewing in Cade's eyes told her he agreed. He brushed his fingertips across her forehead and then under her nose. His mouth tightened when he inspected his clean hand. "I don't feel anyone else. You weren't making any noise, either, but that doesn't mean..."

Bridget shook her head. Every sign of magic that should be manifesting on her person wasn't. Bile stung her throat. "What's happening to me?"

Because it had to be more than just dreams. Everything about them felt so *real*. Bridget could still feel the heat of the sun in Olysa and the slice of the blade she'd used on herself. Even when she found herself in Cavamyne, scents she shouldn't know lingered in the air.

The muscles on Cade's neck were strained as he said, "I don't know. But we'll figure it out. We leave for Andarre in a few days. Maybe being away from all this will help."

The unwarranted hope and belief on his face almost killed her. Especially when every time she looked at him, the vision he'd shared from his father flashed through her head. Bridget winced as she remembered watching herself kill him. It seemed so impossible, but she couldn't ignore the growing dread in her gut. What if she continued blacking out? What if all her dreams were leading to that moment by twisting her brain into something unrecognizable one by one?

The thought had Bridget shooting up off the bed. "Do you know where Marin is right now?"

"She's probably in her room or with Stellan," Cade said, following her to the door. He grabbed her hand before she could open it and twisted her around to face him. There was a small smile on his face that didn't quite reach his eyes. "Now I know you said you weren't jealous over the whole sham engagement plan with Marin, but there's quite a determined glint in your eyes right now that might make me think differently."

Bridget half-heartedly shoved his chest. "What if I was?"

"Then I guess I'd have to find a way to prove to you that there's no reason to be," he said, pulling her closer.

"And how exactly would you do that?"

Cade's darkening eyes sent heat rushing to her core. "Don't tempt me," he whispered. His lips brushed against hers.

Bridget's breath hitched. The desire for him to show her exactly what he had planned almost overwhelmed her. Her stomach fluttered as she thought how easy it would be to give in and press her lips against his. To shove him back on the bed and let him help her forget about all the dreams plaguing her.

But as her eyes locked with Cade's, the sound of the sword piercing his flesh echoed in her ears. She needed answers. And Marin was the only Shaman who'd always been upfront about their intentions with her. Bridget let out a shaky breath. It was almost painful to pull away from him. "That almost worked."

Cade only looked slightly disappointed. "Do you want me to come with you?"

The question froze her. It was her instinct to say *yes*, but she hated the idea of him knowing just how much the vision had affected her, especially when he was so adamant that it would never come true. She must have paused longer than she thought, because he suddenly leaned forward and groaned against her neck.

"Your rejections are killing me."

Bridget pecked his cheek. "I'll find you later."

She dashed out of the room before Cade could stop her, feet thudding softly against the stone floor. She didn't slow until she rounded the corner past the library. Only then did her breath begin to even out, her muscles gradually uncoiling with every step. As she descended the sweeping staircase to the lower floor, she let her fingertips brush the carved railing.

For the first time, Bridget realized she wasn't hiding as she walked through the palace. She was just... walking freely. It was unsettling how foreign that felt. Vases filled with violet blooms lined the corridor, delicate petals curling toward the light like little crowns. She paused, admiring the rich color, before continuing into the palace's west wing.

This part of the hall was quieter than it should be. There were no indications she was even in the right place. Bridget hesitated at the last hallway, nerves bubbling in her stomach. She was about to turn back, to find someone who actually knew where Marin lived, when a door creaked open beside her.

Marin's pale face peeked out. Shadows pooled under her eyes, and her hair was twisted in a loose, careless knot. She looked exhausted.

For a moment, guilt stabbed through Bridget's chest. She shouldn't have come. Marin was clearly unwell. And here she was, ready to pour more problems onto someone already carrying too many.

"You're not very good at hiding your thoughts," Marin said. "Don't worry, I've known you were coming for a very long time."

Well, *that* wasn't comforting either. Bridget's neck heated as she obeyed the wave of Marin's hand and followed her into the room. It was smaller than Cade's, and darker. There was only one window covered by a deep blue curtain. Tiny yellow lamps were scattered on every surface, creating looming shadows as Bridget sat down on a velvet chaise next to the small table where Marin poured a glass of wine. She handed it to Bridget and sat down in the armchair across from her.

Bridget took a sip of the red liquid and forced herself not to down it in one go. "So how are you doing?"

The corners of Marin's thin lips turned up. "That's not what you came here to talk about... But I'm fine."

Bridget eyed the black mark on Marin's arm. It seemed to have grown since she'd seen it. It now curled up her arm like a snake. Guilt brewed in Cade's eyes every time it was mentioned. "You did that to yourself to protect Cade," she said. She could still hear Archer's screams from the blood spell. "Why?"

Marin stared at the glowing lamp next to her for a very long time. Finally, she tilted her head. "We need him. I've seen more of the future than my father. I'm not afraid of it," she said, her voice calm and matter of fact. "And I'm not blinded by guilt or the past to see it clearly. What we see... It's not always straightforward. Sometimes they come in metaphors. Or riddles. I've perfected untangling them. That's how I knew what to do at Cavamyne."

Bridget's heart flipped in her chest as she remembered the unbearable pain in her side and the air leaving her lungs as she went through the gate. She unconsciously rubbed the scar. *I have to get the timing right.* Marin's words hadn't made sense to her then, nor had her incessant chanting before she'd sent her through to the human realm. Now, it finally hit her that she'd been breaking the curse.

"Thank you for that," Bridget said, chugging the rest of the wine. She wished it was something stronger.

"You're the first to do so."

Bridget cleared her throat. "You tried to tell me before, didn't you? In your own way."

*You're one of the oldest souls I've ever met.*

The signs had been in front of her, the whole time. If only she'd bothered to ask the right questions.

Marin didn't answer. Her silence was confirmation enough.

Quietly, Bridget continued, "So without Cade, we lose against Vega. That's why we were brought back, right? He can use that sword."

Marin sighed. For once, frustration gleamed in her eyes. "It's more than that. Cade's just one part of it... He's one factor that we need for the future I'm working for..."

"Which is what?" Bridget asked, almost holding her breath.

"The future that my father believes doesn't exist." Marin's face softened. "One where he's happy."

Bridget's eyes widened. Her actions revolved around *Stellan*? Half of her understood, she would do anything to ensure Nylah's happiness. But the other half... She glanced at the rotting mark on Marin's arm again. She'd basically ensured her demise for the chance to give him the future she wanted for him. Even if it was without her.

A ghost of a laugh crinkled Marin's face. "Don't worry," she said. "Defeating Vega is a part of that future too."

Relief bubbled in Bridget's chest. At least that was still a possibility. "If you've seen bits and pieces of the future... why did you tell the others you were blocked?"

Marin tilted her head, considering. "It was the easiest way to get them to stop asking questions. I saw what would happen if I told them anything. The future changed in ways that was catastrophic." A low blush lit her cheeks. "Besides, I didn't completely *lie*. There is one more person I'm waiting on to make a decision."

Bridget leaned forward. "What decision?"

"The decision to be brave."

Marin didn't elaborate. The flames crackled softly between them. Bridget glanced down at the black mark on her arm, her skin crawling with unease.

"What about you?" she asked.

"What about *you*?" Marin countered.

"I have a feeling I don't want to know everything."

Now that she was in front of Marin, the idea of knowing the weight of her future made Bridget's hands tremble. If she was truly destined to lose her mind to magic, she didn't want the fact hanging over her head every day until then.

"It's better that way," Marin said. "Don't let anyone tell you differently"

Bridget gave her a forced smile, then took a deep breath. There was still *one* answer that she needed. One answer that she came to Marin for. She couldn't leave without it… she couldn't breathe until she finally *knew*. The question almost got lodged in her throat. "Am I going to kill Cade?"

Marin didn't flinch at the question or give any indication of surprise. In fact, her face remained passively blank. "Like I said, visions aren't always what they seem."

Frustration shot up Bridget's spine. Before she could open her mouth to argue, Marin held up her hand.

"There's no future that I see where you kill him. It's up to you to trust me or not."

Bridget couldn't help but sense another lingering truth in her statement. There was too much forced casualness in her tone. A tightness to her gaze too obvious to ignore. "That's it? There's nothing more to it?"

Suddenly, Marin stood up. "Like I said, trust me or not. Your decision to do so won't change what happens," she said, smoothing out the lines of her pants. She glided to her bedroom door and opened it. "It was a pleasure to know you, Bridget Adams. You have remarkable resilience for a human. I hope you remember that."

Bridget slammed the empty wine glass down on the table and rushed to the door. "What do you mean *it was*?"

A terrible dread settled in her chest. The urge to question Marin further spiked her adrenaline. What else did she know? Was she closer to succumbing to the price of the blood spell sooner than they realized?

"It *is* nice knowing you," Marin corrected. Her pale face forced a tight smile. "I'm sorry. My head has been pounding all day. I really do need to rest, or I'll hear an earful from my father."

Bridget searched Marin's gaze for a lie. Her dark eyes *were* tired and hazy. Still, unease lingered in her bones. Throat tight, she forced herself over the threshold. The icy air of the hallway sent a shiver up her spine.

Marin gripped the side of the dark brown oak panel that was about to separate them. "When the time comes, don't blame yourself, Bridget."

The door closed before Bridget had a chance to ask whether she meant her inevitable surrender to the price of magic or something else entirely.

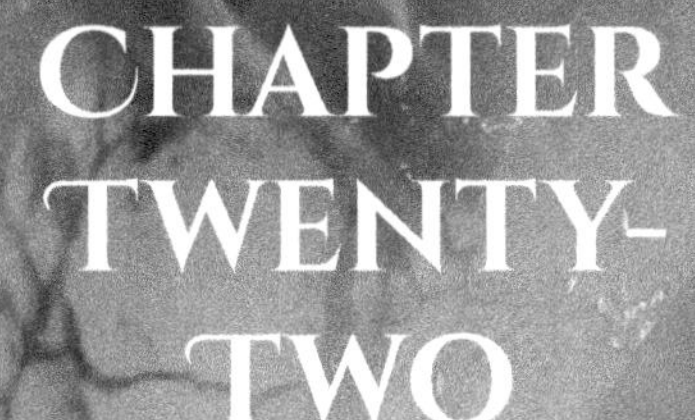

# CHAPTER TWENTY-TWO

"So this is where you lived while you were competing in the tournament?" Nylah asked, pulling on Bridget's sleeve as they entered the contestant apartments on the east end of the palace. It was exactly as she remembered. The rustic staircase hadn't changed and the scent of chocolate muffins still lingered in the air.

"Yeah, my room was right up those stairs and to the left," Bridget said, eyeing the closed door beside her old room. Months before, Quinn had slept there. She wondered if anyone had been inside since then and if any of her belongings were left.

"What a thrilling tour. What's next, a patch of grass where you saw a flower that reminded you of Cade?"

Alexia's deadpanned voice behind them tensed her muscles. For a moment, Nylah's excitement had almost made Bridget forget the other girl followed behind them. Upon her sister's insistence, of course. Apparently, she'd made it her personal responsibility to supervise Alexia at all times.

Nylah scowled at her. "No one asked for your opinion. I like hearing about what I missed. But maybe that's because I actually have people that I—"

"Speaking of things you're missing," Bridget said, cutting her off. She grabbed Nylah by the shoulders and pushed her toward the gym. "Are you okay?"

"What do you mean?" Nylah frowned. "Of course, I am."

The pure ignorance in her sister's gaze tore at Bridget's chest. Taking her on a tour of the palace was the last thing she ever expected to do with her. "Don't you miss school?"

"Are you crazy? Reading about magic and forcing this one to follow me everywhere definitely beats sitting behind a kid who hasn't discovered deodorant while trying to learn pre-algebra," Nylah said, wrinkling her nose.

"What about your friends?"

Nylah shrugged. "I can make friends anywhere. It's not that difficult. It starts with hello and then you keep asking questions until you eventually get to know them."

"But it's not the same."

Elyria *wasn't* Manhattan or Boston. She'd hardly seen any other kids around the palace. And when they did, Nylah ignored them. Since they'd arrived, she'd spent most of her time with *Alexia*. The last person she needed to get to know.

Nylah whirled on her. "Why are you trying to convince me that I shouldn't be happy to be here? We're finally all together again. And we're about to go on a *boat*. Stop worrying about me. I'm *fine*."

Her tight, dark curls bounced as she shoved the door to the gym open. Bridget gaped at her. Those pre-teen years were coming on quick.

"Looks like I did you a favor," Alexia whispered in her ear. "She actually *wants* to be here."

"Shut the hell up."

Bridget pushed her into the gym. The clang of weights smashing together echoed through the room. In the corner, Delphine pressed her legs against a black sheet of metal. Sweat dripped down her face as she scrunched her eyes in concentration.

"Delly!" Nylah squealed, zig zagging through the machines to reach her.

Delphine dropped her legs and twisted around on the seat. She wrapped her arms around Nylah, who'd thrust herself on top of her. "You're still sticking with that nickname, huh?"

"Bridget's taking me on a tour of all the places she used to go."

"Is that right? Then this is the perfect place. I actually taught her how to use this machine."

Nylah grinned. "I think I read that in her notebook."

"What are you doing here?" Bridget asked. Delphine raised a brow. "Well, besides the obvious."

Delphine stood up and wiped her forehead with her sleeve. "I like coming in here. It's peaceful and no one ever bothers me."

Crossing her arms, Bridget didn't fail to notice the quiver in her voice or the way she was avoiding her gaze. Bumping Nylah with her hip, she nodded at the treadmill across the room. "Didn't you learn how to use one of those?"

Nylah's brows furrowed as she followed her gaze. When she spotted the machine, it only took a second for a conspiratorial gleam to take over her features. With a sly smile, she nodded.

"Why don't you show Alexia how?" Bridget suggested.

"If you insist."

Alexia blanched. "I don't think that's—"

Her protests faded as Nylah dragged her across the room. Bridget rolled her lips together. She almost wished she had a camera. Before she had a chance to turn to Delphine, the gym door opened again. This time, Hai and Brynley strode through the door. Their laughter died the moment they spotted her with Delphine. For a second, Bridget felt transported back to five months ago. She'd almost forgotten Cade had told her the tournament had restarted and that the other girls were still living in the palace. She wondered where Alette was. Not that she wanted to run into her.

"Hi," Bridget said, waving her fingers. She shoved her hand behind her back when she realized how awkward the gesture looked.

Brynley almost waved back until Hai slapped her hand down and shot Bridget an annoyed glare. Red faced, she pulled Brynley out of the room. The door slammed behind them.

"Why did Hai look so peeved to see me?" Bridget asked. "I know they were told that I was back and that they wouldn't be competing anymore... But I don't think Cade ever even spoke to her."

Delphine shrugged. "Who knows. Maybe she got her hopes up when the king tried to restart the tournament."

Bridget watched her fiddle with the leg press again. "So why are you really here? Even during the competition, I don't think I saw you this focused on any of these machines."

Delphine's composure broke. Her lips trembled as she lowered her gaze and stared at a speck on the floor.

"Does it have something to do with why you didn't want to use your magic last week?" Bridget asked. "I could tell something was wrong."

It took a long time for Delphine to answer. "After what happened in Cavamyne... It's like I can still feel it every time I jump. The pain. Even with Cade's pendant, I think I still almost got us lost in the void. It wasn't enough. My magic hasn't been the same since then... I just thought, if I could get stronger, maybe it would get better."

Bridget swallowed hard. Hadn't she been doing the same thing in Boston? No matter what she did, nothing felt like it was *enough*. She squeezed Delphine's hand. "You could have died. No one is going to blame you for being wary. Have the others not noticed?"

"I like to pretend they haven't, but it's impossible to miss the questioning stares. And the judgement practically wafts off Cassia every time I see her." Delphine chewed on her lower lip. "I'm so sorry, Bridget. You needed me the other day and I couldn't bring myself to help."

"It's okay. I shouldn't have expected you to save Nylah for me."

If she would've left with them, Quinn wouldn't have found her. She would be sleeping at night instead of being struck awake constantly by the thought that she might be losing her mind, just like her. All she had done was distract Cade and waste time before Castor and Marin fixed the protection spell around the wall.

"What was Quinn even after?" Delphine asked.

*It's time for us to go.*

Bile stung Bridget's tongue. "I don't know. The running theory is that she finally tried to get to Cade so she could take another shot at breaking the curse on the Sanguis. The Bloodstone has changed her, though... she didn't seem stable."

Delphine's brows pinched. "What do you mean?"

Across the room, Bridget watched Nylah push a few buttons on the treadmill. Alexia let out a strained huff as the incline increased. Once the knot in her throat released her voice, she asked, "Have you ever seen anyone change because of magic? Not just go power hungry and get consumed by it, but really *change...* like blackout and forget who they are?"

Taking a sip of water, Delphine thought for a long moment. "Honestly, no. I've always been under the assumption it would kill you before it got that far. Obviously, I was wrong. That Wraith working for Quinn proves that. If you think blackouts are happening to Quinn... it has the price of blood magic, right?"

"Yeah, it must be," Bridget said, forcing her gaze to the black matted ground. She could think of two blood magic spells that had been done to her. One had left scars on her stomach. The other had broken a centuries-old curse. Was that enough for her to pay that same price?

"Now it's my turn for a weird question," Delphine said. She fiddled with the top of her water bottle. A hint of pink filled her cheeks. "How did you know Cade was the one?"

The turn of conversation almost gave Bridget whiplash, but Delphine's eager eyes told her the question had been weighing on her a long time. "I wish I had something really eloquent to say, but... I just knew. Every time I look at him, I feel peaceful, but exhilarated at the same time. Like my heart could burst out of my chest, but I know he would be right there to catch it. I don't know if that makes sense."

Delphine couldn't hide the disappointed pinch of her face. Still, she smiled wryly. "That was more eloquent than you think."

"Is this about Castor?" Bridget asked. Anyone with eyes could see the way Delphine looked at him. But they could also see the way he and Cassia seemed to orbit each other like magnets. Bridget wasn't sure if they even realized it, the way they stayed in sync.

"Is it that obvious? He's been in love with Cassia since we were ten. Everybody knows that. But for a while, I thought..." Delphine let out a hollow laugh, her voice hoarse. "I don't know what I thought, actually. I think I let a couple of butterflies trick me into thinking it could be more."

"I don't know their history, but I do know you deserve more than just a couple of butterflies. There is someone out there who is going to match the absolute greatness that is you," Bridget said. "And if it's not Castor, he's definitely missing out."

"I am pretty great, right?" With a half-hearted smile, Delphine lifted her chin. Her watery gaze cut to the other side of the room. Alexia stumbled off the treadmill, gasping for breath. "Should we go save her now?"

Fighting a laugh, Bridget shrugged. "Maybe in a few minutes."

Bridget had never attended a more awkward dinner in her life.

According to Cade, his family used to eat together every night. It used to be one of his favorite traditions. Until Riker died. And then he left for three years. Since then, he'd avoided it like the plague. Every dinner either turned into a fight about the future or the tournament, according to him. Bridget eyed the twelve-year-old she wanted to throttle. Sitting between her and Cade, Nylah stuffed a piece of chicken in her mouth. They were here because of her. She'd turned her big brown eyes on Cade the moment she'd heard the unwanted invitation from Cassia.

So far, the talking had been minimal. The few short conversations that had transpired all revolved around Quinn, the army, which cities were being reinforced, and a letter Cade needed to deliver to the King of Andarre. Bridget took a sip of wine and forced some mashed potatoes in her mouth. The swirling tension in the windowless room was ruining her appetite. And the long sleeved, blue dress she'd borrowed from Cassia itched her elbows.

"Why is the letter so important?" Cade asked. "It's not like he replied or acknowledged anything from you in the past."

Deckard raised a brow. "I'm surprised you ever noticed my efforts between the adolescent partying and escape to the human realm."

A shuffling to Bridget's right distracted her from Cade's terse reply. Nylah pulled a folded piece of paper out of her pocket and gently smoothed it out.

"What's that?"

"I drew this earlier," Nylah whispered. She tilted the paper. On it, a poorly illustrated man sat on a throne. His wild hair resembled snakes and his nose took up most of his face. A bolt of lightning shot out of a hand the size of a quarter. The crown sitting atop the man's head was Bridget's only clue that she'd drawn Deckard. She'd certainly taken creative liberties. And clearly, Cade hadn't given her any tips when she asked to borrow his sketchbook.

"That is... something."

Bridget tried to push the paper further into Nylah's lap. Deckard looked like a troll. She imagined him flipping over the table if he saw it.

"I'm going to give it to him," Nylah said, jumping out of her seat before Bridget could stop her.

Falling into her sister's velvet chair, Bridget's mouth fell open as she watched Nylah skip around Cade and plant herself next to Deckard at the head of the table. The king immediately stopped talking. Cade and Cassia dropped their forks. Bridget lost her ability to form words. If she wasn't so horrified, the absolute bewilderment on his face would probably make her laugh.

"I don't believe I summoned you over here," Deckard said.

Nylah handed him the paper. Silence pierced the air as the king's dark eyes roamed over the drawing. Bridget held her breath and braced herself for a growl or blast of magic or—

A deep, hearty noise escaped Deckard's throat. It grew louder the longer he stared at the paper. He was laughing. Bridget couldn't believe the amused lines forming around his eyes or the way his chest shook. Next to him, Cassia paled like she'd seen a ghost.

"I haven't gotten one of these in a long time," Deckard said. After one last chuckle, he put the paper on the table next to his plate and continued to eat.

Bridget locked eyes with Cade. He looked just as confused as she felt. *What the hell*, he mouthed. With a satisfied smile, Nylah plopped back in her seat between them.

Cassia craned her neck to look at the drawing. Her nose wrinkled. "Is that what passes for art in the human realm?"

"Aren't stick figures your specialty?" Cade countered.

The room fell into brief, pointed silence.

Deckard's gaze swept over the table before landing squarely on Cassia. His brow furrowed. "Why are you wearing gloves?"

Bridget's eyes darted to silk white gloves lacing Cassia's fingers. A bold choice for dinner.

Cassia glared. "Why do you think?"

Between bites, Nylah cut them off. "What happened to your hair?" she asked Deckard. Her words were slightly muffled by the food in her mouth. "I saw an old painting of you. It used to be brown."

Bridget remembered the exact one. They'd passed by it during their tour. She'd never seen it before and hadn't been able to give her any answers. For all she knew, his long white hair had always been that color.

Any previous humor left on Deckard's face disappeared. His mouth fell into a straight line. Gripping his knife in his right hand, he said, "When my youngest son succumbed to the effects of magic, I tried to save him. Despite my efforts, it didn't work. I couldn't channel enough power. Consequently, my hair reflected my actions. The spell I tried to perform drained my hair of its vibrancy. It seems something similar happened to your sister."

Surprise jolted through Bridget's. She hadn't expected the honest words, nor the acknowledgement of her. He'd been avoiding speaking to her all night. Peeking at Cade over Nylah's head, Bridget's heart twisted. The hard lines of his face were steeled into a cold mask.

Across from him, Cassia wasn't as composed. Her lower lip trembled. "What are you talking about? What spell did you try to do?"

Deckard cleared his throat and roughly sliced his knife through a large piece of chicken. "It doesn't matter now. It was a terrible accident and..."

"That's what you're calling it now?" Cade growled, his voice low and harsh.

As a flicker of rage began to brew on Deckard's face, darkness consumed them.

# CHAPTER TWENTY-THREE

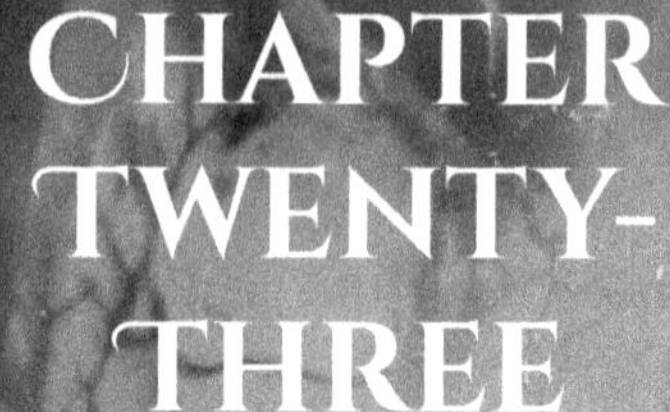

Bridget reflexively reached for Nylah's hand. The moment small fingers met hers, she relaxed a bit, despite the harrowing blackness surrounding her. Silence pressed in from all sides. The usual low hum of palace life had vanished, replaced by something far more unsettling.

"What the hell is this?" Deckard's voice cut through the dark.

Bridget heard Cade scoff nearby. "The power went out."

A knife slammed hard against the table.

"I *understand* the electricity is off," Deckard snapped. "I want to know *why*."

At the head of the table, two glowing eyes flickered to life. Deckard muttered something under his breath as a faint shimmer of blue lit his face. Magic, no doubt, as he whispered a message to someone across the palace. At least the light emanating from his face allowed Bridget to vaguely see the profile of her sister's contemplative one.

"Maybe eating in a windowless room wasn't such a good idea," Nylah said. "Too bad I left my lighter in my room."

Bridget balked. "Who gave you a lighter?"

It had to be Archer. Asking for forgiveness and not permission was his specialty. Just like the time he'd let Nylah drink a Red Bull after dinner.

A shriek penetrated Bridget's ears. Goosebumps erupted over skin as it echoed throughout the palace, reaching their location in faint, haunting waves. Her chest twisted. The noise was familiar and tensed her muscles. A prick shot through her forehead.

*Is it just me, or did that sound like the Wraith?* Cade asked.

*It's not just you.*

She felt his grimace. *I was hoping I was wrong. It shouldn't be possible. Not with the protection spell.*

"What was that?" Cassia asked, her voice a nervous whisper.

A frustrated hum reverberated from Deckard's chest. "Whatever it is, it will be dead soon enough."

*I think we need to stop doubting Quinn and what she can do with the Bloodstone. She must have found a loophole*, Bridget told Cade.

Before he could respond, Deckard shoved back his velvet chair with a scrape of wood against stone. At the same time, the dining room doors burst open. Torchlight from the hall spilled in, finally illuminating the room in flickering orange. A guard dressed in black stepped inside, gave a curt bow, then snapped to attention.

"It seems to be only the palace affected by the blackout. One of the lieutenants found the solar powered generator in the east wing blown to bits. The rest of the city still has power. We should move you to a more secure location while we work on fixing the issue."

"You want me to hide in my own palace?" Deckard sneered. The dagger at his hip shimmered as he yanked it from its sheath, its edge catching the firelight. "I don't think so. If that beast from the wall has made it inside, then I want to deal with it myself."

Cade stood, matching his father's glare. "You didn't fight the Wraith at the wall. *I* did. You're going to need more than a rune. Fire was the only thing that seemed to deter it until the protection spell returned."

Deckard scoffed. "This dagger can still cut off a head. I've never seen anything survive that, not even a Shaman." He turned to the guard and snapped his fingers. "We'll take the east side. My son will take the west. Let's see which one of us gets to it first."

Another unearthly wail rippled through the walls. It was closer this time. Everyone stilled. Bridget's heart thundered. Still connected to Cade, she sensed his annoyed trepidation. A hint of plan echoed down the bond. Another windowless room. A tunnel. A fireball by Stellan. Power began to glow under his skin.

*Stellan and Marin are going to meet us on the first floor.*

Before Bridget could argue, his presence disappeared with a sharp pop. Blood dripped down her nose. She felt Nylah's gaze burning a hole through her skin as she quickly wiped it away with the sleeve of her dress.

"Can you not do that while she's wearing my dress?" Cassia snarled to Cade. "That blood will be impossible to get off."

Nylah pulled on Bridget's hand. "We stick together this time. I know you two just had a secret conversation."

Lips turned up slightly, Cade ruffled the top of her tight curls. Despite the knot constricting her throat, Bridget said, "I promised you that wouldn't happen again."

And she'd basically made the same unspoken promise to Delphine. Nylah was her responsibility. No matter how much she wanted to help, she wouldn't abandon her again.

Deckard rolled his eyes, a dark scowl settling on his face as he paused at the doorway. Out of the corner of his eye, he appraised the guard. "What's your name?"

"Barrett," the guard stammered.

Deckard's lip curled. "Barrett, give my son your sword."

The king stormed into the hallway. The guard's cheeks reddened as a series of strangled noises escaped his throat. After a moment, Cade flicked his wrist. The sword attached at Barrett's side flew to his hand. He caught it midair.

"I don't need this, but it's better for you if he thinks you listened," Cade said coolly. "You better hurry before you lose him and the Wraith finds you first."

Barrett swallowed hard, nodded without a word, and hurried after Deckard. Once their footsteps faded down the hall, Cade turned and pressed the sword into Bridget's hand. Then he scooped up Nylah, placing her carefully on the closet chair.

"Hop on, we'll be able to move faster if I carry you," he said. "Cass, grab one of the torches from the hallway and make sure it doesn't go out."

Nylah jumped on his back and wrapped her arms around his neck. Bridget's knuckles turned white as she gripped the sword's handle. It felt heavy and foreign in her hand. And too similar to the one in the vision. As it swished in the air, the whistling made her stomach churn. She suddenly wanted nothing more than to throw it out the window. "I'm much better with a dagger, you know. Besides, I can hardly move in this dress. This won't do me any good."

Bridget tried to give it to Cassia. The blonde traitorously held up her hands.

"You need it more than me. While my magic is a little erratic at the moment, it's more than you have."

"Just hold on to it. Please," Cade said, eyes softening. "Cass has a point. You need to have something and that dress leaves little to the imagination. I know you don't have any daggers on you."

Heat traveled up Bridget's neck as she reluctantly nodded. The moment they arrived at the tunnel she'd seen in Cade's head, she was dropping the damned thing.

Silence wrapped around them as they stepped into the dim hallway. Shadows flickered along the walls, making the paintings seem almost alive. Cassia pulled a torch from the wall, the metallic *click* of its release echoing far louder than it should have. Nylah pressed a finger to her lips, silently shushing her, and Cassia shot her a sharp glare. Following Cade toward the main stairwell, Bridget cast a glance over her shoulder at the empty corridor behind them. Her heart pounded loudly in her ears.

"How do you think it got in?" Bridget whispered. "Quinn has to be with it, right?"

Her fingers nervously tugged at the soft green leaves of the fichus tree planted in the center of the double staircase, half-expecting Quinn to leap out from behind it.

"Now I normally don't mind being alone in a dark room with a man, but the shrieking killed the mood."

Heart leaping to her throat, Bridget whirled around and snapped the sword upward. Metal clinked as Finn blocked the weapon with his own before it reached Archer's neck. Adrenaline buzzed through Bridget's veins as she let out a frustrated huff and hit the Warlock on the arm.

"Why did you sneak up on us like that?"

"Why did you jump behind a plant?" Archer countered, brow raised. "Your boyfriend summoned us. Again, can we try a note next time?"

"Because that would be such a great use of our time," Cade replied scathingly.

"I can't pinpoint the Wraith's location," Finn said. "Every time it wails, it sounds like it's coming from a different direction."

"Fantastic," Cassia grumbled. Her anxious gaze darted to the dark space behind Finn and Archer. "Where's Castor?"

Finn glanced at Cade before he answered. "Once we heard the Wraith, he and Delphine went to help secure the servants quarters and get them out. And no surprise to anyone, Alexia followed."

Cassia nodded, face transforming into steel. Bridget lowered her gaze when she noticed the subtle bob of her throat. She didn't envy the unsurety of not knowing how the person you cared about felt.

Archer tossed a small metal item to Nylah. "Here you go, kid."

Bridget narrowed her eyes at the lighter in her sister's hands. "I knew it was you."

"There's a safe room on the bottom floor. It leads to a tunnel," Cade said, propping Nylah up higher on his back. "I'll get you all there and then help Stellan deal with the Wraith once and for all."

Bridget tried to catch Cade's gaze, but he wouldn't meet her eyes. So staying with her and Nylah obviously wasn't part of the plan. Dread spiked through her chest at the thought of having to transverse the tunnel out of the palace without him. Especially if fire was involved. There was no guarantee they could control it if it started to spread.

Luckily, Finn voiced her thoughts. "So he has a plan? If we use as much fire as you did last time, you're going to burn the palace down."

"An idea of one, apparently," Cade said, leading them down the stairs. "I haven't decided if it's a good one or not."

Bridget stared at the back of his head and willed him to connect to her mind. She could tell he felt her gaze by the tense set of his shoulders. Before she gave in and poked him, his presence pinched her temple.

*If you stare any harder, I'm going to catch on fire before we even find the Wraith.*

*That's not funny. What is Stellan asking you to do?*

Cade's gaze flickered to his sister beside him. *Use Cassia.*

With a quick pop, he was gone. Bridget watched Cassia twist her hands. They'd barely learned anything about her Druid abilities. *She* barely knew anything. Except for the terrifying warning that her powers, if overused, could annihilate everything around her. What did Stellan expect her to do? And what would the price be?

Blinding light flashed throughout the hallway, temporarily blinding Bridget and illuminating the west courtyard to their right. Moments later, thunder rumbled, shaking the palace walls and rattling her bones. The wind howled fiercely, shattering a pane in the glass doors that framed the golden-red and green tree she remembered from the first day of the tournament. Thick, humid air drifted in, heavy with the scent of rain, as lightning struck again, illuminating the trembling timber outside.

Finn tensed, his gaze darting along the corridor. "A storm isn't going to help us track anything."

"Are we almost there?" Nylah asked, her voice trembling.

With a tilt of his head, Cade urged them forward. "It's around the next corner."

Tightening her grip on the sword, Bridget sped up her steps. Another roll of thunder made her jump. "I haven't heard the Wraith since we made it downstairs."

"Maybe it left," Archer said.

Cassia rolled her eyes. "Unlikely."

At the end of the hallway, Cade stopped in front of a gray metal door with no handles. "We still need to figure out how it made it to the palace in the first place," he said, waving his hand over the hinges. "I can still feel the protection spell around Astraeus."

"So can we."

Stellan's deep voice echoed from behind them. Bridget whirled around to meet his steady gaze. Beside him, Marin took a deep breath and shoved her trembling hands behind her back. Narrowing her eyes, Bridget opened her mouth to ask if she was okay, but Cade's voice cut her off.

"Once I show Bridget the right way through the tunnels, you need to explain exactly how you plan to use Cass against this Wraith," he said, kicking open the now unlocked safe room door with his heel.

Cassia paled. "*Me*? Absolutely not. I can't. Not if it means I could hurt—"

At the end of the hall, the girl from Bridget's dreams appeared between lightning strikes. With a taunting smile, she wiggled her fingers.

Bridget flung herself backward, colliding with Stellan's chest. His hands closed around her shoulders, steadying her as her whole body shook.

She squeezed her eyes shut. Thunder rolled overhead, low and menacing. When she opened them, the girl would be gone. She had to be.

"Are you okay?" Stellan asked.

Bridget's hands trembled as she forced her eyes open. The space where the girl had stood was empty now—utterly, impossibly empty. She couldn't bring herself to meet Cade and Nylah's worried gazes. Her voice broke as she whispered, "I saw her. She was right there."

Cade's throat bobbed as he swallowed hard, eyes fixed on Bridget. "There's no one there," he said gently, his voice laced with worry.

Cassia's gaze swept the hallway, sharp and tense. "What the hell is she talking about?" she hissed, her fingers twitching at her side.

Archer grabbed her arm. "Bridget, now is not the time for your little—"

"Watch out!"

Nylah's scream tore through the hall.

A blur of shadow surged from the ceiling. Skeletal limbs and smoke trailed as the Wraith dove straight for Bridget. Stellan yanked her back just in time, his arm slamming across her chest as the creature's claws scraped the air inches from her face.

Finn drew his sword in one fluid motion. "That thing can walk on the ceiling now?"

Before he could lunge, a second figure stepped from inside the safe room. Quinn's eyes glowed like burning coals, and blood seeped from her palms, swirling into twisted, pulsing threads as she gripped the Bloodstone. "Oops, was this room supposed to be secured?"

"Move!" Cade shouted, shoving Bridget backwards. He dropped Nylah beside her and raised his palms. His eyes crackled with glowing silver as he turned to face Quinn.

The Wraith let out a piercing shriek, an inhuman wail that rattled the walls. It launched again, this time at Stellan, who barely ducked, trying to knock Marin out of the way. His blue tattoos glowed as he summoned an ember and launched it at the Wraith. With a flick of his wrist, Cade did the same. The Wraith shrieked as the fire collided with its form, staggering it midair. But it didn't fall. It crawled along the wall with spider-like limbs, eyes glowing like coals.

"Hello, friends," Quinn said. Suddenly, the Witch raised her bleeding hands and sent a wave of magic down the hall. It slammed into them, knocking them all off their feet. Glass and torches shattered around them.

Again, Quinn raised a bleeding hand, the Bloodstone pulsing in her grip. With a flick of her fingers, a jagged line of fire ripped down the hallway, splitting the floor between the group and sealing off their path to the safe room. Bridget stumbled back, nearly falling into Nylah as Cade threw up a shield just in time to block the blaze. Heat radiated from the wall of fire, forcing them into a tightening circle.

"Stay behind me!" Cade shouted, dragging Nylah behind him as the flames roared.

Quinn stepped through the smoke unfazed, the Bloodstone pulsing with dark light in her grip. With a sharp flick of her wrist, she drew a bleeding line down her forearm, feeding her power. Another line of fire erupted in a jagged streak across the hallway.

"She's trying to box us in," Stellan growled, sweat beading at his temple as he tried to reflect the heat from their bodies. Marin stepped forward, her own magic humming. She launched a swirl of icy wind and sharp shards that shattered against the Wraith's form.

Through the flames, Quinn smirked and stepped through her own fire as if it were nothing. She moved inhumanly fast, darting past Cade and Stellan in a blur. Before Finn could react, she was in front of him, hand raised.

"Finn!" Bridget cried, lunging forward, but Cassia pulled her back.

Quinn reached him in a blink. Her jagged and black as obsidian nails sliced clean across Finn's neck.

He stumbled, a strangled cry ripping from his throat as blood streamed through his fingers. "You—" he gasped.

Quinn tilted her head. "Still breathing? Pity."

Archer charged her with a roar. "Get away from him!"

But Quinn turned and flicked her hand. A blast of energy slammed into Archer, throwing him across the hall. He hit the stone with a sickening crack and slumped to the ground, unmoving.

Bridget gasped and turned to Nylah. The girl trembled against her side, eyes wide with fear.

"It's okay," Bridget whispered, even though her voice shook. "I've got you. I won't let anything happen to you."

"Bridget—*run!*" Cade shouted, fire roaring from his palms as the Wraith launched toward him again. Stellan flanked him, casting another glowing barrier to hold it back.

The Wraith screamed, then dove at Cade and Stellan, its claws raking through the air as they countered with bursts of magic. Marin summoned a tempest of ice, swirling it around the Wraith to slow its deadly strike.

But Quinn's magic surged again, slamming into the floor beneath their feet with a violent crack. The marble shattered, a chasm tearing open between Bridget and Cassia and the others.

Dust and rubble exploded as the ceiling groaned, then crashed down in a deafening roar, sealing off the side corridor.

"No!" Bridget screamed, pounding on the stone wall.

A sob tore through Nylah's chest. "What happened to Archer?"

Gripping Bridget's arm, Cassia urged, "That won't do any good. We have to keep moving and find another way around to help them. Or we need to find my father. We can't just stand here and idiotically pound at the rubble."

Bridget's heart hammered as she clutched Nylah tighter. The flames flickered behind them, the Wraith's shrieks echoing in the distance. She was right. The stones were too heavy to move. There had to be another way through the palace. Gripping Nylah's hand, Bridget grabbed the sword from the floor and chased after Cassia's already retreating form.

Bridget stumbled through the narrow hallway, sword whooshing through the air as she led Nylah along the twisting, shadowed passage. Dust choked the air, and the distant roar of collapsing stone faded behind them, swallowed by the heavy silence.

"Where are we going?" Bridget breathed. "Stellan said he needed *you*. We're moving further away from them."

"The west courtyard," Cassia said without hesitation. "I know this palace better than you. There's another path we can take that will lead us back to them."

Lightning cracked overhead as they pushed open the heavy iron doors, rain lashing like cold knives against their skin. Thunder rolled low and deep, vibrating through the stone beneath their feet.

Nylah whimpered, pressing herself against Bridget's side. Bridget wrapped an arm around her protectively, shielding the girl from the biting wind. For a moment, the chaos of the fight seemed miles away. Only the storm's wild howl and the pounding rain.

A cold, rattling shriek shattered the moment.

The Wraith dropped from the roof's edge, landing between them and the broken wall that led back inside. Its hollow eyes burned like embers, limbs twisting unnaturally as it advanced.

Bridget's breath caught in her throat. She moved to stand in front of Nylah, every muscle tense. "How the hell did it find us?"

Cassia didn't answer, only stared up at the Wraith with wide, horrified eyes. The creature darted forward.

"Cassia, move!" Bridget shouted, shoving her and Nylah out of its path.

The creature scuttled up the ancient ash tree, leaving a trail of black sludge oozing down the bark. Its claws dug deep into the timber, gouging through as it climbed, rain hissing against its form. Bridget raised her sword and swung, but the weight of her soaked dress clung to her legs, restricting every movement. They just had to attend that damned dinner.

The Wraith leapt again. Cassia moved this time, barely dodging as the clawed limb raked through the space where her head had been seconds before.

"You have magic!" Bridget snapped, eyes burning as she backed Nylah away from the tree. "*Do something!*"

The moment the harsh words escaped Bridget's mouth, the glass doors leading out to the courtyard shattered. Bridget twisted toward the sound. Quinn stood in the shattered doorway, untouched by the storm. Her tattered dress clung to her like blood, the Bloodstone clutched in her palm glowing a deep, pulsing red.

A cruel, satisfied smile flickered on her face. "Found you."

Bridget tightened her grip on her sword. "What do you want?" she snapped. "You can't win here. No matter what you try, Cade is *not* ending up in Cavamyne."

Dread curled like smoke in her gut. Where the hell was he?

Quinn didn't answer. She stepped through the shattered doorway, the Bloodstone in her palm glowing like molten coal.

"Now's not the time for reason, Bridget," Cassia muttered, ducking as the Wraith slashed through the air again, inches from her head.

Bridget refused to back down. "Is Vega controlling you? Did she send you for the Tuathan artifacts?" The others had to be close. She refused to believe any other options. "Well, guess what. They're not here. Looks like you wasted your time."

*Lie.* There was one. Bridget pushed Nylah further behind her. Like hell was that crazy Witch getting anywhere near her sister. She desperately hoped Nylah had left the stone somewhere in her room.

A harsh laugh escaped Quinn's throat. Blood streaked down her wrist. "Do you still think this is about the artifacts? Vega wants so much more."

Quinn raised her palm. Magic pulsed from her hand, power crackling like the lightning surrounding them, ready to strike. But just as Bridget raised her sword, glass shards knocked Quinn to the ground.

Glowing with powers, Cade stepped through the far stone archway. He raised his hand again, sending more glass toward the Wraith circling Cassia, Stellan and Marin at his sides. Stellan's tattoos blazed with magic, and Marin's cloak whipped behind her in the wind, her eyes fixed on the Wraith.

The Wraith shrieked, piercing the roar of the storm. It lunged toward Nylah, claws slicing through the air. Bridget shoved Nylah behind her, shielding her with her body as the creature veered toward them. But Nylah stepped out from behind her, chin lifted.

"Nylah, *don't—*" Bridget started.

Nylah pulled the small lighter from her pocket, her thumb sparking it to life with shaking hands, and then *threw* it. The lighter arced through the air and landed at the Wraith's feet.

Fire burst upward.

A searing, unnatural scream tore from the creature as its legs caught flame. The blaze clung to it, hissing and devouring the shadows snaking up its arms. The Wraith staggered forward, writhing in the storm, its hollow eyes locked on her sister. Bridget swung at the beast, but it dodged her. With a flick of its wrist, it knocked her to the ground. Stone dug into her back and rain choked her as she gasped for breath.

"Cade, stop it!" Bridget begged, voice hoarse as she used all her strength to pull herself to her feet.

Instead, Marin surged forward without hesitation, throwing herself between Nylah and the Wraith. A blast of frost exploded from her palms, holding the creature off. But its claws whipped around, slashing deep across her back and shoulder.

She screamed, but stayed standing.

Bridget couldn't breathe. It was exactly what she'd seen in Stellan's head.

"*Marin!*" Stellan faltered, eyes going wide. His eyes lit up with blue fire, he caught Marin before she hit the ground. With a blast from his palm, he sent the Wraith hurtling back toward Cassia.

Suddenly, Quinn stepped toward the tree like death itself, Bloodstone glowing hot in her palm. Her eyes locked on Bridget.

And then she moved.

Bridget barely registered it before Quinn was in front of her, arm raised, power blazing.

But Bridget was faster. She lunged, sword clenched tight, and drove it up under Quinn's ribs. Steel tore through flesh. Quinn gasped, face twisting in fury and pain. She dropped to her knees.

Stunned at what she'd done, Bridget dropped the sword and stumbled backward. She ran into Cade, who wrapped his arms around her waist before she fell. "It's okay, I've got you," he whispered.

The Wraith shrieked again, half-burning but still dangerous.

Cassia stood frozen, her hands trembling at her sides as it crawled toward her.

"Cassia!" Stellan shouted, still holding Marin. "*Now!* You're the only one that can."

A determination Bridget had never seen suddenly consumed Cassia's rain-streaked face. The air seemed to vibrate around her as her blue eyes began to fill with something cold and bright. When the Wraith lunged again, Cassia reached for it.

The moment her palms touched the creature's wrists, a horrible squeal pierced Bridget's ear. Jaw dropping, she watched as Cassia sucked life and magic straight from the Wraith. It buckled, howling, its form unraveling as if pulled apart from within.

Seconds later, it stilled, then collapsed into dust in between Cassia's fingertips.

Cassia lowered her hands slowly, chest heaving and white as snow. Silence followed, broken only by thunder in the distance. Bridget turned her head, scanning until she found Nylah, who stood wide-eyed beneath the scorched ash tree. Relief pierced through her haze. But only for a second. Twisting out of Cade's arms, Bridget dropped to her knees beside Quinn's shaking body. The Bloodstone pulsed weakly in the witch's trembling hand, and without hesitation, Bridget tore it free. The stone burned in her grip, slick with blood and humming with residual power. Wordlessly, she pressed it into Cade's waiting palm. Their fingers brushed, but she couldn't feel anything past the cold in her bones.

Quinn convulsed the moment the Bloodstone left her palm. Crimson gurgled up from her throat, staining her lips. Her breath rattled. Her body shook.

Bridget grabbed her by the shoulders and shook her. "What were you after?" Her voice cracked. Adrenaline buzzed through her veins as the sight of Quinn's broken body churned her stomach. "Were you here for Cade? Or something more?"

She didn't care that Quinn's skin had turned waxen. She didn't care that every part of her wanted to run. She *needed* an answer. Especially when the Wraith's disappearance hadn't ceased the darkness still swirling above their heads.

Quinn coughed. She took one last gasping breath. "I'm sorry," she croaked.

Seconds later, her body stilled. Hazy dark eyes froze, forever staring into the distance. Bridget sat back, numb. She barely noticed Cade kneel beside her, his hand landing gently on her shoulder. His voice was there, soft and steady, but it couldn't hear it. The only thing she could hear was her own heartbeat, a furious drumbeat behind her ribs.

"Bridget..."

It was Nylah's voice that pierced through, fragile and trembling. She turned her head slowly. Nylah stood staring toward the far corner of the courtyard, where Stellan knelt in the mud, cradling Marin in his arms. Marin's eyes were barely staying open. Her head lolled against his shoulder

Bridget rose stiffly. As lightning lit the sky again, the glint of her old amethyst necklace on Quinn's neck caught her eye. Without thinking, she ripped it from the witch's neck and shoved it into her pocket. Then

Cade helped her to her feet. She took Nylah's hand, holding it tighter than necessary, and crossed the courtyard in aching steps.

As they passed the ashen tree, Cade caught Cassia gently by the elbow. "Cass..."

She yanked away like he'd slapped her. "Don't touch me," she whispered, eyes wild. "I don't know how to control it. I don't want to hurt you."

"Cass," Cade said quietly, brow furrowed, "you saved us."

But his voice didn't reach her. She turned and bolted from the courtyard, disappearing into the castle's dark halls without a glance back. Bridget barely had time to process it before Marin let out a ragged, shuddering breath. The black veins spreading from the slash down her back were climbing higher and already creeping toward her neck.

"No," Stellan whispered, shaking his head, rocking slightly. "Stay with me."

"You know what to do next," Marin murmured, her voice a thread. "You have to find the crown. She won't stop until she gets what she wants."

Her hand, weak but deliberate, reached up and touched Stellan's cheek. A moment passed. Finally, she said, "Be happy."

"You have to be here for that to happen," he choked. His voice broke on the last word. "Please, Marin..."

She gave the faintest smile. "No, I don't."

Her eyes slipped closed. Her hand slid from his face, landing soundlessly on the stone.

Stellan bowed over her. A broken sob escaped his chest, full of raw pain. Bridget wrapped an arm around Nylah, pulling her close as her own eyes blurred. Marin had jumped in front of Nylah. She'd saved her. A heavy wave of guilt and sorrow washed over her. Her eyes darted to Stellan, whose face was pale and twisted with grief so deep it seemed to shatter the silence. Then she looked to Cade, whose clenched jaw and haunted eyes spoke of his own quiet torment.

Above them, the storm finally broke. One ray of sunlight pierced through the dark clouds to rest on Marin's still form.

# CHAPTER TWENTY-FOUR

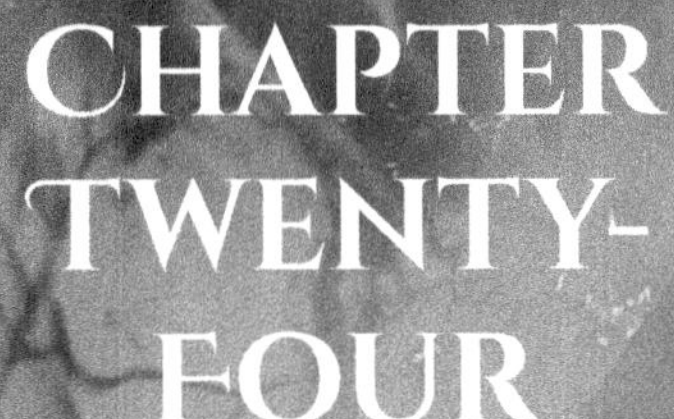

Heat pounded against Bridget's back as she stood motionless beneath the shower, steam curling around her like a second skin. She had no idea how long she'd been standing there, frozen in place, letting the water scald her until her skin tingled. It didn't matter. Nothing could wash away the images etched into her mind like scars: Archer flying into the wall. A burning Wraith. Endless black sludge. Blood. Constant blood. Marin and Quinn's crumpled bodies.

Deckard and a legion of guards had barged into the courtyard seconds after Marin took her last breath. Their bodies had quickly been removed. She didn't know where to.

She didn't understand it—how the sword had felt like an extension of herself, how her hands had moved as if answering muscle memory she didn't know she had. It had been instinct. Like something ancient had woken up inside her. Despite the heat of the water, she shivered.

Archer and Finn were fine, she told herself. They were both in the other room with Nylah, playing a game and trying to make her laugh despite the heaviness in the air. Cade had turned on the shower for her... had placed a soft kiss against her lips and whispered that he'd be waiting for her. But Stellan...

A sharp ache coiled through her chest. His grief had been unbearable to watch. When her body had been lifted from the ground, he'd stormed out of the courtyard before anyone could stop him. She wondered where he was now and hoped someone was with him. And with Cassia, too. Castor had paled when they'd told him what happened and rushed to find her.

Bridget drew in a slow breath and finally reached for the knob, shutting off the water. The silence afterward rang louder than the storm. She dried off with aching limbs and slipped into a pair of leggings and a dark blue sweater. Her damp hair clung to her skin, soaking into the wool. Heavy bags hung beneath her storm-dark eyes. She couldn't remember the last time she'd slept. And couldn't think of a reason to try. The day felt endless, and the moon had only just begun to rise.

She laced up her boots with stiff fingers and padded back into Cade's room.

Archer, Finn, and Nylah sat on the floor in front of one of the fireplaces. A board game she didn't recognize lay between them. Bandages were wrapped around Finn's neck and Archer held up a bag of ice to his temple given to him by the healers in the infirmary. They were both too busy arguing about the rules to notice Nylah sneaking a peak at their cards.

But there was one thing missing. Cade. The power was still out so Bridget grabbed a flashlight from his desk drawer. The guilt on his face had been impossible to ignore. She needed to find him before it ate him alive.

Nylah noticed her movements and placed her cards face down on the floor. "Where are you going?"

Despite her assurances that she was *fine*, an underlying fright hadn't left her gaze. And it was no longer full of blissful innocence. The thought made Bridget's stomach twist. She glanced at the amethyst necklace she'd forced around her sister's neck. At least she was protected now.

"The attic," Finn answered. His knowing gaze cut to Bridget. "There's a ladder to the roof in there."

Bridget nodded, hoping Finn sensed the overwhelming gratitude rushing through her veins that he knew where to find his best friend. Clicking on the flashlight, she took off to the servant stairwell hidden behind the library. The stone steps groaned beneath her boots, the air growing colder the higher she climbed.

The attic greeted her with a musty hush, dust thick in the air. She sneezed as it hit her nose, brushing cobwebs away with one hand as she carefully made her way through the maze of draped furniture and forgotten trunks. At last, her beam of light caught the outline of a steel ladder stretching up through a half-open skylight.

It looked barely functional. The metal was rusted and rickety. But she didn't hesitate.

The metal groaned in protest as she climbed.

When Bridget emerged onto the roof, wind tore at her damp sweater and lashed her hair across her face. Her gaze locked on Cade. He sat near the edge, his back to her. His feet dangled off the narrow stone ledge as if the drop below didn't exist. Gravel crunched softly beneath her boots as she stepped forward. He didn't turn. Wordlessly, Bridget lowered herself beside him and mirrored his pose. Shoulder to shoulder, legs hanging into the darkness.

Finally, his golden-brown eyes met hers. Frowning, Cade brushed the ends of her damp hair.

Reading his mind, Bridget said, "That's an old wives' tale. I went without heat for a long time in New York one year to figure that out."

Silence enveloped them. Bridget laced her fingers between his and laid her head on his shoulder. Her heart ached as she waited for him to speak. She could feel the weight of the day hanging between them.

After a long moment, Cade turned his head and pressed his lips into her hair. Hoarsely, he whispered, "This is where I came after Riker died.

It was the only place that could get rid of that final terrible moment out of my head." His voice broke. After clearing his throat, he continued, "Right after it happened, I lost control of my abilities. Everyone's thoughts invaded my mind, including their grief. It didn't silence until I crossed the gate."

Bridget bit the inside of her cheek, the sting behind her eyes burning harder. Cade rarely spoke about Riker. About what came *before*. She didn't dare move.

"I came here after Cavamyne, too. You went through the gate and I wasn't sure..." Cade paused again. His grip on her fingers tightened. "I used to sit here and think it should've been me. I should've been the one taking that bullet. I would look down at my hands and still see your blood."

Bridget finally turned her head. "Cade..."

His jaw was clenched, hard enough to tremble. The look in his eyes twisted something deep inside her.

"Marin could've survived if she already wasn't so weak from taking that damned consequence from me," he muttered, voice rough with guilt. "Maybe if the powers I supposedly used to have weren't buried somewhere inside me, I could have helped her."

"You don't know that," Bridget said softly. She reached up and stroked his cheek, flinching at how cold his skin felt under her fingers. "Besides, she *chose* those things. She chose to protect you. And Nylah."

Bridget closed her eyes, the image of Marin jumping in front of Nylah like a knife to her gut. Quietly, she confessed, "When I went to find her yesterday, she said she was working toward a future where we win. This must have been part of it."

*Don't blame yourself.* Is this what she had been talking about? Had she seen the cost of protecting Nylah and chosen it anyway?

Cade stared out at the horizon, jaw taut. No stars were visible through the dark clouds. "Everything I've done has been with the sole intent of making sure you don't lose your family like I did... Now I did that to Stellan."

Bridget's hand tightened around his. She knew those words would haunt him longer than anything Vega could conjure.

"At least you're safe now," she whispered. "And we have the Bloodstone. No one can use it to break the curse on the Sanguis anymore."

He nodded faintly.

"We'll take it back to the vault tomorrow. It'll be sealed and out of reach from anyone else Vega tries to use from Iegorus." His voice dropped. "But that doesn't mean it's over. You heard what Marin said. We still have to find the crown. Vega won't stop."

Cade looked at her, eyes rimmed with exhaustion, but something steadier beat beneath it.

"Then let's start right now," Bridget said. "Let's make sure her final wishes come true."

She leaned in and pressed her forehead against his, eyes fluttering shut. She didn't know how they'd find the crown—or if Stellan would ever be willing to help them again. But for now, in this fragile moment between grief and what came next, she let herself breathe and hope that fate wasn't in complete control.

The palace halls were quiet as Bridget followed Cade to Stellan's room. Her boots echoed softly on the stone floor as they entered the east wing, past shuttered windows and darkened sconces. Every room they passed felt like it was holding its breath. They didn't dare look into the ruined courtyard as they passed.

"What if he's not there?" Bridget asked. There was a chance he wouldn't even speak to them. If he didn't, she wouldn't blame him. She couldn't imagine what she'd be doing if it had been Nylah taken in the courtyard.

"Then we track down Castor and Cassia and figure out a new plan," Cade said, shoulders tense. "If you really were the last person to see the crown, then there has to be a way to access your memories."

When they reached Stellan's door, they both hesitated. Cade took a deep breath, then knocked. Once. Twice. "Stellan?"

Silence.

Bridget reached for the handle and twisted it. Without any resistance, it popped open.

The room was dim, lit only by moonlight streaking through the tall windows. Stellan sat in a chair by the fire that had long since gone out, Marin's cloak clutched in his fists like it was the only thing keeping him tethered to the earth. His shoulders were hunched, his head bowed. He didn't look up.

"What are you doing here?" Stellan asked, his voice low, hoarse, and frayed at the edges.

Cade placed a hand gently on the small of Bridget's back, guiding her forward before stepping in behind her and quietly closing the door. "We need your help."

Stellan gave a bitter, hollow laugh. "Is that right?"

He finally turned to face them. His normally sharp blue eyes were bloodshot and rimmed with red, his expression carved from grief.

"If you hadn't noticed," he said, voice rising, "my daughter just died. The girl I swore to a dying man to protect." He shook his head slowly, eyes shining with anger and sorrow. "You'll have to come back later."

Bridget stepped forward. "We wouldn't be here if it wasn't important."

Stellan's gaze snapped to her. "Important?" he echoed, the word sharp with disbelief. "Is that what this is? Some mission that suddenly outweighs the fact that Marin is gone?"

Cade flinched, but Bridget didn't. Even though she wanted to. Her chest ached just looking at him. "She died saving Nylah," Bridget said quietly. "And I will never forget that. I will never stop being grateful. But Marin didn't give her life so you could disappear again. She asked us to find the crown. Like she said, Vega won't stop. We should try before she sends someone else."

Stellan looked away, hands balled at his sides. "No."

The word hit like a door slamming shut.

Cade reached for Bridget's arm, a silent plea to stay back, but she shook him off and stepped forward, her voice rising. "This is what she wanted."

"How would you know anything about what Marin wanted?" Stellan snapped.

"I spoke to her yesterday," Bridget said. She hated that her voice began to shake. "She told me about her visions... About how she had mastered decoding them and was using them to work toward a future where we win." She hesitated, but the words pressed on her chest like a weight that needed to be set down. "A future where *you* would be happy."

Stellan's breath caught, but he said nothing.

Cade finally stepped forward, quiet but steady. "You think she didn't know what helping us would cost? She saw the end. And she still chose this path."

Bridget's throat tightened. The echo of her words on the roof melted her chest.

He paused, letting the silence settle before adding, "Don't make her sacrifice meaningless. We need you... not just to find the crown, but because she believed you were the one who could figure out how. She wouldn't have requested it if she didn't think you had an idea of where to find it."

After a long, heavy moment, Stellan rose to his feet. Bridget watched the war behind his eyes as the weight of history pressed down on him. And for a flicker of a second, she could've sworn he was seeing them not as strangers shaped by distance and pain, but as the Bridget and Cade he used to know. The ones who hadn't yet lost him.

"You don't understand what you're asking," Stellan said quietly, reaching for a weathered, leather-bound book on the table next to where he'd been sitting.

Cade stiffened. "That's the grimoire with all the blood spells," he said, his voice flat, guarded.

The one he'd used to possess Archer through the gate. Bridget's eyes flicked to the fireplace, where the embers had long since died, then to the now empty space on the table where the book must have been. A chill slid down her spine. Had he been planning to burn it before they arrived?

And then she realized why.

"The blood spell," Bridget whispered. "It's the only way to access my memories... isn't it?"

Cade's head snapped toward her, eyes wide with alarm. A dull ache pulsed along her side, right where the old scars still lingered. The truth settled like ice in her chest. The location of the crown was what Quinn had been searching for inside her, all those months ago.

Stellan's eyes remained on Cade. "It's the only way."

The muscles in Cade's throat tightened. "You don't understand," he said, voice rough. "There was so much blood. I thought she had *died* when I finally found where they'd been keeping her. It's too dangerous."

A knife sliced through Bridget's chest, but Stellan stayed calm.

"That was before the curse broke," he said. "The memory was buried then under magic so strong, no one could touch it. Now? It should be closer to the surface. Easier to reach."

Bridget stepped forward, her voice steady despite the weight behind the question. "And the price?"

Stellan's lips curled into a faint smile. It didn't quite reach his eyes. "Well, it's a good thing we've got a Druid on our side."

"I can't do this."

Cassia paced in front of her bed. She'd repeated the same words for the last five minutes, despite the pleas and reasonings of the others in the room. Even Castor's calm voice and reassurance that he wouldn't let her push herself too far couldn't calm her down. Bridget leaned heavily against one of the carved bedposts, her head pounding. Cassia's relentless movement was starting to make her dizzy.

"Yes, you can," Stellan said, though fatigue edged his voice. "I'll walk you through it step by step. You'll draw from the Bloodstone. That way, you won't accidentally take too much for one of us."

"Besides," Bridget muttered, "you're not the one getting poked and prodded."

She shot Cade a look, tired and pleading, silently urging him to say something that might break through. If anyone could get through to Cassia, it was him.

"You're the only one who can do this, Cass," Cade said, squaring his shoulders to meet his sister's panicked gaze. The silence between them crackled with unspoken meaning, a twin language Bridget had learned not to interrupt.

"And this can't wait until morning?" Cassia asked aloud.

"We don't know that Quinn was the only one out there creating Wraiths or working for Vega," Cade said. "Based on the attacks on the Kastronian border, there has to be more than just one of those creatures out there. We should get ahead while we can. Marin didn't die for us to just sit around and wait for something else to happen. And since Bridget and I are leaving for Andarre in a few days... It's now or never."

Stellan's throat bobbed at his words, his expression tight with restrained grief. Cassia still looked unconvinced, her arms wrapped tightly around herself like armor.

Castor stepped forward. "I know what you're worried about, but what you did to the Wraith doesn't make you evil or like Vega. Your powers are unique and it doesn't make you dangerous... It makes you powerful. That isn't a bad thing. It's time to embrace it."

The gentle conviction in his voice softened something in Cassia's posture. Her arms loosened at her sides. She didn't respond, but she didn't pace anymore either.

Bridget glanced sideways at Delphine. Her friend stood still as stone, but her lips trembled ever so slightly. Bridget reached over and gently squeezed her forearm in silent support.

"Cass... please. I wouldn't ask if I didn't trust you."

Cade's pleading tone finally seemed to crack something open. Cassia drew in a long breath, rolled her shoulders, and closed her eyes like she was bracing for a storm.

"Okay," she said, exhaling. "Fine. But don't blame me if this doesn't work or if I accidentally dig up some intimate memory none of us will be able to unsee. Especially the kind that'll make it really awkward to look you in the eye every day."

Her tone was dry, but the tremor in her voice betrayed her false bravado.

Bridget prompted Stellan to open the grimoire. "Let's get this over with before I change my mind."

Wordlessly, Stellan set the leather-bound book on the edge of Cassia's bed. The moment it touched the blanket, the cover snapped open with a sharp crack. Pages flipped wildly on their own, stirred by a wind that hadn't come from anywhere. Then, suddenly, they stilled. A single page shimmered with inky black script, glowing faintly in the firelight. The air shifted, thickening with something ancient and electric. A heavy weight settled in Bridget's stomach like a stone.

Well, that wasn't ominous at all.

Delphine frowned, eyes narrowing. "Is it supposed to do that?"

Before Stellan could respond, the bedroom door creaked open. Bridget's heart jumped as Finn slipped through the narrow gap.

"Whoa," he said, pausing mid-step. His gaze landed on the grimoire. "What's going on?"

"We're going to try to find the crown in Bridget's memories," Cade explained, his jaw tight. His gaze moved to the empty space behind him. "Why aren't you with Nylah and Archer?"

Finn shrugged as he stepped further into the room, eyes still flicking warily between the grimoire and the increasingly tense group. "She thought Bridget had been gone too long. I told her I'd come check."

Bridget sighed. "Way to make me feel guilty before I go under."

She hadn't even thought to go check on her before rounding up everyone they could find to get this spell done as soon as possible. But in a way, she was doing this *for* her. Quinn had been just the beginning. If Vega had control over more creatures, they'd all be targets. Even in Andarre.

Cade turned to her, his voice quieter now. "Are you sure you want to do this?"

Throat tight, Bridget gave a small nod. "Yes."

If Marin thought finding the crown was the key to defeating Vega, then they had to search for it. No matter the cost.

Stellan gestured toward the bed and pulled out a silver dagger from his pocket. "Lie down, just at the edge. Cassia will need to access—"

"Absolutely not."

Cassia's voice sliced through the air like a blade. She stepped forward, her face a mix of horror and protest. "Not on my *bed*."

Bridget watched as Cade tipped his head back and stared at the ceiling, clearly calculating whether murder or meditation would bring him more peace.

Castor sighed, despite the twitch of his lips. "Cassia…"

"There's obviously going to be blood," she added, glaring at the grimoire like it was personally responsible. "You are *not* ruining my favorite pair of sheets."

Bridget ran her hand across the top comforter. She guessed she couldn't blame her. They were annoyingly soft.

A muscle in Stellan's jaw twitched. "Then what do you suggest?"

Before Cassia could fire back, a loud crash echoed through the room. Bridget jolted as every item on Cassia's desk flew off and scattered across the floor.

Cassia spun around, jaw slack, as Cade calmly lowered his hand.

"There," he said scathingly. "That'll do."

Despite the tight knot of anxiety twisting in her chest, Bridget had to press her lips together to keep from laughing.

Stellan's cheeks flushed as he stiffly moved the grimoire from the bed to the newly cleared desk. Bridget could practically feel the frustration rolling off him in waves. Not wanting to add to it, she crossed the room and lay down on the desk.

Cade moved beside her head without a word, tension radiating from every line of his body. Delphine slid up next to him, voice low and steady.

"If the bleeding gets out of control, I'll be here to help," she murmured.

It didn't seem to help. Worry still tightened the corners of his brow.

Stellan placed the grimoire beside her. Bridget inched away slightly, suddenly uneasy about how close it was.

"Like I was saying," Stellan continued, voice quieter now, "you'll need to read the spell and channel through the Bloodstone. Once it starts, you'll need access to Bridget's blood. It might be easiest to use the scars she already has from Quinn's previous attempt."

Bridget's gaze flicked to the dagger, heart lurching. For a second, she thought she saw something flicker in Stellan's expression. Guilt, maybe. Or doubt. But it vanished before she could name it.

Cade slipped the Bloodstone from his pocket and held it out. Bridget turned her head away. She didn't want to look at it. Didn't want to *feel* it. The magic thrumming from it already made her skin crawl.

It seemed like Cassia felt the same way. She stared at it for a long time before she finally took it from Cade's outstretched hand. She inhaled sharply when it hit her skin. Moments later, Castor appeared behind her, lowering his voice as he leaned in close. Whatever he whispered, Bridget couldn't hear, but the tension in Cassia's shoulders eased. Barely.

Bridget opened her mouth, ready to call the whole thing off. Her instincts screamed at her to stop it, to yank the grimoire off the table and forget the crown. But then Stellan and Finn moved to stand at her feet, silent and focused. Before she could say anything, Cassia wrapped her hand around the Bloodstone and began to chant.

Her voice was unrecognizable. It was low and ancient, echoing in a rhythm that pulsed in Bridget's veins. Cassia's eyes glazed over and began to glow. They weren't white like Cade's, but golden. Bridget couldn't look away. There was something hauntingly familiar about it, like a dream she'd half-forgotten.

The chant abruptly stopped. Cassia vibrated, as if the spell transformed into something else entirely. In a fluid motion, she picked up the dagger with her free hand and drew it across Bridget's abdomen.

Bridget gasped, pain slicing through her like fire. Cade flinched beside her, his hand tightening near hers but not daring to touch. Blood poured freely, hot against her skin.

Then Cassia's fingers plunged into the wound.

The world around Bridget disappeared. Darkness consumed her as Cassia's presence infiltrated her mind. The pure power connected to her left Bridget writhing and reeling from the sheer force of it. It felt like she couldn't breathe.

Suddenly, a single thread appeared in her mind, tight and sharp. Colors bloomed. Shapes formed. Memories unraveled as she dug deeper and deeper.

The thread looped around her brain like a fishhook. She could feel it. It swiveled back and forth, pressing against things Bridget couldn't believe she'd witnessed. Like a glittering frozen lake in the Elder Woods and a tavern that looked like it belonged in one of Archer's favorite television shows. But then she saw *her* face. The girl from her dreams. Just for a second. But it was enough. Bridget knew her.

Reflexively, she tried to catch it. She wanted to see… to finally know whether she'd been real or not. The hook stopped. A wave of realization rushed over her. She could control it. Bridget let her consciousness wrap around the thread.

*Bridget, stop!*

She ignored Cassia's panicked voice. Because at that moment, she decided she didn't just want the memory of the crown. She wanted *everything*.

Bridget pulled harder on the thread and tunneled further down. Her entire life passed before her eyes. She saw her childhood, a waterfall, a dark tavern, dark blue eyes, *Cade*, a glittering ballroom. And then the memories got darker. Sadder. More devastating. Blood. Screams. Pain so raw it stole the breath from her lungs. She wanted to look away but couldn't. It was *hers*. All of it.

Her body trembled beneath the weight of it.

It was too much. She wanted to cry out. To scream. To thrash. But before she could, she found it. The crown. The memory she needed. And as it wrapped around her like mist, Bridget let herself succumb to the past.

# CHAPTER TWENTY-FIVE



The moment the door closed behind her, Bridget sprinted for the armoire. She'd spotted what she needed in there yesterday, when she'd been summoned like a dog to Vega's room. Their conversation hadn't been pleasant, but somewhere between the insults and threats, a glimpse of the crown had fueled Bridget's hopes of a possible win. Even though time was running out, she just needed one more chance in the room alone. After that, she'd watched Vega long enough to know what to do next.

Luckily, Vega was stubborn enough to repeat her mistakes.

She knew what Vega wanted her to do. She wanted her to beg. To plead. To somehow validate the prickle of guilt Bridget knew lived in her *somewhere* with words of regret. And since Vega relentlessly pursued what she wanted, she summoned Bridget. Again. And left her alone, unbound and free, until she deemed Bridget had waited an appropriate amount of time to be graced with her presence.

Almost flinging the wooden door off its hinges, Bridget clawed the space inside until splintered wood grazed her fingertips. Carefully, she pulled out an old chest. Scratches adorned the sides and the engraved heart on its top was faded and barely visible. To anyone else, it was a piece of junk. But Bridget knew exactly what lay inside.

Once she got the chest open, the Tuathan crown gleamed in the dim light of Vega's bedroom, like it was almost daring her to pick it up. Air fled the room, leaving Bridget's heartbeat echoing in her ears. After searching for it for so long, and being beaten to it, she couldn't believe the object was within her grasp. It was even more beautiful than legend had described. The blackness of the metal was deeper than any night sky and the cut of the diamonds placed along its curves outshined every jewel she'd ever seen. Trepidation ran down Bridget's spine. Only something with so much raw, dangerous power would be so appealing.

Footsteps sounded from the hallway. Stuffing the crown inside the deep inner pocket of her cloak, Bridget slammed the chest and armoire closed. Hurrying over to the ornate table in the center of the room, she zeroed in on the other object she needed for her plan. Pages from Vega's book of spells. Bridget cringed as she flipped through the thick book. It had grown in size the last few months and a few of the pages were stained with fresh blood.

The door creaked open. Hoping she remembered the pages right, Bridget ripped out a handful and slid them into the waistband of her pants. Now, part two of her plan had to be enacted. Whipping around, she crossed her arms and acted bored. Vega's favorite maid wheeled in a cart of tea, too busy fretting over the glass cups to notice Bridget's actions. Poor Helga. She knew Vega treated her poorly. She'd seen it with her own eyes during the few weeks she'd been held prisoner in what was technically her own castle. Not that her and Cade would ever live here. Vega had seen to that.

Bridget watched Helga shakily pour steaming black liquid into one of the cups. The girl's black hair fell over her face as she added a lump of sugar and a squeeze of lemon. Vega's preference. Which meant the Druid herself wasn't too far behind.

Helga placed Vega's cup on the table, inches away from Bridget's hip. With a shaky smile, she trotted back over to the tiny cart. "Would you also like some tea, Your Highness?"

"What did you just call her?"

The hiss from the doorway made Helga drop the empty glass in her hand. Bridget grimaced as she took in Vega's appearance in the doorway. Mask on, like it always was nowadays, the material so thick that her pupils were barely visible. Metal claws extended from her fingertips, attached together at her wrist by thin silver strings. The dark blue gown was new, though, despite the bright red drops of blood scattered across the bottom. Where exactly had she come from?

"I thought... I thought that was her title," Helga answered, her voice a squeaky whisper. "She's married to the Prince and she's—"

Vega's hand was wrapped around Helga's throat in a flash. The girl's heels left the ground. "With or without her recent marriage, she's still a bastard. She's never had a title. Not a real one." Once her claws began to draw blood, she dropped the maid to the ground. "And she never will. The Prince's claim to the throne is useless now. Now. Get. Out."

Gasping for breath, Helga scrambled to her feet and darted out of the room.

"Was that necessary?" Bridget asked. "Believe me, I know where I stand in the grand scheme of things." When Vega ignored her, she knocked the full teacup off the table. "Oops."

Bridget could almost see the curl of Vega's lips under her mask. "That was the last of the tea from Suza."

"If you wanted more, maybe you and your *Sanguis* shouldn't have razed it to the ground." The name tasted ugly on her tongue. It separated them from what they'd done too much. In reality, they were Druids who'd destroyed their homeland by absorbing too much power. After all, all magic had a cost.

"A necessary loss," Vega argued, her gravelly voice muffled from her mask.

Right. Absorbing enough power to destroy thousands of Tuathans was *necessary*. A knot formed in Bridget's throat. Behind Vega's head, the hills of Cavamyne sat, scorched and burning. Last time she'd been outside, the air had been almost unbreathable. The city's beauty had long disappeared. "Cavamyne is next."

"I'm already working on a solution."

Bridget tilted her head. The words surprised her, enough that she almost asked what she meant. But she held her tongue. Vega *wanted* her to ask. And pleasing her was the last thing she wanted to do. Bridget scoffed. "Can I go now? I would rather not spend my final hours making small talk with you."

She'd been told about her execution yesterday. It's why she needed to get out of the room and on with her plan as soon as possible. There were only hours left. Wordlessly, Vega moved to stand in front of her. Thick silence enveloped them. For a split second, Bridget believed Vega knew her plan and was about to stop her. Instead, the Druid picked up her left hand and examined the bleeding cut on her index finger.

"The teacup," Bridget lied.

The Druid loosened her grip. Bridget almost breathed a sigh of relief that Vega hadn't questioned her further, until the Druid began clawing at the fourth finger on her left hand. Bridget curled her fingers and desperately tried to escape her grip. "What the hell are you doing?"

Bridget screamed when Vega's nails clawed the back of her hand. The burning pain loosened her muscles, allowing the Druid to slip off what she didn't want her to steal. Her wedding ring.

"Give it back," Bridget snarled, darting forward to snatch it out of Vega's hand. Before she could reach her, she was flying backwards. An electric shock radiated through her back as she slammed into the armoire, then flopped to the ground. Sometimes, she really hated magic. "What do you even want with it?" Bridget demanded. Her vision focused in time for her to see Vega drop it into a vial before muttering a spell.

Bridget's heart dropped. She was using it for the curse. She had to be.

After a moment, Vega threw the ring back at her. "You know, I've been quite nice. I've let you stay in your old room. Didn't your Prince have it *specifically* picked out for you?"

"I don't know if you've ever truly been nice a day in your life," Bridget said, spitting a lob of blood out of her mouth. Somewhere between the armoire and the ground, she'd bitten her tongue. "You put me in my old bedroom because you want something."

Before she stood up, Bridget gazed at her wedding ring on the stone floor in front of her. Vega wanted to use it for the curse, that much was obvious. If she left it, or refused to put it back on, it was a way to thwart her plans. Even though she knew what Vega wanted was inevitable. But then she remembered the moment she'd first tried it on in front of Cade.

Bridget slipped the ring back on her finger.

"Is that what you really think?" Vega asked.

*Yes*, Bridget wanted to argue. But if she was going to be successful, she needed to stay focused. "Put me in the dungeon."

Underneath the mask, Vega's eyes narrowed. "I thought I told you what happens tonight."

"If you're going to kill me like a prisoner, then treat me like one." Even though her ankle now throbbed with every step, Bridget made sure she was directly in front of Vega when she demanded, "Put me in the dungeon."

A hint of a laugh escaped Vega's throat. "Do you really want their screams to be the last thing you hear?"

The Druid returned her attention to the tea cart. The whispers of what Vega had turned the dungeons into were endless around the castle. Wailing could be heard throughout the night and persistent rumors of escaping Wraiths kept people indoors.

"Will it be the last?"

Bridget's words had Vega placing the teapot back down before pouring a drop. "So you've figured out what I plan to do."

"If you didn't want me to, you shouldn't have left out your creepy book of spells."

Not only had Vega shown her the crown yesterday, she'd been left alone in her room for almost a half hour… the outline of the curse clear as day on the table. Along with a few others she planned to use afterward.

"It doesn't have to be like this," Vega said. The plea in her voice was just as fake as her actions.

"Yes… it does." Bridget knew her loyalty wasn't the only thing Vega wanted. Like the sword, the crown came with a test. A price. And the Druid wanted to use it on more people than just her. "You can't get it to work otherwise."

With a flourish, Vega raised her hand and snapped her finger. Helga and a burly guard came running in. She should have known that the meek Nymph hadn't gone far. The guard's archer ears and iron clad wrists told Bridget he was just as much a prisoner as she. "Take *Her Highness* to the dungeon," Vega taunted. "Let's see if she lasts the hour."

Bridget stomped down the tiny bit of satisfaction that coursed through her veins. A jaunt in the dungeons was exactly what she needed before tonight. The guard grabbed her elbow and pushed her toward the hallway. The crown heavy in her pocket, Bridget stood her ground in front of Vega. There was one last thing that needed to be said.

"Goodbye, Vega."

Bridget put every ounce of meaning she could into her words. For a moment, she wished she could see Vega's face. But it didn't matter anymore. After this, there was no going back. Not between them.

Vega silently watched her leave the room. The hallway was dark and damp as the guard and Helga led her down to the castle's lower levels. The entire place was so different than it had been just two years ago. It was almost recognizable. The memories of following Cade down this very path felt like a distance dream instead of a real event. The walls were no longer adorned with paintings and imported wallpaper, but flickering torchlight and wilted vines. Instead of lavender in the air, decay permeated every room.

Once the door to the cells entered their line of vision, an imposing sight of rusty nails and darkness, Helga slowed down beside her. The dungeon's warden sat in a lofty chair at the end of the hall, picking his yellowed teeth with a quill. Even through the thick, spiked door, a cackle reached their ears. Taking a deep breath, Bridget tried her best to ignore the sudden swirling in her gut.

"A new prisoner for cell seven? And a famous one at that." The warden barked a humorless laugh. With the quill, he jotted down her name on the enchanted roster attached to his hip. Bridget swallowed hard. Her fate was officially sealed. The sign of her name only meant one thing. Her only exit from the dungeon would be her execution.

When the guard and Helga made no move toward the dungeon door, the warden sneered, "What?"

Bridget sighed, nodding her head toward Helga. "She doesn't want to go in there." She glanced at the guard. "And if I'm not mistaken, his brother is in there. I doubt he wants to see what state he's in."

The warden glowered.

Bridget held out her wrists. "Cuff me, if you must. But it looks like you're taking me in there."

With a nasty snarl, the warden snatched his keys from his belt and shoved Bridget toward the door. "That smirk on your face will be wiped off soon enough."

Bridget didn't look back to see the guard or Helga's expressions. She hadn't stood up for them out of kindness. For the most part.

Once the door was open, the warden pushed her inside. It was darker than Bridget remembered. Or imagined. When the Tuathans had been in charge, hardly anyone was kept in the cells. Some of them had been used as storage. Now, almost every cell was occupied. Bridget guessed most of the prisoners she passed were people Vega deemed untrustworthy. They were dirty and ragged, but harmless. In appearance, at least. However, the further they went, the crazier tenants acted. One man, covered in the tell-tale black markings of blood magic corruption, leaped onto his bars to wiggle his tongue at her. Another rocked in a corner, muttering things she didn't quite understand. The stench permeating the air became so strong she could hardly breathe.

Light seemed like a foreign concept by the time they reached her cell. "The whole palace knows about the Queen's big plans for tonight. I don't know what you did to spend your last hours in here, Your Highness," the warned rumbled, "but I do hope you find some enjoyment in this little piece of hell."

Bridget stared at the speck of light shining through a hole in the ceiling until she heard him lock the cell and pad off back to his station. She closed her eyes. She could do this. She *had* to do this. Cade's face flashed through her mind. An ache spread through her bones. She really hoped he forgave her.

"I'm surprised to see you down here, Princess."

The scratchy voice to her right refocused her attention. In the cell next to her, Selene leaned against the bars separating them with narrowed, calculating eyes. She looked worse for wear. The last time Bridget had seen her, she'd been stabbing Cade's stepfather in the back. Literally. Black goo oozed from her mouth and the corner of her eyes. A few of her teeth were missing and almost all of her once long, beautiful blonde hair was gone. The only thing left of her Tuathan nature was her ears. She's transformed into a Wraith in every sense. Apparently too out of control even for Vega to be sentenced down here.

"Don't let Vega hear you call me that," Bridget replied, daring a smirk.

"What more can she do to me?" Selene cackled, waving at herself. The iron shackles on her wrist looked permanently seared on. "She took everything from me so magic would turn me into this."

Bridget couldn't sympathize. It was nobody's fault but her own that she kept giving in pursuit of more magic and power, even her very soul. "I asked to come down here." She eyed Selene's thin body just inches from her. "I need your help."

"I'm not in the helping mood."

"I didn't think so."

Before Selene had a chance to react, Bridget had her first wrapped around the Wraith's throat, a dagger at her throat. One made of pure iron from the mountains. If Selene was cut with it, only magic would heal her. Magic she clearly couldn't pay for without wasting away even more.

"For someone who claims not to trust me anymore, Vega never searches me," Bridget explained.

Despite the dagger digging into her skin, Selene cackled. "Some bonds can never be broken." Black liquid sputtered onto Bridget's shirt. She wanted to gag. "What are you willing to pay?"

"Whatever it takes," Bridget vowed, ignoring the dread creeping up her spine. "We're going to cast a curse."

Removing her hand from Selene's throat, Bridget slowly pulled out the pages and the crown. The Wraith's eyes widened. They widened even more when she pulled out the third item from her cloak. The Tuathan stone. The one she'd hidden from Vega for weeks. Her planned escape from the palace when she'd originally came looking for the crown. But she'd been caught and had stubbornly refused to use it until she'd found out exactly what Vega was up to, much to Cade's dismay. Plus, she hadn't quite figured out how to use it yet.

Selene reached out a shaky hand. "How did you get those?"

Bridget swatted it away. "Don't get too excited. We're about to make one disappear."

Keeping the dagger level, Bridget sorted through the pages. Finding the right one, she shoved the parchment in Selene's face. "This one."

The Wraith froze. The trepidation Bridget found in her dark eyes made her snarl. "Say the words. You can use my blood."

Selene remained silent.

Bridget pushed the dagger harder. *"Say it."*

"We can't use an artifact without its permission," Selene cried hoarsely. "The price will be too great. Using the Tuathan stone as an anchor will curse us both."

"Haven't you heard? I'm already cursed."

Bridget sliced her palm. Blood gushed onto Selene's palm and the crown. Like she predicted, the wraith couldn't resist the pull of blood magic. Seconds later, Selene's eyes darkened as she started the spell. Bridget's blood hummed as it was pulled out of her palm. The stone and the crown began to shake. Metal vibrated around them as a gate tried to form.

Spewing darkness from her throat, Selene growled. "We need more blood."

Doing her best to stay upright by the sheer force of magic booming around her, Bridget stabbed Selene in the stomach, the only place on her body that seemed to have any amount of blood left. The Wraith wailed and hissed, but couldn't let go of the spell. Chanting continued to explode from her mouth. Between them, the stone dropped to the ground. A large crack resounded through the cells. The prisoners around them whooped and hollered as white light appeared like a cyclone out of the stone.

"It's working," Bridget whispered. Her glee soon turned to alarm as fire shot up her arm. Screaming, she dropped the crown inside the cyclone. The moment she did, an explosion shot her away from Selene.

Silence pierced Bridget's ears. Pain sliced up her arm and through her forehead as she tried to sit up. Her chest grew heavier with every breath. Rolling over, she spotted the stone lying on the ground. Reaching out to pick it up, she gasped. The veins in her wrists had blackened. She could see each one snaking up her arm, traveling further growing darker with every passing second.

"I guess what you wanted most was to live through this," Selene taunted weakly before her eyes closed. Only the soft sound of wheezing told Bridget she was still alive.

Bridget knew it was more than that. Of course she wanted to live and see Cade again. But sometimes, magic was too much for a human. She'd seen it dozens of times. She never believed she would be the exception.

Curling into a ball, Bridget lay on the hard ground. She couldn't find the strength to get up or care if the warden had heard them. It was done. The crown was gone. Vega wouldn't be able to use her even if she tried.

Time passed slowly. With each breath, the pain radiating up her arms worsened. Any second, someone would come grab her to take her to Vega. She wondered where she planned to kill her. And if Cade knew. She hoped he didn't. Trying to stop Vega would be useless at this point. She was already dying. The last thing she wanted was for him to share her fate.

"What did you do?"

Bridget's eyes flew open. The voice sounded real… not like the muted ones she'd been replaying in her head to keep her mind off the pain. A blurry figure tried to help her up.

"What are you doing here? How did you get in?" Bridget asked Stellan, even though she already knew the answer. His camouflage skills were one of the strongest abilities she'd ever seen. And he'd grown up in the palace… he knew it almost as well as Cade did. "I told Cade I needed more time. And now…"

How was she supposed to explain what she'd done? She barely comprehended it herself. It had been a spontaneous decision, one built from the fear of finally being fully controlled by Vega. Something she couldn't let happen, especially with nearly all their futures in the balance.

Stellan tried to pull her upright again. "We don't have much time. I'm here to get you out. We heard what she plans to do tonight."

"These cells are spelled with blood magic. If there's no heartbeat inside these walls, Vega and the guard will know," Bridget said. Using Stellan's help, she heaved herself to her feet. The world spun. She stumbled forward.

Stellan caught her. "I know."

Even in the darkness, Bridget read in his eyes what he intended to do. "I can't let you do that."

He wanted to take her place.

"It's what has to be done."

Bridget moved away from him, further into the cell. "No."

Stellan's gaze cut to her arms, where dark veins now covered her entire hands. At least her cloak covered the rest of her skin. "What happened?" he asked.

It took her a moment to answer. "I found out what Vega's plan for the crown was..."

"So she does have it? Just like we thought?"

Despite the knot in her throat choking her, Bridget shook her head. "Not anymore."

Alarm spread over Stellan's features. He darted toward her and pulled up the sleeves of her cloak, only to find her darkening skin. "What exactly did you do?"

"What I had to," Bridget said, voice breaking. "She's going to kill me to enact a curse, one that makes all humans forget who they are... After, she wanted to bring me back with the crown and then use the curse on me so I don't remember her or Cade or what she's done."

Bridget pushed down the sob that threatened to escape her chest. She'd seen what Vega planned to do with her after that. With no memories, she'd be turned into a tool to manipulate Cade and win the war for the Sanguis. And with all her blood being used as one of the anchors, Cade couldn't break the curse or get her memories back. Not without killing her. She'd be doomed forever.

"I couldn't let that happen," Bridget continued. "The thought of being used by her to manipulate Cade and you and everyone and not knowing..."

Who she was. Who Vega was. What needed to be done to defeat her.

"So I sent the crown away. Despite the price. Now she'll lose what she wants most."

*Her*. On her side. Along with the possession of almost all the artifacts.

Stellan's throat bobbed. In all the time she'd known him, she'd never seen him so speechless or distraught. "Where did you send it?" he asked.

"Backwards, I think. Or maybe forward," Bridget muttered, rubbing her temple. Some of the spell she hadn't been able to translate properly. Language had never been her strong suit. And she really needed to sit down. "I'm not really sure."

"You sent it through *time*?" Wide-eyed, Stellan shook his head. "You don't realize what you've done."

"If Vega wants to get it back, she'll have to curse herself with the same spell to chase it." Bitterness rose up Bridget's throat. "It's what she was going to do to Cade, you know. After everything. An unending purgatory he couldn't escape from. Once he handed over the Tuathan sword, of course."

"Bridget, I'm not saying it wasn't a good plan," Stellan said, grabbing her arms. He shook her until her vision refocused. "It's one less weapon for Vega to use. But now you're *dying*."

She blinked at him. This much she knew from every weakening beat of her heart. She didn't understand what he was getting at.

A muscle in Stellan's jaw throbbed. Roughly, he said, "Which means Cade is dying."

Bridget's already crumbling chest shattered. The blurring room tilted. What he said couldn't be true. There was no way he tied his life to hers. Not yet. "No," she croaked. "No. He promised he hadn't... at the wedding, I made him promise he wouldn't until this was all over. We couldn't take the risk, especially when Vega... If he had done it, I would know. I would *remember*. I would..."

"It happened long before that."

"Vassuryn." The word spilled automatically from her lips. It's where they'd found the sword. Together. She'd almost died trying to retrieve it. Until she'd been healed by Cade's magic. Or so she thought. Turns out, it had been a different type of magic entirely. "But that was before..."

Before she'd even realized her feelings for him. Before he'd known her real name. Before *everything*.

Stellan smiled sadly. "I don't think that mattered to him."

Tears welled up in Bridget's eyes. How could he have been so careless to save her like that? When it was his life that mattered the most in the war?

"The moment that happened," Stellan said, nodding at her arms, "he felt it too. It's why he sent me now. Our original plan had been to disrupt the execution and get you out then."

"So I still wouldn't find out what he did?"

At least Stellan had the nerve to look a little guilty. "We can't win this war without him. The sword answers to him. It's the only thing that works on the Wraiths... and the Sanguis. We weren't sure what was wrong. He only knew that you were hurt. We figured if we got you out, he could heal you with his abilities. It's always been one of his stronger gifts. But..."

His abilities had already been fading. Bridget had assumed it was from the relentless use of magic he'd been forced to perform the past year. She knew why now. It was the price of tying his life to hers. Not only did the spell take a Tuathan's extremely slow aging... it took their gifts. Piece by piece. Bridget looked down at her worsening hands. Cade wouldn't be able to save her now. Besides... some magic couldn't be undone.

Bridget's head swirled with possible solutions. This couldn't be how the war ended. Vega *couldn't* win. Not after everything. Not after...

The ripped pages of Vega's book of spells stared up at her. "Another curse."

It was Stellan's turn to blink in confusion. "*What*?"

"You have to curse us. *This* curse." Bridget unfolded the papers to show him Vega's almost unintelligible scribble. "With powerful enough blood, you can send her and the Sanguis away. It's what she wanted to do to the Nymphs that rebelled against her last month. And this one." Bridget waved another piece of paper in his face. The one describing the rebirth curse. "I hadn't figured out who this was for, but it will work, right? It's just like picking us up and moving us to a different time so that we can survive. If you use Cade's blood as the anchor and have a strong enough rune, it should work."

Stellan kept his eyes on her face. "You sound just like her right now."

Bridget flinched. It was the one thing he could have possibly said to hurt her and deflate her ideas. But it's what would have to be done if they had a chance to win the war and save Cade. "*Please*. We can't let her win. If she does, how long is it before she destroys even more worlds?"

Silently, Stellan took the pages from her. He slowly read each spell. "This is blood magic."

"Which you've never done," Bridget argued, her voice sounding a little too hysterical, even to her. "So hopefully the price won't be that steep."

Shame pricked her chest. It was such an unfair statement. She had no idea what blood magic would cost him. But she needed him to try.

"What if Cade doesn't agree?"

"He will."

Stellan didn't bother to argue. They both knew Cade well enough to know that if she hadn't been the one to come up with the dangerous plan she was currently proposing, he would've.

"If I do this…" Stellan took a deep breath and put the pages in his pocket, "there's no guarantee that you'll be reborn at the same time. Or in the same world. Or that you'll figure out what happened at all. There are so many things that could go wrong. I don't think I can risk…"

"*When* you do this... you'll find us one day. The spell says whoever's cursed will have to be reborn in the same bloodline... you'll know where to look. Stay with Cade's family and send Bronwyn with mine. I'm sure she'll agree." Bridget reached out and grabbed his cold hands. "And when we see you again, you'll tell us everything. We'll have a head start. Vega will be trapped in another realm. We'll have all the time in the world to figure out how to get rid of her once and for all. You'll find me, find *us*, and then tell us everything. Promise me."

Stellan's tortured gaze remained unsure.

"*Please*," Bridget begged. "Promise me."

After a long moment, Stellan closed his eyes. Suddenly, he pulled her into his arms. "I promise."

Bridget quickly squeezed him back before she knelt down to grab the Tuathan stone from the hard cell ground. "Keep this safe until we figure out how to use it."

Not looking at her, Stellan put the stone in his pocket.

"Don't let Cade watch the execution," Bridget requested quietly. "And tell him that I'm sorry. And that I love him."

It was all she could manage to get out. If she thought about how she wouldn't get to see him again or say goodbye... then she wouldn't make it out of the cell in one piece. She wouldn't be able to face Vega and accomplish what needed to be done.

With a quick poof, Stellan appeared on the other side of the cell bars. He slowly backed down the hallway, keeping his eyes on her. "I'll do my best."

Once he was out of sight, Bridget sank to her knees. The plan was dangerous, and would cost Stellan dearly, but it had to work. And knowing that there was a plan in place to save Cade made the thought of facing Vega one last time a little easier.

Minutes, or hours, passed before the warden appeared again. Hardly able to stay upright, Bridget barely registered her surroundings as he led her to Vega. Only when cool night air hit her face did she realize where she was being taken. The thrones and the gate to the human realm buzzed as they arrived, like even the very earth knew a large amount of magic was about to be unleashed.

As she was shoved in front of Vega, a familiar shiver vibrated over Bridget's skin. She turned to the hills behind the palace, where she knew she would find Cade. Of course he was here, despite her request. If the roles were reversed, she wouldn't have stayed away either. Even from far away, she could tell what he was thinking. Bridget shook her head. He couldn't interfere. Not now. Not if they wanted a chance. She mouthed *I love you*. She hoped he saw it.

"Is there anything you'd like to say to me?" Vega asked. Somehow, her ceremonial mask was even worse than the one she usually wore.

Bridget glared at her. "Just get on with it."

The blood red mask seemed to glare at her. "Bring it forward."

The chest from Vega's room was dropped in front of Bridget. The chest she knew was now empty. She couldn't stop a tiny smile from forming on her lips.

The Sanguis surrounding her began to chant. A slow, deafening build. The reality of what was about to happen suddenly hit her. Hands trembling, Bridget kept her eyes glued to the bottom hem of Vega's gown so she wouldn't do anything stupid like try to run away. She thought of Cade, and the time he'd shown her around Cavamyne before war tarnished every single moment... then of her sister, swimming in the lake when they were ten. The only thing they cared about then was finding peace together one day. Two perfect memories. Two perfect days.

Vega raised her knife.

Then, with one quick blow, it struck Bridget's heart.

Pain like she'd never known radiated throughout Bridget's body. She couldn't breathe. She couldn't even blink as Vega left the knife in her chest, letting her bleed out slowly. Falling forward, her head struck the ground and rattled her teeth.

The world began to fade.

With one of her metal claws, Vega sliced her left index finger. Blood dripped onto the engraved heart centered on the chest's top. Seconds later, it popped open. Through blurry vision, Bridget stared at the identical wound on her own hand. Spelling objects with her own blood had always been one of Vega's favorite tricks. It guaranteed only she could use them.

Or someone that happened to share her blood.

A horrible scream pierced the air.

"WHERE IS IT?"

In a rage, Vega thrust off her mask, as if doing so would allow her to see the crown back in its box. When she still couldn't find it, she grabbed Bridget by the neck. The knife dislodged from her chest as she was pulled upward. Hot liquid poured out of the center of her body, filling every cavity inside and out. Darkness was a breath away.

"What did you do?" Vega snarled.

There was no more strength left in her body for a reply. Weakly, Bridget smirked as she stared into the Druid's furious, accusatory eyes.

The eyes of her *sister*.

Her *own* eyes. The only identical trait they shared.

And for the first time since they were six, Bridget swore she saw fear.

# CHAPTER TWENTY-SIX

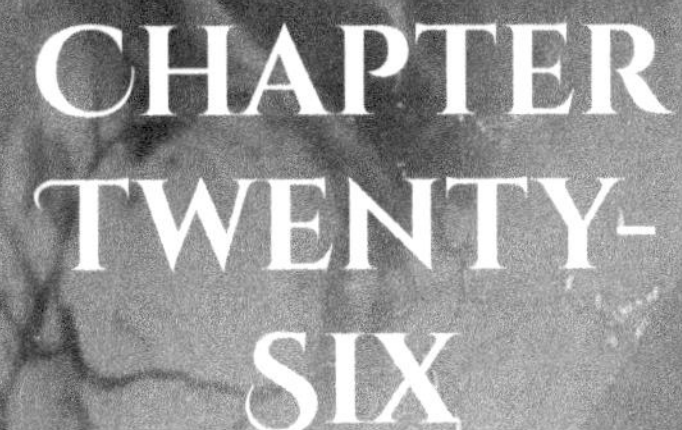

Bridget gasped for air as she broke away from the memory. The pain in her side from Cassia's fingers was nothing compared to the fire still searing her chest. There was no longer a knife or a gaping hole in her chest. She was fine. She was *alive*. But the onslaught of memories still racing through her brain disoriented her.

She knew exactly who she was.

And who Vega was.

Her *sister*.

The realization hit like a punch. Bile surged up her throat as guilt clawed at her insides. Everything had been her fault.

Above her, Cassia's face contorted in agony as she fought to release the spell. Her golden hair clung to her damp skin, wild and tangled, teeth clenched as she tried to tear herself free. When she let out a guttural moan, Castor grabbed her by the shoulders and yanked her backwards. Cassia screamed as her fingers finally tore free, and with a sharp, audible pop, the hum of magic vanished. The silence that followed was deafening. Cassia collapsed into Castor's arms, slick with sweat and barely conscious.

"What the hell is wrong with you?" Castor hissed, holding up Cassia under her arms so she wouldn't fall. "She's barely beginning to understand her magic. You asked her to do too much."

As Delphine's hands pressed against the hole in her side, Bridget searched for an apology she knew she should offer, but it wouldn't come. Regret wouldn't stop Vega. The past was the only weapon they had against her now, and Vega was something else entirely: a brutal combination of magic and vengeance. A force *Bridget* barely understood.

Cade leaned over her protectively. "Back off," he growled. "Cass was in Bridget's head for barely a minute. Besides, she wasn't the one at risk of *bleeding to death*."

A *minute*? An entire lifetime had passed.

"I needed to know," Bridget muttered, the world around her spinning like a ride at Coney Island. Vega. Her sister. The ghost that had been haunting her dreams. Or slowly infiltrating her mind from Iegorus. The second option seemed more likely. She'd been taunting her the entire time.

Drained of color, Cassia whispered, "I could've killed you."

"I'm fine." Pressing her hand over Cade's, Bridget struggled to sit up. At the end of the table, Finn and Stellan stood by her feet. Finn gave her a puzzled look, no doubt from the onslaught of guilt he was receiving from her.

But Stellan... There was an odd mix of anticipation and dread. What exactly did he not want her to know?

Cade pushed back her damp, sticky hair from her face, sending a rush of goosebumps over her skin. "Don't push yourself too hard. You're still bleeding."

His touch sent another thousand memories flying through her head. Ones that overpowered the stench of blood that still lingered in her nose. Slowly, Bridget grazed her fingers over his cheek. He was so different, yet exactly the same. "Cade," she cried, throwing her arms around him. Bridget buried her head in his neck, desperate to feel his skin against hers.

There's nothing she wanted more than to bury the last memory she had of him, standing broken on a hill, ready to watch her die.

*He* was alive. It had worked. They were both here. Now all they had to do was find the rest of the artifacts before Vega could from Iegorus.

"I was supposed to find the memory, not you," Cassia argued, finding enough strength to point her finger at Bridget. "Instead, you took *everything*."

Cade's hand on her lower back froze. He pulled back to look at her. "Everything?"

Bridget's chest twisted. There was so much *hope* in eyes that it almost made her sick. It was clear he wanted to know their shared past too... to see what their life had been like. But there was so much he *couldn't* know. Not yet.

"You remember everything?"

Forcing her gaze away from Cade, Bridget turned to Stellan. Trepidation had taken over his features. At least she wasn't the only one feeling that way.

Bridget swallowed hard. "I took my entire life back."

As if on cue, a sharp pain sliced through her temple. How many lives had she reclaimed now? It seemed to be a never-ending cycle. Who exactly was she now? Cade's wife? An illegitimate princess with a complicated sister? An orphan from New York?

What in the world was she going to tell Nylah? That she had an evil older sister?

The sudden thought of Vega and Nylah in the same vicinity made her stomach twist.

No.

Only over her dead body would she ever let Vega near her.

Bridget barely had time to catch her breath before Cade's voice cut through the haze.

"Do me next."

Her head snapped toward him.

He was looking at Cassia with an unreadable expression. Bridget felt the shift like a thunderclap in her chest. Her stomach twisted. *No. He couldn't. Not yet.*

Cassia blinked, visibly reeling from the aftershocks of the spell. Her skin looked ashen in the firelight, and her hands still trembled faintly at her sides. Before she could respond, Castor stepped forward, voice sharp and unyielding.

"She's too weak for that right now."

Cade's eyes narrowed. Bridget recognized the stubborn tilt of his chin. He was about to push back, to insist like he always did when something mattered too much to let go.

Delphine moved first, cutting him off with a gentle touch on his arm. "He's right," she said softly, her gaze flicking to Cassia. "She needs to rest. For real."

A swell of relief rushed through her when he didn't push again. He simply nodded, voice clipped but final. "Tomorrow then."

"Bridget's memories should be enough," Castor replied. He turned to her. "What does Vega want? Do you know where the crown is? Why did she kill you?"

This time, a faint glow began to hum under Cade's skin. "I said *back off*. She's going to need a minute to sort everything out."

Cassia moved, as if to step between them, but the door creaked open. They all slammed their mouths shut as they simultaneously whipped their heads to the left.

"Don't shoot the messenger," Archer said, holding up his hands. "But there's a girl who is very concerned about some screaming we just heard."

Of course Nylah had heard. Bridget didn't doubt she'd been sitting in the hallway close by the entire time.

"I'll go check on her and explain what happened," Finn said, giving Cade a supportive pat on the back before exiting the room. Archer saluted him.

Glancing at the Bloodstone strewn on the floor, he asked, "Should I keep an eye on that for now? Or do we really just want it laying there?"

Bridget glanced at Cade, then Cassia and Castor. It was clear none of them wanted to pick it up after what had just happened.

"I'll take that as a yes," he said before leaving the room in a quick flourish.

"I apologize, Bridget," Castor said through a locked jaw. "I know you must be very overwhelmed right now, but you need to explain what exactly you discovered."

Bridget took a deep breath.

"Vega is my sister."

Silence penetrated the room, thick and suffocating. Bridget didn't even think anyone was breathing. Even Cade, who usually took everything in stride, was speechless. His mouth fell open, then closed, then opened again as he stared at her. Bridget glanced at Stellan, curious if he'd been withholding that information, but he was clearly stunned. So *that* wasn't the source of his dread.

"How?" Stellan asked. "She's a Druid."

"And technically, the rightful heir to what was the human throne in Astraeus," Bridget added, causing another sharp intake of breath from everyone. "Her mother was a *very* powerful Druid from Suza, happily married to our father in hopes of bringing prosperity to both Kingdoms. At the time, the land in Suza was slowly dying and no one knew why. Eventually, we figured out it was the Sanguis drawing too much power without thinking of the consequences. But I can tell on your faces that part doesn't really matter right now... Okay, long story short, our father had an affair with my mother. Both of them were entirely human. I didn't meet Vega until we were six, when both our mothers died in an accident. After that, I lived here but..."

But she'd lived like an outsider. A sister and daughter, but excluded from being a true member of the family. For the most part. Bridget gazed around at the room. The part of the palace they were in hadn't been built when she'd last considered Astraeus her home. She had a sudden urge to visit her old room.

"That's how Quinn knew how to get past the protection spell through the tunnels. It was built by our father. Vega must have told her," Bridget said, pinching the bridge of her nose. They had been at a complete disadvantage. Vega knew the palace like the back of her hand.

Silence enveloped the room as everyone processed their shock.

"You're a *princess*?"

With her nose wrinkled in dismay, Bridget wasn't sure she'd ever seen Cassia look so revolted.

"No, not really…"

"But your father was the king?" Castor asked. His gaze cut to Stellan's. "Does that mean she's that missing princess from Andarre? That would be her bloodline, correct?"

What. The. Fuck.

On top of everything else, the present-day complications with her family wasn't something she could deal with at the moment.

Archer let out a low whistle. "Alexia's going to *love* that news…"

Bridget sent him a droll look.

"She can't be your sister," Cade said, beginning to pace. "Every story I've been told about Vega says she killed the human girl—*you…*" He ran a distressed hand through his wild hair, like he couldn't believe what he was saying, "because I wouldn't marry her."

"There was a verbal agreement between our parents that you were going to marry her long before we met…" Bridget cringed at the sudden disgust on his face. "It obviously didn't happen. I was the homewrecker in that situation. And we were married for at least a year before she executed me. I don't know where in history it suddenly got mixed up."

"It was the story Bronwyn told me when I finally woke up," Stellan finally said, his voice a bit rough. "She must have been trying to protect you."

Bronwyn. Her mother's best friend—*Tuathan* best friend, who'd been with her since she was born. Where was she now?

"What about the crown?" Castor asked. "Do you know where it is?"

Bridget took a deep breath. She kept her eyes on Cade. Out of everyone, he would be the one to understand why she cursed the crown. "Yes. We had a feeling Vega had it, so I snuck into the palace in Cavamyne to find it... she'd taken it over six months prior. But I got caught. Vega held me there for weeks until she finally showed me the crown and told me what she wanted to do with it."

Cade seemed to be holding his breath. "Which was?" he asked.

"She was going to use it to bring me back after she killed me," Bridget said. "Then use the curse she killed me for to wipe memories so I didn't remember you or what she'd done. She'd have me all to herself."

"A perfect happy family," Archer muttered under his breath.

"So you hid the crown," Delphine interjected. "To keep her from using you like that."

"In a way..." Bridget mumbled. "This is where it gets complicated. While I was there, I found a spell in Vega's things that would send something or someone through time." She couldn't look at their faces. "From what I read, it was designed to be an endless cycle, where whatever it was would never be allowed to stay in one spot for long. She wanted to use it on Cade once she found the Tuathan stone. That was a key element of her spell. A key element she didn't know I had... I thought it was the best way to get rid of the crown without her finding it again. And even if she did, she wouldn't be able to break the curse on it. I would already be dead..."

"Taking the blood she would need with you," Cade finished grimly.

A wave of anxiety lashed up Bridget's spine as she waited for their reactions. Cade squeezed her hand and gave her a small smile. It didn't reach his eyes, but it was enough to calm the squeezing in her chest.

"A brilliant plan stupidly foiled by the idiot who decided it was a great idea to bring you and Cade back five hundred years later," Cassia sneered. "News flash. Your blood is hot and ready for any wannabe Sanguis member to use."

Cade glared at her. "Seriously, Cass?"

"Hey, it's not just mine that's needed," Bridget argued indignantly. "Selene's blood was part of the curse too. I kind of... stabbed her in the stomach to get it. I assume she's dead."

"Who the hell is Selene?" Archer asked.

"A Wraith in the cell next to mine. She used to be this high ranking Tuathan that worked for Cade's mother until she got wrapped up in blood magic."

Cassia rolled her eyes. "Of course you were in prison."

"Just so we're clear..." Castor sighed, his nose pinched between two fingers. "We need this crown to stop Vega and these Wraiths that seem to be able to slip between realms?"

"Marin seemed to think so," Stellan replied.

Even Castor, with stress lines etched in his forehead, didn't want to argue with that.

Cassia crossed her arms. "If Marin had all these important visions, why did she even send us after the crown if it's basically inaccessible?"

"Marin said the visions weren't always straightforward or clear," Bridget argued. "Maybe finding out the reasons *why* Vega wants the crown are just as important as finding it physically. Now that we know that she's my sister and I remember how she thinks, it will be easier to stop her from here."

Cassia still didn't look convinced. "Does it matter if we have it? This Vega bitch is still trapped in Iegorus. As long as she stays there, she can't get the crown. And I don't think any of us are planning to sacrifice Cade to let her out any time soon. Unless I've missed a vital part of the plan."

Cade rolled his eyes. "Thanks, Cass."

"That hasn't stopped her from using other people to get what she wants. She clearly has a foothold," Bridget said. Even now, she was afraid Vega would pop into her mind any second.

"I.e. Quinn," Archer added.

Bridget froze. It wasn't only Quinn she'd been contacting. She been speaking to her. For months.

*You're not remembering the right words.*

In her dream, Vega had shown her the time curse. Had repeated the spell over and over until she'd forced herself awake.

"What's wrong?"

Stellan's question broke Bridget out of her sudden reverie. His eyes were glued to her. The realization she'd just come to must have been written all over her face. "I think she's already figured it out," Bridget said.

"The dreams," Cade finished for her, straightening his spine. Without her having to ask, he flicked his wrist. Seconds later, the door flew open and her all-things-Elyria notebook shot into his hand. Wordlessly, he handed it to her. She knew exactly what page she was looking for. It had only happened a few weeks ago.

"This," Bridget said, pointing to the spell on the page. "This is the curse that she wrote. The one that sent the crown away. She knows. She practically told me. She *taunted* me with it."

"What do you mean she practically *told* you?" Stellan growled.

"Bridget's been seeing her. Ever since the curse broke," Cade said, sending Archer a very unfriendly glare.

Archer visibly paled, but Bridget couldn't blame him. She would've had trouble believing herself, too.

"Look, it's not the time to discuss who thought I was going crazy or not," Bridget said. "It's fine. Cade couldn't even feel her. She figured out when we were kids that she could use our shared blood to communicate without hurting me or leaving any magical evidence. Honestly, until now, *I* thought I was going crazy. The important thing is that Vega knows... which means someone needs to go after the crown before she does."

Stellan cursed and moved to stand in front of the window.

"I'm assuming it's another blood magic curse," Castor said. Throughout the conversation, his stance next to Cassia hadn't changed. Protective. Loyal. Unwavering. Cassia seemed just as stuck in his orbit as he was in her, though they both seemed oblivious to it.

Bridget nodded, and then looked down at the grimoire next to her hip "This was hers..." She couldn't believe it hadn't gotten lost in history. It looked exactly the same. It still brought the same unease to her stomach. Bridget shoved it to the floor. "I don't want it near me. But, please, someone else needs to take it and figure out how she was controlling Quinn even with the amethyst rune. All her spells are in there. Except the one I used for the crown."

Grimly, Stellan picked up the grimoire and tucked it under his arm.

"That one is in your notebook?" Delphine asked.

"Yes."

Castor quietly examined the page from her notebook before throwing it down on the table. "If Cassia is going to try to replicate the curse on the crown, she's going to have to do more than just utter a few words. You can't ask her to do this."

"Stop," Cassia ordered quietly. "I can do it."

Bridget stared at her for a long moment, a little stunned by the seriousness in her demeanor. "He's right. Even if you can, you'll need more than this. Luckily... I know where I left the page."

It only took Cassia a second to understand her meaning. "We're not going to Cavamyne."

"I never said we were. Obviously, we can't," Bridget said, sneaking a glance at Cade. Cavamyne was the last place he needed to be. And she knew he wouldn't let her go without him. "Besides, that's what she wants."

Cade let out a hollow laugh. "She's daring you to go after it before she does." His golden eyes searched her face. Reading her intentions, the smile dropped from his face. "It can't be you."

"It *should* be me," Bridget corrected. She was the one that sent it away. It should be her responsibility. However, there was another pressing responsibility she had to take care of first. "But we also need to go to Andarre."

Nylah needed to be healed. Fully. The longer they relied on Stellan's potions, the higher her anxiety rose. Besides, she was getting tired of Alexia breathing down her neck about the issue.

"At least the sword is there, right?" Castor added. "Cade can claim it while you're there. You get to save your sister, and our asses."

"And the crown?" Cassia asked.

"It's too dangerous. At least right now," Cade said. "As long as Vega stays trapped in Iegorus, no one needs to be jumping through time."

Stellan suddenly whirled on them. "Then I'll think of something. I agreed to help because it was what Marin wanted."

"That was before we found out it's tumbling through time," Cade snapped, jaw tight. "Subjecting someone to the same curse is going to be a last resort. Unless you're volunteering?"

"I will if I have to. She said to find the crown, so that's exactly what I'm going to do," Stellan hissed. "Marin showed me what she saw right before she died."

Bridget stilled. "What? Why didn't you mention that sooner?"

But even as the question left her lips, the answer settled over her like a shadow. Marin's hand on his cheek. He *wanted* to keep it secret. To hold onto that last private piece of her... something just for him.

Frustration and fire brewed behind Stellan's blue eyes. "She saw the crown here in Astraeus. Not five hundred years ago. *Now*. We need it. It's the only way."

He stormed past them. The slam of the door behind him rattled the room's wooden table and fireplace mantle.

"Not that he was always a joy to be around," Archer said, breaking the silence, "but is he always going to be such a grump now?"

Cade narrowed his eyes. "His daughter died."

"Right."

"Well, since we all can't exit the room in a dramatic fashion, I need my satin pillow and my favorite wine," Cassia corrected, rubbing her forehead. "I feel almost as bad as I did when you crashed the monstrous machine last year."

Bridget glared at her. "*You* crashed it."

"I've got an idea," Cade said, wrapping an arm around Bridget's waist. "Instead of blaming each other, let's blame Archer for the death of my baby. He *was* the one that chased you."

Archer wasn't amused. "Ha. Ha."

"I think that's our cue," Delphine said, gaze flickering between Castor and Cassia. Cheeks slightly pink, she helped Bridget off the desk. "And we should get you bandaged up."

After Archer made an excuse to leave, Bridget followed. But once they were in the hallway, Cade's hand, still on her waist, stopped her. "We should check on Nylah," she said, watching the others turn the corner.

Bridget hated that she almost didn't want to be alone with him. As she braved a look at his face, her heart wanted to burst out of her chest. Past and present memories mended together into an electric shock consuming her as she fell into his gaze. How was it possible to feel so connected to someone? She'd fallen in love with him so many times... had fought and *died* for the chance of a future with him. There was no one in the world who made her feel more whole. More *alive*.

And now she was going to have to lie to him.

"Can I see?"

The question was innocent enough. The memories she had regained were partly his, too. But as he lifted his hand to her temple, Bridget flinched.

"No."

The word came out harsher than she intended. The slightly wounded shock on his face was worse than she could have ever imagined.

"I just mean not now," Bridget corrected, then leaped toward him. She plastered her lips on his in a searing kiss. When he immediately responded, she tried to pour every ounce of longing she'd felt for him when she'd been trapped with Vega. The goodbye kiss she wished she would've been able to give to him.

When she finally pulled away, her entire body was on fire. "I'm sorry," Bridget said, hands trembling. "I just need some more time to process it all. Promise me you won't look until I'm ready."

With his cheeks flushed and breath hot on her face, it was so hard not to tell him everything.

"I promise," Cade said.

One day, when it was all over, she would let him see. Until then, she had to keep him out of her head.

# CHAPTER TWENTY-SEVEN

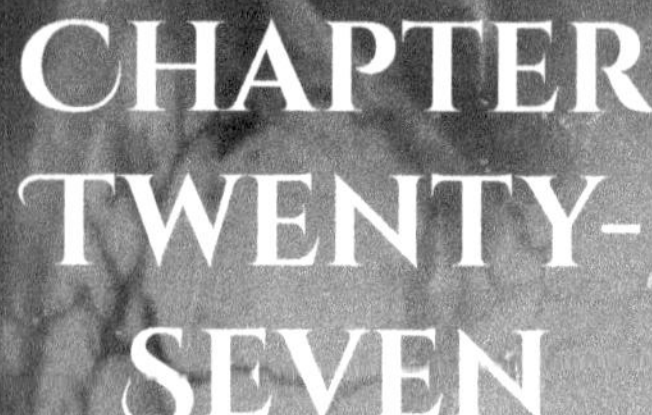

Bridget's father stared back at her.

Well, not literally. A painting of him did. The moment Cade had finally drifted off to sleep beside her, she'd hopped out of bed. Tiptoeing across the hall, she'd peeked inside Nylah's room. Her sister had been knocked out like a rock under a giant comforter. Alone, but Bridget had told herself that was okay. Finn *had* said she'd drifted off to sleep soon after he'd checked on her. After that, her feet had taken her to the throne room before she had even processed what she was wanting to find.

Bridget grabbed the nearest flickering torch. Even though it was the middle of night, the king still kept the few scattered on the onyx columns burning. She held it above her head and squinted her eyes to get a better look at the painting looming on the marble wall. The last time she'd been in the throne room, she'd met Cade's father and been forced into the tournament. Even with his intimidating gaze on her, she almost hadn't been able to take her eyes off a faded portrait of a man with a mustache.

The portrait of her father.

Or her *Before* father. She wasn't sure what to call him. There was still a man out there who could claim the title, too. Bridget couldn't believe there was evidence of him at all in Astraeus. It was shocking that the old Tuathans, or whoever was left of Cade's family, hadn't scrubbed all evidence of humans from the palace once they took over. They'd already been halfway doing that before she was killed. But he had built and designed the throne room—an ode to his new wife and agenda, right after she'd turned sixteen. Perhaps it was their one last thanks to him before he disappeared to Andarre. Supposedly.

She wondered what he would say if he could see her and Vega now, both alive and still fighting five hundred years in the future.

"Where's Cade?"

Bridget whipped around at the sound of Stellan's voice. Unlike her, he hadn't changed into any night clothes. Instead, his usually tidy blonde hair was sticking up at the temples, like he'd been wracking his brain as he read a difficult book. Or thinking about Marin.

"He's asleep."

Stellan froze. Frustration pinched his brows. "Then why did you ask me to meet you here?"

After placing the torch back in its rightful spot, Bridget met him underneath the glass chandelier. "You really did forget everything I needed you to remember."

The words tasted bitter. Her entire plan had hinged on knowing who Vega was to her from the start. But she hadn't. Now Vega was one step away from returning, and there was no one to blame but herself, no matter how she tried to dress it up as accusation.

Stellan frowned. "What are you talking about?"

"I need to show you what you missed."

He was the only person who could help her do what needed to be done. But she knew him well enough—at least, the old version of her did—to know that if he was going to agree, he needed every angle of the story. When he remained frozen, Bridget grabbed his hand and held it up to her temple. Stellan tried to pull away, but she tightened her grip. "Just do it."

After a long pause, he entered her mind. A million needles traveled from her forehead to her spine as she focused on the memory she wanted to show him. Her nails dug into her palms as she relived casting the curse on the crown and him entering her cell. Once he disappeared out of sight, Bridget flung herself away from him.

"Wow."

Rooted to the spot, Stellan stared at her wide-eyed, his voice almost a faint whisper.

A little dizzy, Bridget wiped away the blood dripping from her nose. "I'm so sorry I made you do that."

She hadn't understood then the extent of what she'd asked him to do. Not until she'd witnessed it from his point of view. He'd had to kill his best friend. He'd lost years of his life from the cost of blood magic. It didn't matter if Cade had already been dying or they were going to come back. She'd forced him to do the unthinkable.

Eyes still a bit glassy, like he couldn't stop replaying what he'd seen, Stellan said, "It's what had to be done."

"It didn't have to happen," Bridget said, shaking her head. She needed him to understand. "Everything Vega did was because I chose Cade over her."

She'd spent hours analyzing every detail of her past. And all her ruminating had led her to the inevitable conclusion: it was her fault. She had been the only person in the world with the ability to stop the war and she'd made all the wrong choices.

Stellan opened his mouth, clearly about to argue, but Bridget cut him off.

"Don't try to correct me. It's what everything boils down to..." Bridget said. "I chose him over my sister. I could've tried harder. I could've stayed with her when she asked me to... Maybe if I had, I could've stopped her."

She bit the inside of her cheek before she did something ridiculous like let the moisture stinging her eyelids fall to her cheeks.

"Vega made her own choices long before she found out about you and Cade."

"Maybe." Yes, Vega had already formed the Sanguis before that whole debacle played out, but she could've stopped her from doing any more damage. Rolling her neck, Bridget tried to compose her face into a neutral expression. "But that's not why I asked you to come down here. After I got my memories back, I could tell there was something you didn't want me to remember."

She paused, giving him a chance to deny it, but he remained silent. "It's that Cade tied his life to mine, isn't it?"

Stellan's throat bobbed his bright blue eyes radiating sadness. "I still remembered that because I knew long before those final days. I figured it out the first day you arrived in Cavamyne. It was obvious. To any Tuathan, at least. However, that's where certain events started getting hazy."

"Because Vega was there too." Bridget realized now almost every memory he had of her was probably muffled if Vega was involved. Her stomach twisted. It was hard to believe there was a time when she and Vega entered Cavamyne together as *sisters*. Bridget could still remember every detail, including Cade's expression as she stepped out of the carriage behind Vega. While that had been his first time meeting the *real* her, he and Stellan had known her long before that.

"I don't blame you for trying to run away from all this," Bridget said, referring to their conversation outside the cabin in Connecticut. "I know you wanted to stop interfering... but I understand now why you couldn't stay away. If you hadn't been there that day in the woods after Quinn shot me, Cade would've died."

Despite Archer's efforts, Stellan was another reason why she'd made it out alive. He'd been the one with the phone. The whole reason she'd been brought back with the curse was because of her connection with Cade.

The thought of him dying because of her, even if she hadn't known, made her nauseous. Knowing they were connected that very second made her want to go hide in a padded room.

Stellan's expression suddenly shifted. "I showed up that day to save you."

And then Bridget saw it. The thing she hadn't allowed herself to see… or *couldn't* see when Cade's presence attracted the attention of every single atom in her body. The disguised longing. After all, camouflage had always been his specialty. Another inevitable conclusion barreled through her. The why behind the curse taking his memories surrounding those final events. Above all, he'd wanted to keep his promise… to her.

"I'm sorry."

The words clawed their way out of Bridget's throat, low and broken. The three syllables didn't feel like enough for what he'd been through. She'd never wanted to hurt him. He'd been a constant friend and companion to her, even before she'd permanently become part of his life. But she could never give him what he wanted.

Stellan's expression shuttered close. Within seconds, he'd transformed back into the well-mannered, closed book he always presented himself as. Bridget wondered if she'd ever catch a glimpse of what was truly inside ever again.

Clearing his throat, Stellan asked, "Are you going to tell him? If he knew…"

It took Bridget a moment to realize he was referring to the bond. "If Cade knew, he wouldn't want to break it." She read the trepidation and anxiety in his eyes. "But I agree with you. We *should*."

"Bridget…"

"Because of a vision, Deckard has always believed that I'll kill him. Marin said that I wouldn't, but what if it's metaphorical?" Bridget whispered. "What if he dies because of the bond?"

Stellan's silence told her he'd already suspected that possibility.

"You already tried to break it, didn't you?" Bridget held up the pale ends of her hair. "The old me was a lot more versed in magic. I know the signs. And I know you probably thought the excess power soaking the air from the curse being broken was a good starting point."

A fact she knew from Vega. It was why she would go back to the same place, over and over again, to recharge her abilities.

"After they revived you, I thought it would be weak enough that I could snap it," Stellan admitted. "Then I realized the bond was probably the only thing that kept you alive long enough for the paramedics to arrive. All I did was almost kill you again."

"Why didn't it work?"

"I don't think it's possible from your end. You're not the one who created the bond. Cade did. It's why Tuathans are the only ones affected by it... why they're the ones who have to pay the price for it or die with the other person."

Bridget grimaced. Acid filled her mouth. She understood the *why* behind the bond. If you want to spend your life with someone, you do what it takes. It worked... in a perfect world. If they weren't *them*, the bond would be the most precious thing to her. But they didn't live in a perfect world. Cade *needed* what he'd given up for her. "If we're going to have a shot against these Wraiths or whatever else Vega sends our way, he needs to have all his abilities back. He'll get them back if it breaks, right?"

Because Vega was *not* leaving Iegorus. Cade's death over a stupid rock to bring her sister back wasn't something her brain could even conceive. The moment it tried, she zapped it into oblivion.

"Theoretically." Stress lines returned to Stellan's forehead. "Maybe we can figure out another way. He might not be able to do everything you remember, but he's still powerful. It might not be necessary to—"

"It *is* what's necessary." Pausing, Bridget sucked in a sharp breath. Her eyes closed from a wave of disgust. The words sounded so *Vega*. Hadn't she used the same excuse so many times? *This is different*, she told herself. She was trying to learn from her mistakes. This was their one shot at a do-over.

Taking a deep breath, she continued, "This whole time I've been thinking things will work out because how could they not? I love him. We found each other. We beat the odds... But it's not going to be enough. It wasn't the last time."

Last time, she'd so blindly believed in a happy ending, in being *right*, she'd inadvertently walked right into Vega's plans, without a thought to the consequences. She'd almost doomed them all. "What we did is buy ourselves enough time to realize that," Bridget finished, her voice barely a whisper.

Mouth turned down in a grim line, Stellan processed her words for a long time. Eventually, he sighed. The sound was heavy with the past. "The only instances that I know of the bond being broken is through the Tuathan's death."

When Bridget flinched, Stellan held up a calming hand, continuing, "That's obviously not an option. If the bond is going to be broken, it's going to have to come from him."

"How?"

Bridget knew the answer before the terrifying question left her mouth. She'd have to do something to make it waver. Something that would make him subconsciously pull back on it. She'd have to hurt him.

For a split second, she wanted to fall to her knees and scream that she couldn't. But she tried to smother the twisting in her gut with logic. He needed the entirety of his Tuathan abilities.

And she couldn't risk him dying if Vega suddenly decided to kill her again.

Eventually, Bridget choked out, "I'll see what I can do."

Entire body on the verge from collapsing from the inevitable torture she was about to force on it, Bridget turned to flee the room. She needed time alone to process how it was going to be possible. How she was going to get through this and still manage to look him and Nylah in the eyes.

Before she made it to the throne room's double doors, Stellan's deep voice rattled her bones. "No matter what you do, he's not going to accept it. I don't think he'll ever let go of you enough that the bond can be severed."

That was exactly what she was afraid of.

"He's going to have to."

For years, she'd watched everyone around her give up so much to the war... to fight Vega. To *win*.

It was about time for her to do the same.

# CHAPTER TWENTY-EIGHT

Bridget picked at the apple in her hand. She knew she should take a bite. It had been hours since she'd eaten. Even more since she'd slept. With a frustrated sigh, she threw the fruit down the hallway. She'd watched the night fade into morning as she tried to fade the slicing pain in her chest. Nothing had worked. Instead, she decided to torture herself more by tracking down the painting of her, Cade, and Vega. It was still exactly where she'd stumbled upon it with Cade the first time, right outside the southern garden.

Whoever created it, clearly had never met them. They looked nothing like themselves and Vega never actually ripped out her heart. The thought gave her shivers. Still, she couldn't help but stare at it in hopes it would give her some sort of answers for what she should do next. Faint morning light highlighted the dark-haired woman in the middle. She was regal and cold.

Okay, maybe some features were right.

"What are you planning?" Bridget murmured.

It was cowardice to ask the painting instead of Vega herself. Bridget knew if she closed her eyes and drifted off to sleep, her sister would probably pop in, all too willing to talk. However, Bridget was willing to bet there was an extremely small chance the answers she would receive would actually be the truth.

Seconds later, she caught Cade in the corner of her eye. She didn't look at him, opting to keep her gaze glued to the painting instead. But the closer he came, the more her hands trembled. Even though she'd pondered what to do all night and had even convinced herself she was ready, one glimpse of him, of the warmth in his eyes, had every certainty unraveling.

Bridget kept her arms crossed tightly and forced herself not to move until he reached her. When he finally did, she felt the weight of his gaze shift from her, to the painting, and back again. After a beat, his arm slipped around her waist as he tucked her into his side

Cade kissed the top of her head, his voice muffled against her hair. "You look like you're obsessing."

"I feel like I'm obsessing."

For a moment, Bridget leaned into Cade and let herself savor his warmth. Keeping her arms crossed, she craned her neck to look at him. For someone she'd left sleeping in bed, he looked almost as tired as she felt. There was a hint of purple under his eyes and his thick hair was wavier than usual. At least he was in regular clothes. She was still wearing the shorts and old Yankees shirt she'd pretended to go to bed in.

As if reading her thoughts, Cade tugged on the fraying hem of her shirt. "You should get some rest." His golden eyes cut to the apple at the end of the marble hallway. "Or eat something. It's a shame someone just let a perfectly good apple roll right into a spider's web."

He'd noticed that? Bridget gave him a droll look before she sighed. "I can't."

She just *knew* the moment she closed her eyes, she was going to be pulled into Vega's makeshift dreamworld of Cavamyne.

Cade fiddled with the white edges of her hair before he tucked a few strands behind her right ear. "If you want to sleep, I won't leave your side. That way, if Vega—"

"I don't want to see her right now."

The words came out harsher than she intended. Cade just cocked his head.

"What do you think she's going to do?"

*Ask me too many questions. Try to use Nylah. Figure out that I remember. Realize you're bonded to me and use it to kill you.*

Every logical answer got trapped in her throat. She wasn't supposed to be confiding in him. She was supposed to be pushing him away.

For a moment, she couldn't breathe.

She didn't realize she was clenching her fists until Cade gently uncrossed her arms and pried her fingers loose. Red, crescent shaped marks were embedded in her palms.

"Bridget, I want to help."

There was so much damn *worry* and love in his eyes, she wanted to obliterate herself into a pile of ash on the floor. It was now or never. She had to get it over with it. Like ripping off a Band-Aid. Or she never would.

"I know," Bridget finally croaked. "I just..."

Her throat tightened up, like it was almost physically impossible for her to actually say the words. Chest thundering, she tried to make herself swallow.

After a long moment, Cade asked, "What is it?"

Bridget used all the strength she had to push her voice to a whisper. "There's just so much going on right now and I..."

If she managed to get through this moment, how in the hell was she going to keep this up? She was already being a coward by using the easiest and lamest plan she could come up with. Maybe she really should have gotten some sleep.

With his thumb, Cade wiped away the stray tear that had traitorously left her eye. "Hey, it's alright. I know finding out Vega is your sister has messed with your head and that whatever happened in the past is worrying you. But you don't have to go through it alone. I'm right here."

The confident, supportive smile on his face flickered when she didn't answer. "If you don't want my help, at least talk to Nylah."

"I think we should break up."

The suggestion tumbled from her lips in such a hoarse, jumbled mess, Bridget was surprised Cade understood her at all. *Break up*. It didn't even seem like the right words for what they were. It was too insignificant. But it was the only thing she could think of that would be the first step in creating separation.

Time seemed to slow down as she watched Cade's expression battle between shock, confusion, and anger. Eventually, downright *furious* conquered his features. "No."

Bridget blinked a few times. She didn't have an answer for *no*. "Yes," she stuttered.

"No," Cade bit out, jaw clenched. "You can't be serious."

Why did she ever expect he would make this easy on her? She'd never seen him so outraged. And the stubborn draw of his brows told her she wasn't going to win the conversation. "We have to."

Cade scoffed. "*We have to*. Do you hear yourself?"

Yes. And she was now regretting even thinking that this tactic could work.

Without breaking eye contact, Cade grabbed her left hand and held it up. "You want to break up with me, but you moved your ring to your other hand?"

Bridget snatched her hand away. Heat flooded her cheeks. She had no idea when she'd moved her wedding ring to the correct finger. Her memories were now such a jumbled mess, she kept having to remind herself which *time* she was in.

"I didn't mean to do that," she whispered, twisting the broken emerald around her finger to pull it off.

Fire flashed through Cade's darkening expression. "Don't you dare move it back."

Bridget slowly dropped her hands. Lowering her gaze, she picked a tile to stare at her and hoped the world would stop tilting around her. If she was going to push him away, she needed to move the ring back to her right hand or keep it in a drawer or *something*. But Cade's statement had melted her into an unmoving mess.

"Why?" he asked.

Bridget snapped her gaze back to Cade's. The calm question was so opposite of the ire still brewing in his golden eyes, it almost left her out at a loss for words again. "Why what?"

"Why do *we have to*?" Cade asked. "What happened in the past that's making you try to push me away?"

"I can't tell you. If you trust me at all—"

"But you can tell Stellan."

Bridget's mouth fell open. Panic licked up her spine. His haggard appearance suddenly made sense. "You followed me?"

"Of course, I did. Something is obviously wrong. You could barely look me in the eye last night," Cade argued. "And while my father has seemed to accept we're together, that still doesn't mean it's safe to wander around here in the dead of night all by yourself."

"You don't understand..." Bridget began, thinking only of her conversation with Stellan about the bond. He couldn't know. But then she saw what he was trying to hide. *Jealousy.* "It's not what you think."

She slammed her mouth shut. For someone trying to break up with him, she was letting every good excuse roll right out the window.

Confusion marred Cade's features before his mouth curled in irritation. "Fuck, Bridget, give me a little more credit," he growled. Letting out a tired sigh, he grabbed the sides of her face. His thumb ran over her cheekbone.

"I know that you love me... which is why you need to help me understand why you can trust him, but not me."

Bridget wanted to scream that she did trust him. More than anyone. But the panic paralyzing her limbs choked her. Cade couldn't know about the bond. Not yet. Even if the urge to just tell him was growing by the second.

Especially when there was a nervous lilt to his voice when he asked, "What did you show Stellan?"

"Were you listening the whole time?" Bridget whispered—half terrified of the answer, half hoping he just already *knew*.

"I don't have supersonic hearing." Frustration returned to Cade's gaze. Again, he asked, "What did you show him?"

Relief soared through her limbs. At least they still had a chance to get his abilities back. At least they—

An all too familiar cloak floated through Bridget's line of vision behind him. With a sour look on her face as she glanced at the giant portraits of Cade's ancestors, Alexia pulled up her hood and eyed the open archway to the southern garden.

"Alexia," Bridget mumbled, brain sputtering with all the pieces it was trying to put together.

Cade stared at her like she had two heads. "*What?*"

"What time is it?" Bridget asked. Alexia shouldn't be alone. Since they'd arrived in Astraeus, Nylah had made it her life's mission to ensure that didn't happen. *Since she poisoned me, I'm going to pester her*, she'd said.

"I don't know. I think around eleven..." Cade said, wildly looking around for a clock. Once he spotted Alexia, he paled. The same conclusion she'd spun to obvious on his face.

How was it already that late? Bridget pushed past him and darted toward Alexia. She grabbed the other girl's arm and ripped her backwards before she made it to the courtyard.

Alexia sneered. "Get your hands off me."

"How did you get past Nylah?" Bridget demanded.

"What in the hell are you talking about?" Alexia's now wary gaze darted between her and Cade, who'd followed her maniacal sprint.

"She's been guarding you like it's her damn job," Bridget muttered through gritted teeth. "You know, kind of like what you used to do to me."

Having the gall to look affronted, Alexia ripped her arm back to her side. "Is that why the little twerp won't leave me alone?"

Bridget's stomach sank to the floor. Something was wrong. Something was *very* wrong. She knew it in her bones. Nylah never slept late. Without a word, she took off toward the main staircase, Cade hot on her heels.

Taking the round, carpeted staircase two steps at a time, Bridget's lungs burned by the time she made it to the fourth floor. Sprinting past the library, she skidded to a halt in front of Nylah's door and slammed it open.

The same large lump she'd seen in the middle of the night still lay in the center of the bed. Cade grabbed her arm, clearly saying something, but the sharp ringing in her ears drowned out every noise except her own heartbeat. Bridget flipped the covers off the four-poster bed. Two fluffy pillows stared up at her.

For a split second, it was like every single atom of her body had imploded and escaped through a gaping hole in her chest. When specks of light began to flood her vision again, Bridget found herself collapsed in Cade's arms. Her entire body trembled as a singular, slicing message erupted through her brain: Nylah was gone.

# CHAPTER TWENTY-NINE

## CASSIA

The throne room was a mess of voices, movement, and too many people Cassia couldn't name. Not that she cared to. She lingered near the corner, half in shadow, observing more than participating. Watching. Listening. It was easier that way. She'd perfected the art of fading into the background, of being the silent one no one noticed until she decided to let out a brash comment.

Plus, the last thing Cassia wanted to do was touch someone. Or something magical. The lingering hum of the Bloodstone's power still clung to her fingers, even through the gloves she'd hastily pulled back on. Too intoxicating. Too addictive. Her hands ached with the memory of it... of how natural it had felt, how much she'd wanted more.

A shiver slid down her spine.

Cassia clenched her jaw and stared at the floor. She hated remembering what she'd done. The image of her fingers buried in Bridget's side was still too fresh. So was the sound of her scream. And now, on top of that, she was stuck in her least favorite room... crammed in with a crowd, hemmed in by firelight and walls that swallowed all trace of sunlight. Windowless. Airless. Smothering.

Or maybe the feeling was caused by a certain person. Her eyes drifted to her father. He stood across the room, speaking in clipped, stern tones to one of his advisors. She'd barely come to terms with the revelation that he'd known what she was for *years* and tried to smother it. Despite his claims his actions had stemmed from his desire to protect his children, she wasn't sure she could forgive him. Even if he did seem like he was trying to help. With a rough flick of his wrist, her father summoned Orion away from him with a growl.

"I've checked the kitchens and eastern apartments. Everyone there is accounted for," Delphine said, hurrying into the room with her dark hair messily wrapped atop her head. She made a beeline for Cade and Bridget.

Cassia almost wanted to laugh. So the girls still trapped on the palace grounds because of the tournament wouldn't be joining them? She glanced at Bridget and Cade pressed together by one of the marble columns. Actually, it was probably a smart move by her brother to keep them away. Bridget already looked like she was one breath away from combusting. For the last ten minutes, she'd been staring at nothing, her expression carved from stone.

"You're turning blue. I don't know if you've heard of this thing called air, but..."

The whispered words from Archer to Bridget earned him a tired glare from Cade.

Cassia strained her ears to hear Cade's low reply, but a presence to her left sent her heart rate spiking. She didn't have to look to know it was Castor. The mere inch between them buzzed with more tension than she could handle. Her body ached to close it. Just lean over, touch his arm, and feel something real. But she couldn't tell if that pull was hers or the magic still simmering beneath her skin, greedy for more.

Instead, she asked him, "How did this happen?"

The palace grounds were under protection spells, and her father had almost the entire army stationed inside. The tunnel Quinn and the Wraith had entered from were still covered by rubble. A little girl couldn't have just disappeared.

"She must have wandered off," Castor said.

She didn't think that was the case. Cade had basically sent the entire palace into a lockdown. She'd learned a long time to always trust her brother's hunches.

"I don't think so."

Tapping into the lingering current of magic in her veins, Cassia reached out to Cade's mind. With a sharp pop of energy, she slipped inside. The weight of his thoughts nearly knocked her flat. His mind was in chaos. For a second, she almost couldn't breathe from the frantic flashes of memory, fear, and the burn of responsibility gnawing at him.

*Do you have any ideas?*

*No.* His voice was tinted with frustration. *And Bridget won't let me in her head to know what she's thinking.*

"Ah," Castor said. "Have you two ever thought some of these conversations would be better said aloud?"

Cassia ignored him.

*Why?* she asked.

Two deep lines marred Cade's forehead as he watched Bridget and Delphine exchange whispers. *There's something she saw in the past that she doesn't want me to know.*

Cassia sent him the bits and pieces she'd seen. A dungeon. A waterfall. Ballrooms and dresses. A brief image of him in a tavern.

Cade sent her a droll look over his shoulder. *That's all very vague.*

*Like I said, she did most of the searching.*

"Wait, where's Finn?"

Archer's question landed like a dropped blade.

Cassia's eyes snapped to Cade, just as his posture stiffened. His glowing irises sparked to life as he searched for Finn's presence in his head. After a moment, his brows furrowed.

"I can't find him," Cade said slowly, like the words were unfamiliar in his mouth.

Cassia's pulse quickened. That wasn't possible. The energy in the throne room seemed to shift. She glanced at Bridget, who still looked lost in thought.

"Did anyone see him after he checked on Nylah?" Delphine asked, a nervous lilt in her voice.

Archer rubbed the back of his neck, eyes narrowed in thought. "Briefly. In the hallway. He passed me like I wasn't there… He didn't even react to the joke I told him."

"I doubt it was funny," Cade said, trying for lightness, but the tension in his voice betrayed him.

But then Bridget moved. Cassia saw it first on her shoulders. A flinch, a tremor, and then the widening of her eyes.

"That wasn't Finn," she said, voice low and broken.

The room stilled in an instant. Even the torches flickered low, as if the castle itself were holding its breath. A chill spidered up Cassia's spine. She could tell by the rising panic on Bridget's face that the next words out of her mouth were going to be bad.

Bridget swallowed hard. "It was Vega."

All the air in the room vanished. Everyone in the room seemed to tremble at the name. Even her father, who rarely showed emotion, sat straighter on the throne. His shoulders squared. His eyes darkened as they locked on Bridget, as if he could interrogate the truth out of her with his gaze alone.

Confusion etched across Cade's features. "What do you mean?"

"It was Vega. Finn was cut by Quinn, remember?" Bridget's hoarse words came out in a rush, like she couldn't get them out fast enough. "She's possessing him. That was always one of her favorite tricks, but she could never hold it long. That was a long time ago though and…" She paused and inhaled a sharp breath. "Of course, that has to be what she did to Quinn. She must have written a new blood spell based on how she already knew how to get in my head, without anyone sensing it."

The world tilted on its axis. Cassia didn't need confirmation. Cade's face said it all. Color drained from his skin, and when his eyes met hers across the room, she didn't need to enter his mind to feel the rising panic brewing behind them. Not only had Vega taken Nylah, she also had the Bloodstone. Cassia glanced at Castor. Engrossed in a silent conversation with Cade, the lines of his throat had gone taunt.

Her father let out an exasperated breath, pinching the bridge of his nose. "Are we certain she didn't just run off?" he asked, voice sharp with irritation. But Cassia caught it… a flicker of something beneath the frustration. Concern, she thought, before it vanished behind the practiced mask of a king.

"She wouldn't do that," Bridget shot back sharply. "Besides, she doesn't know this land. She wouldn't know where to go."

Her father's eyes cut to Alexia, who sat curled up in a corner, expressionless. "I assume you can't track her because of the Andarrian rune," he said.

A headache threatened to form in Cassia's head. Earlier, she'd admired that Bridget had chosen to give her sister the necklace instead of wearing it herself. Now, a wave of frustration shot up her spine that she couldn't have waited to give it away just a few hours later.

Cade's neck heated. The frustration was clear on his face, even if she already hadn't caught a glimpse of his thoughts. His gaze drifted from their father, then back to Bridget. "If she possessed Finn to take Nylah, then there's only one place she'll go."

Cassia closed her eyes. She knew Bridget's answer before she said it.

"Cavamyne."

The last place her brother needed to be. The only place where Vega could finally get what she wanted: a way back into their world. Cassia's chest twisted. She wanted to scream at Cade and forbid him to go. But she knew him well enough to know that wasn't an option. He was going. No matter what.

"We can't let that happen. It's too risky," Castor whispered, as if reading her thoughts. His eyes hadn't left her since Cade's grim reply to their father.

"I don't think we have much of a choice," she choked out, fear seizing her. She had to go with them, just in case something happened. But the words to Cade wouldn't escape her mouth.

Their father rose from the glittering throne, his footsteps echoing sharply off the marble as he crossed the room. When he stopped in front of Cade, the fury in his eyes was barely restrained. "You're walking into a trap," he said, voice low but seething.

Cade didn't flinch. His jaw set with quiet resolve. "I know."

Silence pierced the room as they stared at each other. Cassia half-expected an order. Some final act of power to stop Cade from doing what they all knew he would do anyway. But then—

"Then I'm coming too," their father said. "Besides, I can't miss another fight. Any more, and I may have to give up my title."

Cassia froze. Her father's words landed with the weight of finality, more jarring than any shout. The quiet authority in his voice shook something loose in her chest. Every breath caught like it no longer belonged to her. Around her, the room exploded into motion. Voices rose, orders barked, and plans unraveled faster than she could process. And still, she stood anchored in place, untouched by the whirlwind.

They were going to Cavamyne.

And no matter how hard she wished to rewind the last hour, to claw the thread of fate back into her hands—there was no stopping it now.

# CHAPTER THIRTY

Cassia lingered in the shadows of the stables, the scent of old hay and worn leather settling deep in her lungs. Snow dusted the edges of the wooden beams, and her fingers curled tighter around the edge of a stall door as she watched Bridget saddle a horse. She moved like someone who'd done this a hundred times. Saddling the mare, checking straps, adjusting the reins with quiet precision. There was a calmness to her hands, a fluency to the motions that hadn't been there before.

Cassia narrowed her eyes.

She didn't think Bridget even realized what she was doing. She wasn't hesitating. She moved like the knowledge had always lived inside her bones... like it had returned the moment the memories did. Cassia had seen her fumble her way through most things in Elyria. Now here she was, acting like she'd been around horses her entire life.

Which maybe was a good thing for where they were headed. Cassia's stomach twisted again. Her hands hadn't stopped trembling since she'd followed her father and the rest of the search party to the stables to get ready for their journey.

"We've already wasted too much time," Bridget said, cinching the saddle with a final, purposeful tug. "It took me forever to find a damn cloak and boots."

Cassia couldn't make out Cade's reply. His voice was too soft, threaded with worry as he approached. He said something under his breath, hand brushing Bridget's back as he tried to comfort her.

But Bridget didn't soften. She didn't pull away... but she didn't lean in either.

"At least Alexia is staying here. I don't think I can tolerate her snide remarks right now," she muttered.

Then, with a soft pop, the air crackled. Stellan appeared in the center of the stable like a gust of midnight wind.

Bridget whipped around. "Where have you been?"

"I was researching the blood spell Vega must have used on Finn," he said, voice taut with urgency. He held up the old grimoire. "The more we understand it, the easier it will be to find him and break the connection. She's powerful, but she's holding him from another realm. That leaves signs, despite what you or her may think. Dead trees. Dried snow. Things that appear out of the norm."

Cade stepped forward, brow furrowed. "Are you sure?"

Before she could hear Stellan's answer, Cassia sensed another presence slipping in beside her. Castor. The air around them seemed to shift, just like it always did when he was near. She inhaled sharply and tried to remain focused on the threesome still whispering across the stable.

Castor didn't speak right away. Just stood close enough to brush shoulders if she leaned slightly. Finally, he said, "Here, let me help."

She watched him take the straps she had forgotten she was supposed to be adjusting and buckled them tightly around her horse's waist.

"You're still wearing those gloves," he said gently, not quite teasing. "You remind me of Bridget last year."

"At least her bare hands weren't a threat to everyone around her," Cassia said flatly.

"Cassia…"

"I don't want to talk about me right now," she snapped, softer than she meant. Her voice cracked at the edges. "Not when my brother's life is on the line."

"He's going to be fine," Castor said, his voice low and certain.

Cassia didn't answer. She looked past him toward Cade and Bridget again, watching them move around each other like twin flames. The weight of everything that had transpired pressed heavily upon her heart. The pain, the choices, the past… had all led here.

"Everything's led to this, hasn't it?" she murmured, her thoughts swirling and escaping her mouth.

Castor's brows pulled together. "What do you mean?"

"No matter what Cade or Bridget or *anyone* did to try and change the path… we were always going to end up in Cavamyne," she said. "It's like we've been careening toward it this whole time, without even realizing it."

Suddenly, the past stretched out before her, in a way it hadn't before. Every misstep glared back at her… every chance they'd had to change course, every moment they could've chosen differently. Guilt coiled along her spine. If she'd been braver, if she'd stopped running from what she was, maybe she wouldn't feel so useless now. Maybe she could have helped. Could have *been* more.

A long silence settled between them before Cassia added, "I'm sorry I pushed you away. Three years ago. I didn't know how to be with you and fix myself at the same time."

The pain of losing Riker sliced through her chest. But this time, she didn't fight it. She let it linger like it belonged there. Castor's eyes softened, but she didn't let herself look away.

"I didn't just lose Riker that day," Cassia said, voice breaking. "I lost my family. We splintered that day and never got put back together. I lost myself. I lost *you*." She paused, then forced herself to keep going. "I used to think I might hate Cade for leaving me here, but I'm beginning to see it was inevitable. That him leaving was actually some stupid call to destiny. That maybe even Riker's death was just a push to get him to this point."

Her voice broke again, quieter this time. "But if I'd just been braver... if I'd trusted you and let you figure out what I was sooner instead of hiding away, maybe things would've turned out differently. Maybe Vega wouldn't have Nylah or the Bloodstone right now. Maybe we wouldn't be standing here, practically letting my brother offer himself up to that damn Druid."

"You don't know that," Castor said gently.

"I do," she whispered, the words trembling out of her like a secret she'd buried too deep for too long. Her eyes burned, but she didn't blink. Didn't look away. Then, after a heartbeat, she added, "I loved you, you know."

The words were selfish. So selfish. But she couldn't take them back. She *wouldn't*. Not when they might be marching into death. Not when she might never get another chance to say the one thing that had haunted her every day since the moment she let him go. He had to know what he meant to her. That he wasn't the reason it fell apart. That *she* was. She'd been too broken, too angry, too lost in her own pain to reach for him when it counted. And now... now they were standing on the edge of war and she couldn't help but think her weakness had been one of the first dominos.

Castor's dark eyes met her eyes. The understanding there sucked the air from her lungs. "I know," he said.

But Cassia wasn't *her* anymore. And no matter how many pieces of the past she tried to pick up, she couldn't stitch them back into what they used to be. No matter how much she wished she could. Out of the corner of her eye, she saw Castor's outstretched hand, but she couldn't take it. Not without unraveling. So she ignored it, swung herself up onto the horse in one practiced motion, and stared straight ahead. It hurt too much to look at him.

Her gaze cut to Cade and Bridget, now mounted on their own horses, the wind tugging at their cloaks. She knew, without a doubt, they would do whatever it took to save each other.

Cassia tightened her grip on the reins. If it came down to it, she just hoped she'd be brave enough to do the same.

# CHAPTER THIRTY-ONE

## BRIDGET

The Elder Woods hadn't changed.

Even in the daylight, the trees seemed to whisper. Gnarled branches twisted toward the path like skeletal fingers. Fog clung to the mossy undergrowth in loose, shifting veils that made the world look more like a memory than a place that actually existed. Bridget's horse stepped carefully over a half-rotted log, hooves crunching in the silence.

It felt exactly as eerie as she remembered. Only this time, it wasn't just the past creeping in around the edges. It was the present, too.

Her thoughts circled Nylah, over and over. Every few minutes, she checked over her shoulder, half-expecting to see her sister curled up on a blanket behind her or riding beside Cade or Finn with her chin tucked into his back. But the saddle behind Bridget remained painfully empty. And Finn—no, *Vega*—had taken her. The fact churned in her gut. Especially since the potion Stellan had brewed for Nylah to keep her well had been left behind. Another fact she couldn't forget. The longer they took to find her, the sicker her sister would become.

Suddenly, the group of soldiers surrounding the king veered to the left in front of her, moving toward the old path they'd taken to Cavamyne months ago.

But not the path they needed to take now. Not if they were going to catch up with Finn slash Vega before she made it to Cavamyne.

"We're going the wrong way," Bridget said, her voice more breath than sound. In her past life, she'd traveled to Cavamyne more times than she could count and she had always taken the same route. A narrow, hidden path favored by thieves and smugglers slipping across the border unnoticed. It had been perfect for who she was back then. And Vega had known that.

"Yeah, in the 15th century," Cassia shot back. "I would think a bit of the landscape has changed since then."

Despite her scathing words, Bridget didn't flinch. She was too tired.

"I've gone this way before," Archer said from beside her, still intent on following the guards ahead of them. "And it's the way we took last time."

Bridget didn't have to look to know Cade was watching her. She could feel his eyes searing into her like he was trying to climb inside her thoughts and claw out every memory she was still refusing to share with him.

"Vega wouldn't go this way," she stated, ignoring the twist in her chest. "This path didn't exist when we lived here. There's another one, further east through a valley. It's rougher, but you don't have to cut over the mountain. She'll go that way."

The steady crunch of hooves filled the silence that followed, echoing against the gnarled trees of the Elder Woods. She could feel their doubt prickling around her. Castor arched a skeptical brow toward Cade.

But Cade didn't say anything. He just looked at her, gaze heavy with something unreadable. Trust, maybe. Or worry.

Then came the soft click of his heels. His horse surged forward.

"I'll ride up ahead and tell my father," Cade said, already pulling ahead.

Bridget watched him disappear around a bend, past Stellan, who kept to the front of the group like a shadow that didn't belong. He looked stiff in the saddle. But she understood why he stuck with them. In Finn's body, Vega couldn't risk blood magic to teleport herself or Nylah. She was trapped in this realm, on foot. Which meant they could encounter her before they even arrived at Cavamyne.

Or maybe that's just what she hoped.

"Trouble in paradise?" Archer muttered under his breath, but not quietly enough.

Delphine, Cassia, and Castor's gazes all shot to her. Bridget knew the tension between her and Cade was obvious to them. She'd avoided being alone with him since they'd discovered Nylah missing. If she hadn't been so distracted by trying to solve the past and their bond, her sister would still be with her.

After a moment, Bridget admitted, "I tried to break up with him."

Cassia practically almost fell off her horse. "What?" she stuttered.

"Why?" Delphine asked, brows furrowed. She trotted her horse closer to Bridget's.

Bridget didn't have to look up to know every head turned toward her. The tension between her and Cade had been impossible to miss.

Her stomach flopped. If she told them about the bond, Cade would know. And most likely, they wouldn't understand why it was so imperative that it be broken. Without the past, she probably wouldn't understand it herself.

"It's not important right now," she mumbled, shifting her gaze to where Cade and his father were locked in a tense conversation. Their voices started to rise, drawing uneasy glances from the soldiers in front of them. With a resigned sigh, Stellan spurred his horse forward, trotting up to join them. After a moment, Deckard snarled something unintelligible and yanked his reins to veer off the main path, turning east.

Relief coursed through Bridget. At least now they were on the right course and had a chance of finding Vega and Nylah before they reached Cavamyne. She patted the potion bottles in her saddle bag just to reassure herself they were still there.

Lowering her voice, Bridget turned to Delphine. "How strong are you feeling?"

Delphine's throat bobbed. "Does it matter? I'm going to have to get over my fear whether I like it or not, if the past few hours are any indication."

"Good." Bridget cast a quick glance at the others, who were distracted adjusting their course behind Cade and his father. Her voice dropped even further. "If we get close to Cavamyne and we still haven't found them, I want you to jump me there first."

Delphine blinked, hesitation rippling across her face as her hands tightened around her reins. Guilt settled in Bridget's chest. It wasn't fair to ask. But if they didn't find Vega first, then it would be the only way to ensure no one else walked into a trap.

"Are you sure that's a good idea?" Delphine asked.

"It's me that my sister wants."

She'd revealed too much to Vega in her dreams. She'd let her see just how much Nylah meant to her. And if anything was Vega's specialty, it was using the people you loved against you.

Delphine's gaze moved past Bridget. Her mouth twitched slightly as she looked at Cade, who was already riding back toward them. "He asked me the same thing, you know," she said softly.

Bridget's chest tightened. Of course he had. Cade always had a plan. He always tried to stay one step ahead. But this wasn't something he could control. Not this time.

Clearing her throat, she said, "It has to be me."

The words hung in the air just long enough to feel like a vow before silence fell between them. Cade returned to her side, his expression unreadable. Bridget gave him a half-hearted smile, then turned back toward the trail ahead.

As they moved closer to the valley, the trees thinned. Their bark silvered and cracked, as if the land had been drained of life. The path narrowed, turning rocky and uneven, forcing their horses to slow to a careful walk. Gray smoke clung low across the ground like mist, curling between jagged stones and skeletal trees. It didn't smell like fire. It smelled like something older. Forgotten.

No birds sang here. No branches rustled. Even the wind seemed hesitant to enter the valley.

It was exactly as Bridget remembered.

Only worse.

It was completely lifeless. Drained of everything beautiful, but dangerous, about it since the Sanguis had infiltrated Cavamyne so many years ago.

They had just passed a marker she remembered, one that indicated the tavern was ahead, when Cade saddled up beside her. To her luck, the search party had fallen into silence as they traveled. For a long time, the only sound Bridget had heard was her own heartbeat, and the occasional barked order from Deckard.

All morning, she'd been able to ignore Cade's imploring gaze. Until now. He was so close, his leg brushed against hers, stealing her breath. Lowering his voice, he said, "We never finished our conversation."

Bridget tightened her grip on the reins. Her horse instinctively slowed, and Cade matched her pace as they drifted behind the others.

"Now's not the time," she said.

"I think it is."

Bridget's jaw clenched. "You don't understand what she's like, Cade. This isn't going to end well, no matter what you think you have planned."

He hadn't grown up with her. Vega was cold. Vega was *ruthless*. She was everything Bridget dreaded facing. She'd managed to find a scrap of softness buried inside her. Once. But that had been years ago. She wasn't sure if it existed anymore.

"Maybe I *would* understand," Cade said, the frustration bleeding through his voice, "if you'd just tell me about her. Or whatever it is about the past that's making you push me away."

The words hit harder than she expected.

Before Bridget could force an answer past the knot in her throat, Stellan appeared beside them with a quiet pop of displaced air. His horse snorted in protest.

"Is everything alright?" he asked, glancing between the two of them.

Bridget pulled her eyes from Cade and forced a tight nod. "It's fine."

*Lie.*

"It's not, actually," Cade said. "There's something Bridget remembers that she doesn't want to tell me and I think you know exactly what it is."

Stellan blinked.

"That's why you just showed up back here, isn't it?" Cade pushed. "She's asked you to keep it from me too."

Stellan stiffened. Just slightly. But Bridget saw it.

Guilt pricked the back of her throat. She hadn't meant to draw Stellan into this. But there had been no one else she could confide in. There was no one else who knew what the bond really meant. What it could do. What it cost. And now, Cade, with his eyes narrowed in quiet accusation... The gap between them felt wider than it had in days.

Stellan opened his mouth to respond, but before he could speak, a cry cut through the smoke-laced air.

"Over here!" one of the soldiers shouted, voice cracking with alarm.

Cade was already moving. He kicked his horse into a gallop toward the sound. Bridget followed without thinking, Stellan thundering close behind. The others snapped to attention and followed as the company veered sharply off the rocky path and into a copse of brittle, frost-scorched trees.

They didn't have to search long.

Bridget's stomach dropped at the sight.

Finn was slumped against a gnarled tree, arms bound tightly behind his back, blood caked around a gash at his temple. His head lolled to the side, unconscious but alive. The bark behind him was blackened in a perfect circle, burned with residual magic. His cloak had been torn and his boots were missing.

"No one cut his binds," Deckard barked, holding up a hand. "Not yet."

Cade threw himself off his horse and knelt beside him. "Finn?" he asked, urgency flaring in his voice. "Hey—Finn, look at me."

Bridget dismounted, her fingers trembling. The bark behind Finn was charred black in a perfect ring. The ground at his feet was cracked, as though drained by the kind of magic Vega channeled. And Nylah wasn't anywhere to be seen. Her stomach twisted.

He looked like Finn.

But it didn't mean it *was*.

"Wait," she said as Cade reached to cut his restraints. "Don't."

Cade paused, blade in hand. "What?"

"There's a chance Vega is still controlling him," Bridget said, gaze fixed on Finn's eerily still form. "This was too easy. There's no way Vega just let him go."

"He's barely conscious," Delphine murmured behind her. "Wouldn't she need more strength to keep control?"

"If she lost control, wouldn't Nylah be here? She's had time to adjust the blood spell. And she's done it before. I'd bet anything she's still in there."

Bridget turned to Cade, heart pounding. "We have to test him first. Ask him something only Finn would know."

Cade's jaw ticked. "I don't feel anyone else in his mind."

"You didn't feel anything with me," Bridget reminded him. "Or Quinn."

Cade didn't respond. His blade dropped slightly, but the tension in his shoulders didn't ease.

"As much as I don't want to agree with her..." Deckard's gravelly voice cut through the air like a stamp of judgment. "She's right."

For a moment, no one moved.

Finn stirred. Just slightly. Then his head slowly lifted.

"Cade?" he rasped. "I am sure glad as hell to see you. I feel like I've been walking through a nightmare. My head is pounding."

Bridget's heart stuttered. The voice was right. The confusion in his eyes looked real. But Vega was a master manipulator.

Castor stepped forward. "What happened?"

Finn let out a ragged breath. "It's like... I could see everything, but I couldn't control anything. Like I was sleepwalking. No matter how hard I tried to fight, I couldn't wake up." His eyes flicked from face to face. "There was a man. We met him on the road."

Cade crouched lower. "Did he take Nylah?"

Finn nodded slowly. "He took her... after I—after I cut his neck. Then everything went black."

Cassia's breath caught behind Bridget.

"If he was fighting her, maybe she was starting to lose control," Castor said cautiously. "And then found someone else to possess."

*Or maybe she wants us to think that.*

Bridget's thoughts spiraled. Something still felt *off*. Vega was meticulous. She never made mistakes like this... unless they served her.

Cade hesitated. "How do we know it's really you?"

Finn's eyes met his, and for the first time, something familiar sparked there.

"Okay," Finn said, lifting his chin. "There was one time I went out for coffee in New York. When I came back, I walked in on you and Bridget—"

"Okay, it's him," Cade interrupted, voice tight.

Bridget blinked. A muscle jumped in Cade's jaw as he quickly bent and sliced through the ropes binding Finn's wrists. Finn groaned, slumping forward, and Cade caught him before he hit the ground.

But Bridget's eyes didn't leave him. Relief warred with suspicion inside her, and the knot in her stomach didn't loosen. She swallowed hard and stepped forward, voice steady but firm. "We still need to keep him restrained."

Cade looked like he wanted to argue. Deckard just raised his brow at her.

Finn's eyes flickered, but there was no fight in them. Just exhaustion. "I get it," he whispered. "You don't know what's real anymore. Neither do I."

She reached out carefully, pulling the loose ends of the ropes taut again, her hands trembling despite herself. "It's not just about trust. It's about keeping Nylah safe. And all of us."

Finn nodded, his gaze heavy with a mix of gratitude and sorrow. "I don't want to hurt anyone. Especially Nylah."

A silence settled between them, thick and uneasy. Bridget wanted so badly to believe him, but the memory of Vega's cold smile and the way she could slip into someone's mind like water made her fists clench at her sides.

Cade stepped back, watching the exchange silently, his eyes unreadable.

Bridget met Finn's gaze one last time. "We're going to get her back. But until we're sure—"

"Keep me tied up," Finn interrupted softly. "I want that too."

She watched silently as the soldiers handed him a pair of worn boots and secured him to one of the horses. At least this way, every twitch, every glance would be under her scrutiny. If anything about him felt off, if even a shadow of Vega stirred within him, she would be the first to raise the alarm.

Beside her, Cade's unease was unmistakable. He didn't have to say a word. His conflicted gaze spoke volumes, torn between loyalty to his friend and the reality of their situation.

"She left him," Bridget whispered, her voice barely more than breath, the weight of it sinking deep into her chest. "She wanted us to find him."

Cade looked up sharply. "You think it's a trap."

"I *know* it is."

Because Vega always left a message.

And this time, Bridget feared, it had only just begun.

# CHAPTER THIRTY-TWO

The sun hung low, bleeding gold and amber through the thick canopy as their horses picked their way toward a clearing. The fading light revealed the silhouette of a broken-down tavern. Its crooked frame leaning against time and neglect. A cold shiver crawled up Bridget's spine.

She knew this place. Or at least she used to. In the past, she frequented the establishment. Back then, it had been bursting with life and noise. A place to forget about the brewing war that was surrounding the land.

A place where a human and a Tuathan met nearly five centuries ago without knowing what the future held.

The thought made her chest tighten. She glanced at Cade's tired form as the group dismounted silently. Bridget's boots crunched over shattered wood and fallen beams as she pushed open the heavy door, wincing at the creak that echoed through the empty, ruined interior. Her eyes darted across the shadowed corners, searching for any sign of Nylah. But the place was bare.

Only buried memories seem to lay inside. Ones that she couldn't bear to relive at the moment.

A low voice broke through her mounting frustration.

"We should rest here for a while," King Deckard suggested, his gaze sweeping the weary faces around them.

Bridget stiffened. The word *rest* hit her like a punch. How could they stop now? Time was wasting away and Nylah was still missing. She opened her mouth to protest, but Delphine's hand on her arm silenced her.

"We've made good time," Delphine said softly. "We won't get far without some rest. Even just a little sleep will make a difference."

Her eyes met Cade's across the firelight. There was a quiet understanding in his gaze. And the subtle nod of his head silenced something stubborn inside her. Swallowing the rising panic, Bridget forced herself to relent, though the knot in her stomach tightened with every heartbeat.

Outside, the soldiers began gathering wood for a fire. Flames soon crackled, casting flickering shadows that danced against the tavern's decaying walls. Bridget's eyes, however, remained fixed on Finn, who was tied loosely to a gnarled tree not far from the fire. His expression was unreadable, but she couldn't shake the suspicion or gnawing fear of what Vega might still be hiding inside him.

She swallowed hard and looked away, forcing herself to focus on the firelight instead of the dark unknowns waiting just beyond the camp. From inside the old tavern, she could hear Cade, his father, Stellan, and Castor deep in conversation. Delphine and Cassia had already fallen asleep in one of the upstairs rooms, despite their insistence that Bridget join them. Instead, she remained with the soldiers. Something about their presence now felt familiar.

Archer wrapped his arm around her shoulder and handed her a roll of bread.

"Are you going to go talk to him?" he asked, nodding at Finn. "Or I could. I'm not very good at interrogations, but I think I could ask him the right questions."

Bridget hadn't failed to notice how he'd been watching Finn with concern since they'd found him. He'd even lent him a potion that was supposed to help with the cut on his head.

"No, I'll do it," she said quietly, meeting Archer's gaze. "There's still more I want to ask him about Nylah."

It'd almost been twenty-four hours since she'd last taken one of Stellan's concoctions for her. She desperately hoped her symptoms hadn't gotten too bad.

"Good luck," Archer replied with a half-smile, taking one last glimpse of Finn before heading into the tavern.

Bridget squared her shoulders and stepped closer to Finn, who sat slumped against a tree, hands tied in front of him. The firelight caught the angry red of the wound on his temple.

"How are you feeling?" Bridget asked softly, trying to keep her voice steady despite the knot twisting in her stomach.

"A little better," Finn said, voice hoarse but steady. "Archer's potion helped with the headache."

Relief flickered in Bridget's chest, but it was quickly swallowed by doubt. She pushed forward, questions spilling out before she could stop herself. "What do you remember? How was Nylah? Did she seem... alright?"

His eyes darkened, shadows flickering behind them. "She's fine." The word hung in the air, but something about his tone made her skin prickle. There was a shift... subtle but unmistakable. "I'm glad you came to talk to me, Bridget."

Her heart stumbled in her chest. "What do you mean? You don't usually give answers like that."

Finn was one of the most descriptive people she knew. Direct, and his words never held a second meaning.

A slow, mocking smile curved his lips, one that didn't belong to Finn. "I knew you wouldn't resist getting me alone. It's so like you to act first and think later, especially when it involves someone you love."

A chill slid down Bridget's spine. Before she could scream, Finn surged his hand into Bridget's side, piercing his fingers into the cut still festering from Cassia's blood spell. The pressure wasn't just physical, it was like a dark pulse of power twisted beneath her skin. A sinister echo of the magic Vega wielded.

Burning fire radiated through every vein in her body, until it consumed her completely.

When Bridget opened her eyes, she couldn't feel her body. In fact, she felt like a floating head, watching a televised version of her life. An invisible wall she couldn't break through seemed to separate her and the real world. She tried to scream as she felt herself sit up and brush the dirt and snow from her hair.

*No one may be able to hear you scream,* a voice purred inside her head, smooth and bitter, *but I still can. So if you could keep it down...*

The sound of her voice split something deep inside Bridget. It had been so long since she'd *really* heard her. Not the haunting fragments in dreams, her the full presence.

And even now, some hollow, broken part of her heart ached with familiarity.

She hated it. She hated that a part of her always missed her sister.

But she also had another one to protect.

*Where's Nylah? I'll do whatever you want. Just let the others find her.*

Vega ignored her. Bridget's body didn't freeze or tremble with the words she'd shouted internally, like she wanted. Instead, it moved easily, confidently, like it *belonged* to Vega. The disconnect was nauseating. She couldn't even clench her fists.

A shuffle came from her right. Her head—*Vega's* head—turned toward it, eyes landing on a young soldier jogging up the slope toward her. His breath came in fast puffs, concern etched between his brows.

"Are you alright?" he asked, eyes darting to the snow she'd collapsed in seconds ago. "I saw you fall over."

*Run,* Bridget begged him, voice useless in her own skull. *Get away from me.*

But her mouth curved upward in a soft, reassuring smile. "I came over to talk to him, but he'd already fallen asleep," Bridget heard herself say. "Then I tripped over one of the roots."

Bridget screamed *no* inside her skull, powerless to stop the flick of her lashes or the softness in her tone as Vega—*in her skin*—tilted her head just so.

The soldier blinked. His shoulders eased a fraction. Concern softened into something else... something Bridget recognized instantly...

He was charmed. And completely oblivious.

Nausea curled in her gut.

But her body stood steady, chin lifted in the twilight.

"You sure?" the soldier asked, eyes darting from her face down to the hem of her cloak, where snow clung to the edges. "You scared the hell out of me for a second."

"Truly," Vega replied smoothly, voice laced with sincerity. "Thank you for checking."

Bridget wanted to shake him. But all she could do was watch as the guard gave her a crooked smile.

"You should head inside," he said, gesturing back toward the crumbling tavern. "The fire's going and—"

His voice cut off, his gaze catching on something behind her.

Bridget's body turned slowly. Vega's composure didn't crack, but Bridget's panic spiked the moment she saw what the guard was staring at.

Finn.

He was still slumped against the tree, tied up as they'd left him. But now, a thin stream of blood trickled from his nose, painting a crimson line down the corner of his mouth. Unconscious, his head lolled slightly.

The soldier took a half-step forward. "Is he okay?"

Vega didn't answer right away. Her eyes—Bridget's eyes—lingered on Finn a moment too long.

Bridget's blood turned to ice. *Don't you dare hurt him,* she hissed inwardly.

But Vega only turned back to the guard and smiled again, this time with a hint of mischief. "I'll check on him. You should go warm up. You've done more than enough."

The guard hesitated, but the smile worked again, just enough to send him walking back toward the fire.

As soon as his footsteps faded, Vega turned back to Finn.

And Bridget screamed again inside her own head. *Is he going to be alright?*

*Probably. He won't remember what happened, though. Unfortunately for you.*

Seconds later, Bridget felt the shift in her posture, the smooth grace of her movements as she turned away from the tree and Finn. She didn't rush. She didn't check if Finn was breathing. She didn't look back. She simply started walking.

Each step through the brittle grass and soot-blackened snow felt like a betrayal Bridget couldn't stop. Her limbs moved with easy purpose, like she belonged here. Like she wasn't wearing someone else's life.

The tavern loomed ahead, its warped silhouette caught in the fading gold of the sun. Smoke curled upward from the fire pit nearby, where the soldiers gathered. They stayed seated as she pushed the crooked tavern door open.

Cade was the first to see her.

His head snapped up, golden eyes locking on hers. Bridget felt the crackle of tension that passed between them, even from yards away. He stood quickly, a question rising to his lips. His eyes searched her face.

*Look closer, Cade. Please. You know it's not me.*

She wanted to scream as Vega's gaze slid right past him like he was nothing. Cade's brows pinched together as she walked by without a word.

Deckard stood a few feet behind, eyes narrowing as he noticed the blood at her side and the dried smudge on her cheek. His fingers flexed once at his side, but he didn't speak.

Stellan straightened near the edge of the fire, face unreadable. She felt his magic stir faintly, tasting for something. But Vega slipped past him.

Even Archer, who always saw more than he let on, simply gave her a sideways glance and offered a casual, "You okay?" as she moved by.

But Vega never broke stride. Shadows stretched long across the warped floorboards as her boots clicked softly against the wood of the stairs. Bridget wanted to claw her way out of her own body.

*If you have Nylah and Bloodstone...* she thought, the words echoing inside the prison of her mind, *why did you bring us back inside? Why not run straight to Cavamyne?*

A bitter thought surged up Bridget's spine. One she didn't want to share with Vega, but she was sure she already knew. *Cade wouldn't be far behind once he realized you had us both.*

Vega didn't answer.

She climbed the stairs with slow, deliberate steps. The rotted railing scraped against Bridget's palm, but the sensation felt far away. Her foot pressed into a board that groaned beneath their weight.

Bridget strained against the invisible wall inside herself, desperate to stop. At the top of the stairs, Vega paused in the darkened hallway, letting

Bridget's eyes adjust. Dust floated in the still air. Doors stood half-open, their hinges warped with age. Moonlight slanted in through a cracked window, revealing faded wallpaper and a splatter of black mold creeping up the corners. It smelled of rot and memory.

*We need the grimoire to break the curse. I wrote that spell centuries ago,* Vega said lightly, fingers trailing along the rusted doorknob to her left. *I wouldn't want to mess it up.*

The tone was casual, almost joking, but Bridget felt the sliver of unease pulsing beneath it. Vega was confident. But not invincible. The moment her hand landed on the knob, Bridget felt the whisper of magic ripple across her skin like static.

*I ripped those pages out.*

Bridget hoped the reveal was enough to distract from going into the room where Cassia and Delphine slept. Had Stellan left the grimoire with them?

*Luckily for me,* Vega's voice was syrupy, *Bronwyn put them back in.* She practically spat the name. *She was always putting her nose in places it didn't belong. She thought she was helping by putting the pages you gave to Stellan back together and that no one would find them if they were in my old spell book. But why she left it with Stellan, I'll never understand.*

As Vega's hand closed around the knob, a memory surged to the front of Bridget's mind, unbidden and unwanted. A cold, damp cell. Her fingers shaking as she tucked the page deep into a cracked stone along the wall, sealing it with blood. She'd hidden the curse, the one she'd forced on the crown, where no one could ever find it.

*What was that?* Vega's voice sliced through the silence.

Bridget's blood turned to ice.

She hadn't spoken. Hadn't *meant* to think it so loudly. But the invisible wall between them wasn't just a prison. It was a window. And Vega was listening.

*Nothing*, Bridget said quietly. She pushed the memory as deep as she could. *When did you figure out what I'd done?*

*I'll admit, I spent a few decades trying to figure out where I went wrong*, Vega said as she turned the knob and slowly pushed the door open. Cassia and Delphine slept with straw pillows on the floor. *I even believed you were dead, just like you wanted, for a very long time. That was a long century. It wasn't until I remembered that cut on your finger. It was then I knew that you had done something to the crown.*

A shiver of dread ran down Bridget's spine. The grimoire was next to Cassia, like she'd been trying to read it before she'd fallen asleep.

*And then when you and Cade were reborn, I gained a foothold from Iegorus. The world shifted. In my favor, of course: I couldn't communicate yet, but I could see. I spent the next few years watching and waiting. And then one day... you finally saw me.*

Ice ran down Bridget's spine. *What are you talking about?*

She felt Vega smile. *You were five, I think. It was fun getting to talk to you again around the age you were when we first met. Bronwyn, of course, noticed and ruined everything... like she tends to do. It was her idea to send you to the human realm so that I couldn't influence you. She promised you would be safer there until the time was right.*

*I was sent there because of you?* If Bridget had control of her body, she probably would have vomited. She hadn't randomly been sent away? It had been for her protection? And where had it all gone wrong?

Vega let out a scoff. *I couldn't believe her. Me? A bad influence? You were always the one running around and avoiding all your responsibilities. But I digress. It was a setback, especially since it worked, but it made me realize something... You were the key to my foothold. More specifically, your blood. Our* blood.

Nausea hit Bridget even harder. Even her very blood was a reminder that everything had been her own fault.

*I was so happy when Quinn came along,* Vega went on, her voice dripping with mock affection. *And then Cora. Two minds willing to be shaped. Two lonely people looking for a purpose. So I gave them one. It wasn't long before they figured out how to communicate with me. It was even easier to convince them to use you for blood magic. I told them the spell would search your memories for the crown, but all it did was increase my influence. With a cut and a drop, I was able to slip in and out of their minds undetected. Your blood... my blood... close enough that not even Cade could tell.*

*You destroyed them.* The seething words escaped Bridget's mind before she could stop them. She remembered Quinn cutting Finn's neck. That must have been when she'd gained control over him. And then her, with the open gash on her stomach. Iegorus had given her too much time to perfect blood magic.

*I did what I had to,* Vega replied. *It's not like they weren't willing participants. They enjoyed the power. Didn't you? Weren't you willing to embrace blood magic when it suited you?*

Bitterness rose in Bridget like bile. Rage churned under her skin.

Vega laughed. *No, of course not. You're the hero.* She paced slowly toward the bed and traced her finger along the tattered grimoire. *But it is a little funny that you didn't have a problem using my curses.*

*It's what had to be done.*

The words sounded just like Vega. Bridget hated that it needed to be said. Because she was right. She'd turned to blood magic to get rid of the crown and save Cade. Why did she ever think she was any better for it?

*Sounds familiar,* Vega mused.

Silence stretched between them.

*I'm nothing like you.*

The thought burst through Bridget's mind with raw fury. A truth she refused to surrender. She wouldn't let herself be. She *couldn't.*

*We'll see about that.* Vega picked up the grimoire and opened it to the last page. Her finger traced the sparkling ink of the ancient blood spell, the lines curling and twisting with silent threat. Vega's lips moved as she memorized the words, the cadence of power already thrumming through Bridget's veins like a storm gathering momentum. The spell repeated again and again in her head.

A tremor passed through Bridget's body. Her lungs stung. Her skull throbbed. And then—

A warm drop slid from her nose.

Blood.

It splashed onto the grimoire and stained the gold-edged parchment. Panic slammed through her.

*You can't hold me for long. You'll kill me.*

Vega stilled, eyes narrowing. Then, calmly, she snapped the book shut before the blood could mar the text further. Casually, she walked to the opposite corner of the room and laid the grimoire beside Cassia's sleeping form, brushing a strand of blonde hair from her cheek.

*Maybe that's a price I'm now willing to pay.*

The words gutted Bridget. She went still inside herself, a breath held in a body that wasn't hers to breathe. She had always believed, maybe naively, that somewhere beneath all of Vega's bitterness and madness, there was still some thread of love. Some tether between them that might keep her sister from destroying her completely.

But now... she wasn't so sure.

Vega didn't seem interested in preserving her. Not like before. Not like when Bridget had been a valuable pawn to get what she wanted.

Now she was just a shell. A tool. And completely expendable.

And the terrifying truth was that Bridget wasn't sure how much more her body or mind could endure.

From the shadows, Cassia stirred in her sleep. A soft sigh, then nothing more. With a satisfied smile, Vega left the small room. After she'd slipped through the small crack in the door, she turned to close it quietly.

And then Bridget felt it. A pulse, not in her chest, but deep in the core of herself.

Cade.

He was behind them. Standing at the top of the stairs.

Bridget didn't have to see him. She could feel his presence the way she'd always felt it. Before magic, before the bond, before everything between them had turned to ash and grief. It was the ache of knowing someone down to the marrow. It was something she knew Vega never understood, no matter how deeply she clawed into Bridget's skin.

But at that moment, Vega smiled.

*Well, well,* she purred inside Bridget's mind. *Let's see if he can tell the difference.*

A surge of panic bloomed in Bridget's chest.

*He's mad at me,* Bridget said, half-hoping Cade wasn't there to talk to her. Even though she knew he was.

Vega let out an unbelieving hum. *Yes, he looks positively enraged.*

Bridget fought to pull herself forward, to take back one limb or a breath. But her body didn't move. All she could do was watch through her own eyes as Vega tilted her head and turned to face him.

Cade stood at the end of the hall, one hand still gripping the bannister. The firelight from below flickered across his face, shadowing the line of his jaw and the storm building in his golden eyes.

For a heartbeat, he didn't speak.

He was watching her.

Watching *them.*

Bridget didn't dare try to speak again. Didn't want to tip Vega off to how close she was to breaking. But Vega must have felt the spike of fear, because she smiled wider.

"You know," she said aloud, Bridget's voice soft and sweet, "you really should stop sneaking up on people. It's unnerving."

Cade's eyes narrowed slightly, flicking down her body, then back up again. Suspicion bloomed at the edges of his expression. He didn't move, not at first. But Bridget could see the moment he shifted into something quieter, more dangerous. His shoulders relaxed, but it was the wrong kind of relaxed. It was tense beneath the calm.

"Couldn't sleep?" he asked. "Although it seems like you didn't try for more than a minute."

"Too much on my mind," Vega replied easily, tilting Bridget's head to the side with a faux-casual shrug. She took a slow step toward him. "And I thought I heard something strange upstairs. I went to check it out."

Cade nodded once. His gaze moved to the closed door. "Really? That's strange. I didn't hear anything."

He didn't say it accusingly, but it was still a little too casual for Bridget's liking. And then she wanted to scream as she watched her own body inch closer to him.

"You've been avoiding me."

He said it so quietly, Bridget almost missed it.

Vega tilted her head, feigning a frown. "Only because you've been impossible to talk to."

Cade let out a single, short laugh.

"Maybe," he said.

His voice was strange now. And there was something behind his eyes that Bridget couldn't quite read. She couldn't tell if it was hurt... or doubt.

Vega must have sensed it too. She closed the final step between them and touched his chest.

"Why don't we stop fighting?" she said gently.

And then she kissed him.

Rage shuddered up Bridget's spine. She wanted to shove Vega out of her skin. She wanted to scream. To claw her way back to Cade. But her limbs remained still. Her lips pressed against his.

Cade didn't move. Not at first. Then, slowly, he kissed her back. Just for a moment. Bridget's world spun. The betrayal cut so deep she could hardly breathe. But then he pulled away.

His eyes had changed.

*He does kiss you differently than he ever kissed me,* Vega mused. *But still, not bad.*

Bridget wanted to throttle her. But she was too busy trying to see if Cade realized she wasn't *her*.

"Are you sure you're alright?" he asked softly.

Vega blinked, masking the hesitation with a smile.

"Why wouldn't I be?"

Cade didn't respond. He stepped back instead, putting a bit of space between them.

Bridget's breath caught in her throat. Not because she could finally breathe, but because something in him had shifted. She couldn't name it, but she *felt* it.

*He knew.*

But Vega didn't seem fazed. She turned from him with a hum and moved back down the hallway, murmuring something about heading outside to the fire and needing rest.

Bridget felt herself walk away.

But Cade's eyes stayed with her, burning into her back the entire way down the hall.

If he knew, why was he letting her walk away?

The door creaked softly on its hinges as they slipped out of the tavern. Cold air slapped Bridget's cheeks. The fire had burned low in the center of the camp, its embers flickering like dying stars. Most of the soldiers were curled in their cloaks, faces half-hidden, unaware that anything was wrong.

Bridget scanned the camp with Vega's eyes. The horses shifted in their sleep, steam curling from their noses into the chill. Shadows clung to the trees.

*I guess he doesn't know you as well as you thought,* Vega said with a fake pout.

Bridget said nothing, but the ache in her chest pulsed sharper with each step.

*It's almost disappointing,* Vega continued, trailing her fingers along one horse's mane. *I expected more of a fight. And yet...* She gave a soft, venom-laced laugh. *He let you walk away.*

Bridget clenched inwardly. Vega was testing her, pushing on every bruise she knew how to find. After glancing at the unassuming soldiers behind her, Vega's fingers curled around the reins, her boot slipping into the stirrup.

Bridget felt it... the tension in her own muscles, the way her limbs didn't belong to her. Her body was tired, sore, her bones aching from fighting what she couldn't control. But Vega didn't hesitate. She moved with purpose.

She was going to run.

And then Cade's voice shattered the night.

"Don't let her leave."

Vega froze mid-motion. Slowly, she turned her head. Cade emerged from the tavern's shadows, his golden eyes seething and glowing with power. Behind him came Deckard, Castor, Archer and Stellan, fanned out like a warfront. Every face was taut with fury.

Bridget's heart stuttered. *He knew.*

A pulse of magic burst from his palm, a shield-breaking blast meant to disarm, not kill. Vega whipped around and threw out a hand of her own, meeting his spell with one of her own. The force knocked Vega back from the horse. Her heels skidded against the snow-packed ground. Pain tore through Bridget's body like knives in her ribs.

A pulse of raw power exploded from Deckard's hand, followed by another from Stellan. The air around Bridget crackled as their magic converged into a shimmering dome of force rising around her, locking her in.

The wind howled in protest, slamming into her like a wall. Her knees buckled. Then another blast hit her. It felt like her lungs had collapsed. She couldn't scream, couldn't breathe.

Cade lunged forward, but then he stopped. Bridget knew why.

Vega's hand trembled now, her other arm wrapped around her middle. She coughed once. Then twice. Blood dripped from her mouth. Bridget's *own* blood.

"You want to try that again?" Vega rasped. "One more hit like that, and she's gone."

The camp stilled. The guards reached for their weapons, but Cade threw out a hand, commanding, "Stand down. Don't touch her."

His voice broke on the last word. Vega straightened slowly. Her body swayed slightly with exhaustion, but Bridget felt the smirk on her face.

"You can't be serious," Deckard hissed. "Take her now."

Swords lifted and bows creaked. But Cade's fingers twitched and with a whisper of power, every weapon flew from the guards' hands and clattered to the snow.

"No one touches her," he said, barely audible. His eyes never left Bridget's face.

"Let me go," Vega hissed. "You might get to say goodbye this time. Or you might not. But if you take me out now, no one will find poor little Nylah."

The thought had Bridget wanting to scream.

Cade's hands curled into fists. "You're bluffing."

"Try me," Vega whispered. "Let me go now and I'll make sure Nylah makes it to Cavamyne in one piece."

The pain seared again through Bridget's chest. Her body ached. Her vision blurred. Somewhere in her skull, she could feel Vega digging deeper, cementing her place like a root cracking through stone.

But even through the haze, she saw Cade step forward anyway. "Take me. I'm the one you want," he said, voice steady now, gaze locked on Vega. "I'm the one you need to break the curse."

Behind him, his father paled and gripped his dagger tighter.

"Tempting," Vega purred, licking the blood from her lip. "But I'm afraid I'm not done with my little sister just yet."

She stepped back toward the horse, blood still dripping. And though she smiled, Bridget felt it. Vega was weakening. The hold was breaking. Slowly. And definitely painfully. But it was happening. She just needed to hold on a little longer.

"Cade." Stellan's voice came from the edge of the firelight. He stepped into the circle of flame-glow, eyes fixed, not on Vega, but on Cade. "Let her go."

Cade whirled on him. Fury flared in his golden gaze. "Are you out of your mind?"

"We'll find another way," Stellan said, calm despite the storm brewing around them. "Let her go for now. We'll follow. She's burning through Bridget's body to stay tethered. Push her any harder and we won't get Bridget back at all."

His eyes flicked toward Vega—toward *her*—and for one breathless second, Bridget swore she saw it. Desperation. Not for himself, but for her. Especially with their secret hanging between them. They couldn't risk Vega killing her. Not yet.

A crack split through her chest, invisible but deep. She wanted to scream. Or beg. Or reach out. But she was trapped in silence.

"It looks like you both don't have what it takes," Deckard snapped, raising his hand to strike, but Stellan lifted his palm first, summoning a wall of force between the king and Vega.

"You'll have to go through me," he warned, magic humming in the air.

Cade's jaw clenched. His hands shook. "I can't just let her—"

"You have to," Stellan said. "You've done everything you can. Trust me now."

Those words finally landed. Because for one breath, Cade's face cracked. But then he exhaled and stepped back.

Vega smiled. Blood still on her lip, dark and drying. "Smart boy," she said.

She swung herself onto the horse and turned toward the trees. No one moved as they vanished into the smoke-laced trees. But then Bridget heard Cade whisper, so low she wasn't sure Vega even noticed: "I'll find you."

And somehow, she knew, even as every part of her screamed for him to stay away—

He meant it.

# CHAPTER THIRTY-THREE

## CASSIA

The fire crackled like bones snapping beneath booted feet. Cassia didn't flinch. She stood just outside the circle of heat, arms folded. She let the icy wind bite at her cheeks. It grounded her and cleared her head. She didn't even bother to listen to Delphine's attempt at a calming speech as she watched her father and Cade argue by the horses.

She'd awoken to shouts and blasts of magic, unsure if she was still dreaming or not. When she'd run out of the musty old tavern, the entire camp had been thrust into chaos. And still remained that way. Cassia glanced at Archer and Castor trying to revive Finn. He was breathing, they hadn't been able to wake him. Blood dripped down his face.

Across the clearing, her father and Cade continued to bellow. Chest twisting, she hoped Cade listened to reason. The closer he was to Cavamyne, the more danger he was in. The more danger they were all in. If he died there, an evil they couldn't comprehend would be unleashed.

An evil she was technically connected to.

Cassia pulled her gloves back on. The more she thought about the Sanguis and Vega and Druids, the less controlled she felt. Ever since she'd searched Bridget's memories, it was like the inside of her skin yearned for the power again. For magic.

"Don't you see? *This* was the vision all along. If you go to Cavamyne, you will die," their father hissed, his voice low and blistering. "It's a suicide mission. I don't care if you think you're doing it in the name of *love*, or whatever bullshit you want to encourage yourself with, your death will unleash a power you don't understand. As king, I can't—"

"And what about as my father?" Cade shot back. The air between them crackled. "But I assume you don't have an answer for that. You haven't prioritized that role in a very long time. I'm going. Whether you like it or not."

Cassia didn't bother stepping between them. Not yet. She was too busy watching Cade. His shoulders were tense and his eyes were alight with a mad fury. He wasn't hearing anything. At least not the things that mattered. And she'd seen that look on his face before. It was the same one he wore the day he'd left for the human realm. And again, when their father had surprised him with Bridget at the start of the tournament, after months of searching.

"Mark my words, I won't let you leave here," their father growled, lifting his hand. A flicker of magic shimmered in his palm.

But Cade was faster. He caught their father's wrist and flung it to the side with a brutal snap. "I don't have time to fight with you right now. Believe me, I *would* win. But right now, you're not worth wasting the energy."

Cassia stepped forward to intervene. She'd never seen her father's face so purple. But Delphine's hand on her forearm stopped her. Cassia jerked away instinctively. Even that small touch seemed to stir magic under her skin.

Delphine didn't seem to notice. Her gaze was locked on the argument still transpiring. "He wants me to take him there now," Delphine whispered, voice barely audible. "To Cavamyne. I don't know how to say no. You should grab Castor and leave now so you're ahead of the others."

"Can you do that?" Cassia asked. She didn't know what she was more surprised about... Delphine *actually* willing to use her powers, despite the clear reluctance that had hindered her for months. Or the fact she was suggesting she go with Castor without her.

"We've already been there. We're close enough it wouldn't hurt too much," Delphine replied with a slight tremble. "I could do it."

Cassia shook her head. "He needs us as backup. Especially Stellan."

Turning toward the tree line, Cassia let her gaze find Stellan. He stood still as stone, leaning against a particularly snowy tree with arms crossed. At a glance, he looked bored. But Cassia knew better. There was a stiffness to his shoulders and a subtle flare of energy under his skin that was unmistakable. He was just as anxious as the rest of them.

"You have to stall him," Cassia demanded. "Stellan may be able to follow, but if something happens and we're not there in time..."

She couldn't even finish the sentence. A blinding pain killed the words in her throat.

Delphine's expression broke. Her dark eyes reflected a truth Cassia already understood. "You know I won't be able to," she said.

The stupid knot tightened again. Cassia tried to swallow it down. Eventually, she muttered, "I know."

The only person who could possibly convince Cade *not* to go to Cavamyne... was the one already gone. She'd already almost drowned in his emotions when Nylah had been taken. With Bridget gone... there would be no stopping him.

As if reading her thoughts, Delphine added, "Bridget doesn't have much time left. I saw a glimpse of her, when he connected with my mind." A shudder pulsed through her body. "There was already so much blood."

The words hung in the air like ash.

From across the clearing, Stellan's gaze snapped to them. His stare locked on Cassia, unreadable. Something tightened in his expression.

Beside her, Delphine swallowed audibly. "I think he wants to talk to you," she murmured. "I should be helping with Finn anyway. I just... thought you looked like you needed someone."

Cassia used all her strength to keep her mouth from falling open. The observation hit her harder than she expected. It had been a long time since anyone had taken the time to see her. Really *see* her. Besides Castor, she wasn't sure anyone ever had.

She rolled her lips together, fighting the sudden prick of tears. Her voice came out steadier than she felt. "Thank you."

Delphine gave a single nod, then turned and jogged toward Finn's unconscious form near the tavern. Cassia exhaled slowly and closed her eyes. When she finally opened them, Stellan was standing directly in front of her.

"Was that necessary?" Cassia snapped, rubbing her temple. The pound of her heartbeat fueled the growing ache in her head. Especially since her father hadn't stopped berating Cade. Her brother ignored his rageful remarks as he strode off to join the others with Finn.

Cassia's patience, already paper-thin, ripped.

"Why don't you stop them?" she hissed. "It's just like in his study. You could probably overpower them both but you choose not to."

The accusation burned hotter than she intended. But deep down, part of her meant it. He could *stop* this. Knock them out or freeze them. He was *Tuathan*. Weren't they supposed to be more powerful than any of them combined?

Stellan didn't flinch. His voice was maddeningly calm. "My interference would only make things worse." His resigned gaze drifted toward the campfire, toward Cade. "Besides, it's time."

Cassia's heart stopped. "Time for what?"

He didn't answer right away. Instead, he just stood there, strangely still. "Time for the moment I've spent five hundred years dreading," he finally said. "I thought I could stop it. Once." His mouth curled into a broken smile. "Everything I did only made it worse."

He wasn't looking at her anymore. His eyes had locked onto Cade, who now whispered something to Delphine, his whole body practically vibrating with barely restrained urgency.

"What we are," Stellan murmured, "is a blessing and a curse. I know he's frustrated he doesn't have his full abilities yet, but he should consider himself lucky he doesn't see what I do."

The urge to ask him just what he saw overwhelmed Cassia, but for once, no remarks formed in her mouth. There was such a heavy weight in his eyes. For a split-second, she was afraid of carrying it too. Of knowing exactly what the future held and being unable to stop it.

After a moment, Stellan added, "And you should consider yourself lucky too."

"What do you mean?" Cassia asked, blood running cold.

Stellan turned his full attention to her, and the shift in his expression made her stomach tighten. "I spent a long time trying to figure out your existence too," Stellan admitted. "You're an anomaly. You were born when you shouldn't have been. Cade was never a twin. Why would he be reborn as one?"

Cassia had no idea. Magic had been the bane of her existence for so many years. Because of that, she'd deliberately avoided most books about it. She'd tuned out every conversation that might have been worthwhile to her now.

"And then I began to realize..." Stellan continued. "Magic loves balance."

"I don't feel very balanced." Cassia couldn't help but snap. What ran through her veins felt anything *but*. Her skin felt like a live wire desperate for power.

Stellan's lips twisted, just slightly. "Vega... she disrupted everything. Her pursuit for power broke entire lands. I think nature wanted a way to put things right." He reached into his pocket and pulled out a folded piece of paper. "That's why I think you're the only one who can do this. Blood magic won't affect you like everyone else."

Cassia refused to take it from his hand. "What's that?"

"It's the curse Bridget used to send the crown away. At least, the part Vega told her, apparently," he said, still holding it up for her, like he knew she would eventually take it. "But it should be enough. And it won't take that much blood if you channel something else just as strong... Like the site of three life changing curses."

Air evaporated from her lungs. Cavamyne. She couldn't feel her body as she slowly took the paper from him. Once it was in her fingers, Cassia recognized the notebook paper. Bridget's handwriting was a scribble, but it was enough. Her brain couldn't imagine actually doing what he implied. She couldn't comprehend using the curse in her hand on herself and willingly jumping through time for an *object*.

"Why are you giving this to me?" Cassia asked, despite already knowing the answer. If that's what he wanted her to do, then she wanted to *hear* it. Loud and clear.

"Maybe it's time for you to embrace your fate, too."

# CHAPTER THIRTY-FOUR

## BRIDGET

Smog swirled in the air as Vega paced around the two thrones of Cavamyne, the heels of her boots ticking like a clock against cracked stone. Torches and moonlight gave an eerie glow to the ceremonial courtyard that was hollowed by time and half-swallowed by vines. With each passing moment, Bridget had slowly begun to feel the burning of her muscles. The squeeze of her chest. The piercing iron claw around her mind as her sister's control wavered. She'd been under the influence of magic too long. If Vega didn't let go soon, her heart would stop.

As Vega circled again, Bridget fought to find any sliver of muscle she might be able to move on her own. But her body remained trapped behind the force of Vega's will. Her own thoughts sounded distant, like echoes bouncing off glass. She wondered if Vega was purposefully trying to tune her out.

When she saw the body lying motionless across the courtyard floor, she nearly shattered.

Nylah.

She was curled at the base of the flat altar stone, arms limp and dark hair a tangle of shadow across her cheek. From this distance, Bridget couldn't see her chest move.

*Can you please just go check to see if she's breathing?* Bridget begged, hoping Vega felt the anxiety rushing through her veins.

Vega stopped and faced the half-way shattered gate. The boulder sat almost split in half at its center. Crimson stained one side. Her blood, most likely. Bridget glanced at the hills behind it. Her stomach twisted. There was still no sign of Cade or Stellan or—

*You've got to learn to relax, Bee. She's fine*, Vega answered, the words dry and casual. Bridget didn't need to be looking at her to know she was rolling her eyes.

*Then why isn't she awake?*

*Do you want her to interfere with my plans?* Vega snapped.

Bridget didn't answer. The last thing she wanted was to say something to make Vega act impulsively. She'd learned a long time ago that her sister's worst decisions came from her trying to prove a point.

With a sigh, Vega hopped down the carved stone steps and began to move toward Nylah. Her pace was too slow for Bridget's liking, but when she crouched beside Nylah and hovered a hand over her mouth, Bridget dared to believe that maybe she was actually checking her breathing.

*I'm surprised you care*, Bridget said.

*I don't.*

The response came without hesitation. Vega's hand dropped from Nylah's face and trailed to something hidden just behind her. Bridget warily eyed the oblong shape swaddled in worn red velvet. Vega gripped it and began to unwrap it with deliberate care.

*But if you don't make it through this, maybe she'll want to be my new sister,* Vega added, her tone turning playful.

Bridget seethed. When Vega turned her back on Nylah again, it took everything in her not to scream. *Is that your plan?* she hissed. *Possess me long enough to kill me? Which in turn would kill Cade in the place you need him to.*

*Whatever do you mean?*

The simpering mock-innocence clawed under Bridget's skin. She could practically feel Vega smiling.

*Don't pretend like you haven't figured out about the bond.*

Bridget tried to ignore the slicing of her ribs as she thought about the bond she simultaneously hated and loved. The one that tethered Cade's life to hers like a second heartbeat. If Vega hadn't pieced it together before, Stellan's willingness to let her leave in Bridget's body should've made it obvious. Bridget had felt her thoughts about it slip. She knew Vega had heard them.

*I'll admit, it took me a while. It wasn't until I saw how diminished Cade's powers were that it hit me. You remember what he was like.* Vega clicked her tongue, as though disappointed. *Such a waste.*

Bridget's retort vanished as the velvet cloth fell to the stones with a whisper of finality. Vega held the sword aloft. The blade shimmered silver in the moonlight, sleek and impossible. Rubies glittered in its hilt like fresh blood, arranged in the shape of an ancient sigil that was unmistakable.

Her breath locked in her throat.

It was *hers*.

The one she'd carried five hundred years ago. The one she thought couldn't possibly exist anymore. She hadn't seen it since Vega had taken her prisoner, right before the curse.

*Where did you find that?*

Bridget didn't mean to ask. The words broke free, quiet and trembling with dread. She couldn't keep her eyes off of it. There was something else about it that tugged at her mind. A pulse of a warning she couldn't shake.

*It was exactly where I'd locked it up after I found you roaming about my palace,* Vega purred, her voice soaked in venomous pride. *Didn't Cade have this made for you? How sweet. Was he still betrothed to me at the time? I don't remember... but it's not like that fact ever mattered to either of you.*

Bridget couldn't breathe. A flicker of memory surged behind her eyes. Dread rose up her spine. It was the same sword from the vision... the blade she'd used to tear through Cade's chest. She hadn't recognized it without her memories.

And then she realized why Marin had said *she* wouldn't kill Cade.

Because it wouldn't be her. Not really.

A scream clawed at her soul, but her mouth didn't move. She was trapped. Utterly trapped and unable to stop the past and the future from coming full circle.

*You can't.*

Bridget could barely get the words out. Even without control of own body, she felt like she would collapse any second. The roar of her own heartbeat began to drown out all reason and logic.

*Oh, Bee. Don't you see? You're not in the position to demand anything right now.*

Suddenly, the wind shifted. The air split with a hollow echo. Vega turned, sword still raised. Her eyes narrowed toward the top of the hill overlooking the courtyard.

Cade.

Cloak whipping in the wind, his hair was tousled and wild. His brown eyes blazed beneath the low-slung clouds. Behind him, Delphine stood breathless, one hand braced against her knee.

Bridget's heart surged in her chest.

*Cade. No. No, not now. Please—*

She wanted to warn him. To scream. To beg him to turn around. But she couldn't do anything.

And Vega was already moving.

The sword glinted in her hand as she turned toward him, a smile crawling across Bridget's face that wasn't hers.

"Oh good," Vega called, loud enough for him to hear. "Right on time. Any longer and I don't think Bridget would have made it."

Cade's expression didn't flinch, but his body went taut with unspoken rage. He gave Delphine a small nod. With a snap, she vanished. Bridget's entire body trembled. She had to be going back for the others, right? For anyone that could stop Cade's determined descent toward them.

*Please don't make me do this. I'll do anything you want.*

She'd used the same words on her sister before and they'd worked. But this time, Bridget felt a hardening between her and Vega's presence.

Cade crossed the threshold into the courtyard, slow and steady. His eyes never left hers. Or... Vega's. But Bridget could feel it. He was assessing everything, from Nylah's unmoving form to the weapon in her hand to her stance.

Vega laughed softly. *You see, Bee, I realized a long time ago I went about my original plan the wrong way. I tried to force you to choose. I tried to do everything myself.* She swung the sword in a loose arc, its rubied hilt catching the firelight with a glint that twisted in Bridget's stomach. *I underestimated how far you would go to save him. Now it's his turn to prove the same.*

The reality of her sick, twisted plan slammed into Bridget like a freight train. Her mind thrashed inside her own body, teeth bared against the iron grip of her sister's control. She tugged at the frayed seams of magic, desperate to loosen the claw latched around her consciousness. A searing fire bloomed down her spine, but still, she couldn't make her hands drop the sword.

As Cade took another step closer, the air behind him snapped. A second pulse of magic tore through the haze, and Stellan appeared, his form coalescing from shadow at the hill's crest. Deckard was with him. His dark eyes locked immediately on Vega.

Vega's hand flew up.

Flames exploded into existence around the outside of the courtyard, rushing skyward with a hiss of searing magic. A wall of fire roared to life, twisting and blocking Stellan and the king's path entirely. Its heat smothered the air. The stone beneath it glowed red. They skidded to a stop just short of it, lifting their arms to shield their faces.

Bridget's soul twisted as magic tore at her mind like barbed wire. Blood slid from her nose and down her lip. Moments later, Delphine appeared again, sweaty and breathless from the magic it had cost. Cassia and Castor clung to her shoulders, holding her upright. But it didn't matter. They were trapped on the other side and still too far away. They would be forced to watch her do the unimaginable. They couldn't stop her unless Vega let go or killed her first.

A sob tore through Bridget's chest. *Please don't do this.*

*It's the only way,* Vega hissed.

Then she surged forward. The sword slashed through the air, silver glinting with cruel familiarity. Cade's reflexes snapped to life. He twisted out of the way just in time, the blade missing his ribs by inches. The sword felt different in Bridget's hands than the one she'd carried and used to kill Quinn with. Every motion seemed to be carved with the muscle memory of a life that had ended in blood.

Vega lunged again, sweeping low. Cade ducked, sliding across the stone with a pivot. His foot braced, twisting his body just out of reach as the sword struck the ground where his head had been a heartbeat earlier. Sparks scattered and cracked beneath the Tuathan blade. Bridget screamed from within her own skull, thrashing against Vega's control.

Cade circled back, his breaths quick, but even. He still hadn't pulled out the sword dangling at his own hip. Instead, he raised his empty hands. "If you think I'm going to fight back and risk hurting her, I won't. I can do this all night."

He sidestepped again as Vega feinted left, then pivoted toward his shoulder. Bridget flinched internally, but the motion wasn't hers. Her muscles screamed from within the prison of her own body. Seconds later, blood spurted out of Bridget's mouth with a hacking cough. The tether between her and Vega was fraying, Bridget could almost *feel* the blazing air around them, but Vega continued to pull harder.

The fire wall around the courtyard flickered, just slightly, but not enough to break.

Cade's expression darkened. "Release her now," he demanded, his voice cutting through the night. "I know you care about your sister. You wouldn't be doing this if you didn't. You're killing her by holding onto her and the spell around us."

"Don't pretend like you know me or what I want," Vega hissed, then struck again.

Cade sidestepped quickly. Vega slashed again, and again he dodged. Each time she struck, he read the angle a breath before it came. Her left shoulder dipped, and he twisted. Her weight shifted, and he dropped low.

From somewhere near the stone behind them, a weak cough echoed. Bridget's heart lurched.

*No.*

Nylah stirred, lashes fluttering.

*Please don't let her watch this.* Bridget's thoughts came out like a sob.

*Weren't you just begging me to wake her up?* Vega snapped. *Besides, I'm beginning to realize maybe it's not you he's going to die for.*

Another wave of heat crushed Bridget's ribs. Her vision pulsed at the edges. She couldn't breathe. And then came the blood again. More than before. It slid over her teeth and dripped down her chin. The taste of iron filled her mouth.

Cade tensed. "You won't kill her," he snapped, voice taut with rage.

"Maybe not," Vega said coldly. "But I will kill *her*."

The sword snapped toward Nylah. Cade's hand flew to his hilt and unsheathed his blade in a blur of silver. The two swords met with a teeth-shattering clang. Sparks shot into the air as the blades locked. Vega bared her teeth and shoved, but Cade planted his feet and held firm.

Behind her, Bridget heard Nylah gasp. A sob ripped through her chest, soundless and strangled. Inside her skull, she tore at the seams of Vega's grip, clawing for any fraying edge of control she could reach. Suddenly, she could feel the crack of steel reverberate up her arms. A flicker of something moved under her fingertips. Bridget clung to it.

She flung herself back, out of striking distance. Her legs buckled beneath her. The impact of her own weight jarred through her bones like lightning. Every nerve screamed in protest. Pain exploded across her ribs. Her lungs refused to work.

Cade's eyes widened. The hope blossoming there shattered her heart. Coming closer, he demanded, "Keep fighting her."

*I'm trying*, she tried to scream. But Bridget's mouth remained set in a hard line. A vice clamped around her skull. The pressure bloomed into agony as Vega shoved her way back in. Flames erupted behind Bridget's eyes. Her limbs convulsed, and the strength she'd scraped together unraveled in an instant.

"I can't," Bridget managed to mutter before the fire overwhelmed her.

With a wave of agonizing pain, she lost control. Vega entered her mind with a fury. She was locked inside again, screaming and begging.

Cade flinched as she—*Vega*—lunged again. He twisted at the last second, blocking the downward slice that would've cleaved into Nylah's shoulder. Vega grinned and spun low, slicing toward his legs. Cade leapt back, boots skidding across the worn stone. But Vega was relentless. She spun and struck again. Steel rang against steel as he threw his full weight into the clash, driving her back. His expression was grim, his movements increasingly desperate as he tried to keep her from Nylah behind him.

Bridget could only watch from inside her own body as her arm moved and her wrist snapped, moving the blade forward. Faintly, she heard screaming from outside the courtyard. The wall of fire surrounding them wavered, its height suddenly shrinking as if its magic was leaking away. She forced her gaze through the haze, desperate to spot Cassia, but all she saw was flickering orange.

Moments later, a fresh torrent of blood gushed from Bridget's mouth. Her lungs burned as she hacked, wheezing out crimson rivulets. Blood poured from her nose in a frantic river, each heartbeat a hammer blow in her chest as Vega fought to reignite the barrier.

Bridget drew in a ragged breath.

She was dying.

She could feel her heartbeat stuttering and slowing. Every second that Vega held on consumed her bit by bit.

Hesitating, Cade froze and lowered his sword slightly. His frantic eyes darted from her to Nylah, now conscious and watching in horror, and then back again. And then Bridget saw it. A resignation spread on his face, along with a terrifying calm.

No. No. NO.

"We can't leave Nylah alone with her," Cade said.

The truth in his golden eyes struck Bridget's soul. Her vision blurred and her pulse roared in her ears. *He knew.* He'd known about the bond the entire time. Whether from Marin or the conversation he'd overheard with Stellan, it didn't matter. He *knew.* And it was too late to change it or the silent goodbye layered beneath every breath.

"I love you," Cade said, voice hoarse and low. But it struck Bridget like lightning. It wasn't for Vega. It was *for her*, buried beneath the rage and ruin of her sister.

And then Bridget knew what he was going to do.

She thrashed inside herself. Clawed at her own muscles. Tried to push Vega out. Tried to scream or shake her head and stop it. But Vega only smiled. Her grip tightened on Bridget's mind like a vice and twisted hard.

Blood dripped from Bridget's ears.

Cade dropped his sword. "I'm sorry."

*NO—*

Bridget's arm lifted.

The sword hovered in the air for a heartbeat of eternity. She begged every fiber of her being to stop. To drop the blade. To miss. To *do anything but this.* But her muscles obeyed Vega.

She drove the blade straight into Cade's chest.

# CHAPTER THIRTY-FIVE

## CASSIA

Cassia had always thought of herself as a helpless person, unable to help or do anything of value. She'd lived with the feeling her entire life. But it had never utterly consumed her. Until now.

She stood just beyond the courtyard's edge, the fire wall hissing inches from her outstretched hands. Its heat stung her cheeks and fingers. She could have pushed harder. Could have drained it faster. She should have. But she hadn't. She'd frozen.

While her brother bled. While Bridget wheezed and fought and broke beneath the weight of something she never should've had to carry alone. And now it was too late.

Bridget's hand moved, slow and mechanical, like something guiding it from inside. Her fingers slipped into her coat pocket and withdrew a small, shimmering red stone. The Bloodstone.

Cassia's chest caved in.

"No," she whispered. Her hands shook as she finally drew more of the flame into herself, draining it with reckless abandon. But the air was already shifting, thickening with ancient magic. It was happening.

Bridget—*Vega*—lifted the stone high. Cassia surged forward, the fire crumbling around her, but not fast enough.

"Don't!" she screamed.

But Bridget's hand closed into a fist and crushed the stone as she muttered something under her breath. Magic exploded outward in a brilliant, blinding shockwave. The sound cracked like thunder as a web of glowing fissures snaked across the courtyard floor. The blood-soaked stone behind Nylah split with a shuddering groan. A distant rumble echoed beneath their feet. The air howled.

Cassia stumbled against the earthquake building beneath their feet. Seconds later, Bridget collapsed beside Cade's still form. A gust of wind rushed past them. And then Cassia *felt* it. The shift in the air. The change in Bridget's body. Vega was gone. Back to her own, most likely. Ready to appear before them.

Cassia didn't wait. She ran. Behind her, she heard Castor yelling for Delphine. Stellan shouted something to their father. But all she could see was her brother lying bleeding and unconscious, while Bridget curled around his body like she could will him back to life.

And then Bridget screamed.

It wasn't human. It was raw and grief stricken; it shattered something inside Cassia's ribs. Tears streaming down her face, Nylah squeezed Bridget's shoulders, nearly falling from the rumbling beneath them, but she wouldn't move. Cassia dropped to her knees beside them as Castor skidded to a stop behind her.

"What do we do?" she breathed. "There has to be something we can do."

Castor just stared in shock as her father stumbled to the ground beside her. He was pale as Bridget clawed at Cade's tunic, blood staining her hands. Cassia followed their gazes and faltered. Cade no longer looked entirely human. The spell that had masked his true self was gone. His once-rounded ears were now sharply arched. His features had shifted slightly. They were more defined, otherworldly. Tuathan.

"No," Bridget sobbed. "I didn't—I couldn't stop—he—he—"

"Bridget," Delphine whispered, touching her shoulder, but she didn't flinch. She just screamed again, and the sound cracked across the broken courtyard like a curse.

Cassia's heart pounded against her ribs like it wanted to escape. Her eyes swept the courtyard, taking in the ruptures spreading across the ground. Glowing lines of magic split the stone, the sigils carved into the courtyard now crawling with bloodred light.

"They're coming," Stellan said behind her.

Cassia turned to see him standing in the center of the courtyard, eyes trained on the growing rift. His face was pale.

"The Sanguis," he continued. "All of them. Including Vega."

Cassia's stomach twisted. "We have to run."

But her words were drowned out by a sound she hadn't expected: a broken sob. Her father was kneeling at Cade's side now, his hands cradling his son's face. Tears cut tracks through the grime on his cheeks. His lips moved in silent denial.

Then he looked up. Straight at Stellan.

"Help me," he whispered.

Stellan hesitated. His hands clenched at his sides.

"Please," Deckard rasped. "The spell. The one you refused when Riker died."

Cassia's blood ran cold. What in the hell was he talking about? She turned to Castor, searching his face, but he looked just as stunned. Nylah stood frozen beside Delphine, pale and wide-eyed. Delphine wrapped an arm around her without speaking.

Stellan stepped forward slowly, his expression carved from stone. "There will be consequences. Not for you, but for *him*."

"I know," Deckard said. "But at least he'll be alive. Take it. Take my life in exchange for his."

Cassia couldn't breathe. Her father, usually unmovable and unshakable, was begging. She couldn't believe it. She didn't even *want* to believe it. But then Stellan knelt. One hand on Cade's chest. One on Deckard's heart.

A tremor rolled through the courtyard. Moments later, magic began to hum between them, white-gold and flickering. The wind stirred violently as energy pulled into a spiral, bending the broken air around them, even as the courtyard continued to splinter. The earth groaned beneath their feet.

Cassia turned away, unable to look. Grief threatened to snap her spine in half. She turned toward Bridget, still curled against Cade's chest. Her fingers were locked in his shirt as if letting go might make it final.

"We need to move before the Sanguis come through," Castor said, his voice tight with grief. "The stone... Nylah, do you have it with you? Lead us out."

Nylah's trembling hand closed around something in her pocket. Her face crumpled. "I—"

"I can do it," Delphine said softly. "I'll take her to Finn and Archer first, and then come back for you and Cassia."

Cassia looked up, startled. Blood stained the bottom of her nose from her trip with them here. She'd felt the weakness in her body as they'd moved through space.

"What?" Nylah turned to her. "But—"

Delphine's gaze lingered on Nylah's tear-streaked face. Her jaw tightened. "I can do it."

Another roar tore through the stones. The fissures widened. Cassia watched Stellan draw the last threads of life from her father's body. For a second, his eyes locked with hers. And suddenly, she *understood*.

Their conversation from earlier came hurtling at her with full force. She'd never acted fast enough in her life. For anything. Had never done what it took to truly save something or make a difference.

But now she could.

Wordlessly, she reached into Nylah's pocket and pried the Tuathan stone from her curled fingers. The girl didn't resist as she slipped it free and walked toward the two stone thrones. If she was going to attempt the curse, she didn't want anyone near her in case destruction followed in her wake.

"What are you doing?" Castor asked, his voice shaking.

"Delphine, get Nylah out. Then come back for Bridget and Castor," Cassia said, already pulling a blade from her belt.

Delphine hesitated, but only for a second. She wrapped her arm around Nylah's waist. Nylah screamed, "*No!* I'm not leaving her—"

A pop of magic cut her off as they vanished. The ground rumbled again. The crack in flat stone widened. For a split second, Cassia thought she saw a hand trying to claw through.

She took one step forward and faced the cracked gate, still splintering open. Stellan still knelt between her father and Cade. Tears blurred her vision as she watched life slowly fade from her father. He drew a shuddering breath. Then his dark gaze met hers. His lips opened slightly, like he wanted to say something, but his eyes glazed over. Cassia's heart fractured with a soundless scream as his body stilled. Seconds later, Cade's chest began to rise with slow, shallow breaths. But he didn't open his eyes.

The spell had worked.

Cassia's knees nearly buckled as she raised the knife to her palm. She sliced and let blood drip on the Tuathan stone. Closing her eyes, she began to pull from the ground. Power answered instantly. Magic surged upward through her bones like lightning trapped inside her veins. It hummed in her blood and ignited a power inside her gut that sparked into her muscles. Too much. Almost too much.

Castor stepped toward her, panic flooding his face. "Cassia, wait—"

She looked at him, tears burning down her cheeks. Her grip tightened on the stone, blood already slipping between her fingers.

"It's my turn to be brave," she whispered.

Cassia began to mutter the curse she'd had memorized the moment Stellan gave her the paper. The words felt foreign on her tongue. A tornado of energy cracked open at her feet, roaring loud and swirling into a silver-blue funnel. A doorway through time. All she had to do was jump.

She glanced one last time at her father's lifeless body. Then Stellan's eyes met hers. He gave the smallest nod. Then, with his hands still on Bridget and Cade, they shimmered with a brief light and vanished. Relief crashed over her. Stellan had taken them back. Delphine would return for Castor and then—

The flat stone in the center shattered into a million pieces. The Sanguis were coming through. And it was about time someone beat Vega at her own games. Cassia drew a ragged breath.

With a pop, Delphine appeared again, ready to take Castor.

*Now or never.*

Cassia bent her knees and leapt. Wind ripped at her body as magic seized her limbs. She was light and shadow all at once, falling upward through time. But just as she passed the threshold, a hand grabbed hers.

"*No!*" she cried out.

She looked down.

*Castor.*

His determined eyes met hers just as her blood smeared across his arm.

The curse, meant for *her*, bound them *both*.

"No," Cassia gasped, horror crashing through her. "You weren't supposed to—"

But it was too late.

Cassia dug her nails into Castor's palm, trying to hold on to him. Seconds later, darkness consumed her as the curse began to drag them through time.

# CHAPTER THIRTY-SIX

### Bridget

Bridget sat on the edge of the armchair, her fingers twisted in the hem of the oversized blanket someone had draped over her after they'd returned. Her eyes were fixed on the slow, steady rise and fall of Cade's chest. He hadn't stirred since they'd arrived back in Astraeus.

They'd brought him back to his room, hopeful that a familiar setting would calm him whenever he awoke. She knew it wouldn't be easy. That he'd be unsettled. Confused. Maybe even angry.

Even though relief pulsed through every inch of her body, she could hardly look at him. Every time she did, she felt the sensation of the sword piercing through his chest. Heard the sound of his flesh being ripped open. A fresh wave of nausea churned in her stomach as her gaze drifted over his body again. Her eyes lingered on the bandages wound around his chest, dark with dried blood.

She turned her face away and pressed her knuckles to her mouth. It didn't matter that it hadn't been her, not really. It had been her hand. Her body. Her theft of Vega's curse that had sent them down this path.

Beside him, Nylah slept curled on top of the blankets, one arm thrown over his chest. She hadn't moved since they returned. But Bridget couldn't blame her. The thought of being separated from him right now almost destroyed her, too. And the room was too quiet. Too full of things left unsaid. The tick of the clock on the wall sounded like a heartbeat.

At the far end of Cade's room, Stellan stood near the window. His silhouette was as still as glass. His arms were crossed and tension radiated from every inch of him. His eyes tracked something beyond the mountains. Maybe beyond the reach of Astraeus itself. He hadn't spoken much since they'd returned. But he hadn't left their side either. Bridget was grateful for that. Delphine and Archer had rushed to help Finn, still unconscious and fighting whatever threads of Vega's magic lingered in him.

And Cassia and Castor, cursed and traveling through time for the crown. She closed her eyes and hoped they both knew what they were doing. That she'd told them enough.

With a deep breath, Bridget's eyes moved back to Cade. She didn't realize she was crying until a tear slipped onto her wrist. She quickly wiped it away.

"Do you think the bond is broken?" Bridget asked softly, her voice barely more than a whisper.

She still remembered the brittle snap inside her chest when his heart had stopped beating. A sudden emptiness, like someone had cut the cord tethering her soul to the world. But whether it was the bond breaking or her own heart shattering, she couldn't say.

Stellan finally turned from the window. His gaze slid to Cade, then lingered.

"Based on the energy coming off of him," Stellan answered roughly. "Yes, I think it's broken."

Bridget tried to mask her tears with a laugh. "That's good."

It was. It *had* to be. So why did it feel like something inside her had been hollowed out?

Thunder grumbled low in the distance, rattling the windowpanes. The storms hadn't stopped since they got back. She couldn't remember the last time she'd seen the sun. Vega's doing, most likely. They were close to Cavamyne. Whatever blood magic she was twisting to restore herself the Sanguis was seeping into the earth, poisoning everything in its path.

Bridget looked back at Cade, her hand inching closer to his, though she didn't dare touch him. "What do you think it cost him?" she asked quietly.

Dread pulsed through her veins. Even though Stellan said it was normal for him to still be asleep, that he was *recharging*, whatever the hell that meant, she couldn't help but think something was wrong.

Stellan didn't answer at first. His jaw clenched as he stared at Cade, his throat bobbing with the weight of whatever he wasn't saying. "Whatever he wanted most," he murmured at last.

Bridget's chest twisted. The statement could mean so many things. But she'd learned enough about ancient spells to know that desire could be a dangerous currency. Magic didn't choose kindly. It took what it could twist.

But whatever had changed about him when he woke up, it didn't matter. Bridget glanced at the dark clouds behind Stellan. Vega was out there. Gathering strength.

Cade *had* to wake up. Sooner rather than later.

Because darkness was rising. And Vega was coming with it.

# ACKNOWLEDGEMENTS

First and foremost, I want to thank God for the gift of stories and for carrying me through every moment of doubt along the way. To my husband, Vance, thank you for being my constant, for believing in me even when I struggled to believe in myself, and for supporting this dream in all the ways, big and small. I couldn't have done this without you. To my family, thank you for your unwavering love and encouragement. Thank you to my best friends, The Five Wives and The Real Book Club, for listening and cheering me on. No matter what, each and every one of you always show up and remind me of how lucky I am to have you in my corner.

To my editor, Friel Black at Grey Moth Editing, thank you for your incredible insight. You helped shape it into something better than I ever could have on my own. To my copyeditor, Ramona, thank you for your attention to detail and for helping me polish this story. Thank you, Maribeth at Legends Literary Management and my street team, for your enthusiasm and support. You make navigating social media so much easier.

Finally, to my readers: thank you for taking a chance on this story, for spending your time in these pages, and for making all of this possible.

## ABOUT THE AUTHOR

Amy Woodruff is a Texas-based fantasy romance author who writes stories where magic comes at a cost and love complicates everything. She holds a master's degree in Library Media and works as a librarian, surrounded by stories every day. She lives in Dallas with her husband and their twin dogs.

For more information about her or the rest of the Blood and Curses series, visit www.awoodruff.com

9 798218 858209